Which Witch? and The Secret of Platform 13

Eva Ibbotson writes for both adults and children. Born in Vienna, she now lives in the north of England. She has a daughter and three sons, now grown up, who showed her that children like to read about ghosts, wizards and witches 'because they are just like people but madder and more interesting'. She has written four other ghostly adventures for children. *Which Witch?* was runner-up for the Carnegie Medal and *The Secret of Platform 13* was shortlisted for the Smarties Prize.

Also by Eva Ibbotson

The Great Ghost Rescue
The Haunting of Hiram
Not Just a Witch
Dial A Ghost
Monster Mission
Journey to the River Sea

Which Witch?

The Secret of Platform 13

Eva Ibbotson

MACMILLAN CHILDREN'S BOOKS

Which Witch?
First published 1979 by Macmillan Children's Books
This edition published 1992 by Macmillan Children's Books

The Secret of Platform 13
First published 1994 by Macmillan Children's Books
This edition published 1996 by Macmillan Children's Books

This double edition published 2002 by Macmillan Children's Books
a division of Macmillan Publishers Limited
20 New Wharf Road, London N1 9RR
Basingstoke and Oxford
www.panmacmillan.com

Associated companies throughout the world

ISBN 0 330 48908 9

5 7 9 8 6 4

A CIP catalogue record for this book is available from
the British Library.

Phototypeset by Intype London Ltd
Printed and bound in Great Britain by Mackays of Chatham plc, Kent

Which Witch?

for Alan

One

As soon as he was born, Mr and Mrs Canker knew that their baby was not like other people's children.

For one thing he was born with a full set of teeth and would lie in his pram for hours, chewing huge mutton bones to shreds or snapping at the noses of old ladies fool enough to kiss him. For another, though he screamed with temper when they changed his nappies, his eyes never actually filled with tears. Also – and perhaps this was the strangest of all – as soon as they brought him home from hospital and lit a nice, bright fire in the sitting room, the smoke from their chimney began to blow *against* the wind.

For a while the Cankers were puzzled. But as Mr Canker said, there is a book about *everything* if you only know where to look, and one day he went to Todcaster Public Library and began to read. He read and he read and he read, and what he read most about was Black Magic and Sorcery and how to tell from a very early age whether someone is going to be a wizard or a witch. After which he went home and broke the news to Mrs Canker.

It was a shock, of course. No one *likes* to think that their baby is going to grow up to be a wizard, and a black one at that. But the Cankers were sensible people. They changed the baby's name from George to Arriman (after a famous and very wicked Persian sorcerer), painted a frieze of vampire bats and newts' tongues on his nursery wall and decided that if he had to grow up to be a wizard they would see to it he was a good one.

It wasn't easy. Todcaster, where they lived, was an ordinary town full of ordinary people. Though they encouraged little Arriman to practise as much as possible, it was embarrassing to have their bird-table full of gloomy and lop-sided vultures and to have to explain to their neighbours why their apple tree had turned overnight into a blackened stump shaped like a dead man's hand.

Fortunately, wizards grow up quickly. By the time he was fifteen, Arriman could take a bus to Todcaster Common and raise a whirlwind that had every pair of knickers on every washing line in the area flying halfway to Jericho, and soon afterwards he decided to leave home and set up on his own.

The search for a new house took many months. Arriman didn't want a place that was sunny and cheerful or a place that was near a town, and though he wanted somewhere ruined and desolate, he was fussy about the kind of ghost it had. Never having had a sister, Arriman was a little shy with women and he didn't fancy the idea of a Wailing Grey Lady walking back and forth across his breakfast table while he ate his kippers, or a Headless Nun catching him in his bath.

But at last he found Darkington Hall. It was a grey, gloomy, sprawling building about thirty miles from Todcaster. To the west of the Hall was a sinister forest, to the north were bleak and windswept moors and to the east, the grey, relentlessly-pounding sea. What's

2

more, the Darkington ghost was a gentleman, and the sort that Arriman thought he could well get on with: Sir Simon Montpelier who, in the sixteenth century, had murdered all seven of his wives and now wandered about groaning with guilt, moaning with misery and striking his forehead with a plashing sound.

And here Arriman lived for many years, blighting and smiting, blasting and wuthering and doing everything he could to keep darkness and sorcery alive in the land. He filled his battlements with screech owls and his cellars with salamanders. He lined the avenue with scorched tree stumps like gallows and he dug a well in his courtyard from which brimstone and sulphur oozed horribly. He planted a yew tree maze so complicated and devilish that no one had a hope of coming out alive, and he made the fountains on the terrace run with blood. There was only one thing he couldn't do. He couldn't raise the ghost of Sir Simon Montpelier. He would have *liked* to do this; Sir Simon would have been company. But bringing ghosts back to life is the blackest and most difficult magic of all and even Arriman couldn't manage it.

The years passed. Though he seldom left the Hall, Arriman's fame was spreading. People called him Arriman the Awful, Loather of Light and Wizard of the North. Stories began to be told about him: how he could make the thunder come before the lightning, that he was friends with Beelzebub himself. But Arriman just went on working. He had grown to be a tall and handsome man with dark, flashing eyes, a curved nose like the prow of a Viking ship and a

3

flourishing moustache, but despite his fine looks, he was not at all conceited.

In the years that followed, Arriman set up a private zoo in which he kept all the nastiest and ugliest animals he could find: monkeys with bald faces and blue behinds, camels with sneering lips and lumpy knees, wallabies with feet like railway sleepers which kicked everything in sight. He turned the Billiard Room into a laboratory in which fiendish things bubbled all day long giving off appalling smells, and he called in rain clouds from the sea to drip relentlessly on to his roof.

Then one day he woke feeling completely miserable. He knew he ought to get up and throw someone into his well or order a stinking emu for the zoo or mix something poisonous in his laboratory, but he just couldn't face it.

'Lester,' he said, to the servant who brought him his breakfast. 'I feel tired. Weary. Bored.'

Lester was an ogre; a huge, slow-moving man with muscles like footballs. Like most ogres, he had only one eye in the middle of his forehead, but so as not to upset people he wore a black eyepatch above it to make people think he had two. Before he came to be Arriman's servant, Lester had been a sword swallower in a fair and he still liked to gulp down the odd sabre or fencing foil. It soothed him.

Now he looked anxiously at his master. 'Do you, sir?' he said.

'Yes, I do. In fact I don't know if I can go on much longer. I thought I might go away somewhere, Lester. Take a little room in some pretty market town perhaps and write a book.'

4

The ogre was shocked. 'But what would happen to Blackness and Evil, sir?'

Arriman frowned. 'I know, I know. I have a duty, I see that. But how long am I supposed to go on like this? How long, Lester?' The frown deepened and he waved his arms in desperation. 'How *long*?'

Lester wasn't the stupid kind of ogre who goes round saying 'Fe Fi Fo Fum' all the time. So now he looked at his master and said, 'Well, I wouldn't know, sir. Ogres can't tell the future, you know. Gypsies can, though. Why don't you go and have your fortune told? There was a gypsy where I worked. Esmeralda, they called her. Knew her stuff, she did.'

So the following week, Arriman and Lester drove into Todcaster to find the fair.

They found Esmeralda's caravan quite easily. You could tell it from the other gypsy caravans because the people who came out of it looked as though they didn't know what had hit them.

'She tells the truth,' explained Lester, sniffing happily at the remembered fairground smells: fried onions from the hamburger stall, hot engine oil from the dodgems . . . 'None of that garbage about dark strangers and journeys across the sea.'

Esmeralda was a frizzy-haired lady in a pink satin blouse. Arriman had left off his magician's cloak and changed into a grey pin-stripe, but the look she gave him was very sharp indeed.

'For you it'll be a fiver,' she said. 'Sit down.'

She pocketed the money, took a swig from a bottle labelled *Gordon's Gin* and began to stare into her crystal ball.

She stared for a long time. The she pushed the

ball away and lit a fag. 'It's all right,' she said. 'He's coming.'

'Who?' said Arriman eagerly. 'Who's coming?'

'The new bloke,' said Esmeralda. 'The one that's going to take over from you.'

Arriman looked bewildered. 'What new bloke?'

Esmeralda closed her eyes wearily. 'Do you want me to spell it out for you?' She put on a posh voice and droned, 'Soon there cometh a great new wizard whose power shall be mightier and darker even than your own. When this Great New Wizard cometh, you, Arriman the Awful, will be able to lay down the burden of Darkness and Evil which you have carried for so long.' She opened her eyes. 'Got it?' she said nastily.

'Oh, yes, yes!' said Arriman happily. 'I suppose you don't know *when* he cometh?'

'No,' snapped Esmeralda, 'I don't. Next customer please.'

After his visit to Esmeralda, Arriman was a happy man. Just to fill in time he planted a briar hedge whose thorns oozed blood, ran an oil tanker aground on the cliffs nearby and invented a new spell for making people's hair fall out. But most of the time he spent by the main gate, watching and waiting for the new wizard to come.

It was cold work. Darkington Hall was as far north as you could get without bumping into Scotland and when after a week, Arriman found a chilblain on his left toe, he very sensibly decided to make a Wizard Watcher.

For the Wizard Watcher's body he used a sea lion

shape but larger and furrier with a sloping and rather cuddly chest. The Watcher had four feet and one tail, but it had three heads with keen-sighted and beautiful eyes set on short stalks. And every day at sunrise this gentle and very useful monster would waddle down the avenue, past the blackened trees shaped like gallows, past the oozing well and the devilish maze, and sit in the gateway watching for the wizard.

It watched in this way day after day, month after month, year after year, the Middle Head looking north over the moors, the Left-Hand Head looking west across the forest and the Right-Hand Head looking east towards the sea. Then, on the nine hundred and nintieth day of just sitting there, the Wizard Watcher lost heart and became gloomy and annoyed.

'He cometh not from the north,' said the Middle Head, as it had done every day for nine hundred and eighty-nine days.

'He cometh not from the west neither,' said the Left-Hand Head.

'Nor from the east doesn't he cometh,' said the Right-Hand Head. 'And our feet are *freezing*.'

'Our feet are blinking dropping *off*,' said the Left-Hand Head.

There was a pause.

'Know what I think?' said the Middle Head. 'I think the old man's been had.'

'You mean there ain't going to *be* no new wizard?' said the Left-Hand Head.

The Middle Head nodded.

This time the pause was a long one.

'Don't fancy telling him,' said the Right-Hand Head at last.

'Someone's got to,' said the Middle Head.

So the monster turned and lumbered back to the Hall where it found Arriman in his bedroom dressing for dinner.

'Well?' he said eagerly. 'What's the news?'

'The new wizard cometh not from the north,' began the Middle Head patiently.

'Nor from the west he doesn't cometh,' said the Left-Hand Head.

'And you can forget the east,' said the Right-Hand Head, 'because the new wizard doesn't cometh from there neither.'

Then, speaking all together, the three heads said bravely, 'We think you have been taken for a ride.'

Arriman stared at them, aghast. 'You can't mean it! It isn't possible!' He turned to Lester who was getting ready to trim his master's moustache. 'What do you think?'

The ogre rubbed his forehead under the eyepatch and looked worried. 'I've never known Esmeralda make a mistake, sir. But it's been a long— '

He was interrupted by a terrible shriek from Arriman who was peering forward into the mirror and clutching his head.

'A white hair!' yelled the magician. 'A white hair in my curse curl! Oh Shades of Darkness and Perdition, this is the END!'

His shriek brought Mr Leadbetter, his secretary, hurrying into the room. Mr Leadbetter had been born with a small tail which had made him think he was a demon. This was a silly thing to think because quite a lot of people have small tails. The Duke of Wellington had one and had to have a special hole made in his saddle when he rode to battle at Waterloo. But Mr Leadbetter hadn't known about the Duke of Wellington and had wasted a lot of time trying to rob banks and so on, until he realized that crime didn't suit him and he became Arriman's secretary instead.

'Are you all right, sir?' he asked anxiously. 'You seem upset.'

'Upset? I'm finished! *Devastated*. Don't you know what a white hair means? It means old age, it means death. It means the end of Wizardry and Darkness and Doom at Darkington. And where is the new wizard, where, where *where*?'

The monster sighed. 'He cometh not from the north,' began the Middle Head wearily.

'I know he cometh not from the north, you dolt,' snapped the Great Man. 'That's exactly what I'm complaining about. What am I going to *do*? I can't wait for ever.'

Mr Leadbetter coughed. 'Have you ever, sir, considered marriage?'

There was a sudden flash of fire from Arriman's nostrils, and from behind the panelling, Sir Simon gave a gurgling groan.

'Marriage! Me, marry! Are you out of your *mind*?'

'If you were to marry, sir, it would ensure the succession,' said Mr Leadbetter calmly.

'What on earth are you talking about?' snapped Arriman, who was feeling thoroughly miserable and therefore cross.

'He means you could have a wizard baby, sir. Then

9

it could take over from you. A son, you know,' said Lester.

Arriman was silent. A son. For a moment he imagined the baby sitting in his pram, a dear little fellow tearing a marrow bone to shreds. Then he flinched.

'Who would I marry?' he muttered miserably.

But of course he knew. All of them knew. There is only one kind of person a wizard can marry and that is a witch.

'It wouldn't be so bad, maybe?' said the Left-Hand Head encouragingly.

'Wouldn't be so *bad*!' yelled Arriman. 'Are you out of your *mind*? A great black crone with warts and blisters in unmentionable places from crashing about on her broom! You want me to sit opposite one of *those* every morning eating my cornflakes?'

'I believe witches have changed since—' began Mr Leadbetter.

But Arriman wouldn't listen. 'Running along the corridors in her horrible nightgown, shrieking and flapping. Getting egg on her whiskers. Expecting her pussy cat to sleep on the bed, no doubt!'

'She might not—'

'Every time I went to the kitchen for a snack she'd be there, stirring things in her filthy pot – rubbishy frogs' tongues and newts' eyes and all that balderdash. Never a decent bit of steak in the place, I expect, once she came.'

'But—'

'Cleaning her foul yellow teeth in my wash basin,' raged Arriman, getting more and more hysterical. 'Or worse still, *not* cleaning her foul yellow teeth in my wash basin.'

'She could have her own bathroom,' said the Middle Head sensibly.

But nothing could stop Arriman who stormed and ranted for another ten minutes. Then, turning suddenly very calm and pale, he said, 'Very well, I see that it is my duty.'

'A wise decision, sir,' said his secretary.

'How shall I choose?' said Arriman. His voice was a mere thread. 'It'll have to be a Todcaster witch, I suppose. Otherwise there's bound to be bad feeling. But how do we decide which witch?'

'As to that, sir,' said Mr Leadbetter, 'I have an idea.'

Two

The witches of Todcaster were preparing for a coven and they were very much excited. Covens are to witches what the Wolf Cubs or the Brownies are to people: a way of getting together and doing the things that interest them. And this one wasn't to be just an ordinary coven with feasting and dancing and wickedness. Rumours were going round that a most important announcement would be made.

'I wonder what it'll be,' said Mabel Wrack. 'Some new members, perhaps. We could do with them.'

This was very true. Todcaster now only had seven proper witches. If Arriman had known what a state witchcraft had got to in the town of his birth he'd have been even more miserable than he was, but fortunately he didn't.

By day, Miss Wrack kept a wet fish shop not far from Todcaster Pier. She was a sea witch and never liked to be too far from the water. Miss Wrack's mother, Mrs Wrack, had been a mermaid: a proper one who lived on a rock and combed her hair and sang. But sailors had never been lured to their doom by her, partly because she looked like the back of a bus and partly because modern ships are so high out of the water that they never even saw her. So one day she had simply waddled out on to the beach at Todcaster Head with some sovereigns from a sunken galleon and persuaded a plastic surgeon who was on holiday there to operate on her tail and turn it into two legs.

It was from her mother that Mabel Wrack had her magic powers. From her father, Mr Wrack, she had the shop.

Today she closed the shutters early, put a couple of cods' heads into a paper bag and set off for her seaside bungalow. She was just turning into her road when she saw a group of children paddling happily in the surf.

'Tut!' said Miss Wrack, pursing her lips. She closed her eyes, waved her paper bag with the cods' heads and said some poetry. Almost at once a shoal of stinging jellyfish appeared in the water and the children ran screaming to their mothers.

'That's better,' said Miss Wrack. Like most witches, she hated happiness.

When she got home she went straight into her bedroom to change. Covens are like parties; what you wear is important. For this one, Miss Wrack slipped into a purple robe embroidered all over in yellow cross-stitch haddocks, and fastened her best brooch – a single sea slug mounted in plastic – on to the band which kept her frizzy hair in place. Then she went into the bathroom.

'Come on, dear,' she said, bending over the bath. 'Time to get ready!'

What lived in Miss Wrack's bath was, of course, her familiar. Familiars are the animals that help witches with their magic and are *exceedingly* important. Miss Wrack's familiar was an octopus: a large animal with pale tentacles, suckers which left rings of blood

13

where they had been, and vile red eyes. It was a girl octopus and its name was Doris.

'Now don't keep me waiting, dear,' said Miss Wrack. She had fetched a polythene bucket from the bathroom cupboard and was trying to stuff Doris inside. 'Tonight's going to be an important night.'

But Doris was in a playful mood. As soon as one tentacle was in, another was out, and it was a rather bedraggled Miss Wrack who at last fixed on the lid, loaded the bucket on to an old perambulator and set off for the coven bus.

Ethel Feedbag's familiar was not an octopus; it was a pig.

Ethel was a country witch who lived in a tumble-down cottage in a village to the west of Todcaster. She was a round-faced, rather simple person who liked to hack at mangel wurzels with her spade, make parsnip wine and shovel manure over absolutely everything, and just as people often grow to look like their dogs (or the other way round), Ethel had grown to look very like her pig. Both of them had round, pink cheeks and very large behinds. Both of them moved slowly on short hairy legs and grunted as they went along, and both of them had dun-coloured, sleepy little eyes.

Ethel had a job at the Egg Packing Station. It was a boring job because the eggs she packed were mostly rotten anyway so there was nothing for her to do, but she filled in by giving the sheep husk and turning the cows dry as she bicycled home of an evening. As for the plants in the hedgerow between the Egg Packing Station and Ethel's cottage, there was scarcely one

14

that wasn't covered in mould or rust or hadn't clusters of greedy greenfly sucking at its juices.

But tonight she rode straight home. Ethel was not a snappy dresser, but to make herself smart for the coven she rubbed down her Wellington boots with a handful of straw and changed her pinny for a clean one with felt tomatoes (showing felt tomato blight) stitched to the pocket. Then she started looking for something she could take to eat. There didn't seem to be anything in the kitchen, but on the hearthrug in the living room she found a dead jackdaw which had fallen down the chimney.

'That'll roast a treat!' said Ethel, scooping it up. Then she went down to the shed at the bottom of her garden to fetch her pig.

Nancy and Nora Shouter were twin witches who worked at Todcaster Central Station. They were an unusually disagreeable pair who hated passengers, hated each other and hated trains. As soon as Nancy went to the loudspeaker and announced that the Seven Fifty-Two to Edinburgh was approaching Platform Nine, Nora rushed to *her* loudspeaker and cackled into it that the Seven Fifty-Two had engine trouble and would be ninety minutes late and then it wouldn't approach Platform Nine at all but would come in at Platform Five, *if* they were lucky.

So now, when they should have been getting ready for the coven, they were standing in their underclothes in the bedroom of their flat in Station Road, arguing about which of their familiars were which.

'That is *so* my chicken!' shouted Nora, tugging at the tail feathers of the unfortunate bird.

'That is *not* your chicken,' shrieked Nora. '*That* is your chicken over there!'

It was a most ridiculous argument. The Shouter girls were identical, with dyed red hair, long noses and smoke-stained fingertips. They dressed alike and slept in twin beds and they both had chickens for familiars which lived in wicker crates beneath their beds. And of course the chickens too, were very much alike. Chickens often are – fidgety brown birds who would peck your fingers as soon as look at you. But none of this made any difference to the Shouter twins, who went on bickering so long that they were very nearly late for the most important coven of their lives.

For many years now, the witches of Todcaster had met on Windylow Heath, a wild, wuthering sort of place with a few stunted thorn trees, a pond in which a gloomy lady had drowned herself on her wedding eve, and a single rock on which the Ancient Druids had done some dreadful deeds.

To get there, the witches hired a bus – the *Coven Special* – which left the bus depot at seven p.m. (No one had flown on a broomstick since a witch called Mrs Hockeridge had been sucked down the ventilation shaft of a Boeing 707 from Heathrow to Istanbul and nearly caused a very nasty mess indeed.)

The Shouter twins were still quarrelling when they got to the depot, but they stopped when they saw, standing on the pavement beside the bus, a small brown coffee table.

'It's her again,' said Nancy.

'Silly old crone,' said Nora.

'I've a good mind to stub out my fag on her,' said Nancy, who as usual had a cigarette dangling from her lips.

They glared at the squat, round table which seemed to be swaying a little from side to side.

''Tis a pity when they go simple like that,' said Ethel Feedbag. She had loaded her pig on to the trailer and now came over and prodded the table leg with her Wellington boot.

The coffee table was in fact a very old witch called Mother Bloodwort who lived in a tumbledown shack near a disused quarry in the poorest part of town.

When she was young, Mother Bloodwort had been a formidable witch of the old school, bringing people out in boils, putting the evil eye on butchers who sold her gristly chops and casting spells on babies in perambulators so that their own mothers didn't know them.

But now she was old. Her memory had gone and like many old people she got fancies. One of her fancies was to turn herself into a coffee table. There was no point in her being a coffee table: Mother Bloodwort did not drink coffee which was far too expensive, and since she lived alone there was no one who might have wanted to put a cup and saucer down on her. But she was a cranky old witch and every so often she remembered the spell that changed her from a white-haired, whiskery old woman into a low, oak table with carved legs and a glass top, and then there was no stopping her. What she did *not* often remember was how to turn herself back again.

17

'Oh, come along,' called Mabel Wrack from inside the bus. 'Leave the silly old thing where she is.'

From her mermaid mother Mabel had inherited rather scaly legs which dried out easily and itched, so she wanted to get to Windylow Heath where the air was damp and cool.

But just then something happened. Two sparrows who'd been squabbling in the gutter lifted their heads and began to sing like nightingales. A flock of golden butterflies appeared from nowhere, and, drifting through the grimy bus station, came the scent of primroses with morning dew on them.

'Ugh! It's her!' said Nancy Shouter. 'I'm off.' And she threw her chicken into the trailer and climbed into the bus.

'Me too,' said her twin. 'I can't *stand* her. I don't know why they allow her in the coven. Really I don't.'

Belladonna came slowly round the corner. She was a very young witch with thick, golden hair in which a short-eared bat hung like a little wrinkled prune. There was usually *something* in Belladonna's hair: a fledgling blackbird parked there by its mother while she went to hunt for worms, a baby squirrel wanting somewhere safe to eat its hazel nuts or a butterfly who thought she was a lily or a rose. Belladonna's nose turned up at the end, making a ledge for tired ladybirds to rest on; she had a high, clear forehead and eyes as blue as periwinkles. But as she came up to the bus she hesitated and looked troubled and sad, for she had learnt to expect only unkindness from the other witches.

18

Then she saw the coffee table and forgot her own troubles at once.

'Oh, *poor* Mother Bloodwort! Have you forgotten the undoing spell again?'

The table began to rock and Belladonna put her arms round it. 'Try to think,' she said. 'I'm sure you can remember. Was it a rhyming spell?'

The table rocked harder.

'It was? Well, I'm *sure* it'll come back in a minute.' She leant her cheek against the glass top, sending healing thoughts into the old witch's tired brain. 'It's coming back, I can *feel* it coming back . . .'

There was a swishing noise, Belladonna tumbled backwards and there, standing before her, was an old woman in a long mouse-bitten cloak and felt bedroom slippers with the sides cut out.

'Thank you, my dear,' croaked Mother Bloodwort. 'You're a kind girl even if you are—'

But she couldn't bring herself to say the dreadful word – no black witch can. So she hobbled to the bus and began to heave herself aboard, clutching to her chest a large, square tin showing a picture of King George VIth's Coronation on the lid. The tin *should* have gone in the trailer – there was a rule that all familiars travelled separately – but Mother Bloodwort never let it out of her sight. Inside it were hundreds of large white maggots which, when you blew on them, turned into a cloud of flies. *One* fly is no good for magic but a cloud of flies – flies in your hair, your eyes, your nose – that makes a very good familiar indeed.

Belladonna was the last to get into the bus. She alone of all the witches had no familiar. For white magic you do not need one. It was another thing that made her feel so very much alone.

Three

Belladonna had always been white. Even as a tiny baby she had used her witch's teeth only to bite the tops off milk bottles so that the bluetits could get at the cream, and as she grew older her whiteness grew steadily worse. Flowers sprang up where she walked, bursts of glorious music fell from the air, and when she smiled, old gentlemen remembered the Christmasses they had had when they were children. As for her hair – from the age of six or so when it had reached her waist, there had always been *someone* resting in Belladonna's golden hair.

Belladonna herself longed for blackness – to smite and blast and wreck and wither seemed to her the most wonderful thing in the world. But though she could heal people and charm the flowers out of the ground and speak the language of the animals, even the simplest bit of evil like, say, turning a pale green cucumber into a greasy black pudding with bits of fat in it, was more than she could manage. Not that she didn't try. Every morning before she went to work (she was an assistant in a flower shop) Belladonna would stand by the open window and say, 'Every day and in every way I am getting blacker and blacker.'

But she wasn't, and the worst thing she had to bear was the scorn and spite of the other witches. Belladonna really dreaded coven days when she was ignored and despised and had to huddle by herself out of the warm circle of firelight and feasting with only the familiars for company. The only reason she went was that she hoped, one day, some of the blackness might rub off on her.

The bus had left Todcaster now. There was one more witch to pick up on the way. She was a thin, pale witch whom the others called Monalot after a lady on a wireless programme who was always complaining. Monalot's real name was Gwendolyn Swamp and she played the harp in the Todcaster Palm Orchestra. Miss Swamp came from a family of banshees, which are the kind of witch that wails and sighs about the place and tells people when something awful is going to happen. Banshees have never been a healthy bunch, and Monalot was so often ill that to get her to the coven at all they usually stopped the bus specially by her house.

'She's not at the gate,' said Mabel Wrack, impatiently. The air-conditioning in the *Coven Special* was making her legs itch unbearably.

So Belladonna, who always took the messages and ran the errands for the others, climbed out of the bus and walked through the garden of Monalot's little villa with the name *Creepy Corner* written on the gate.

The door was open. Belladonna ran up to the bedroom, knocked on the door – and saw at once that Monalot would not be coming to the coven. The poor witch was completely covered in small red spots.

'It's the measles,' she moaned. 'All over me. Percy too.' She waved a limp hand to the corner of the room where her familiar, a large, sad-looking sheep, was lying. A sheep with measles is unusual, but where there is witchcraft anything is possible.

Belladonna was very upset

'Couldn't I help?' she began.

But like most witches, Monalot hated the word 'help'. 'No,' she moaned. 'Just go and leave me. No one wants me anyway, nobody cares.'

So Belladonna poured her a drink, plumped up her pillows and went out, passing, on Monalot's dressing table, wax images of her doctor and the district nurse, both stuck full of pins.

'I'm afraid it's hopeless,' she reported, back in the bus. 'Miss Swamp has the measles.'

'Stupid old banshee,' snapped Nora Shouter.

'They were always delicate, the Swamps,' said Mother Bloodwort. She had opened her tin with the Coronation on the lid and was stirring her maggots with a long and bony finger. She was still stirring and muttering when the bus got to Windylow Heath.

Two hours later the coven was in full swing. In the middle of the heath the bonfire roared and crackled, lighting up the Great Rock on which the Ancient Druids had done their dreadful deeds. The smell of burnt feathers from Ethel Feedbag's roasted jackdaw rose hideously on the night air; clouds passed to and fro across the fitful moon. The witches had finished feasting and singing rude songs (the kind where 'owl' doesn't just rhyme with 'howl' but with things like 'bowel' or 'foul') and were dancing back to back, or trying to. Ethel Feedbag's Wellingtons did not help, nor the size of her behind as she lurched round with Mabel Wrack.

'You're going the wrong way, you stupid faggot,' yelled Nancy over her shoulder to her twin. 'It's widdershins we should be going.'

'This *is* widdershins, you half-witted cow-pat,' Nora screamed back.

Mother Bloodwort did not dance any more. She sat as close to the fire as she could get, her mouse-bitten robe turned back so that the heat could get at her gnarled old legs. Every so often a handful of the flies that buzzed drunkenly round her head fell into the flames and vanished.

As for Belladonna, as usual she was left out in the cold. No one wanted to dance with her and anyway, like mothers who hand their children over to nannies and nursemaids, the witches had told Belladonna to take their familiars away to a little clump of thorn threes and keep them quiet.

This was easier said than done. As soon as the familiars saw Belladonna they always went to pieces. Ethel Feedbag's enormous pig had collapsed like a felled tree and was lying on its back, its legs in the air, squealing for her to scratch its stomach. The Shouter chickens, who hadn't laid anything in years, began to puff out their feathers and squawk, trying to please her with an egg, and Doris the octopus stuck a tentacle out of her plastic bucket and laid it softly on Belladonna's knee.

Meanwhile, over by the fire, the witches grew wilder and wilder. Mother Bloodwort was knocking back a bottle of black liquid labelled *Furniture Polish: Not for Human Consumption*. Mabel Wrack was

24

kicking her scaly legs higher and higher, showing off her garters of lungfish skin. The Shouter twins were hacking at each other's shins.

And then, suddenly, something happened.

First there came – from the very depths of the earth it seemed – a low and sinister rumbling. Then the ground began to shake and shiver and a dreadful crack appeared beneath the Great Rock of the Druids.

'It's an earthquake,' yelled Mabel Wrack, and the witches threw themselves on the ground, gibbering with fear.

Next came a thunder clap, louder than any they had ever heard, followed by a streak of forked lightning so brilliant that it turned night to day.

'The thunder before the lightning!' wailed Mother Bloodwort, and began to beat her white old head against the ground.

After that came the fog. A great, yellow, choking, blinding fog which rolled across the heath, enveloping everything in its cold and smothering darkness.

'It be t'end of the world,' wailed Ethel Feedbag.

'It's the Creeping Death,' shrieked Nora Shouter.

Only Belladonna was still on her feet, trying to comfort the terrified familiars.

Then, as suddenly as it had come, the Great Fog rolled away, there was a last clap of thunder – and the witches gasped.

For there, standing astride the Great Rock of the Druids was a figure so splendid, so magnificent, that it quite took their breath away.

Arriman had taken a lot of trouble with his clothes. He wore a flowing mantle embroidered with the constellations of the planets, his trousers were of gold lamé and he wore not just horns but antlers which Lester had fastened most cunningly behind his ears. With his devilish eyebrows, his soaring moustache and the sulphurous glow that surrounded him, he presented a vision from which one simply could not tear one's eyes.

'Greetings, ye foul-mouthed hags and lovers of darkness!' boomed the Great Magician.

'Greetings!' croaked the witches, rising slowly to their feet.

Arriman could not see Belladonna who was hidden behind a thorn tree, but he could see Mabel Wrack whose sea slug had fallen over one eye and Ethel Feedbag, a burnt jackdaw feather sticking to her chin. He could see Mother Bloodwort and he could see the Shouter twins, and when he'd seen them he turned and tried to scramble down the rock.

'Steady, sir,' said Mr Leadbetter, who was standing behind the rock with a sheaf of papers.

'The Cankers have never been quitters, sir,' said Lester, placing a huge hand on his master's shoulder.

Seeing his retreat cut off, Arriman reluctantly climbed up the rock again. The witches meanwhile were getting dreadfully excited. They had begun to realize that they were in the presence of the Great Wizard of the North, whom nobody had seen for years and years and years and whose power was the greatest in the land.

'Know ye,' Arriman went on bravely, 'that I am Arriman the Awful, Loather of Light and Blighter of the Beautiful.'

'Know we. I mean, we know,' croaked the witches.

26

'Know ye also that, obedient to the prophecy of the gypsy Esmeralda, I have waited nine hundred and ninety days for the coming of the new wizard to Darkington Hall.' He caught a whiff of manure from Ethel Feedbag's Wellingtons and staggered backwards.

'Bear up, sir,' came Lester's voice from the darkness behind him, and with a great effort, Arriman pulled himself together and went on.

'Know ye also that the aforesaid wizard not having turned up, I, Arriman Frederick Canker, have decided to take a wife.'

The excitement of the witches grew to a frenzy. They began to mutter and nudge each other and to cackle fiendishly because it was known that Arriman had sworn never to marry. Only Belladonna went on standing quietly in the shelter of the trees, her periwinkle eyes fixed wonderingly on the great magician.

'Know ye,' Arriman went on, bracing himself, 'that for my bride I have decided to choose a witch of Todcaster and that whichever witch I choose shall reign—' His voice broke. 'I can't do it,' he murmured, passing a hand across his eyes. He had just caught sight of Mother Bloodwort's fly-stained whiskers in a sudden spurt of firelight.

'No use turning back now, sir,' came Mr Leadbetter's quiet voice. But both the secretary and the ogre, peering out behind the rock, were very much upset. They had had no idea that things had got so bad in Todcaster.

So Arriman made a last desperate effort. 'Know ye,' he went on, 'that to choose which witch shall be my bride I have arranged a Great Competition in the grounds of my estate at Darkington during the fearful week of Hallowe'en. And know ye that whichever witch does there the vilest, darkest and most powerful piece of magic shall be my wife!'

Pandemonium now broke out. Arriman waited for the lurching, cackling and hiccuping to die down and then he said, 'Mr Leadbetter, my secretary, will stay behind to give you your instructions for the contest. And remember,' he said, throwing out his arms, 'that what I am looking for is power, wickedness and evil. Darkness is All!'

And with a sigh of relief, Arriman vanished.

When the witches had calmed down again, Mr Leadbetter stepped out from behind the rock and handed everyone an entry form for the contest. Mother Bloodwort, who couldn't read, held hers upside down, and the Shouter twins immediately began arguing about how many days there were to Hallowe'en.

'What about that lady over there?' said Mr Leadbetter. He had caught sight of the pale glimmer of Belladonna's hair between the trees.

'Oh, you don't want to bother with *her*,' said Nancy Shouter.

'She's not one of us,' said her twin.

'Still, she is a witch,' said Mother Bloodwort, spitting out a couple of flies. She was the only one who sometimes had a kind word for Belladonna. So Mr Leadbetter walked over to the clump of trees where Belladonna was still trying to calm the familiars.

'Oh dear,' he said when he had introduced himself. 'How *very* unfortunate.'

For he realized as soon as he saw her what was wrong. The little, short-eared bat hanging so tenderly in her hair, the chickens roosting on her feet, the scent of primroses with morning dew on them. 'Have you . . . er . . . always been . . .?'

'White?' said Belladonna sadly. 'Yes. From birth.'

'Nothing can be done, I suppose?'

Belladonna shook her head. 'I've tried everything.'

'You won't be going in for the contest, then?'

Belladonna shook her head. 'What would be the use? You heard him. "Darkness is All," he said.' Witches cannot cry any more than wizards can, but her eyes were wide with sorrow. 'Tell me, is he really . . . as marvellous as he looks?'

Mr Leadbetter thought. Pictures came into his mind. Arriman shrieking with rage when he lost his suspenders. Arriman filling the bath with electric eels and giggling. Arriman ordering twelve stinking emus for the zoo and leaving his secretary to unpack them . . . But there was nothing mean or small-spirited about Arriman and it was very sincerely that Mr Leadbetter said, 'He is a gentleman. Most truly a gentleman.'

'I thought he must be,' said Belladonna, sighing.

'Well, I'll leave you one of these anyway, in case you change your mind,' he said. 'And perhaps you'd be kind enough to see that – Miss Swamp, is it – gets hers too?' He had turned away when he remembered something. 'I'm going to vanish in a minute,' he said. 'At least I hope I am. I don't have any magic powers myself so I hope the Great Man will remember. But when I do there'll be some presents on the rock – one for each witch. Make sure you get yours.'

'Oh, thank you, I will,' said Belladonna. Then she added shyly, 'I hope you don't mind my saying so, but when you walked away just now I thought how *very* good-looking it was. Your tail, I mean. Mostly the backs of gentlemen are so flat and dull.'

Mr Leadbetter was very much moved. 'Thank you, my dear; you've made me very happy. Of course the moonlight is flattering. By daylight it can look a little crude.'

He pressed her hand gratefully. It was on the tip of his tongue to tell her about his childhood and the shock of finding that he was not like other boys, but just then Arriman found he needed his secretary. There was a little puff of smoke and Mr Leadbetter vanished.

Almost at once, the other witches began to shriek and yammer.

'Look! Over there, on the rock!'

'Something glittering!'

The next second they were all scrambling at a pile of oval handmirrors, very beautiful ones, set in frames of precious stones. But when they looked into the mirrors' shining surfaces they did not see their own ugly faces. They saw the face of the great Arriman with his flashing eyes and curving nose and magnificent moustache. What was more, the mirror showed the witches what Arriman was doing at any moment in time so that they could get to know him and his habits and know what awaited them at Darkington if they should win.

'What a smasher!' said Nora Shouter.

'Well, you're not going to win, *I'm* going to win!'

'Cor, I wouldn't mind being married to 'im,' said Ethel Feedbag. 'Give the sheep the staggers, I will, when I get up there – an' the cows the bloat.'

Mabel Wrack smiled pityingly. The daughter of Mrs Wrack, who'd been a mermaid, was such an obvious winner that she had nothing at all to worry about. 'Mabel Canker, Wizardess of the North'. It sounded good.

'I never thought I'd be glad I buried poor Mr Bloodwort,' said Mother Bloodwort. 'But I am because now I can go in for the competition.'

'You!' shrieked the Shouter twins. 'You're far too old!'

'I am now,' said Mother Bloodwort, 'though there's a lot of men as likes an older woman. But I've got a turning-myself-young-again spell. It's on the tip of my tongue, and when I remember it I won't half make things hum!'

Belladonna had crept shyly forward and picked up one of the two mirrors that still glittered on the rock. Arriman was taking off his antlers – she could just see Lester's huge hand undoing the sellotape. The great man looked tired and discouraged. Oh, if only she could be there to stroke his forehead and comfort him!

'What are *you* hanging round for?' said Mabel Wrack. '*You* won't be going in for the competition.'

'That'd be a joke. Blossoming roses in the snow! Golden singing birds! *Yak*!' said Nora Shouter.

Belladonna said nothing. In silence she helped the other witches pack up their picnics, lifted Doris into the trailer, soothed Ethel Feedbag's pig. But when the

31

bus was ready to leave she did not join the others. It was a long walk back to Todcaster in the darkness, but she welcomed the idea of it. More than anything, she wanted to be alone.

She was sitting quietly on the rock where He had stood, gazing into the mirror when a high and irritable voice said, 'Well, I think you're just being wet. Wet and feeble.'

Belladonna sat up, startled. Then she realized that the voice had spoken not 'human' but 'bat' and had come from her own hair.

'Not to say spineless,' the little bat went on. 'Why don't you at least have a *try*?'

'Don't be silly,' said Belladonna. 'You know perfectly well that I can't even make a toad come out of someone's mouth and that's the corniest piece of blackness that there is.'

'People change,' said the bat. 'Take my Aunt Screwtooth. She was the most useless old bat you can imagine – couldn't suck juice out of an over-ripe pear without her husband to hold her claw. Then they took a holiday in some place abroad. Transylvania or some such name. She fell in with a family of vampires and settled over there. You should see her now, sucking blood as if it were mother's milk. Fairly sozzled with the stuff she is. And if my Aunt Screwtooth, why not you?'

Belladonna was bending over the mirror again. Arriman was in his pyjamas now. Yellow silk, they were, edged with black braid.

'Is that really true? About your Aunt Screwtooth?'

The little bat blushed in the darkness. He had

32

made the whole thing up because he loved Belladonna.

But Belladonna did not see. She was thinking. If she went in for the contest she could at least *see* him again. He'd be one of the judges for sure. And once she was there, maybe she'd find *some* way to help and comfort him.

She stood up. 'All right,' she said, 'I'll do it. I'll have a try.'

Four

Mr Leadbetter was very fond of watching television. In spite of his little stump of a tail he was a very ordinary person, and when the magic and goings-on at Darkington were too much for him he liked to go quietly to his room and watch the box.

One of Mr Leadbetter's favourite programmes was the one that showed the Miss World competition. Mr Leadbetter knew, of course, that it was silly for girls to let themselves be prodded and measured like cows or turnips at an agricultural show, but all the same he very much liked all the contestants coming from different countries and staying together at a hotel and appearing first in their National Costumes and then in their Evening Dresses and then in their Swim Suits, and when the most beautiful one climbed on to the platform and had a crown put on her head, Mr Leadbetter always felt a lump come to his throat.

So when it was decided to hold a competition for the Blackest Witch of Todcaster, Mr Leadbetter decided to organize it rather in the way that the Miss World contest was organized. Not, of course, that he thought of making the witches parade in their swim suits. Even before he saw Mother Bloodwort and Mabel Wrack and Ethel Feedbag he had not thought of *that*. But it seemed to him a good idea that the witches should be brought together in a hotel first and get their clothes and their table manners sorted out before they got to Darkington. Above all, he wanted to make sure that they knew the rules and that no hanky panky went on between them. Any witch casting a spell on another witch was to be disqualified *immediately*.

So he rented the Grand Spa Hotel on the outskirts of Todcaster. It was a very grand hotel with a cocktail lounge and a ballroom and a terrace with stripy deck-chairs, and the Manager, who was quite used to conferences of politicians and schoolteachers and clergymen, rather welcomed the idea of a conference of witches.

But after his first day there, Mr Leadbetter began to feel that he had made a terrible mistake. Mother Bloodwort and the Shouter twins and Ethel Feedbag just did not *behave* like Miss Australia and Miss Belgium and Miss U.S.A. In fact, as Mr Leadbetter said to Lester, who had come to help him, if it wasn't for Belladonna he'd have had a good mind to chuck the whole thing and let Arriman get on with choosing his own wife.

Belladonna, who had arrived earlier carrying a straw basket with her toothbrush, her nightdress and the magic mirror, had been wonderful. It was Belladonna who had tactfully removed Ethel Feedbag's wellies and hosed them down in the pantry when the Manager complained about manure on his carpet. It was Belladonna who had sellotaped up Mother Bloodwort's tin with the Coronation on the lid and persuaded the old woman that at the best hotels one did not come down to dinner in a Cloud of Flies. And when Mabel Wrack got into the bath fully clothed because her legs were drying out, causing Doris (who liked to be alone) to squirt her all over with inky fluid, it was Belladonna who cleared up the mess and carried the irritated animal to her own bathroom and quietened her.

Not that she got any thanks for it. 'It makes my blood boil,' said Lester, 'the way those witches talk to you.'

'Oh, well,' said Belladonna. 'It's hard for them, me being . . . you know . . .'

They were in the office, which the Manager had kindly lent to Mr Leadbetter, snatching a quick cup of tea. Lester, who'd been badly hit by the sight of the witches in daylight, was prowling round looking for a sword to swallow. Mr Leadbetter, like everyone who organizes things, was shuffling his papers and worrying.

'Maybe you're just *fancying* yourself white,' Lester went on. He found the Manager's umbrella, looked at it and put it down again. There wasn't any real skill in swallowing umbrellas and if they came unfurled inside it could be messy.

'I'm afraid not,' said Belladonna. As usual she was looking into the magic mirror which she carried with her everywhere. Arriman was sitting hunched up in what seemed to be a broom cupboard.

'*Try!*' said Lester, who'd set his heart on Belladonna as mistress of Darkington Hall. 'Look, see that typewriter on the desk? Bet if you really put your mind to it you could turn it into a nest of vipers or something. I mean, you've got to *believe* in yourself.'

Belladonna sighed. She knew it was useless but she hated disappointing people so she got up and felt in the pocket of her skirt for a magic wand or something of the sort. There wasn't anything, of course – only a handful of healing herbs, the identity disc of a carrier pigeon who was playing truant from his loft and a baby field mouse. So she put everything back and just closed her eyes, waved her arms over the typewriter and thought of the blackest things she could think of, such as uncooked liver and shoelaces and open graves. Then she stepped back.

'Oh dear!' said Mr Leadbetter.

The typewriter had not turned into a nest of vipers. It had turned into a pot of pink begonias; charming, sweetly-scented flowers, each cradling a golden bee.

'Pretty,' said the ogre gloomily.

'I told you,' said Belladonna, very much embarrassed. She turned the typewriter back again and picked up the magic mirror. How dreadfully the Great Man would despise her if he knew!

'Still sulking, is he?' said Lester.

'Oh, no, he could never *sulk*,' said Belladonna. 'But he hasn't perhaps been very . . . *cheerful* lately.'

'You can say that again,' said the ogre.

And indeed, ever since he had seen his choice of future brides at the coven, Arriman had been in a terrible state. He woke screaming from dreadful nightmares, babbling of fly-stained whiskers chasing him down corridors. He was off his food, his moustache had begun to moult and he hounded the Wizard Watcher unmercifully, sending the poor beast out to the gate long before daybreak in a last, desperate hope that the new wizard might still come and he could cancel the competition.

37

'I can't help wondering why he is sitting in a *broom* cupboard,' said Belladonna.

'I'll tell you why,' said Lester frowning. 'Because he's waiting for Sir Simon, that's why. Favourite spot of Sir Simon's, the broom cupboard.'

'Is that the rather dead-looking gentleman he speaks to sometimes?' enquired Belladonna.

Lester nodded. 'Very dead-looking. Died in 1583,' he said. 'Murdered all seven of his wives.'

Mr Leadbetter put down his papers and came over, and together the ogre and the secretary looked over Belladonna's shoulder at their employer. Sure enough, a wavering shadow appeared on the surface of the mirror and Arriman rose eagerly to his feet.

'I don't like it,' said Lester, shaking his enormous head. 'He's been trying to bring Sir Simon back to life for years, but since the coven he's been at it all the time. When I brought him his egg this morning he was sitting up in bed with this huge book – *Necromancy* it was called. Nasty.'

'I wouldn't worry,' said Mr Leadbetter. 'I believe it's two hundred years since anyone managed to raise a ghost.'

But he was a little more anxious than he admitted. Suppose Arriman *did* manage it? A man who had murdered all seven of his wives did not seem to be a good person to have around in a house where there was soon to be a wedding.

An hour later the witches were all assembled in the cocktail lounge of the hotel waiting for Mr Leadbetter to tell them the rules of the contest. They had taken a lot of trouble to make themselves smart. Mabel Wrack had plaited her frizzy hair with a string of dogfish egg-cases, Mother Bloodwort's chin sprouted a brand-new piece of sticking plaster, and Ethel Feedbag had nobly left her wellies upstairs and was in bedsocks.

'Are we all here?' asked Mr Leadbetter, letting his eyes rest for a moment on Belladonna, sitting quietly apart from the others on a stool.

'No,' said Nancy Shouter, jangling her knuckle-bone ear-rings. 'Silly old Monalot's not here.'

Mr Leadbetter sighed. Miss Swamp had sent in her entrance form, but so far there had been no sign of her, and he was a person who hated muddle.

'No point in her going in for the competition anyway,' said Mabel Wrack. 'A flabby old banshee like that.'

'And that sheep of hers. Gives me the bots!' said Ethel Feedbag.

The others nodded. It was true that Percy really was a most depressing animal: the kind that always thinks other sheep are having a better life than he is, and eating greener grass and *doing* more.

'Well, we shall have to begin without her,' said Mr Leadbetter.

But just then the hotel porter came in and whispered something to Mr Leadbetter whose face brightened. 'Show her in please,' he said. 'We're expecting another lady.'

But the new witch didn't seem to be someone one showed in. The new witch came striding in like a queen and as she came the other witches shrank back in their chairs and Belladonna drew in her breath.

Because the new witch was not Monalot. Nothing less like the pale, sickly Miss Swamp could be

39

imagined. The new witch was very tall with black hair piled high on her head. She had long, blood-red fingernails and round her shoulders she wore a cape of puppy skin. Her fingers and wrists sparkled with jewels, but the necklace wound round her throat was, unexpectedly, not of pearls or diamonds but of human teeth. But what startled the others most was the new witch's familiar. Dragging behind her on a rhinestone-studded lead there came a grey, lumbering animal with a snout like a hoover and wicked-looking claws.

'What is it?' whispered Mother Bloodwort, who could never scrape up enough money to go to the zoo.

'I think it's an aardvark,' Belladonna whispered back.

'Good evening,' said the new witch. 'I am Madame Olympia. I have come to take part in the competition.'

'I'm afraid there's been some mistake,' said Mr Leadbetter. 'The competition is limited to the witches of Todcaster.'

Madame Olympia smiled – a smile that sent shivers down one's spine.

'I *am* a witch of Todcaster,' she said.

'How can that be?' began Mr Leadbetter. 'We—'

'I have bought Miss Gwendolyn Swamp's house, Creep Corner,' interrupted the newcomer, dropping the rhinestone lead carelessly on to a chair. 'Too small for me, of course, but not without charm. Miss Swamp found she wanted to travel.'

'Monalot *never* wanted to travel,' said Mother Bloodwort stoutly. 'Travel brought her out in spots

40

an' all sorts. It was all you could do to get Monalot down the road for a bag of bulls' eyes.'

'She is travelling now, however,' said Madame Olympia with another of her sinister smiles. 'Oh, yes, she is definitely travelling now. Somewhere round Turkey I would guess.'

She opened her crocodile-skin handbag and began to powder her nose. And when she saw the vain, proud look that Madame Olympia threw at herself in the mirror, Belladonna suddenly understood what kind of a person the new witch was. She was an enchantress, one of the oldest and most evil kind of witch there is. Morgan le Fay, the one who caused the death of the great King Arthur was one, and Circe, who turned brave Ulysses' men to swine. Enchantresses are beautiful, but it is an evil beauty. They use it to snare men and make them helpless and tear from them the secrets of their power. And when they have got all they want from them, they destroy them.

'Well, madam, I suppose you had better let me have your entrance form,' said Mr Leadbetter. Fair was fair, and if the new witch now lived in Todcaster she was eligible to join. But he felt very unhappy as he wrote her name down on the register. Mr Leadbetter didn't know much about enchantresses, but there was something about Madame Olympia that made his blood run cold.

Not only was Madame Olympia not a witch of Todcaster, she wasn't a Witch of the North at all. She lived in London where she kept a Beauty Parlour. It was a wicked place. Stupid women were lured into it and assured they would become young and

41

beautiful if they let themselves be pummelled and pounded and smeared with sticky creams and have their faces lifted and their stomach flattened. They paid a lot of money to Madame Olympia who would put a little bit of magic into the creams and ointments that she used so that at first they did look marvellous. But it was the kind of magic that wore off very quickly, leaving the women even uglier than before so that they would rush back to her and pay her more money and the whole thing would start again. She was also horrid to the girls she employed and paid them too little and bullied them.

Madame Olympia had had five husbands. All these husbands had disappeared in very odd ways, mostly after they had made wills leaving her all their money. She *said* that they had died, but it was odd that a werewolf with weak, blue eyes and a bald patch had appeared in Epping Forest, very much frightening the inhabitants, just after she had reported her first husband's death. The second and third husbands had vanished within a year of each other, and each time the girls in the Beauty Parlour were struck by the way Madame's necklace of human teeth suddenly got very much longer. The fourth Mr Olympia really did run his Jaguar into a lamp-post, but the fifth . . . well, no one knew for certain what had happened to him, but the coffin in which he was carried to his funeral was most *suspiciously* light.

And now she was after Arriman the Awful, Wizard of the North!

As soon as she had heard of the competition she had come straight up to Todcaster and 'persuaded' Monalot to sell her house. Monalot hadn't wanted to go, of course: she'd sobbed and moaned and pleaded; after all, she wasn't a banshee for nothing. But by the time Madame Olympia had suggested just a few of the things she might do to her, and to Percy, if she didn't, Monalot had been very glad to sell her house and take a nice package tour round the world. Very glad indeed.

Mr Leadbetter had begun to explain the rules of the competition. The witches were to wear black gowns and masks so that the judges would not go by the way they looked but by the blackness of their magic. They were to draw numbers out of a hat and do their tricks in the order that they drew. They were to hand in a list of anything they might need for the contest: dragons' blood, sieves to go to sea in and so on, so that they would be ready in good time . . .

Madame Olympia hardly bothered to listen. One look at the other witches and she had known she would win. The little golden-haired thing was quite fetching, but anyone could see what was wrong with *her*. Oh, yes, she'd be Queen of Darkington all right. And then . . .!

Hardly waiting for Mr Leadbetter to finish, she rose to her feet and stretched. 'See that my aardvark is watered and fed, please,' she ordered carelessly. 'I'm going to change for dinner.'

And she glided out of the room, leaving the other witches boiling and bubbling with indignation.

'Cocky, sneering cow, who does she think she is?' said Nancy Shouter. 'Hope she drops dead.'

And for once, her twin agreed with her.

*

43

It was a long time before Belladonna slept that night. Dinner had been excellent, but even before the piece of sticking plaster fell from Mother Bloodwort's chin into her mushroom soup, Belladonna had not been really hungry. Then there was a fuss about Ethel Feedbag who had a double bed and wanted to share it with her pig, and when Belladonna got to her room at last there was still Doris in the bath, waving to her and wanting to be noticed.

But it was none of that that worried Belladonna. It was the glimpse she had had, passing an open door, of Madame Olympia, standing in a gold négligé, her black hair falling round her shoulders, the aardvark cowering at her feet. She was looking into the magic mirror that had been left for Monalot and laughing – a low and truly evil sound.

'You wanted Power and Darkness, you Wizard of the North,' Belladonna heard her say. 'Well, Power and Darkness you shall have!'

And it was with the sound of the new witch's horrible laughter still in her ears that Belladonna fell asleep at last.

Five

Belladonna was still worried when she awoke. It seemed to her certain that Madame Olympia would win the competition and become Mrs Canker, and she feared most dreadfully for Arriman.

She got up and went to the open window and at once a family of bluetits flew on to her shoulder and started telling her a long story about a nesting box which wasn't fit for a flea to sleep in and the shocking way that people carried on, taking their milk bottles in too soon and keeping cats.

Belladonna sighed. She could cope with one bluetit in her hair, but a whole family always gave her a headache.

'You can stay, but in my straw basket,' she said, managing for once to be firm.

Doris, fortunately, was still asleep, her body bleached to the whiteness of the bath, her vile eyes peacefully closed. Belladonna cleaned her teeth and went downstairs. The rooms were deserted and silent still. She didn't feel like the other witches this morning; she didn't feel like anybody. And slipping out of a side door into the street, she began to walk away from the hotel.

She walked and she walked and she walked, letting her feet carry her where they would, and presently she found that she had left the pleasant gardens and smart shops which surounded the Grand Spa Hotel and was in a poor and slummy part of the town where the houses were neglected and dirty, orange peel and broken glass littered the gutters and mangy dogs foraged in the dustbins.

She crossed a mean little square with a few dusty laurel bushes, a boarded-up lemonade stall and a public lavatory, and found herself in front of a large, grey building with curtains the colour of bile. A flight of mottled stone steps led from the side of the building into a patch of gravel and scuffed earth which might once have been a garden. And there, hunched on the low wall which ran beside the pavement was a small boy. He was looking down at something that he held cupped in his skinny hands and making that kind of hiccuping noise that people make when they are trying not to cry.

What was cupped in the boy's hands was an earthworm. And the name of the boy – a name he hated – was Terence Mugg.

When he was a very small baby, Terence Mugg had been found wrapped in a newspaper in a telephone kiosk behind the railway station. The newspaper had smelt of vinegar, and the lady who found it had thought at first that it was a packet of fish and chips. However, when the fish and chips packet burst and put out a small, pink hand she screamed and ran for a policeman.

At the police station, Terence was fed and clothed and photographed in the arms of a pretty police lady. But when his picture appeared in the paper no one said, 'Ooh!' and 'Aah!' and 'Isn't he sweet?', and no one wrote in offering to adopt him (though an old gentleman wrote in offering to adopt the police lady). Terence just wasn't that kind of baby. There were even people cruel enough to say they might have left him in a telephone kiosk themselves.

So poor Terence was sent to the Sunnydene Children's Home in the most dismal part of Todcaster and Matron christened him 'Terence' after an actor she fancied at the time and 'Mugg' because she said, 'With a mug like that, what else can he be called?'

Babies in children's homes usually get adopted quite quickly, but not Terence. Not only was he an unusually plain baby, but he spent the first five years of his life getting not only chicken pox and whooping cough but really quite unusual things like brain fever and dermatitis and croup. Naturally nobody wants to adopt a baby whose entire head is swathed in banadages or whose face is covered with spots or who can't digest cheese without turning as yellow as a lentil. By the time he was five and had started at the local school, Terence had quite given up hope of finding a family of his own to love him.

'We'll have *that* one with us for life,' Matron would say nastily as Terence crept past her like a battered little snail. 'No Mrs Right's going to come along for *him.*'

People who are lonely and unloved often turn to animals for company and that was what Terence had done. Only, of course, at the Sunnydene Children's Home, Matron did not allow proper pets. So it was little things – small spiders and hurrying woodlice and shiny beetles – that Terence played with when he was out in the waste patch they called a garden, or found under paving stones on the way to school.

It was in this way that he had found Rover.

Rover was an earthworm, a pale pink, slender animal with a mauve bulge in the middle, a pointed end and a peaceful way of crawling along the ground.

Terence had liked him immediately. There was something a little special about Rover. He did not seem quite like other worms who often appear to have no notion of doing anything beyond burrowing down into the soil. Rover would curl into knots around Terence's fingers or lie quietly in the palm of his hand, and sometimes he would rear up his pointed end in a most intelligent way. Terence had found him in a tub of earth outside a chemist's shop and he'd sneaked him into the Home and found a place for him in the garden – a jam jar filled with leaf mould which he was careful to keep damp because his teacher had told him that earthworms breathe through their skins and should never get dry. He'd buried the jam jar behind a pile of bricks and told no one – only Billy who was deaf and hadn't been adopted either. Billy was another person who didn't bother living things.

And there Rover had lived as happily as anything until last night when Matron had found Terence and Billy talking to him when they should have been inside getting ready for bed.

'How *dare* you!' she had shouted, charging down the garden like an ill-tempered camel. 'Come inside at once! And throw that disgusting, insanitary worm away immediately!'

And when Terence did not instantly do what he

was told she snatched Rover's jar and turned it upside down, scuffing at the leaf mould with her sharp and spiky shoes.

She had hurt Rover. Hurt him badly. He was no better this morning: there was a wound in his middle where the skin was broken and his inside was spilling out in a terrible way. Rover wasn't moving, either; he just lay there, perfectly still and stretched in Terence's hand.

He was going to die.

'Hello!' said a soft and musical voice above his head, and Terence, looking up, saw the most beautiful girl he had ever seen – a girl he would have been frightened of except that her blue eyes looked sad, and sadness was something Terence knew about. 'My name is Belladonna,' the gentle voice went on. 'What's yours?'

The little boy flushed. 'Terence Mugg,' he said, staring up at her through his big, steel-rimmed spectacles. 'And this,' he swallowed, 'is Rover. Only,' he said, keeping his voice steady with an effort, 'I think he's going . . . to die.'

Belladonna looked carefully at the worm. She did not think Rover was an odd name for an earthworm. She knew at once that he was called Rover because Terence dreadfully wanted a dog and knew he would never get one. And she knew too, that Terence was right. Rover was very, very sick.

'May I hold him for a moment?' she asked.

Terence hesitated. When somebody that belongs to you is going to die you feel you should hold on to him and help him right to the end. But when he saw the look on Belladonna's face he carefully opened his hand and gave her his worm.

Belladonna bent over Rover and her hair fell like a golden curtain, inside which the wounded worm lay snug and warm. Then she began to croon a little song.

Terence had never heard a song like the one that Belladonna sang. It was about dampness and the soft darkness of the rich earth and about the patient worms who had turned it through the years. It was a song about pinkness and wetness and roundness, and while she sang it, Terence felt that he too, was an earthworm and understood the soul of all earth-worms and always would. Then she blew three times on her cupped hands and parted them.

'Let's see now,' she said.

'Oh!' said Terence. '*Oh!*'

The little jagged place where Matron's shoe had hit the earthworm's side was quite closed over. Rover's skin was smooth again, there was no scar, and even as Terence gazed at him, Rover reared up his pointed end in just the jaunty way he used to do.

Terence was possibly the ugliest little boy that Belladonna had ever seen, but now his face was shining like an archangel's. 'He's better! He's all right again! You *healed* him! Oh, Rover, you're fine again, you're better than before!' He looked up at Belladonna. 'Only you didn't give him any medicine or anything. Are you a vet, then?' But his face was puzzled because he had seen vets and they did not look like Belladonna.

'Well, not exactly,' said Belladonna. 'But sometimes I can—' She broke off and flinched. Quite the most

50

unpleasant voice she had ever heard was coming at her from the top of the steps.

'Where is that dratted boy,' it whined. 'Skulking in the garden again! Really, I don't know why they bothered to fish him out of the telephone kiosk, he's been nothing but trouble since the day he arrived.'

The unpleasant voice belonged to a tall, bony woman with a yellowish skin and a nose you could have cut cheese with.

'It's Matron,' whispered Terence and drew closer to Belladonna.

'Oh there you are, you wretched boy! Well, come in at *once* or you'll have no lunch. And if you've still got that slimy worm I'm going to flush him down the lavatory, and you after him!'

She began to charge down the steps, and Belladonna could feel Terence shrinking beside her. 'No,' he said. 'Please. I'll put him away.'

Matron took no notice at all. She had reached the bottom step and was coming at them along the gravel path. 'As for you,' she said, glaring at Belladonna, 'I'd like to know what you're doing, trespassing in a private garden.'

'Will you take him?' Terence whispered.

Belladonna nodded and slipped Rover into her hand. Then she put her arm round Terence's shoulders. And as she felt the shivers that shook his thin little frame, a great anger shot through her. Belladonna was almost never angry, but she was angry now. Very angry.

Belladonna closed her eyes. She took a deep breath. And then she called on a god that white witches do not usually call on. 'Oh, great Cernunnos, you

51

Horned One, please help me halt this *revolting* woman!'

Matron was coming closer. Closer still ... Then suddenly she stumbled and looked back at her left foot. She tugged at it. She pulled. Nothing happened. Matron's left foot would not move.

'Oh!' gasped Terence. '*Look!*'

A little bulge had appeared at the tip of Matron's left shoe. Then the leather burst open and a green root appeared and began to snake along the ground and bury itself in the soil. From the side of the shoe came another root, and another ... The roots grew thicker and stronger; gnarled they were now, like the roots of an ancient beech and always pushing down, down into the ground.

'Help!' shrieked Matron. 'Help! *Eek!*'

It was happening to the other foot now. From her heels, her toes, her ankles, her knobbly knees ... Roots that began soft and green and became thicker and more twisted as they grew downwards; roots like great creepers, like ropes – and all tethering Matron as if with bands of steel to the ground.

'Help!' shrieked Matron again. But no one heard her and now the roots were coming out of her waist, her arms ... And then she could shriek no more because a tendril had sprung out of her upper lip and was snaking down towards the ground, closing her mouth as firmly as a trap.

'*Oh!*' said Terence once again. He was still nestling against her skirt, but when Belladonna looked down she saw that he wasn't frightened, just amazed. 'You did it!' said Terence, 'I know you did it. You're magic, aren't you? You're a witch!'

52

Belladonna nodded. She too, was very much excited, because rooting people to the ground is magic all right but it is not really very white. Rooting a begonia or a cabbage or a clump of wallflowers is white because begonias and cabbages and clumps of wallflowers like to have roots and cannot live without them. But rooting Matrons is a different matter. If it wasn't actually *black* magic, it was certainly fairly grey, and Belladonna's eyes were shining as she looked at Terence.

'You've brought me luck,' she said. 'You and Rover. That's the blackest thing I've done, *ever*.'

'You mean you usually do white magic, like healing people and so on?' said Terence. It struck Belladonna that he seemed to have a natural feeling for magic and not to show any of the fears one would expect in so nervous a boy. 'But do you *want* to be black?'

'Yes I do. I do terribly,' said Belladonna. And she explained about the competition and Arriman. She was too shy to tell Terence that she loved Arriman, but she thought he had probably guessed. He was that kind of little boy. Suddenly a thought struck her. 'Terence, you don't think . . .' She looked down at the worm, now distinctly perky and inclined to tie himself into knots round her finger. 'You don't think that Rover . . . that he might be a *familiar*. I never had one, you know. The other witches did, but I didn't. Do you think,' – Belladonna was growing very excited now – 'do you think it was because I was holding Rover that I managed to root Matron?'

'It might be.' Terence was as excited as she was.

'Only I thought familiars were usually black cats and hares and goats and things?'

'Oh, no.' And Belladonna explained about the octopus called Doris, and Madame Olympia's aardvark and the Cloud of Flies.

'He's so little,' said Terence. There was a pause, broken only by a furious, suffocated grunt from Matron, up whose legs a large black spider was steadily marching. 'But if he has helped you,' Terence went on bravely, 'then you must have him. Take him with you so's you win the competition.'

Belladonna was incredibly touched.

'I couldn't, Terence. I couldn't separate you two. You belong together. Anyway, I haven't a hope of winning the competition even so.'

But Terence now was clutching her arm and looking up at her, his eyes pleading.

'If you couldn't separate us, couldn't you . . . Oh, please, *please* couldn't you take me with you? Witches have servants, I know they do. Imps and . . . fiends and things. I'd do anything for you, *anything*.'

'Oh, Terence, I'd love to, but how can I? I'm staying in this posh hotel and they'd never let you come. And anyway, witches don't really mix with ordinary people, you know. It never comes right.'

But her voice trailed away as she said it, for what was 'right' for Terence about the Sunnydene Children's Home? And what would happen to him when Matron stopped being rooted? Belladonna had absolutely no idea how long the spell would last and the glitter in Matron's eye as she tugged uselessly at her roots boded extremely ill for Terence.

Terence did not say anything. He just stood there,

54

dejected and beaten, but still holding out to her his worm.

'Oh, heck,' said Belladonna suddenly, making up her mind. 'Let's just *do* it. It may come right.'

She climbed over the low wall and turned, stretching out a hand to Terence. Then, followed by the strangled grunts of the rooted Matron, they ran together down the road.

Six

When Belladonna got back to the hotel, she took Terence straight to the Manager's office to see Mr Leadbetter and the ogre.

She found them in a bad way. There had been a row about Ethel Feedbag's pig, which was not house-trained, and when the Manager complained, Ethel (who had not been well brought up) said, 'Oh, go and teach your grandmother to suck eggs!' Unfortunately she had been clutching her hazel wand at the time and the next moment the Manager found himself in a Nursing Home in Bexhill-on-Sea holding out a raw egg to his mother's mother, a frail old lady who had been looking forward to her morning Bovril and was very much annoyed.

The muddle had taken a long time to clear up and then it was discovered that Mother Bloodwort, who had been riding up and down in the hotel lift all morning, had got jammed between floors. Trying to remember the spell for making things go up in the air, she had got mixed up and become a coffee table once again, and since coffee tables cannot press Emergency Buttons, she had caused a great deal of trouble to the engineers.

But when they saw Belladonna, the secretary and the ogre both cheered up and greeted Terence most politely.

Belladonna lost no time in explaining about Terence and the horrible Home. 'And he's brought this absolutely *marvellous* familiar!' she went on. 'He made me able to do a really quite black thing. Me!'

The ogre and Mr Leadbetter looked round the room, wondering if they had missed a stampeding bufflalo or a wolverine with slavering fangs, but all they could see was a small and skinny boy, his gaze fixed wonderingly on the ogre's single eye.

'Show them, Terence,' said Belladonna.

So Terence felt in his pocket and lifted out Rover and put him carefully down on Mr Leadbetter's blotter. The secretary and the ogre bent over him and their hearts sank. A small, pale worm whose bristles as he crawled across the paper made a delicate soughing noise like autumn leaves stirred by the softest of winds. And for a moment they'd really hoped!

'Shall I try the typewriter?' said Belladonna eagerly. 'Like you wanted me to yesterday? A nest of vipers, wasn't it? Come on, Terence.'

So Terence picked up Rover and stood beside her and Belladonna rested her fingertips lightly on the little worm's mauve and slightly bulgy middle and closed her eyes. And, lo and behold, the typewriter vanished with a puff and there on the desk was a writhing mass of hissing vipers with darting tongues and slitty, yellow eyes.

'Poor little things,' said Belladonna, forgetting her blackness for a moment. 'They look awfully dry.'

'Vipers is born dry,' said Lester, 'so don't you go fretting yourself.'

But the look he exchanged with Mr Leadbetter was

eager and excited. If Belladonna could get black so quickly, there was hope yet!

'Amazing!' said Mr Leadbetter. He looked at Rover again to see if he had missed anything: a hidden poison sac, a lethal sting – but the worm now crawling peaceably up Terence's sleeve was exactly what he seemed: gentle, modest and moist.

'So I was wondering,' said Belladonna, putting her arm round Terence's shoulder, 'if Terence could *possibly* stay for a bit? Rover belongs to him and though he offered to give him to me, I just *couldn't* take him away.'

Mr Leadbetter looked worried. What would the Manager say to another guest? And what about the other witches? Would it start an absolute avalanche of witch friends and relations coming to stay at the hotel? Fishy little Wracks and quarrelling Shouter cousins and small Feedbags in nasty Wellington boots?

Terence said nothing. He just stood there, waiting. He was not a boy who had ever hoped for much.

Mr Leadbetter cleared his throat. 'It so happens,' he began, 'that I have a sister. Amelia, her name is. Amelia Leadbetter.'

The ogre and Belladonna looked at him anxiously. They knew how hard he had been working and that overwork can drive people a little mad.

'She didn't, in fact, marry,' Mr Leadbetter went on. 'But she might have done. There was a swimming bath attendant who was very fond of her.'

The others waited.

'I'm not saying that the swimming bath attendant was called Mugg,' the secretary went on, 'because he wasn't. His name, actually, was Arthur Hurtleypool. I remember it because jokes were made about hurtle-ying into the pool, that kind of thing. Still, if he *had* been called Mugg and if he had married my sister Amelia and if the marriage had been blessed with a son, then this son,' finished the secretary, 'would undoubtedly have been my nephew.'

'Your nephew, Terence!' said Belladonna, seeing the light.

'Precisely. And what more natural than that my sister, Amelia, having to go into hospital to have her appendix out, should send Terence to stay with me?'

'Oh, Mr Leadbetter, you're wonderful,' cried Bella-donna, throwing her arms round the secretary, a thing he very much enjoyed.

Terence looked as though he'd swallowed a lighted candle. But when he spoke it was to say haltingly, 'If I was your nephew shouldn't I have . . .' He was too shy to finish, but his eyes went to the back of Mr Leadbetter and lingered there. The secretary was a modest man, so much so that he usually wore his stump inside his trousers, but Terence was a boy who noticed things.

'A tail?' said Mr Leadbetter.

Terence nodded.

'I could make him a little one,' said Belladonna. 'Even without Rover. Making tails is *growing* magic and there's nothing whiter than that. But I don't know . . . I feel Terence is sort of perfect as he is.'

Terence looked up quickly. Surely Belladonna was mocking him? But no – her periwinkle eyes were very clear and very loving as she looked at him and he had to turn away because a lump had come up in his throat.

'Quite honestly, Terence,' said Mr Leadbetter, 'if you *can* manage without one, it would be better. There is, you see, the problem of sitting down. And my sister Amelia – your mother that would be – was perfectly tail-less, as far as I recall.'

Terence didn't keep on about it after that. To be able to be near Belladonna, to know that *his* worm might help her to gain her heart's desire, was happiness enough. Only someone really greedy and undisciplined would also expect a tail.

'I'll tell you one thing, though,' said Lester. 'I wouldn't say anything about Rover being such a powerful familiar. I'd let Terence look after Rover and pretend he was just a pet, that's what I'd do. If it gets round that Rover's giving Belladonna even half a chance of winning the competition, I wouldn't give a fig for his chances.'

'Oh, no, *surely*, no one would hurt an innocent worm like that!' said Belladonna.

'Now, Belladonna, try *thinking* black as well as acting it. There's already been some hanky panky with Doris. Lurching about the bath she was, drunk as a lord and a nasty pea green colour with it – and Miss Wrack saying Doris never touched a drop and someone must have forced it down her throat.'

'Oh, *poor* Doris – is she all right now?' cried Belladonna.

'Well, it seems she'd been on the bath salts. But it just shows,' said Lester darkly. 'I wouldn't trust any of those witches as far as I could throw them, let alone that Madame Olympia.'

A chill spread round the room as they remembered the enchantress's cruel smile and the necklace of human teeth.

'And what about those Shouter chickens? You know how they follow you about. One peck at Rover and you'll be back to bloomin' begonias,' the ogre went on.

Belladonna saw the sense of this. 'They wouldn't *mean* to, of course; they'd feel dreadful afterwards, but all the same . . .' She turned to Terence. 'All right, you shall be Rover's *bodyguard* and keep him, and when I want to do some magic you can come over and stand beside me and I'll touch Rover without anyone seeing.'

'That's the ticket,' said the ogre.

It was decided that Terence should sleep on a camp bed in Mr Leadbetter's room and make himself useful generally until it was time to go to Darkington, and when Belladonna had turned the vipers back into a typewriter again, she and Terence went to wash their hands for lunch.

In the afternoon, Mr Leadbetter took the witches to a big department store called Turnbull and Buttle to buy the long, black gowns and hoods that they were to wear for the competition. He had hoped to have Lester to help him, but Arriman had sent for the ogre, spiriting him away just as he was about to lift a spoonful of banana fritter to his mouth and it was Mr Leadbetter alone who had to shepherd the witches up to the third floor and stop Mabel Wrack from leaping on to the fish slab and return the cigarettes that had mysteriously flown through the air into the handbags of the Shouter twins and explain to the young man behind the glove counter that he couldn't immediately marry Belladonna.

Fortunately the gowns were waiting for them: black ones with hoods like schoolteachers used to wear, and long enough to reach right down to the ground and cover Mother Bloodwort's slippers and Ethel Feedbag's wellies, so that with the black carnival masks which Turnbull and Buttle had ordered specially, there really was no way of telling which witch was which.

But when it came to Madame Olympia's turn to try on her gown, she made a nasty scene. All day, the enchantress had kept snootily to her room, insisting that meals be sent up to her, ordering incredible delicacies for the aardvark and putting out seventeen pairs of shoes for the poor boot-boy to clean.

Now she looked at her plain cotton gown and said:

'Are you out of your *mind*? Do you imagine I can perform magic in that *rag*!'

'I'm afraid all the witches have to be dressed alike,' said Mr Leadbetter. 'It's one of the rules of the competition.'

'Then the rules must be broken,' said the enchantress, fixing Mr Leadbetter with an evil and glittering eye.

It is impossible to say what would have happened next, but just at that moment Mother Bloodwort, who had been resting on a low gilt chair, gave a shriek of excitement.

'It's me toe! Me big toe! It's happened. I can feel it!'

Belladonna put down her gown and hurried over to her. 'What has, Mother Bloodwort?'

'It's my turning-myself-young-again spell! I've been working on it all week and just now me big toe gave this splutter. More of a *spurt* it was, really. Like a spring chicken it felt, rearin' to go.'

She began to scrabble under her musty skirt, removed her stockings, shook off a couple of the small, grey bandages which clung like dead mice round her ankles and stuck her naked foot into the air.

The stunned shop assistants drew closer; the witches clustered round.

'It is ... *pinker* than the others, I'm almost sure,' said Belladonna at last. 'And sort of ... fuller-looking.'

'Rubbish,' said Nancy Shouter. 'It's exactly like the others and nasty with it.'

'You've made the whole thing up,' said Mabel Wrack, pursing her cod-like lips.

'And your toenails need cutting.'

The unkind remarks of the other witches came thick and fast. And it had to be admitted that Mother Bloodwort's toe did look exactly like all the others: yellow and bent with little tufty hairs.

But Mother Bloodwort was not to be put down. 'You'll see one day, all of you. When I get the rest of the spell, you'll see, I'll be so young you'll have to put me into nappies!'

But she allowed Belladonna to help her on with her stockings and lead her back to the bus. It had been rather an exciting day.

When Lester found himself spirited away to Dark-ington in the middle of his banana fritter he had a feeling that his master was up to no good, and he was right. Arriman had sent for him to tell him that the witches couldn't stay at the Hall during the competition.

'But sir—' began Lester.

Arriman, who was in his library, waved a hand.

'Don't try to persuade me, Lester. Even if they stay in the East Wing as you suggested, even if they're completely covered in their hoods and gowns, I just can't face it.'

Lester tried not to show it, but he was annoyed. It seemed to him that Arriman was doing everything he could to make the contest as difficult as possible. After all, if you wanted a black witch what was the use of fussing about a few warts with whiskers on them or a sea slug over someone's eye? For a moment, he wondered whether to mention Madame Olympia. Arriman hadn't seen her yet and she might be more his type. About Belladonna he decided to say nothing. The disappointment if she didn't win would be bad enough without raising any hopes.

'Well, where are they to stay, then?' he asked.

Arriman brightened. 'I had a good idea. I want them to camp in the West Meadow, the one opposite the main gate. They'll be out of the way there. Just buy everything you need – those pretty orange tents with little plastic porches and primus stoves and those cunning canvas huts they have to spend a penny in. Buy everything,' he said grandly, 'and send the bill to me.'

'But it's October, sir! They'll be freezing!'

'No, no – not at all. Braced is what they'll be. Toned up. Those nylon sleeping-bags are very good, I hear.

You'll have to excuse me now, Lester – I have the judges arriving tonight.'

As he came away from the library, Lester met the Wizard Watcher.

'How do you find him?' asked the Left-Hand Head.

'Off his chump,' said the ogre. 'Wants the witches to camp in the West Meadow. Won't have them in the house.'

The monster sighed. 'He's taken it hard,' said the Middle Head. 'You can imagine how we feel, letting him down.'

'Still, if the wizard didn't cometh, what could we do?' remarked the Left-Hand Head.

'And cometh he definitely didn't,' the Right-Hand Head said.

The monster then told Lester that it had asked for a holiday during the actual contest. It was just going to take a rucksack and go walkabout.

'We'll be back for the wedding, of course,' said the Middle Head. 'But everyone'll be better for a break.'

Lester nodded. He could see that, in spite of itself, the Wizard Watcher felt it had somehow failed in its task and wanted to be alone till it felt better.

'What's with Sir Simon?' he said. 'Seems to me the old man's seeing a bit too much of him, eh?'

He had no sooner spoken than there was a moaning sound, followed by the clank of leg armour and the hollow, gloomy spectre of the wife-slayer passed through them in the corridor.

'Gone to watch the old man noshing,' said the Middle Head disapprovingly.

'Thick as thieves, they are,' said the Left-Hand Head.

'Gets me down, all that beating his blinking forehead,' complained the Right-Hand Head. 'I mean, if you've murdered your wives, you've murdered them and that's *it*.'

Lester's great craggy brow was so furrowed that the eyepatch seemed to be riding a storm-tossed sea.

'I don't like it,' he said. 'There's something fishy going on between those two, you mark my words.'

He sighed and pulled a sabre out of the umbrella stand. There was never anything decent to swallow at the hotel.

'Ready, sir,' he called upstairs to Arriman.

And with a whoosh, was gone.

Seven

The news that the witches were to camp hit Mr Leadbetter extremely hard. Once, before he came to work for Arriman, he had taken a camping holiday in the South of France. He could remember a huge ironmonger's daughter from Berlin who had lost her way back to her tent at night and fallen like a felled ox across his guy ropes. He could remember an old Greek lady cutting her toenails into the sinks for washing up, and three sunburnt Italian men who had stumped up and down with blaring transistors clamped to their oiled stomachs. He remembered the dead toad caught in the slatted floor of the shower block and the hairy housewife from Luxembourg who had sat on the steps of her caravan shaving her legs. And when he remembered that these were *ordinary* people, the thought of what the witches would make of camping made him groan aloud.

'Sometimes I don't know what I've done to deserve it, Lester, honestly I don't,' he said to the ogre.

But of course he went out, good secretary that he was, and ordered everything he could think of: tents and sleeping-bags and folding chairs, and had the stuff sent up to Darkington. Then he borrowed the Manager's top hat and wrote the numbers one to seven on bits of paper and put them inside the hat and left it on the piano stool in the ballroom ready for the witches to draw lots on the following day for their place in the contest.

'Perhaps Madame Olympia would care to draw first?' he suggested, when he had gathered them together after breakfast.

So the enchantress, dragging her aardvark by his rhinestone collar, came forward and put her hand into the hat.

'Is this some sort of joke?' she said disdainfully, putting the thing she had just pulled out on to the piano stool.

It was an egg.

There was only the shortest of pauses and then it began:

'That is an egg laid by *my* chicken,' said Nancy Shouter.

'Oh, no it isn't. That is an egg laid by *my* chicken. I could tell that egg anywhere.'

The other witches came closer. There is always excitement when a familiar lays an egg. There could so easily be a small dragon inside or a dark stain which could be trained to grow up into a fiend – anything – and for once they could see what the Shouter twins were quarrelling about.

Mr Leadbetter sighed. He did so want to get on with drawing lots.

Ethel Feedbag now stepped forward. Working at the Egg Packing Station she was reckoned to be an expert.

'That egg,' she pronounced, 'be, simply – an egg.'

This, of course, set the Shouters off again.

'How *dare* you suggest that *my* chicken could lay an ordinary egg.'

'Not your chicken! *My* chicken!'

Ethel shrugged. Nancy Shouter picked up the egg. Nora Shouter tried to pull it away from her. The next second they were all peering down at the mess of yellow yolk, transparent white and bits of shell sploshed across the carpet.

Ethel was perfectly right. Whichever of the chickens had laid it, the thing was simply an egg.

When at last they got round to drawing lots it worked out like this: Mabel Wrack was Number One which meant that she would be the first to do her trick. Ethel Feedbag was Number Two and the Shouter twins had drawn three and four. Mother Bloodwort was Number Five and Madame Olympia was Number Six. And the witch who would do her trick last, on the actual night of Hallowe'en and who had drawn Number Seven – was Belladonna.

'Fine Hallowe'en that'll be,' sneered Nancy Shouter. 'Blinking nightingales all over the place and angels singing the Hallelujah Chorus, I shouldn't wonder.'

Once, those words would have hurt Bellodonna badly, but not now. Only half an hour earlier, with Rover and Terence, she had turned the ashtray in her bedroom into a hideous, grinning skull.

There was only one more thing for the witches to do, and in a way it was the most important of all. They had to decide on which piece of magic they were going to do and make lists of all the things they needed for it so that they could be got ready and waiting for them at the Hall. All the other witches seemed to know – you could hear them plotting and whispering and hiding bits of paper from each other all over the hotel – but not Belladonna. Being black needs a lot of practise and a completely different way of thinking to being white, and when she tried to imagine a trick foul and vicious enough to please Arriman her mind just went completely blank.

'Oh, Terence, I *wish* I knew what to do,' she said to the little boy who was sitting beside her on the bed.

Even in the two days since he had left the Home, Terence seemed to have changed. His mud-coloured eyes had grown bright and eager, his hair was no longer plastered to his head but bounced with life, and he wore his spectacles at quite a jaunty angle on the end of his nose. Happiness is almost as good as magic for altering a person's looks.

'I suppose Mabel Wrack will do some watery, fishy kind of trick,' Belladonna went on. 'And Ethel Feedbag's sure to do something country-ish, and Madame Olympia . . .' But the thought of Madame Olympia's trick was horrible in a special sort of way and Belladonna left her sentence unfinished.

She picked up the mirror. Arriman was playing patience – not cheating exactly but sometimes rearranging the cards a little. The look on his dark, brooding face, the white hair in his curse curl, made her heart turn over. She was just going to put the mirror down again when a grey, wavering shape passed over its surface and she saw Arriman look up eagerly.

'Is that Sir Simon?' asked Terence. It was his first sight of the wicked spectre.

Belladonna nodded. 'He's his special friend.'

'Why is he banging at his forehead like that?' Terence wanted to know.

'It's guilt. Because he killed all his wives. It makes a plashing noise, Lester says, but we can't hear it because the mirror's silent.'

'Is that all he does?' Terence asked. 'Can't he speak or anything?'

Belladonna shook her head. 'You've got to remember he's been dead for four hundred years. Whatever it is people speak with must have got very withered up by now.' She sighed. 'It must be so *lonely* for Arriman, having a friend who can't say anything. I mean, a plashing sound is not the same.'

Suddenly Terence gave a little cry and Belladonna saw that behind his spectacles his bright, mud-coloured eyes were positively sparkling with excitement.

'Belladonna, I've had a *marvellous* idea! For your trick. Why don't you raise Sir Simon? Bring him back to life?'

Belladonna stared at him. 'Terence, I *couldn't*. Not *possibly*. That's the blackest magic in the whole world. Witches didn't just get burnt at the stake for that, they got hung and drawn and quartered and rolled up into little balls of *dung*.'

Terence didn't seem to think this mattered. 'But you want to be black, don't you? What's the point of being just a little bit black? If you're going to win, surely you have to do the most awful thing there is?'

'Yes, but I'd never *do* it. Arriman hasn't been able to do it and Lester says he's tried and tried and tried.'

'Arriman hasn't got Rover,' said Terence.

Belladonna was silent. The little boy's faith in his worm was somehow catching.

'Oh, Terence, do you really think I could?'

'Of *course* you could. And think how happy you'd be making Arriman. That's what you want when you love someone, isn't it? To make them happy?'

So he *had* guessed her secret.

'Yes,' said Belladonna quietly, 'that's what you want.'

She got up and went over to the wooden box which Terence had fitted out for Rover to live in when he wasn't in the matchbox in his pocket. Just to know that the worm was there, cradled deep in layers of damp, rich earth, made her feel at once more evil, more wicked and more dark.

'What shall I put on my list, then? There are awful things you need for necromancy. Warm sheep's blood, I think and . . . *pits* . . . and things.'

Terence considered. 'I wouldn't bother with all that,' he said. 'I think all that stuff's just for people who haven't got Rover. I reckon you've just got to *think* black.'

So Belladonna got a sheet of hotel note paper out of the bureau and wrote, *Witch Number Seven: Nothing*, and went downstairs to give it to the secretary and the ogre.

Mr Leadbetter had just finished reading the lists handed in by the other six witches, after which he had done something most unusual. He had sat down. Not even the pain as his stump grated against the seat could keep him on his feet. He had expected the witches to want a few things like crucibles and thuribles (whatever they were), a bit of wax for making images, perhaps a spot of moonwort or of mercury – that kind of thing. But no; the witches had really gone to town.

'Seven princesses!' cried Mr Leadbetter, holding up the list that the chambermaid had written out for Witch Number Five. 'What does she think I am?'

Lester pulled skilfully at the handle of the sabre sticking from his mouth and drew it from his gullet.

'These'll have to go up to the Hall,' he said, coming to stand behind the secretary. 'We'll get the easy stuff, but the old man'll have to magic up the rest on the day. *I'm* not going into Turnbull and Buttle's to ask for Seven Princesses of the Blood Royal, and nor are you.'

Mr Leadbetter nodded. Much as he hated failing Arriman, he could see that Lester was right.

It was just then that Belladonna knocked and slipped in quietly with her list.

'The dear girl,' said Mr Leadbetter when he'd read it. 'She's never any trouble.'

But secretly, the orge and the secretary were anxious and dismayed. Did it mean that Belladonna had gone white again? That she wasn't even going to try? What kind of magic could one do with, *Nothing*?

Meanwhile, at Darkington Hall, the visiting judges had arrived.

When the competition had first been suggested, Arriman had thought of having a whole panel of judges as they do for the Miss World contest or the Olympic Games. But people who really knew about magic were getting hard to find, and anyway now

73

that he had *seen* some of the witches, Arriman felt so gloomy that he just wanted to get everything over in the simplest way possible. He had written to a lady called The Hag of the Dribble to ask if she would come and be a judge but she hadn't answered – probably there wasn't any writing paper in Dribbles – and what he was left with was an extremely old rather frail ghoul called Henry Sniveller and a genie called Mr Chatterjee.

Mr Chatterjee, like most genies, lived in a bottle out of which he swooshed if someone said the right words and remembered to unscrew the top. He was an Indian genie and felt the cold so dreadfully that mostly he liked to stay inside the bottle and talk through the glass. As his Indian accent was rather strong, this made it difficult to understand him, but he was a very fine judge of magic, having lived so long in the East where they do a lot of interesting things like sending people up on Flying Carpets and then bringing them down suddenly so that their behinds become impaled on spikes.

Mr Sniveller was a very different sort of person: a dark-faced, silent ghoul who lived behind a slaughter house in a Satanic northern town and spent the night foraging in dustbins for unspeakable, blood-red things, some of which he ate and some of which he collected. Ghouls are not particularly good at magic, but there is nothing darker, gloomier or more evil than a ghoul, and Arriman knew that he had been very lucky to get him.

So now the three of them sat at dinner round the carved oak table in the Great Hall, where the firelight flickered, the ravens croaked in the rafters and, on a rug, the weary Wizard Watcher rested its head. Arriman was in low spirits – the witches were due to arrive in a couple of days – and kind Mr Chatterjee, who was dining inside his bottle because of the draughts, was doing his best to cheer him up.

'Oh my goodness, it will not be so bad, I think, to have a wife,' he said in his soft, sing-song voice, sucking up a piece of spaghetti which Arriman had dropped in for him. Although tiny, he was most beautifully dressed in a white turban and a scarlet tunic frogged with gold.

The ghoul did not see it like that. 'Yak!' he said. And presently, when he had swallowed a fish finger, 'Ugh.'

Arriman was just beginning to explain about the contest and how it should be judged when there was the usual plashing and moaning and Sir Simon appeared through the tapestry and thrust his pale and ghastly face at Arriman.

'You see,' said the wizard gloomily. 'He's trying to warn me. Seven times he's been married and each time his wife drove him to murder. Quite simply *drove* him.'

'Oh, dearie me!' said Mr Chatterjee, very much upset. 'How has he been murdering so many, please?'

Arriman shrugged. 'The usual methods, I suppose. Drowning, stabbing, strangulation – that kind of thing.'

'Then it is good he is only a ghost,' said the little genie, 'or your new wife will perhaps be Number Eight.'

Arriman threw him a sharp look from beneath his devilish eyebrows. 'It's only his *own* wives he kills,' he said. But for a while he stared abstractedly into the fire as though turning a new and important idea over in his mind.

'Well now, gentlemen,' he said at last. 'To business. I thought each witch should be given ten points. Two for darkness, two for power, two for presentation . . .'

There was a swoosh and Mr Chatterjee came out of his bottle, growing almost to normal size as he did. Like most genies, he was very serious about his work.

And for the next hour, while the shadows lengthened and the Wizard Watcher slept, the judges of the Miss Witch of Todcaster contest bent over their task.

Eight

The witches' camping wasn't as bad as Mr Leadbetter had thought it would be. It was worse.

Not that there was anything wrong with the campsite. The campsite was very nice. Mr Leadbetter had ordered a caravan for Mother Bloodwort, who had seemed to him too old to do well under canvas, and tents and a toilet block with showers and absolutely the latest kind of chemical loo. But the witches hadn't been in the West Meadow outside the main gate at Darkington for twenty-four hours before pandemonium set in.

For a start, Mother Bloodwort never got into her caravan at all. Madame Olympia nabbed it straight away, no one knew how, and sat inside it with the aardvark, despising the other witches and refusing to take her turn at any of the chores. Nancy and Nora Shouter spent the first night quarrelling about which of them had the better camp bed and ended by sticking pen knives into each other's lilos. Ethel Feedbag's pig escaped from its pen and crashed into Mother Bloodwort's tent, sending the old witch flying just as she was trying to fix a mouse-blood poultice under her nightdress, and Mabel Wrack insisted on using the cooking cauldron to give Doris a bubble bath which made the breakfast porridge taste very strange indeed.

It was Belladonna, of course, who was left to fetch the water and do the cooking and the washing-up, and however hard she tried to please everybody – braising cod's eyes for Mabel Wrack and roasting squashed hedgehogs on hot bricks for Ethel Feedbag – she got nothing but grumbles and sneers for her pains.

And Belladonna had her own troubles. Mr Leadbetter and the orge were back in their old rooms up at the Hall and as Terence was supposed to be Mr Leadbetter's nephew he had been given a little room beside the secretary's in the servants' wing. This meant that Rover too, was far away at the end of the long drive, sleeping in his wooden box under Terence's window. And with her familiar out of reach, Belladonna's old trouble was coming back, and coming back badly. The very first morning she had woken to find that her sleeping-bag had come out in a rash of passion flowers – great, pollen-loaded things that tickled abominably and made her sneeze, and when she opened the flap of her tent she found six twitch-eared, bright-eyed baby rabbits waiting for her, their paws in the air.

'I'm not a white witch now, you know,' she said crossly. But of course she let them in and conjured up a patch of lettuce for them out of her groundsheet, and it was clear to everybody that they were to stay.

But if life was hard on the camping site in the West Meadow, it wasn't exactly easy at the Hall. Mr Sniveller, the ghoul, who was sleeping in the Tapestry Room, found it difficult to break the habit of years and spent the night scooping fungus off the cellar walls and filching raw mince from the refrigerator and taking them to bed. This meant that he was usually very tired during the day and fell asleep all over the place, waking up suddenly to say things like, 'Blood!' or, 'Slime!' which made it difficult to carry on a sensible conversation. Poor Mr Chatterjee had caught a cold and sat inside his bottle sneezing miserably so that the glass misted up and he couldn't see out. As for Arriman, well, as Lester said, 'Anyone would think he was goin' to have his bloomin' head chopped off instead of getting hitched, the way he's carrying on.'

In the bustle and fuss that led up to the start of the competition, Terence turned out to be worth his weight in gold. He ran errands, found the wizard's socks, removed the bits of sticking plaster with scabs on them from Mr Sniveller's bed and stuffed Mr Chatterjee's bottle with paper tissue so that the little genie could blow his swollen nose. And everything he did, he did happily and with delight because Darkington, with its devilish maze and stinking laboratory and ghastly zoo seemed to him the most enchanting place in the whole world.

But what Terence did whenever he could be spared was to study Sir Simon Montpelier, and quite soon he knew as much about the wicked wife-slayer as Arriman himself. He learnt that the spectre usually appeared first in the broom cupboard, where he limbered up with a couple of groans, half a dozen eerie thumps and a wail or two, before settling into the serious business of smiting his forehead with a plashing sound. Then, still plashing for all he was worth, the unhappy phantom would set off through the

79

laundry room, up the stairs to the library, pass through a couple of book cases and a stuffed bison, and end up in the Great Hall, popping out through a tapestry of a man being stuck full of arrows while being burnt at the stake, and ruining the appetite of whoever was at dinner.

'You'll see,' said Terence to Belladonna, who was stirring the witches' supper over the campfire. 'He'll be absolutely terrific when he's raised. When you get close to him, his face is all sort of loathsome and ruined-looking. When he bursts through the wall, *alive*, it'll be a sensation.'

'Oh, Terence, I do hope so,' said Belladonna. The baby rabbits hadn't gone, nor had the passion flowers and the tree behind her tent was bearing golden pears. 'Tell me,' she went on, 'how is He? Is he still so sad?'

She meant Arriman, of course. The great magician was seldom from her mind.

'Well, he is a bit. But you've got to remember that he's never seen you and that he doesn't know you're going to win.'

'No,' said Belladonna. 'He certainly doesn't know *that*.'

But already she felt blacker and more hopeful. It was always like that when Terence came.

And so, at last, after all the preparations and the fuss, the first day of the contest dawned.

Mabel Wrack – Witch Number One – had got up early and stood for two hours under the shower so that her legs did not dry out on her big day. She had dressed with care, fastening the sea slug brooch beneath her gown, but she was not nervous. Owing to Mrs Wrack having been a mermaid, Mabel was one-quarter fish and, as is well known, fishes are cold-blooded and never get excited.

As everyone had expected, Mabel had decided to do her trick beside the sea. The place she had chosen was called the Devil's Cauldron: a sandy bay flanked by brooding granite cliffs and strewn with jagged rocks to which dark seaweed slimily clung.

Backing the sand was a strip of turf and it was here, at a trestle table which Lester had dragged out for them, that the judges sat. Arriman the Awful, wearing his robe with the constellations on it, was in the middle; Mr Chatterjee (inside his bottle on account of the nippy breeze) was on the magician's left, and on the right – pale and exhausted after a night of hideous wandering – dropped Mr Sniveller. The other witches, gowned and masked so that Arriman couldn't catch even an accidental glimpse of them, were huddled behind a clump of gorse bushes – all except Madame Olympia who had stayed snootily inside her caravan.

Arriman now got up to make a speech. He declared the Miss Witch of Todcaster contest open and welcomed all the competitors. He reminded them of the rules – any witch practising black magic on another witch or her familiars would be disqualified, the competitors must not show their faces and the judges' decision was final. Then he sat down and Mr Leadbetter, shouting through a megaphone like a film director, said:

'Witch Number One – step forward!'

There was clapping from the other witches, and

from some villagers who had come up the cliff path, and Mabel emerged from behind the gorse bushes. Only the lower part of her face showed beneath the mask, but it was enough to make Arriman hope frantically that she was going to go to sea in a sieve and drown.

'Present your list!' ordered Mr Leadbetter, and Mabel went up to the judges' table with her piece of paper. In the neat hand of a practised shopkeeper, Mabel had written:

1. *One gong (loud)*
2. *Some golden rings*
3. *A drowned sailor*

'The Manager of the hotel was kind enough to lend us his gong,' said Mr Leadbetter. 'And we got the golden rings from Woolworths. But there is this matter of the drowned sailor.'

'Hm,' said Arriman, looking rather sick. There is a place called Davy Jones's locker under the sea, where the bodies of drowned sailors are supposed to be kept, but he had never fancied it. Messy, it sounded, as though things would have been nibbled at, and, of all things, Arriman hated a *mess*.

Then he had an idea and smiled. 'Hand me my wand, Leadbetter,' he said, and shut his eyes. The next second a large grey skeleton stuck together with bits of wire swirled through the air and landed at the sea witch's feet

'I wanted a *fresh* one,' complained Miss Wrack. 'One with some meat on him. It's for bait.'

'If Witch Number One is not satisfied,' snapped

Arriman, fire shooting from his nostrils, 'she may withdraw from the contest.

'Oh, all right,' said Mabel sulkily. 'But he's a very funny shape.'

This was certainly true. The skeleton had, in fact, belonged to the Biology Lab of a large Comprehensive School in the Midlands, and the poor gentleman hadn't exactly been a sailor but an undertaker who liked messing about in boats and had fallen, in the year 1892, into the Shropshire Union Canal. Owing to the carelessness of the children, and the fact that the Biology master was the kind that couldn't keep order, the skeleton had got badly jumbled. The skull was back to front, three finger bones were missing and for some reason he seemed to have had three thighs.

'Announce the trick you will perform,' Mr Leadbetter shouted through his megaphone.

Mabel Wrack turned to face the judges. She had taken Doris out of her bucket and thrown the familiar's tentacles carelessly round her shoulders like a mink stole, while she held the animal's round body under her arm, squeezing it for power and darkness like someone playing the bagpipes.

Then she spoke.

'I SHALL CALL FORTH THE KRAKEN FROM THE DEEP,' she said.

There was a stunned silence. The Kraken! That dread and dangerous monster that has lain since the dawn of time beneath the surface of the sea, dragging ships to their doom, creating by its lightest movement, tidal waves that could drown cities!

83

'Oh, Terence,' whispered Belladonna, 'I'm scared, aren't you? Fancy Mabel Wrack being able to do *that!*'

And indeed all the onlookers were a little bit ashamed. They had never taken the fishy witch too seriously and now . . .

Even Arriman the Awful was impressed. 'Instruct Witch Number One to proceed,' he said.

Mabel Wrack stepped forward to the edge of the ocean. The sea witch was no slouch and she had prepared her act with care. She would begin by peppering the sea with golden rings to fetch up the underwater spirits who were known to be extremely fond of jewellery and would then come and help her when she called them to her aid. As for the drowned sailor, he was meant to lure the Kraken from his lair and so make it easier for the spirits to find him.

She put Doris back in her bucket and threw the rings one by one into the foam. Then she raised her arms, and the skeleton of the undertaker who had liked messing about in boats rose slowly up in the air, turned a somersault and tumbled into the waves.

'Levitation,' said Arriman. 'Quite neat. Give her a mark for that, don't you think?' The thought of seeing a Kraken had quite cheered him up.

Next, Mabel picked up the gong and thumped it with a resounding wallop, which sent the sea birds flying up in terror. Then:

> *Mighty Spirits of the Deep*
> *Pray you waken from your sleep*
> *Come as fast as you are able*
> *Come and help your sister, Mabel,'*

84

chanted Miss Wrack. She had decided to go into poetry for the contest. This may have been a mistake. Some witches have a feeling for poetry, some haven't. Miss Wrack hadn't.

> 'From thunderous reef and mighty grot
> The dreaded Kraken must be got . . .'

'What's a grot?' whispered Mother Bloodwort pettishly from behind the gorse bushes.

'It's short for grotto, I think,' Belladonna whispered back. 'Sort of a cave.' Though she knew that she had no chance of winning now – who could do anything more terrible than call up a Kraken – she was looking at Miss Wrack with shining eyes. There just wasn't a mean streak anywhere in Belladonna.

The pause which followed was an anxious one. Even Arriman wondered if he had been hasty. Would there be flooding? Whirlpools? Cannibalism? There are too many stories of witches summoning up evil forces which they cannot then control.

The pause lengthened. The ghoul, unable to take the strain, dropped off to sleep, and still the wind soughed, and the grey sea foamed and boiled against the rocks.

But now there was a change. The sky seemed to darken. The white crests of the waves died away to leave a creeping, wrinkled skin of water. The wind dropped. The sea birds fell silent.

What came next was a strange heaping up of the water into a mound which grew and grew and became a huge tower topped with foam. And now the tower reared upwards, bent, and turned to race –

85

a great tunnel of boiling, churning water – towards the shore.

The witches huddled together. Terence's hand crept into Belladonna's, and at the judges' table, Arriman reached for the genie's bottle and screwed on the top.

Just in time. The towering wave had landed with a thunderous crash upon the strand. And when the foam and turmoil had died down, the onlookers blinked.

Miss Wrack had called on the Spirits of the Deep to help her find the Kraken and it was perhaps natural that these should be mermaids. But the four ladies who now sat on the beach were fleshy and no longer young, and they seemed to be rather pointlessly clutching a large black handbag, each of them holding on to it with a pudgy arm. The rings which Miss Wrack had sent them glistened on their fingers, and their lower halves were sensibly covered in tail cosies of knitted bladderwrack, but all of them were topless and Arriman had already flinched and closed his eyes.

Miss Wrack stepped closer – and her mouth opened in horror.

'Septic suckerfish!' she swore under her breath.

And indeed it was the most appalling luck! Of all the mermaids in the ocean, she had managed to call up her mother's four unmarried sisters: Aunt Edna, Aunt Gwendolyn, Aunt Phoebe and Aunt Jane!

For a moment, Mabel panicked. There is probably nothing less black or magical in the whole world than a person's aunt. Then she remembered that the top half of her face was covered by a mask. With luck, she would not be recognized. There had been a bit of a split in the family when her mother had opted for legs. So, disguising her voice as well as she could, she began:

> 'Summoned here, I bid thee hearken,
> You have been to fetch the Kraken
> Search the corners of the ocean—'

She broke off, trying to find a rhyme for 'ocean', and also wondering a bit whether an ocean really *had* corners. But she needn't have bothered because all four of her aunts were talking at once, taking no notice of each other or of her.

'My dear, we're so glad you called! We've been worried *sick*!'

'Not knowing what to do for the best, you see.'

'When that oil rig went through his mother's head—'

'Skull shattered; not a hope, poor soul—'

'It's *meant*, I said to Edna, didn't I, dear?'

'You did, Phoebe. It's *meant*, you said.'

'*Someone* knows what's right.'

The aunt who had just spoken broke off, edged closer, peered at Mabel Wrack. 'Funny, I'd swear I'd seen you before. Those nostrils . . . that mouth . . .'

Still clutching their handbag, the mermaids waddled towards her on their tails.

'It can't be, of course. But isn't she the *spit* of poor Agatha!'

'The spit!' echoed Aunt Jane.

Mabel Wrack retreated backwards, but it was too late.

'It *must* be Agatha's little girl. The one she had with

87

the fishmonger after the operation. It *is* her, I'm sure. Mabel, wasn't she called?'

'Mabel! Dear little Mabel!'

Terribly excited, the aunts dropped their handbag at last and surrounded their niece with a great flopping of tails and waving of pink, plump arms.

'Stop it!' hissed Mabel furiously. 'This is a competition. Keep *away*! And speak in verse, you're disgracing me.'

There was a moment of outraged silence while Mabel continued to glare angrily at her relations. It was a silly thing for her to do. Mermaids are famous for being touchy, and so, of course, are maiden aunts.

'Oh, very well,' said Aunt Edna haughtily. 'We know when we aren't wanted, don't we?'

'It was you that called *us*, you know.'

'Such airs – just because her father had legs and a shop.'

As they spoke, the mermaids began to waddle huffily away, speaking over their shoulders as they went.

'We were going to stay and give you a few hints, but we won't bother now.'

'Don't blame *us* if you don't know how much sieved sea quirt to give.'

'Speak in verse, indeed!'

And with a last, offended sniff, the four mermaids dived back into the water and were gone.

'Stop!' shouted the desperate Miss Wrack. 'Come back! You've left your handbag!'

It was a dreadful moment. The mermaids had gone, the mighty Kraken still slumbered beneath the deep, and on the face of Arriman the Awful there was a look that froze the marrow in one's bones.

And now this handbag . . .

Only, was it a handbag? For even as they watched, the object on the sand seemed to give a kind of judder. Next it puffed itself out into a round, smoothed dome like the top of a tadpole or of a small and very squidgy flying saucer. In the middle of this dome two slits now appeared and a pair of shining, tear-filled, sky-blue eyes stared upwards at Miss Wrack.

'Oh, my Gawd,' said Lester, with whom the penny had already dropped.

The thing now went into a kind of private struggle and from its round, dark blancmange of a body there appeared, one by one, eight wavery, wobbly legs each ending in a blob-shaped foot. Peering closer, the onlookers could see, at the rim of the saucer, a round hole from whose reddened edges the little finger bone of the undertaker sadly hung. Aunt Jane had given it to him to help him with his teething.

Even with the evidence there before their eyes, no one could quite believe it. They watched in silence as the 'handbag' raised itself once more, tottered a few pathetic steps and fell in a despairing, quivering heap before Miss Wrack.

'Mummy?' it said in a piteous voice. 'Mummy?'

The sea witch stepped back in disgust. Terence clung tightly to Belladonna to stop her running forward, the ghoul woke suddenly and said, 'Spittle!' and Arriman the Awful rose from his seat.

'What in the name of devilry and darkness is that THING?' he thundered.

He knew, of course. You could say a lot about Arriman, but not that he was thick.

'That, sir,' said the ogre, 'is a Kraken. A baby Kraken. A very young baby Kraken indeed.'

Hearing voices, feeling himself unwanted by the very witch who had called him from the sea, the Kraken, his eyes, his whole body streaming with tears, now began to totter wetly to the table where the judges sat. Three times he fell, his legs hopelessly knotted, and three times he rose again, leaving each time a glistening pool of water, until he reached the chair of Arriman the Awful, Wizard of the North.

'Daddy?' said the Kraken, rolling his anguished eyes upwards. And again, 'Daddy?'

Everybody waited.

Arriman looked downwards and shuddered. 'Take it away, Lester. Remove it. Throw it back into the sea.'

The orge did not move.

'You heard me, Lester. It is dribbling on my feet.'

'Sir,' said the ogre. 'That Kraken is an orphan. Its mother's had an oil rig through her head. It'll be two thousand years before that Kraken is old enough to swallow as much as a canoe. If you throw it back now, it'll die.'

'So?' said Arriman nastily.

Over by the gorse bushes, Belladonna closed her eyes and prayed. Mr Chatterjee tried to swoosh out of his bottle, hit his head on the screwed-on-top and fell back, his turban over his dark, kind face.

'Daddy?' said the Kraken, his voice only a whisper now – and raised from the top of his body, a tiny, trembling and hopeless-looking tail.

'Oh, a plague on the lot of you,' cursed Arriman,

and scooping up the Kraken, which immediately began to squeak and giggle because it was extremely ticklish, the furious magician left the judges' table and strode away towards the Hall.

Nine

Mabel's marks were announced that night. She had scored four out of a possible ten – a low mark and one that would have been lower if Arriman had had his way. But as kind Mr Chatterjee pointed out, she had called up the Kraken from the Deep and it wasn't her fault that the thing had turned out the way it had.

The low score pleased all the other witches, and Ethel Feedbag, whose turn came on the following day, was heard lurching and roistering round the camp fire until long after midnight, hiccupping over her parsnip wine and falling asleep with her head on her pig and her wellies dangerously close to the embers. Belladonna, of course, couldn't help feeling a bit sorry for Mabel, who had retired huffily into her sleeping bag with wet towels round her legs, but Terence didn't pretend to be anything but pleased.

'You'll see, Belladonna, you'll win; you're bound to!'

He had brought Rover down earlier, and just by touching the slender, peaceful body of her familiar, Belladonna had been able to turn the passion flowers into bloodshot eyeballs and the golden pears into thumbscrews. She'd left the baby rabbits because, as she said to Terence, it was knowing that she *could* turn them into decayed appendixes that was important.

'How is . . . you know . . . He?' she asked now.

Terence said that Arriman was a little bit upset. He could have said more, but he knew that Belladonna was in love and that nothing hurts people more than to think that someone they love is not altogether perfect. In fact, Arriman had been creating like nobody's business on account of the Kraken. Absolutely nothing could persuade the Kraken that Arriman was not his father and the magician had had to change his shoes three times between tea and supper because the thing insisted on sitting on his feet. Krakens make their own wetness from the inside and can breathe in air as well as in water so there was nothing to stop the dreaded Denizen of the Deep from trying to climb on to Arriman's lap or shedding tears all over his trousers, and the Great Man was taking it very badly.

'Oh, why didn't the New Wizard Cometh!' he raged at dinner. 'I'd have been spared all this. Lester, take it away!'

'It's you he wants, sir,' said the ogre reproachfully. But he scooped the Kraken up and put him in a soup tureen, for what with Sir Simon wailing in the wainscot, Mr Chatterjee sneezing in his bottle and the ghoul dribbling raw liver from his mouth, he did feel that perhaps his master had had enough.

The following morning they were up early to see what Witch Number Two was going to do.

Ethel had chosen to perform her trick in a grassy and very beautiful hollow in which, beside a bubbling brook, there grew an oak, an ash and a thorn.

These three trees have, since the beginning of time, been special trees. Even separately they are special

93

but when they grow together . . . well, anything can happen in a place like that.

'Witch Number Two – step forward!' shouted Mr Leadbetter, and Ethel, still wearing beneath her gown the three mouldering jerseys she'd slept in, lurched out from behind a rock, pushing a wheelbarrow and calling to her huge and mucky pig.

'Hand in your list!' Mr Leadbetter ordered, and Ethel walked over to the judges' table, which Lester had set out on a level patch of grass, and put down a crumbled piece of paper in front of Arriman.

The magician read it and passed a weary hand across his forehead. Witch Number Two wanted: *A man, a woman and a child*.

'More fuss,' he murmured. And then, 'Fetch the telephone directory.'

So Terence ran up to the Hall and came back with the Todcaster and District Directory, and Arriman closed his eyes, flicked the pages, and stubbed his finger down on what turned out to be the B's.

It is not difficult to work a telephone directory. Any wizard worth his salt can do it. You just press your finger down hard on a telephone number, say the right spells and immediately you can see in your mind's eye the family that lives at that address. After that, summoning them by levitation is just child's play. So now Arriman ignored a Colonel Bellingbotter sitting pinkly in his bath at Todcaster 5930, passed over the Brisket sisters doing Keep Fit exercise at 2378 and found in the Bicknell family at Todcaster 9549, exactly what he was looking for.

*

Mr and Mrs Bicknell and their daughter, Linda, were sitting at breakfast in their small semi at 187 Acacia Avenue. Mrs Bicknell was still in her hairnet and curlers, Linda was dressed for school. Linda was fat and her mother was thin; Linda was eight years old and her mother was thirty-five, but what they both liked best was being nasty to Linda's father, Mr Bicknell, and they were doing it now.

'Why did you put on that stupid shirt?' said Mrs Bicknell. 'It makes you look like an ostrich with the croup.'

'Your hair's getting awfully thin on top, Daddy! You'll be bald soon. Won't you look silly when you're bald,' said Linda.

'Mrs Pearce across the road is getting a new washing machine. I suppose you know I've had *my* washing machine for three years?'

'Davina's daddy's buying her a doll that can clean her own teeth. Why don't *you* buy me a doll like that?'

Mr Bicknell, a small, rather stooped man with a thin, tired face and a lined forehead, just went on quietly eating his cornflakes. He worked hard all day in his grocer's shop helping the people he served to make their money go further and when he came home at night he went on helping. He helped his wife with the washing up and fixed shelves and dug the garden, but whatever he did, it made no difference. His wife and his daughter just nagged and nagged and nagged.

'You didn't clean the budgerigar out properly,' said Mrs Bicknell, piling her toast with marmalade. 'There's bird seed stuck to the corner of his cage.'

95

'Davina says being a grocer is *silly*. Only *silly* people are grocers, Davina says.'

'And I wish that just for once you'd—'

But at this point the windows began to rattle violently. Then they burst open and the room was filled with a whirling, roaring wind which lifted Mr and Mrs Bicknell and their daughter, Linda, and sent them up and out of the house . . . up and away . . . to land, in what seemed to be just a moment in time, at Ethel Feedbag's feet.

The country witch peered down at them and nodded. Then she stuck her boot under the shrieking, twitching Mrs Bicknell and the howling, kicking Linda and turned them over on their backs. There was no need to turn over Mr Bicknell who already lay quietly, looking upwards at the sky.

'Announce your trick!' commanded Mr Leadbetter through his megaphone.

Ethel took the straw from her mouth, burped, and said:

'I BE GOIN' TO SHUT THE WOMAN IN THE ASH TREE AN' THE MAN IN THE OAK TREE AN' THAT BAWLIN' BRAT IN THE THORN TREE.'

A whisper passed through the audience and they looked at Witch Number Two with a new respect. Imprisonment of human beings in trees is very old magic and it is as black as night. The Druids did it, and the witches of Ancient Greece and Rome. Even now there are gaunt willows and shuddering alders from whose insides their own spirits have fled, to be replaced by some boastful traveller or careless shepherd who has lain there trapped in slumber for a thousand years.

Only Belladonna, hiding with the other witches, was unhappy. 'Those *poor* trees!' she murmured.

And indeed the trees were worth worrying about. The oak was one of those trees that are a whole world of their own: its great scarred trunk was full of clefts and hollows in which squirrels lived, and mice and little scurrying beetles. It stood rooted in a pool of soft green moss; delicate acorn cups clung to its mazed branches and its crown was a mass of autumn gold.

The ash was as tall, but slender, the smooth grey bark seemingly like silver against the pale blue sky, the keys hanging in bunches from its upward-sweeping boughs. A younger tree than the oak, but proud and regal as a queen.

And lastly, the hawthorn, a most powerful and knowing tree with its writhing trunk, its blood-red berries clustered round the fierce black barbs.

Ethel Feedbag, meanwhile, had fetched a sack from her wheelbarrow and humped it to where the Bicknells lay. It was labelled *Mangel Wurzel Meal*, but it was better not to ask what was really in the powder she now sprinkled over the bawling, slug-faced Linda, her twitching mother and the tired body of the grocer. Whatever it was, within seconds all three of them lay unconscious on the grass.

Grinning happily, Ethel now pulled up her gown, fumbled under her skirt, and from the elastic of her brown woollen knickers, drew a long black-hilted witches' knife. And as she did so, Arriman gasped and turned a chalky white. He had seen, clear as daylight, the dreaded wellies beneath the gown.

For a moment, it looked as though the great magician would cut and run. But the ogre and the secretary had already closed ranks behind him, and with a groan he sank back in his seat.

Ethel, meanwhile, was smearing the bark of the thorn tree with a slimy blood-coloured paste. Then she picked up her knife and made a single, long slit in its side.

'Oh, Terence, I can't *bear* it!' whispered Belladonna.

'I don't suppose it feels any pain, Belladonna. I expect that's what the ointment was for. To stop it hurting.'

They watched breathlessly as the slit, of its own accord, grew wider . . . wider . . . and became, at last, a gaping hole which led to the tree's very heart.

'Not bad,' said Arriman, struggling to be fair. 'Though I prefer lightning myself. Neater.'

Ethel grunted, whacked her pig and came back to stand with her knife poised over Linda.

'Is she going to kill her?' asked Terence hopefully.

But Ethel was crouching over Linda, murmuring a spell in a language so ancient and peculiar that none of them could make out a word. Over and over again she chanted, and then slowly the fat, nasty little schoolgirl rose from the grass, stuck her hands in front of her and began to sleepwalk, like a bewitched suet pudding, towards the tree.

'In!' ordered Ethel, putting a boot in Linda's bottom.

And, lo and behold, Linda wobbled forward into the thorn tree and the sides of the tree came together closer . . . closer . . . and the slit vanished and she was gone.

Next, Ethel went over to the ash. Again she rubbed the tree with ointment, again she made a slit in its side and again the slit widened to show the dark centre of the tree. And now it was Mrs Bicknell who rose and walked in a trance into the tree and the tree closed round her, and she was gone.

Ethel was just going to start the oak when there was an extremely angry *rustling* noise which began at the hawthorn tree and moved over to where Ethel stood. A second, even angrier rustle, followed. What these were, were the Spirits of the Thorn and of the Ash, and they were in a very nasty temper indeed.

'It is not at *all* convenient for me to be out this morning,' said the Spirit of the Ash.

'You might have *asked*,' said the Spirit of the Thorn.

One cannot actually see tree spirits – they are simply a rustle – but one knows that if one could, they would be green, female and easily upset.

'Didn't ask you to shift,' said Ethel. 'Plenty of room for everybody.'

'Stay in with that repulsive child!' said the Spirit of the Thorn. 'You must be joking! I'm going home to Mother.' And she rustled off in the direction of an old hawthorn standing on the hill, followed by the Spirit of the Ash, still yammering with indignation.

Ethel shrugged. It took more than a couple of rustles to upset a Feedbag. She had made a slit in the oak tree now and stood back as it opened, groaning and creaking and sending the squirrels and dormice scampering away in terror.

Then Ethel went to fetch Mr Bicknell and he too, got up and walked into the tree and the tree closed over him and he was gone.

The judges, going over to have a closer look, were pleased. True, the thorn tree bulged at the bottom because of the fatness of Linda's thighs, and its bark had come out in bumpy knots like boils. The golden leaves of the ash too, were shrivelling fast. Still, no passer-by could possibly have guessed that three frantic, tortured human beings were imprisoned in this peaceful dell.

But of course there was no question of giving out marks just yet. A true witch must be able to loosen an enchantment as well as weave it.

'Undo the spell!' ordered Arriman.

Ethel had slumped down beside her pig. Now she got up and waddled over to the thorn. Again she made a slit in the tree, again the slit widened – and out on the grass like a crumpled maggot, rolled Linda Bicknell.

Next, Ethel slit open the ash and the lovely tree seemed to sigh with relief as Mrs Bicknell, sticky with sap and minus three of her curlers, fell out on to the turf.

Smirking now, Ethel went over to the oak. Again she slit it, again she stood back and waited.

Nothing happened.

'Out!' ordered Ethel, jerking her head.

Still nothing.

Beneath the mask, Ethel's round face flushed with temper.

'Out!' she said, stamping her foot. Silence. Then, from the depths of the great tree, a quiet voice said, 'No!'

Ethel's face darkened to beetroot. 'It's over,' she hissed. 'You come on out!'

But inside the oak tree, the tired grocer did not stir. What did come out of the tree was its spirit. Like the Spirits of the Ash and of the Thorn, the Spirit of the Oak was simply a rustle but an older and a wiser one.

'Leave him be,' it said to Ethel Feedbag. 'He wants to stay. He likes it in there. Says he'll come out when his wife's ninety and in a wheelchair and can't nag, and his daughter's left home for good.'

'Stay in t' tree?' roared Ethel, angry as a bull.

'That's right,' rustled the Spirit. 'Says he's never been so happy in his life. He's no bother to me, he just wants to sleep most of the time. His wife used to snore and kick him round the bed, you know how some women do. I don't mind him, he's company – and you can see *He* doesn't mind.'

This was true. Unlike the thorn which had come out in boils, or the ash whose leaves had shrivelled, the great oak tree stood calm and undisturbed by the grocer in his depths.

'Just do us up again, dear,' ordered the Spirit. 'It's getting draughty. He'll be all right in there for fifty years or so; I'll see he doesn't go mouldy. Then someone can let him out and the poor bloke can lead a decent life.'

So Ethel closed the tree up again. What else could she do? But when Linda and her mother had been sent back to Acacia Avenue and Ethel's marks came through, they were low; four out of ten, the same as Mabel's. What else could one expect? There is nothing black about shutting someone into a tree who simply loves it there.

But if Ethel was furious, Arriman was as happy as

a sandboy. Whatever else happened, he wouldn't have to marry the witch with the wellies. All through supper he laughed and joked – until he went upstairs, heard the steady drip-drip of water, and found that the Kraken had climbed on to his bed.

Ten

No one ever forgot what happened when Witch Number Three did her trick. It was really very horrible in a way that no one could have imagined, and even Arriman, used as he was to terror and disaster, could never think of it, in years to come, without feeling quite giddy and faint.

Witch Number Three was Nancy Shouter and when she announced her trick there was a great deal of interest.

'I AM GOING,' she said, 'TO MAKE A BOTTOM-LESS HOLE.'

To make a bottomless hole is not easy. A bottomless hole is not a hole that comes out in Australia; a hole that comes out in Australia is a hole that comes out in Australia – it is not bottomless. No, bottomless is something very different. Bottomlessness is a mysterious nothingness that goes on for ever, it is an interminable blackness, it is no echo, no plop when something drops into it, no glimmer of water in its depths. Not only that; a bottomless hole has a demonic and unusual power – anyone coming too close has an almost uncontrollable longing to throw himself into it.

Everyone, therefore, was pleased and Mr Chatterjee, becoming muddled in his excitement, said, 'Oh, that is good! A bottom with no hole!'

So Nancy got to work. She had chosen the East Lawn, quite close to the house, to do her trick and she went about it in a business-like manner, stubbing out her fag, putting her chicken down on the bonnet of the caterpillar tractor that Mr Leadbetter had hired for her and setting the motor in motion so that the heavy rotary blades could dig into the soil.

It was a mild and pleasant day. The other witches were clustered in the little summer house where they could see without being seen by Arriman. Even Madame Olympia had turned out with her aardvark. At the judges' table, which Lester had raised on wooden blocks so that they could see the digging better, Arriman tried to forget the awful night he'd spent with the Kraken, and his anxiety about the Wizard Watcher (who was sending brave but home-sick postcards from places like Brighton and Southend-on-Sea) and prepared to give Witch Number Three a chance.

Nancy certainly seemed to know her job. True, her chicken was against her. All along, the Shouter chickens had been rather a wash-out as familiars. They never crowed thrice or flapped threateningly or erected their wattles, and altogether they looked more like old age pensioners evicted from a battery than the kind of bird one finds in fairy stories or in fights.

All the same, Nancy was doing all right. From working with the railway, both the Shouter twins were good with mechanical things, and after about an hour Nancy drove the tractor away to the other side of the lawn and the real task began.

Because, of course, at this stage the thing was

simply a hole. Nancy had dug up some old drain-pipes, part of a tin bath, an old ham bone of the Wizard Watcher's and masses and masses of shale and sludge. She had made a deep hole, a good hole, the kind of hole little boys stand and gape at on the way to school, but though its bottom was a long way down, it was still *there*.

But now the magic began. First Nancy circled the hole with her wand, scratching a witches' pentacle deep into the surrounding soil. Five times she walked widdershins round the hole and five times she walked *not* widdershins, keeping always to the far side of the magic symbol. Then she put down her wand, picked up her chicken, and raising it aloft, turned to the north.

'Spirits of the Earth, I bid thee *SUCK THE BOTTOM FROM THIS HOLE!*' she intoned.

Then, still holding her chicken, she turned to the west: 'Spirits of Fire, I bid thee *BURN THE BOTTOM FROM THIS HOLE!*' cried Nancy Shouter.

Then she turned to the east and bade the Spirits of the Air *BLOW THE BOTTOM FROM THE HOLE.* But now, the chicken had had enough. It fluttered, squawking, from her arms and it was chicken-less that Nancy turned to the south and commanded the Spirits of the Water to *DROWN THE BOTTOM OF THE HOLE.*

After which she said the Lord's Prayer backwards – and the spell was complete.

It is always hard, the bit between the end of a piece of magic and the time when it is supposed to work. No one is good at waiting, and witches least of all. Nancy had begun most irritably to tap her toes when the scream began.

It was a scream such as no one could have imagined. A scream as if a million giants were being disembowelled with red-hot pincers – a scream that grew louder and more unendurable each second, till everyone present thought that their skulls must shatter with the pain of it.

And how could it be otherwise? For this was the scream of a hole losing the only thing it has – its bottom.

When the noise had died away at last and the pain in their ears had gone, the judges walked over to where Nancy stood. Taking care not to go too close because of the fearsome power a bottomless hole has to draw things into it, they examined, discussed and considered.

And they were pleased. Arriman was nodding, Mr Chatterjee, in his bright turban, was bobbing up and down, and the white exhausted face of the old ghoul had cracked into something almost like a smile.

For while it is true that there is not much you can actually *do* with a bottomless hole, at least it cannot possibly turn out to be someone's aunt like the mermaids, nor can it make anybody happy as Mr Bicknell had been made happy by being shut into a tree. As they returned to the table, it was clear that the judges were going to give Nancy a much higher mark than they had awarded to Ethel Feedbag or Mabel Wrack.

But before they could make an announcement there was a scuffle from the summer house, Bella-donna cried: 'Oh, please, don't!' – and then Nora

106

Shouter, shaking herself loose, catapulated on to the East Lawn, brandishing her chicken as she came.

'You're a cheat!' she screamed, charging up to her twin. 'You're a liar and a twister and a cheat! That's *my* chicken you've got there! You've done your trick with *my* chicken so it doesn't count.'

'I have *not* done my trick with your chicken! I have done my trick with *my* chicken!'

'You haven't!'

'You have!'

Face to face on the East Lawn, the Shouter sisters' fury and loathing reached new heights.

'And anyway,' yelled Nora, 'I don't believe your hole is bottomless. It's just a hole!'

'My hole is *so* bottomless!'

'No, it isn't!'

'Yes, it is!'

Arriman had risen from his seat, his devilish eyebrows meeting in an angry frown, and in the summer house, Belladonna covered her face. But nothing could stop the Shouters now. Both had put down their chickens and stood facing each other with murder in their eyes.

'If you say my hole isn't bottomless once more, I'll finish you, you worm-eaten faggot,' screamed Nancy, forgetting the contest, forgetting everything.

'It isn't bottomless! It isn't bottomless! It isn't bottomless!' screamed Nora, quite eaten up with jealousy and temper.

What happened next, happened with terrifying speed.

Nancy stepped forward and pushed her sister hard, sending her reeling, to fall backwards with her legs in the air. Then, as Nora tried to rise, Nancy pushed her again and she fell, this time inside the magic pentacle.

Even then, Nancy might have saved her twin. But she stood there, unmoving, her face suffused with an evil, gloating triumph as Nora half rose, swayed – and tottered, *of her own accord*, towards the round, black maw . . .

Right at the edge, she managed to pause, and tried desperately to take a step backwards. Too late! There was a hideous, roaring, sucking noise, Nora's arm went up . . .

And then the hole took her and she was gone.

The campsite, that night, was silent as the grave. Arriman, white with shock, had disqualified Witch Number Three and ordered the East Lawn to be cleared. Nancy, though, had hardly seemed to hear what he said, but just stood there, blindly gazing at the spot where her sister had last stood, and in the end it was Belladonna who led her away and put her to bed in the tent she had shared with Nora.

'Doesn't matter which of our chickens is which now, does it?' was all Nancy said as Belladonna settled the sad brown birds into their coops.

And Belladonna, who knew perfectly well which chicken was which, and always had, agreed that it didn't matter now. It didn't matter at all.

The horribleness of what had happened kept everyone in a state of shock throughout the following day, which was the one on which Nora should have done her act. Mr Chatterjee stayed curled in his bottle like a baby that doesn't want to be born, Arriman didn't even notice when the Kraken dribbled into his best elastic-sided boots, and at the campsite the witches stopped bickering for once, shamed by the tragedy that had overtaken them.

But the strangest thing of all was what had happened to Nancy.

Nancy had turned overnight from a loud-mouthed, bossy, chain-smoking witch into a timid, shrunken person who just lay on her camp bed in her vest and knickers refusing to wash or dress or eat, and telling anyone who came near that it didn't matter which chicken was which.

'She's going off her nut, you mark my words,' said Mother Bloodwort. 'I've seen it before. She's flipped.'

Terence couldn't understand it. 'She hated Nora so *much*, didn't she, Belladonna? So why is she so upset?'

Belladonna crinkled her forehead, trying to work it out.

'I suppose . . . hating Nora was sort of a *part* of Nancy. I mean, it was what being Nancy was *about*. And now Nora's gone, she isn't anybody. Just a wraith.'

But however worried they were about Nancy, the contest had to go on. So later that afternoon, Terence and Belladonna set off for the woods behind the campsite and practised with Rover, turning the golden bracken fronds into leprous fingers and conjuring little spitting dragons from a bramble bush. They had discovered that Rover's power was so strong that it could work from *inside* the matchbox even when Terence held it closed, and this was a great

109

help because with the box open, Rover had wandered about rather a lot.

'Funny, I thought I heard someone moving over there, behind those elms,' said Belladonna, as they sat resting in a grassy clearing, letting Rover crawl confidingly across their hands.

They peered through the trees, but there was no one there. Yet both of them had had an eerie feeling of being watched, and by someone far more sinister than lumbering Ethel or fishy Mabel Wrack.

'Perhaps we'd better put him away,' said Terence, scooping Rover back into his box. They had kept his incredible power secret from the other witches and they meant to go on doing so.

And if they could not see the cunning enchantress loping away from the clearing, who could blame them? She had taken on a form much used by witches: that of a fleet and silent hare. But no real hare ever had in its eyes the look that was in this one's: evil and calculating and unutterably cruel.

Eleven

The following day it was Mother Bloodwort's turn. She had spent the whole of the evening before in a last desperate attempt at the turning-herself-young-again spell, rushing from her tent to the toilet block and back again with little jars of crushed gall bladder from the inside of murderers, powdered mandrake picked under a dying moon and a whole lot of other noxious things which she rubbed into herself, croaking weird rhymes as she did so.

But it hadn't helped. As she was announced by Mr Leadbetter and tottered out into the Italian Garden, she was unmistakably Mother Bloodwort, warts, whiskers, Cloud of Flies and all.

Arriman of course, recognized her at once. But to the surprise of Mr Leadbetter and the ogre, he did not try to escape. The reason for this was simple. He had decided that if the witch with the whiskers won the contest, he, Arriman the Awful, would kill himself. He would do this in some very dramatic way, perhaps by plunging over the cliff into the boiling waters of the Devil's Cauldron, or by shooting himself with a silver duelling pistol or by falling onto one of the swords that Lester was always swallowing, but he would do it.

So he was quite calm as Witch Number Five

hobbled towards him and handed in her list, and he stayed calm until he'd read it.

It was Mother Bloodwort who wanted the seven princesses. She was going to do an old-fashioned trick, but a very famous one: the one in which seven beautiful maidens of the Blood Royal turn into seven black swans, doomed to wing their way across the waters of the world through all eternity.

There is probably nothing sadder or more romantic in all magic than this spell. One minute you have these lively bright-eyed girls with all life before them, and often a prince or two in the offing – and then there comes this ghastly moment when their golden hair turns into black down, their rose-bud mouths become beaks, their pretty feet in silver slippers change into webbed toes ... until at last the great black tragic birds fly away into the sunset never to return.

As a setting for this trick, Mother Bloodwort had chosen the Italian Garden which lay beside the lake. Arriman hadn't got round to much blighting and smiting there and it was a beautiful spot with urns, statues and wide gravelled paths which swept down to the shimmering water.

But now the great magician had read her list. 'Seven princesses!' he roared. 'Seven! You must be mad!'

Mother Bloodwort, however, was not to be put off.

'Aye. Seven. Proper ones. Royal.'

'I can't just whirl princesses through the air like commoners, you know,' said Arriman. 'The thing has to be done properly. Decent transport and all that. And they're not in the telephone directory.'

But Mother Bloodwort, obstinate old witch that she was, just stood there, waiting.

Arriman sighed. 'Tell everyone to go away for an hour, Leadbetter,' he said. 'I'll have to go to my laboratory for this. And send me that nephew of yours. He's a useful lad and I could do with an extra pair of hands.'

So Mr Leadbetter took the witches back to the camp, and Terence, beaming with pride, followed Arriman and the ogre into the laboratory with its bubbling crucibles and fiendish flasks.

'Actually there is a *sort* of telephone directory for princesses,' said the magician. 'It's called the *Almanach de Gotha*. Run and get it from the library, boy. It's a big, gold-bound book on the second shelf as you go in.'

Terence was back in no time, his eyes shining with excitement.

'Hm,' said Arriman. 'Let's see. There's a Spanish family descended from Carlos the Cruel, I believe. Yes . . . good, there seems to be a daughter. And we ought to find something in Germany. What about the Hohenstifterbluts – they're royal enough.'

'Can't we have a *British* princess?' said Lester.

Arriman shook his head. 'Not wise, I think.' He continued to flick the pages. 'We shall have to scrape the barrel a bit. Still, let's get to work.'

For nearly an hour, Arriman magicked: murmuring spells, twirling his wand, going backwards and forwards between his potions and his vellum-bound books. Once he said, 'Strange, I feel an unusual force in this room. Things are coming through much faster than usual.' But though Terence exchanged a look with Lester, he said nothing. Rover was in his pocket, but if Belladonna was to win the contest, the worm's special power *had* to be kept a secret.

'Right,' said the magician. 'You can fetch them all back now. The last one's just come through.'

Because, sure enough, there, rather beautifully arranged round the rim of a fountain, were seven princesses. Arriman had kept his word and all of them were of the Blood Royal, but that was as far as he'd been able to go. It was no use pretending that they were a matching set of lovely girls. The Princesses Olga Zerchinsky, for example, a niece of one of the last Grand Dukes of Russia, was ninety-two and crippled with rheumatism so that Arriman had had to conjure her up in a wheelchair. On the other hand, the tiny black African princess, descended from King Solomon himself, was lying asleep in her carved ebony cradle. The Spanish princess, though beautifully dressed in a lace mantilla and low cut gown, unfortunately had a wooden leg and the Red Indian princess was almost invisible in a cloud of smoke from her pipe of peace. There was a young princess from America wearing Levis and a T-shirt emblazoned with *I AM BATMAN'S FRIEND* (her ancestors had left France when Louis Phillipe lost his throne), and there was a middle-aged Austrian one whose nose came down over her chin because she was a Habsburg and they have been famous through history for being the ugliest rulers in the world. And there was an Eastern princess in silken trousers who had Mr Chatterjee swooshing out of his bottle with excitement.

Mother Bloodwort, meanwhile, had announced her trick.

'I AM GOING TO TURN SEVEN PRINCESSES OF THE BLOOD ROYAL INTO SEVEN BLACK SWANS,' she said. Then, feeling perhaps that something was missing, she added, 'TEE HEE,' which was the nearest she could get to evil, cackling laughter.

She then vanished behind a statue of the god, Pan, and returned with a broomstick. It was the crummiest, most moth-eaten broomstick anyone had ever seen – Mother Bloodwort had made it herself from brushwood she had found at the back of the camping site – but everyone was pleased because it meant she was going to do hobby horse magic. This is the kind where you ride round and round your victims going faster and ever faster, dizzying them with your speed and your spells, until the transformation is complete. It is old-fashioned magic, but it can be very powerful.

So now Mother Bloodwort went over to the fountain, blew a hole in her Cloud of Flies and stood peering at the princesses. Then she laid her wrinkled hand on the Spanish one in her lace mantilla and turquoise gown.

'You!' she said, pulling her forward on to the gravelled path.

Arriman had hypnotised the princesses as they came so that the black-eyed Princess Juanita followed the old crone obediently, her wooden leg clacking a little as she walked.

Mother Bloodwort now mounted her broomstick, groaning as she heaved her stiff old legs over the handle, which she had greased with the melted body-fat of maddened skunks, and began to ride round and round the royal Spanish lady.

> *"Hattock away, ye magic broom*
> *Send this princess to her doom!'*

shrieked Mother Bloodwort.

Faster she rode, and faster, sending her hood tumbling back and her white hair screaming, while her Cloud of Flies clung desperately to her flushed face and heaving chest.

So crazy did she look, so exhausted and old, that no one really expected the magic to work. But they were wrong. Strange and terrible things were happening to the Princess Juanita.

Her mantilla had wavered ... vanished ... Her head was shimmering ... and now it was covered in feathers, and her full, pouting mouth was changing ... yes, changing into a beak!

'She's done it, Terence! Mother Bloodwort's done it!' cried Belladonna joyfully from the pavilion.

Once more, Mother Bloodwort circled the doomed princess. Then she dismounted and stood back.

'Drat!' said Mother Bloodwort.

For while it was true that she had completely transformed the princess into a bird, that bird was not a swan. It was a duck. Furthermore, the princess having had this trouble with her leg, it was a *lame* duck.

Everybody stared gloomily at the enchanted bird as it waddled, quacking, towards the water. Why there is such a difference between a duck and a swan it is hard to say. There just is. This one seemed to be a

116

Khaki Campbell and not to be at all the sort of person that a prince might fall in love with, recognizing it for the imprisoned soul it was.

But Mother Bloodwort was not daunted. Leaving the duck to stare moodily at a clump of reeds, she took her broomstick back to the fountain and led out the Eastern princess, lovely as an orchid in her shimmering trousers and golden tunic.

'Oi!' moaned Mr Chatterjee. He had never married, not being sure if his wife would settle in a bottle, and the Princess Shari was all that he desired.

Again the princess followed the old witch meekly, again Mother Bloodwort rode round and round her on her broomstick, reciting her rhyme.

'It's going to work this time,' whispered Belladonna to Terence. 'Look, the feathers are black! It'll be a lovely swan, you'll see.'

They watched, breathless, as Mother Bloodwort slowed down and dismounted.

'I see that I am to be spared nothing,' muttered Arriman the Awful, while beside him, Mr Chatterjee howled with pain.

For the bird now tottering like an overfed alderman towards the lake, was a fat, sleek and foolish-looking penguin.

For a moment, Mother Bloodwort was very much put out. But once more she pulled herself together, and, coughing up a number of dead flies, she re-greased her broomstick and went to fetch the German princess with her flaxen pigtail and her dirndl.

But the Princess Waltraut Hohenstifterbluts did not seem to be as hypnotised as the others.

'Eet iss diss-gussting,' she hissed. 'Ve are beink

117

made schtocking-laughs off. Me, I vill be a black schwann or I vill write to ze newspapers.'

But it was not to be. And of all the heart-rending things they'd had to watch, one of the worst was seeing a great-great-great granddaughter of Atilla the Hun sitting on a branch and saying in that silly way that budgies have, even in Germany, 'Plees to giff Walti a biscuit. A biscuit quickly to Walti, plees.'

It was Belladonna who knew what was going to happen next. Mother Bloodwort had dropped her broom, her shoulders sagged, her Cloud of Flies grew silent.

'Don't!' cried Belladonna. 'Oh, please, Mother Bloodwort, don't!'

Too late. Already the budgie, looking surprised, had hopped on to the thing that now stood, four square, upon the path beside the lake.

The ghoul woke and said, 'Vomit!' Mr Chatterjee shook his turbaned head sadly from side to side. And Arriman the Awful rose from his seat.

'No one,' he said, 'can accuse me of not doing my bit for wizardry and darkness. But there is one thing I will not do and that is *marry a coffee table*!'

And pulling his mantle close about him, the outraged wizard strode away.

Twelve

On the night before Madame Olympia was due to do her trick, Terence had a dream. Not a dream, really – a nightmare – a truly horrible one in which he was back at the Sunnydene Home with all the miseries and cruelties he knew so well.

In his dream, Terence was looking for something. Something terribly important, but he didn't know what it was, and growing more and more frantic, he ran through the drab cold rooms, opening battered locker doors, tearing the lids off serving dishes with their soggy dumplings and clammy meat balls, snatching the rough grey blankets from the iron beds. And all the time, as he searched, he heard the sound of laughter – jeering, taunting laughter. Unable to bear it, Terence ran down the mottled steps into the garden.

'I'll find it,' said Terence, 'I'll find it here.'

He bent down and pressed his hands against the gravel, but the laughter was growing louder and more malevolent, and then, suddenly, rearing up in his path, was the dreaded figure of Matron with her sneering lips and baleful eyes, Matron, grown ten foot tall and still trailing the roots which had tethered her – roots which he saw were now made of plaited, blood-stained *human* teeth.

'I *must* find it!' sobbed the little boy.

'You'll never find it! You'll never find it!' screamed Matron. And as her pointed shoe, sharpened to a saw blade, came up to cut him in half, Terence woke.

At first, just finding that he was in his little room at the Hall, wearing Mr Leadbetter's pyjama top and miles away from Matron, was a tremendous relief. But this dream was one it didn't seem easy to shake off.

What had he been looking for so desperately? What had Matron said he'd never find? And suddenly, awake, Terence knew what he had not known when he was sleeping.

Rover. It was Rover he'd been looking for.

Only that was silly. Rover was safe in his box. Terence had said goodnight to him only an hour ago and he'd been in splendid shape, rippling along the rim of the wash basin like an anaconda.

Still, he'd just make absolutely sure. Jumping out of bed, Terence turned on the light and went over to Rover's box which stood where it always stood, under the window.

He lifted the lid.

'Rover?' he called.

The worm was underground; he usually was, and turning the moist, crumbly earth over with his hands, Terence began to search for his friend.

He was a long way down. And gradually, as he searched, Terence's movement became faster and his breath seemed to stick in his throat.

Even then he didn't panic, but went to fetch a newspaper from the pantry and spreading the sheets out on the floor, upended Rover's box.

In the thinly-spread scattering of earth, the truth could no longer be denied.

Rover was gone.

An hour later, the ogre, the secretary and Terence were in Mr Leadbetter's room, desperately deciding what to do. The ogre had rubbed his eyepatch on to the back of his head. Mr Leadbetter was pacing the floor, and Terence, still in the secretary's pyjama top, was crouched on the bed like a worried fledgling on a nest.

'I suppose it wouldn't be possible to use another earthworm for the competition?' said Mr Leadbetter coming to rest for a moment.

Terence shook his head. 'Belladonna said she'd tried being black sometimes with other worms when I was up at the Hall and it didn't work at all. It isn't *any* worm that makes her black, it's Rover.'

'But if we got another worm and *told* her it was Rover—' began Mr Leadbetter, and broke off because he knew he was being silly. Belladonna could tell each ladybird from all its fellows, call a dozen grimy sparrows on a rooftop by their names. It was as foolish to think that all Chinamen looked alike as it was to imagine that she couldn't tell Rover from every earthworm in the world.

'It's only Friday,' said Terence in a rather shaky voice. To him. Rover had not been just a powerful familiar; Terence had lost a dear and valued friend. 'It's Madame Olympia's turn tomorrow and Sunday's a free day, isn't it. So by the time Belladonna does her trick on Monday night, don't you think

121

Rover might be' – he gulped and pulled himself together – 'might be found?'

The ogre and Mr Leadbetter exchanged glances. Terence believed that Rover was simply lost, and they thought it was better he went on thinking so. They had their own suspicions, but the boy had quite enough to bear.

'I wouldn't bank on it, son,' said Lester, laying his enormous hand on Terence's shoulder.

'I suppose we'll just have to give up all hope of Belladonna winning,' said the secretary wearily.

'*No!*' Terence had jumped from the bed and his voice was strong again. 'No! We mustn't give in. Look – Belladonna's just got to win the actual competition, hasn't she? I mean, once Arriman's seen her he's bound to want to marry her and by that time maybe Rover'll have turned up. So can't we *fake* her trick? *Pretend* to have raised Sir Simon?'

'Get someone to impersonate the ghost, do you mean?'

'That's right,' said Terence eagerly. 'There could be lots of smoke and spotlights and things, like in a pantomine. And then this horrible spectre suddenly appearing – *alive!*'

Mr Leadbetter looked shocked. 'That would be cheating, surely?'

Terence turned to him, surprised. 'Well, cheating's black, isn't it? And blackness is what Arriman wants.'

Mr Leadbetter saw the logic of this. 'But who could we get to take the part of Sir Simon?'

'Ought to be a professional,' said Lester. 'An actor. I used to know some when I was in the fair, but not now.'

'Wait a minute,' said Mr Leadbetter. Now that he had got used to the idea of cheating, his brain was beginning to tick over once again. 'You know my sister Amelia? The one that's Terence's mother and didn't marry the swimming bath attendant?'

The others nodded.

'Well, she keeps a boarding house for theatricals in Todcaster. You know, actors and people connected with the stage generally. I wonder if she could find us someone to impersonate Sir Simon?'

'We'll have to move fast,' said Lester. 'There's only two days and one of them's a Sunday. And I don't really see how I can leave the old man with that Madame Olympia due to do her trick tomorrow.'

'And I can't either,' said Mr Leadbetter. 'She's asked for some most complicated stuff. Strobe lights and amplifiers and goodness knows what. Oh, dear!'

'*I* can go,' said Terence.

There was a pause. Terence had looked wonderfully better since he'd come to the Hall, but he was still the smallest and skinniest boy imaginable. And Todcaster was thirty miles away: it meant a train and then a bus into the town.

'Amelia'd look after you,' said Mr Leadbetter slowly.

'But . . .' His voice trailed away. He was too polite to say that he didn't think an actor or anyone else would take much notice of Terence.

'Wait a minute,' said the ogre. 'I've got an idea. The old man's been making paper money: fivers, tenners, the lot. Says he's sick of humping bags of gold around. I'll just go and have a look.

123

He was back in a few minutes with a large wallet crammed to bursting with notes.

'If you take these you'll be all right,' said Lester. 'No one'll care a stuff what size you are when they see these. And remember, not a word to Belladonna! She's got to believe that she's really raising Sir Simon and that it's Rover she's touching inside his box. However nutty she is on Arriman, she'll never cheat to get him and that's for sure!'

And then, at last, they went to bed to wait for dawn.

But one light still burnt at Darkington. A single lamp in the window of Madame Olympia's caravan where the enchantress sat, gloating over something she held in her cruel, rapacious fingers. Something moist and gentle which, greedy as she was, she prized beyond any jewel.

She had always been certain she would win the competition. But now . . . *No one* could beat her now!

Thirteen

Belladonna woke on the morning of Madame Olympia's trick feeling worried and out of sorts. The bloodshot eyeballs on her sleeping-bag had gone very pink and fragrant in the night and she had a nasty feeling that they might be turning into the begonias she was so often troubled with. Then there was Mother Bloodwort who'd been so upset by the budgerigar that not all Belladonna's coaxing could get her to remember the undoing spell for being a coffee table, and Belladonna had had to drag her into her own tent and just hope she'd come round in time. And being Belladonna, she was worried about the flies. Were they all right inside the coffee table; what did they *think*?

But of course she cooked breakfast for the others and took a cup of tea to Nancy Shouter (who still lay on her camp bed in her vest and knickers telling everyone that it didn't matter which chicken was which) and then she followed Mabel Wrack and Ethel Feedbag up to the Hall.

When she reached the steps leading to the South Terrace, she met Mr Leadbetter and the ogre who told her that Terence had gone into Todcaster to do some errands for Arriman.

'Oh, dear!' said Belladonna. 'He'll miss Madame Olympia's trick and he's so *fond* of magic.'

And feeling ridiculously miserable at the thought of spending the day without the little boy, she went to look for the other witches and find a hiding place from which to watch.

Madame Olympia had chosen to do her trick in the underground vaults and cellars of Darkington Hall itself; a cold, dark, echoing warren of passages which opened into a wide cave, as big as several rooms, where in the olden days prisoners had been tortured to death or left to starve. No daylight ever reached this subterranean maze, and as Arriman strode to his place at the judge's table, holding the genie's bottle under his cloak against the cold, he shivered and pulled his collar round his ears.

But when Witch Number Six strode into the cave, his mood changed. For here, at last, was a witch to be taken seriously.

One moment they were sitting in a dark and gloomy cellar – the next, the cave was aflame with flashing lights which changed from sulphurous yellow to livid green and searing crimson, casting strange and flickering shadows on the walls. Next, the vault was filled with a pulsing, sobbing, shrieking sound as the music of 'The Groaning Gizzards', amplified to screaming pitch, pierced the eardrums of the listeners with a song about greed and wretchedness and hate.

Having thus set the stage, the enchantress walked over to the judges' table and bowed low. She was wearing the hood and gown that Arriman had insisted on, but she did not look at all like Mother Bloodwort or Ethel Feedbag or Mabel Wrack. In the secrecy of her caravan, the enchantress had sewn a thousand jet-black sequins on to her gown which now trembled and glittered in the light of the strobes, as did the rhinestones on the collar and lead of her sinister familiar. Witch Number Six was tall and carried herself like a queen and she had looped her necklace of ninety-three molars, fifty-seven incisors and eleven wisdom teeth so as to make a column of palest ivory round her throat.

'THE SYMPHONY OF DEATH PERFORMED BY A CAST OF THOUSANDS,' announced Madame Olympia.

Arriman nodded. He didn't understand a word but it sounded good, and the witch's low, husky voice sent a most agreeable shiver up his spine.

Madame Olympia stepped into the centre of the cave. Then she closed her eyes and raised, not her wand, but a whip. A whip like no other in the world. Stolen from an accursed Egyptian tomb, its thongs were made of the plaited skins of human slaves; its lapis-lazuli handle had been wrought by an ancient sorcerer so powerful that it had meant death even to know his name.

Three times Madame Olympia laid the whip across the back of the aardvark, charging it with the evil beast's devilish power. Then she cracked the whip – and everybody gasped.

A minute before, the cellar had been empty. Now, from every nook and cranny, from the walls, the ceiling, the floors, from the very air itself, there came tumbling and squeaking and clawing, a hundred, two hundred, five hundred – a thousand huge grey rats.

Not ordinary rats. Lurching, swollen, putrid-eyed

rats with scabrous tails and bloated fleas clinging to their matted fur. Rats with death in their filmed eyes – vicious, maddened, *plague-bearing rats*!

Belladonna, hiding behind a pillar, gasped with terror, turned to take Terence's hand, and remembered that he was not there. The ogre said, 'Cor!' and Arriman the Awful leant forward intently in his seat.

There were so many rats now that they could not all put their diseased and twisted feet on the ground but walked on each other's faces, climbed on each other's backs . . . And now Madame Olympia turned off the music of 'The Groaning Gizzards' and adjusted the amplifier so that it was the squeaks and squeals and hideous scamperings of the rats, magnified beyond bearing, which filled the cave.

Once more she flicked her whip and now, unbelievably, each one of the deformed and frightful animals swelled and swelled . . . grew to twice its size . . . three times . . . Rats the size of large dogs, now, so that the beasts' heavy scaly tails thumped like hawsers against the stones. And the fleas, those dreaded carriers of bubonic plague, fell off them, large as saucers.

Smiling her cruel, complacent smile, the enchantress watched as the sickening monsters in their thousands filled the cave, pressing each other against the walls, stamping each other underfoot, their whiskers flicking like thongs into the oozing eyes and twitching limbs of their fellows. And still more rats appeared, layer upon layer of them till the cave was filled almost to the roof with the mis-shapen, screeching monsters.

Only the ghoul was smiling now. The ogre, though the bravest of men, had pulled Mr Leadbetter away to stand behind Arriman, and the three witches, their differences forgotten, clung together trembling.

Again the enchantress cracked her whip – and they saw that Madame Olympia had not come to the end of her devilry. For even as they watched, the flesh, the hair, the eyes and skin of the giant rats began to pucker up, to shrivel – and then to vanish altogether till the whole cellar was packed with skeletons. But skeletons which still ran and climbed and fought and bit. Eyeless, hairless, tail-less, these were still rats, and on the walls their shadows reared and capered in a grotesque and frightful dance of death.

'Is good, is very good,' said Mr Chatterjee inside his bottle, but he was shaking like a leaf, and Belladonna, almost fainting with disgust, could be glad at least that Terence was not there.

Another crack of the whip, and, lo, the giant rats were clothed in their own flesh again: their grey fur returned, their rheumy eyes, their scabrous tails. But the most horrible part of the trick was still to come. For as they heard the last crack of the whip, all the rats were seized at the same moment with a passionate and uncontrollable desire for *the taste of each other's flesh*. It was cannibalism run riot, cannibalism in its most ghastly form, as the rats sank their yellow teeth into thighs and shoulders and cheeks and slowly devoured each other – crunch by horrendous crunch.

'I can't bear it,' said Belladonna beneath her breath.

There were fewer rats now, and fewer, as more and more twitching bodies vanished into the maws of their fellows. Soon only fifty rats were left, then twenty, then five . . .

And then one . . . A single, huge rat sitting on its torn haunches in the middle of the floor, blood dripping from a wound in his side, and the still-twitching tail of his neighbour vanishing down his gullet.

Even then it was not quite done. For now this last rat was seized with the most terrible madness of all, and, gasping, the onlookers saw it begin, slowly and relentlessly, to *eat itself*.

Madame Olympia waited till the dripping jaws hung in the air. Then she flicked her whip, the jaws vanished – and she turned to the judges and bowed.

'The Symphony of Death is completed,' said Madame Olympia.

And laughed . . .

Fourteen

Madame Olympia got nine out of ten for her 'Symphony of Death', as near full marks as could be. The ghoul loved her trick and though Mr Chatterjee's teeth went on chattering for a long time inside his bottle, he too thought she was very, very clever. Not even the nastiest Caliph in the Arabian Nights had done anything more horrible.

'Why did I only give her nine out of ten?' Arriman asked himself that evening. 'Why not full marks?' Because it was he who held back. The other two had been willing to go the whole hog and give her that last mark also.

What had prevented him, he wondered? For certainly no witch could touch her for darkness. And the style, the flair! Those strobe lights and that single rat left in the middle of the floor eating its own flesh! Standing there in his dressing-gown, Arriman remembered her low and evil laughter – very attractive it was, really – and that proud toss of the head. No, no one would beat her, that was for sure. There was only one witch to go, and from what he'd heard she was just a little slip of a thing, not to be taken seriously. No, Witch Number Six would be Mrs Canker, all right. She'd known it herself.

'That was a very fine show today, don't you think,

Lester?' he called to the ogre, who was running his bath.

Lester came out of the bathroom looking steamy and rather tired.

'Very fine, sir,' he said, his voice expressionless.

'Those flickering lights and the skeletons and those giant fleas. I really liked them, didn't you?'

'Very much, sir.'

'Of course, some people would have thought it wasn't necessary to make the rats actually . . . eat each other up like that. I mean, I myself have never gone in much for that sort of thing.'

'No, sir.'

'But you couldn't have anything blacker. And she was quite good-looking I think? I didn't see any warts, did you? Or . . . er, whiskers? And I'm almost sure she wasn't wearing wellies.'

'No, she wasn't wearing wellies, sir.'

'So I'm very glad she's won. Well, she's sure to have. Very glad indeed. I think she'll make me an excellent wife. I shouldn't think she'll get things to eat each other very much once we're married. There'll be just straightforward blighting and smiting, wouldn't you say?'

'Yes, sir. Your bath is ready, sir.'

'You're not very forthcoming tonight, Lester. What's the matter with you?'

'I'm a little tired, sir.'

'Are you? Well, I'll tell you what, fetch Leadbetter's nephew, Terence. He can scrub my back for me. A nice boy. I'm fond of him.'

'I'm afraid he isn't here, sir,' said Lester after a short pause. 'He's gone to visit . . . . his mother.'

'Has he? Dear me. That'll be Leadbetter's sister, I suppose. Pity. He'd have enjoyed today, I think,' said the magician, untying his dressing-gown cord. 'Er . . . those were *human* teeth she was wearing round her neck?'

'Undoubtedly, sir.'

'Yes. I thought so. It's a new fashion, I suppose. I mean, one must keep up with the times.'

Arriman took off his trousers, his socks and his shoes and was just about to start on his underpants when the usual plashing sound was heard behind the wainscot.

'Oh my Gawd,' said Lester, who was in no mood for Sir Simon.

But before he could make his getaway, the wicked spook came waveringly through the panelling and thrust his pallid, guilty face at Arriman.

'Hello, hello!' said the magician, cheering up as always at the sight of his friend. 'I've great news for you. I've found a truly black witch. Looks like a certain winner.'

The spectre stood in silence, his eye sockets dark and inscrutable.

'I know you aren't into marriage much, but you'll like her. Great style. She did this amazing trick where all these rats . . . ate each other up. Of course, it's not for people with weak stomachs.'

Still silent, the spectre stood and plashed.

'Oh, blast you!' said Arriman, suddenly furious. 'Why don't you *say* something?'

The wizard was in his bath, and Lester, who'd finished scrubbing his back, was out in the corridor talking to Mr Leadbetter, when a cry of anguish rent the air.

'Lester! Come back! It's trying to get in with me. Take it away!'

Lester did not move.

'Aren't you going to go to him?' asked Mr Leadbetter.

'Not likely.'

'But it's the Kraken. It's trying to get in the bath with him.'

'I know it's the Kraken. It always tries to get in the bath with him.'

'But—' began Mr Leadbetter, as another despairing cry came from Arriman.

'Look,' said the ogre, rubbing his eyepatch. 'Last night that bloke sent seven princesses back to seven different countries, and three of them blinking budgies, lame ducks and penguins before he got to them. A month ago he brought down a ton of toads on the tax inspector's Mini. What's to stop him sending the Kraken back into the sea or turning him into an umbrella stand or something?'

'You mean he likes being followed about and so on?'

'Likes it?' said the ogre. 'He loves it. Laps it up. Can't get enough. You mark my words, if he marries and has a kid he'll be the biggest sucker in the world. Anyone calling that bloke "Daddy" and he's a goner, devilry and wizardry or no.'

They both fell silent. The thought of Arriman's marriage lay like a stone on their chests. For Terence hadn't yet returned and even if he managed to hire an actor, was there really any hope that they'd manage to deceive Arriman?

'Will you stay on if he marries... Madame Olympia?' said Mr Leadbetter, who could hardly bring himself to say the enchantress's name.

Lester shook his craggy head. 'Don't think I could,' he said. 'Goodness knows it goes against the grain to leave the poor bloke, but she really gives me the creeps. I wouldn't put it past her to turn me into a bloomin' baboon *and* get me to nosh meself into the bargain.'

'It's the boy I'm worried about,' said Mr Leadbetter. 'If anything happens to Terence, Belladonna'll never get over it.'

'It won't,' said the ogre. 'He may be gnat-sized, but he's got a head on his shoulders, that boy. Even now, I wouldn't put it past him to bring home the bacon.'

'I do hope you're right, Lester,' said the secretary, rubbing his aching tail. 'I do very much hope so.'

Lester *was* right. No harm had befallen Terence, and midday had found him ringing the doorbell of Amelia Leadbetter's terrace house on the outskirts of Todcaster.

At first when he'd seen again the dreary houses and mean streets of the town he'd been so unhappy in, Terence had felt uneasy and afraid. Miss Leadbetter's Boarding House was not far from the Sunnydene Home, and when Terence thought of Matron and her bullying it was as though the last exciting days at Darkington had never been. But then he remembered that he was there to help Belladonna

135

and not to worry about himself, and it was with renewed courage that he rang the bell.

Miss Leadbetter might not have a tail but she was a brisk and sensible woman, and when she'd read the note her brother had written, and given Terence a cup of tea and a bloater paste sandwich, she got down to business.

'Now it says here you want an actor to take part in a show up at the Hall? Someone tall and used to costume work, is that right?'

Terence nodded. 'If he could be used to talking in that old-fashioned way, you know, with "haths" and "quothees" and things in it?'

'Shakespearean.' Amelia Leadbetter nodded. 'Well, there's plenty of unemployed actors around. It's not a comic you want, then? It's straight lead?'

'Oh, yes. He plays a knight in armour. It's a very good part. Sort of a star part.'

'And it's got to be someone who can keep a secret. Now, let's see . . .' She leant across and filled Terence's mug once more with scalding tea. 'There's Bert Danby, but he's a boozer and you can never trust a boozer. Then there's Dave Lullingworth – he's down to doing cat food adverts on the telly – but Dave would tell his life story to a brick wall. Wait a minute! I've got it. Yes, Monty Moon. He's a bit long in the tooth now, but with the right make-up he'll pass. Monty hasn't worked for years, but he was at Stratford once. In fact I'm not sure he didn't play the ghost in Hamlet.'

Terence was very excited. 'He sounds just right!' he said. An actor who was actually used to playing ghosts was more than he had hoped for.

So Amelia rang up Mr Moon, who by great good luck was at home and agreed to come around immediately.

Monty Moon turned out to be tall and pale and stooped, with a large balding head and a way of tucking in his chin so that it didn't show any sags or wrinkles. When he saw Terence he looked surprised and a little stuffy, but when he saw the wallet which Terence had laid casually open on the table he got a lot less stuffy at once.

Five minutes later, they were deep in conversation.

'Now, I understand I'm to play a wicked, wife-slaying spectre who suddenly finds himself brought back to life – is that correct?'

'That's right.'

'Now, fill me in, dear boy, fill me in. I must get right *inside* this part. How many wives have I slain? What sort of armour do I wear? Am I bloodstained?'

So Terence told him everything he could think of about Sir Simon, and Mr Moon wrote it all down in his little notebook.

'And he doesn't wear his helmet or anything,' finished Terence. 'The top of him is clear and so are his hands so that he can beat his forehead with a plashing sound.'

'Like this?' asked Mr Moon, bringing his arm round in a sweep and striking dramatically at his forehead.

'Well, yes, but it makes a softer noise. Sort of sloshier.'

'Don't worry, dear boy. I'll get it right on the night. Now what about the sound effects? Anything special

137

you want when I appear? Howling dogs? Tempests? Crowing cockerels? Just say the word.'

They went on discussing things for another hour and deciding what Terence should get ready in the way of skulls, necromancy incense and so on, for while it had been all right for Belladonna to write 'Nothing' on her list when they had Rover to rely on, now that her trick was to be faked, the more props there were, the better. When Mr Moon heard that he was to get five hundred pounds now and another five hundred if he succeeded in convincing everybody that he was really Sir Simon brought back to life, he promised of his own accord to bring an electrician and a stage manager who had their own van and would help him set the thing up.

'You'll see, dear boy, it'll be a first-rate show. I always did my best work in costume parts. Now just draw a little map for me to show me how we can get into the Hall the night before and rig up one or two effects. A trap door would have been nice, but one can't have everything.'

When they had finished, Terence went to thank Miss Leadbetter. Returning to say good-bye to Mr Moon, he found the actor still standing in the middle of the room, bringing his arm in a sweep round to his forehead, practising and practising his plashing sound. And knowing that he had found somebody who took his work seriously, Terence went contentedly away.

Fifteen

Arriman woke on the Sunday before Hallowe'en with a headache. Like Terence, he had had a dream and a dream with teeth in it. He'd seen this necklace floating in the air with five brand-new molars on it: cusps, fillings and all. Arriman had known at once that they were *his* teeth and he'd started making teeth-calling noises like the noises you call cows in to be milked with, or chickens to be fed. But the teeth wouldn't come to him, they sort of sneered and floated away – and then Arriman woke and had been almost glad to hear, from under the lid of the soup tureen, the muffled cries of 'Daddy! Daddy!' with which the Kraken greeted the dawn.

Mr Chatterjee was already breakfasting inside his bottle, looking cheerful and relaxed. The climate of the North of England didn't really suit him and as soon as Witch Number Seven had done her trick he was going to fly home to Calcutta.

'Well, we've got the day free,' said Arriman, who was always jolly at breakfast. 'Witch Number Seven's not going to do her trick till tomorrow night. Myself, I think I'll do a little smiting and blighting today; I'm getting short of exercise. What about you, Sniveller?'

But the ghoul, sitting hunched and exhausted over his kidneys, didn't answer. He almost never did.

So Arriman went off and blighted some fir trees

and cleft some boulders in twain and called in a thunderstorm from the west – clean, old-fashioned magic which he enjoyed – and thought how nice it had been when the Wizard Watcher had sat peacefully at the gate and his oak trees had not been filled with sleeping grocers and lost witches had not bubbled about in bottomless holes on his East Lawn.

'Well, tomorrow it'll all be over,' he thought. 'Tomorrow I'll know for certain who my wife is going to be. No, I'm being silly. I know *now*.'

After which he went to find Mr Leadbetter to ask him for some milk of magnesia tablets. Magician or no, Arriman had a stomach ache.

Meanwhile, down at the campsite, Belladonna sat wretchedly by the campfire, facing the fact that Arriman the Awful was lost to her for ever. Even before the enchantress did her trick, Belladonna had not really hoped to win, though when Terence was with her she'd sometimes felt confident and strong. Now, all hope was gone.

She reached for the magic mirror. Arriman was gulping down small white pills. He looked tired and anxious, but what was that to do with her? It would be Madame Olympia now who'd comfort him and smooth the curse curl from his furrowed brow.

Her sad thoughts were interrupted by a fierce rocking noise behind her, followed by a scrabble and a swoosh, and Mother Bloodwort crawled out of Belladonna's tent, her flies sticking like a doormat round her head. The old witch had been a coffee table far too long and as she collapsed on to the camp stool that

Belladonna pulled out for her she looked very battered and confused.

'What happened?' she asked, blinking. 'Was the last one a swan?'

'I'm afraid not,' said Belladonna gently. 'It was a budgerigar. A very intelligent one. It asked for a biscuit.'

'Not the same, though, is it?' the old witch remarked. 'Don't know what went wrong. Didn't get a very high mark, I suppose?'

'Well . . . three out of ten. Not bad, really. More than I'll get, anyway.'

Mother Bloodwort kicked off her slippers so that the fire could get at her bunions and stared sadly into the flames.

'It wouldn't have made any difference if you'd managed the swan bit,' said Belladonna, trying to comfort the old woman. 'Because Madame Olympia would have won, anyway. She did this absolutely terrifying thing with rats. The "Symphony of Death", it was called. She got nine out of ten: no one can possibly beat her.'

'The "Symphony of Death", eh?' said Mother Bloodwort thoughtfully, 'I've heard of that. Very black, that is, *very* nasty. There's not too many witches could do that even in my day. I should think she'd gobble up poor Arriman as soon as look at him. Good job he's got nice teeth.'

'Oh, no, *no*! Don't say that!' cried Belladonna. 'Arriman's the mightiest wizard in the world! She couldn't hurt him, she couldn't!'

'Oh, well, maybe not,' said Mother Bloodwort. She sighed. 'I suppose marriage wouldn't really have

141

suited me. I've lost the habit, I reckon, and that turning-myself-young-again spell doesn't seem to be up to much.'

She got up creakingly, went to fetch her tin with the Coronation on the lid, and began to shake her head into it, blowing on the flies as they fell to change them into maggots. 'Best be getting ready for lunch, I suppose.'

But before Mother Bloodwort could move, Ethel Feedbag and Mabel Wrack came lurching up to them, both heaving with rage.

'Look!' said Mabel, putting down the bucket in which she was taking Doris for her mid-day stroll and pointing with a shaking arm at the enchantress's caravan.

'Stuck up, snooty cow!' raged Ethel Feedbag.

Belladonna looked up, frowning.

'How strange,' she said.

Madame Olympia's caravan was the kind with a little stove and a chimney. And of course as she was a witch, the smoke from her chimney was blowing against the wind. But that wasn't what had made Ethel and Mabel so mad. Madame Olympia had magicked the smoke so that it came out in letters: the letter *O* followed by the letter *C* again and again, standing out as clear as could be against the deep blue sky of autumn.

'What does it mean?' asked Belladonna, puzzled.

'What do you think it means?' snarled Mabel Wrack. 'Those are her new initials, of course. Olympia Canker. She's letting us all know she's won.'

'But she hasn't won! She *hasn't*!'

The voice was a new one, and Belladonna, hearing it, sprang to her feet.

'Terence! Oh, I'm so glad you're back! You've no idea how much I've missed you.'

But though he hugged her as lovingly as always, Terence's mud-coloured eyes were fixed on the enchantress's chimney and his jaw was set.

'You're going to beat her, Belladonna. You're going to get ten out of ten tomorrow. You'll see!'

Sixteen

In the Great Hall at Darkington, the clock struck eleven. An hour till the true beginning of Hallowe'en, the Feast of the Dead, when the Shades of the Departed draw closer, for a few dread hours, to those they have left behind.

In a dozen sconces, the tall candles burnt with a sickly flame; logs of gnarled and knotted alderwood, like ancient severed limbs, hissed and spat in the grate, and the wind, howling through the rafters, eerily stirred the tapestry of the gentleman being shot with arrows while burning at the stake.

Belladonna, waiting for her turn, was as white as a sheet under her gown and mask. Terence had taken her through her trick again and again. He'd told her that everything would be ready, laid out on a great refectory table covered with a cloth, and that he himself would be hiding underneath it, ready to hand her Rover at the right moment and prompt her if she forgot anything. And waiting behind a tall embroidered screen with the other witches, she could see that he'd been as good as his word. The table, with its candlesticks, its grinning skull and portrait of Sir Simon, looked just like one of those dreadful necromancy altars she'd seen in books. But that only made her more horribly afraid of the deed she was about to do.

'Witch Number Seven – step forward!' commanded Mr Leadbetter.

The secretary was looking tired and careworn. However much he argued with himself, it seemed to him that cheating was *not* the same as wizardry and darkness. Cheating, whichever way you looked at it, was *mean*. And what if Monty Moon let them down and all they'd done was make Belladonna look a fool?

But Belladonna, trying to stop her knees from trembling, was walking towards the judges' table, and, pulling himself together, Mr Leadbetter said:

'Announce your trick!'

Belladonna turned and bowed low to the judges. Her voice shook a little on the first words, but she lifted her head bravely and her clear young voice reached even to the furthest corner of the hall.

'I AM GOING TO BRING SIR SIMON MONTPELIER BACK FROM THE DEAD,' said Belladonna, allowing herself a lingering look at Arriman as he sat, brooding and a little bored, between the other judges.

But at her words, the magician leant forward, furiously frowning, and a spurt of fire burst from his left ear. Going to do necromancy, was she? A deed so difficult that he, Arriman the Awful, had failed at it again and again. A little slip of a witch, not up to his shoulder. How *dared* she?

For a moment, it looked as though Arriman was going to make a scene. But even as he brought his fist down, ready to bang it on the table, his curiosity got the better of him. It was impertinence, of course, the most appalling cheek. Still, it wouldn't hurt to let her try. Perhaps she had guessed how achingly he longed for his plashing, ghostly friend.

So Belladonna stepped forward to the table with its long cloth and candle-sticks and skull, and as she did so, Terence slipped Rover's closed box into the pocket of her gown. Then she took a pin from her other pocket and jabbing it into her finger, let a drop of blood fall, like a red pearl, into the incense pot. And immediately there was a flash, and a sheet of rose and amethyst and orange smoke rose almost to the roof.

'Thank Gawd,' said Lester, who believed that if you had to cheat it was best to cheat good and proper. He'd heard a van drive into the courtyard at dawn, but that was the only sign of Monty Moon and his crew, and he'd begun to have doubts.

'Let there be darkness!' said Belladonna. And instantly, every candle guttered and went out, and the hall was plunged into inky impenetrable night.

Belladonna let the darkness and silence stay there for a moment, making everyone's flesh crawl a little. Then she took up the hollow skull and walked over to the magic triangle that Terence had chalked out for her below the tapestry.

'Do you hear me, Shades of the Underworld?' cried Belladonna, raising the skull.

They heard her. First came a low and fearful murmuring which swelled to a cacophony of cackling, screaming and screeching, and under the table, Terence sighed with relief, Mr Moon had been as good as his word – and better.

Belladonna's teeth were chattering badly now. It seemed that Terence was right and that with Rover to help her there was no limit to her darkness. But she went on bravely, and putting down the skull, she fetched the portrait of Sir Simon and held it aloft.

'I call upon thee, Shades, to release from eternal torment the spirit of this man!' she intoned.

More screams and yells from the spirits, while in the rafters, the ravens hideously croaked.

'Sir Simon Montpelier, Knight of Darkington, I command thee to appear!' cried Belladonna.

The jabbering and screeching died away, and now, in the black silence of the hall, there appeared a series of white, disembodied lights which bobbed and flickered, giving off at the same time an almost unendurable stench of decay.

'Corpse candles,' murmured Mother Bloodwort, drawing her skirt away from one which had come too close.

Then, all in the same second, the corpse candles went out, and over the hall there spread a coldness such as they had never before experienced: the coldness of the tomb, the grave, of death itself.

'I wonder how he did that?' murmured Lester, whose respect for Mr Moon was growing every minute. 'Some sort of chemical, I suppose.'

But now the coldness was passing and everyone's gaze was drawn upwards to the wall on the left of the chimney breast. For the tapestry of the man stuck with arrows while burning at the stake was beginning to glow and shine and shimmer with a most unearthly light.

Belladonna felt in her pocket for a last squeeze of Rover's box. She was incredibly tired and her knees felt like water, but she wouldn't weaken now. And taking up a wand from the table, she struck the ground thrice and, prompted by Terence, who all the time had whispered the spells along with her, she said the words that are older than any book of magic in the world:

'*Allay fortission! Fortissio Roa!*' cried Belladonna.

The glow round the tapestry grew stronger. The clock struck midnight. And as the last chime died away, there crept round the edge of the hanging, slowly and gropingly – a hand. A white hand, limp and long-fingered, with an emerald riding one knuckle.

For a few moments, the hand just hung there. Then it felt for the sides of the tapestry and with a sudden violent gesture, tore it from the wall and threw it on the ground.

And there stepped from the stone recess – wan and weary, but definitely alive – the figure of an Elizabethan knight.

A shriek of joy from Arriman broke the stunned silence.

'Sir Simon! Is it really you?' he cried, pushing back his chair so hard that it crashed to the ground. And dashing forward he seized the spectre's hands in both his own.

'Aye, 'tis I,' intoned Sir Simon. His voice was high and reedy, like an oboe playing something sad. 'Ye see before ye the guilty, tainted flesh of Sir Simon Montmorency Montpelier.'

'Oh, I can't believe it! But yes, yes, I can feel you; you're solid! And look at that vein throbbing in your left temple! Oh, happy, happy day! What ecstasy! What bliss!'

Sir Simon removed his left hand from Arriman's grasp and brought it up to his forehead. The plashing sound was much, much better than when he'd been a ghost: more solid, wetter, in every way more *real*.

Arriman was quite overcome. 'The talks we'll have! The confidences! The walks! The delights of nature we will share! My dear, dear fellow, this is the best day of my life!'

Then, remembering at last that this was a competition, Arriman turned to the other judges.

'Ten out of ten, gentlemen, are we agreed?'

The ghoul nodded – he'd have liked the whole world to be inhabited by people who were dead – and kind Mr Chatterjee smiled.

But these words were never heard by Belladonna. Overcome by fatigue, terror and strain, Belladonna had fainted.

Seventeen

Belladonna woke in a four-poster bed in a room at the very top of the North Tower at Darkington. Mr Leadbetter and the ogre had carried her there after the end of the competition, while Terence hopped round her, worrying about her and congratulating her at the same time. Belladonna couldn't remember much about it now; only that she'd been anxious about the baby rabbits and about not having a tooth-brush, and that Terence had said he'd go down to the campsite and see to everything.

How long ago had that been, she wondered? It still seemed to be dark, but now she felt refreshed and very happy. She'd done it! She'd won! She was to be the bride of Arriman, to be with him always, to stroke his moustache and massage his ankles if they swelled and share his secrets, his hopes and his fears.

'Oh, glory!' said Belladonna, and smiling, fell asleep once more.

But a *happy* white witch, a white witch blissfully in love, can be a disaster. While Belladonna slept the room began to fill with exquisite saucer-sized snow flakes, each a perfect, six-pointed star and the flakes did not melt but alighted softly on the hangings of the bed, the embroidered rug, the wash stand. An enamelled musical box burst from the chest of drawers and began to play a dreamy Viennese waltz;

strings of gold and silver tinsel draped themselves across the ceiling, and the window sills filled with rows of crystal goblets each brim-full of Knicker-bocker Glories.

But Belladonna, knowing nothing of all this, slept on.

While Belladonna lay dreaming in the Tower Room, Arriman sat in the library talking to Sir Simon Montpelier. Arriman had suggested that the knight might like to slip into something more comfortable than the breast plate and leg armour he had worn for four hundred years, and though he'd murmured something about his underclothes not being quite the thing, the wife-slayer was now wearing Arriman's second-best dressing-gown – a maroon one appliquéd with fiends and pitchforks – and was telling the magician the story of his life.

'So the Lady Anne was the first of your wives?' enquired Arriman, pushing the whisky decanter towards his friend.

Even so,' agreed Sir Simon. 'She was the one I drowned. Ere the cock crew thrice, I drowned her. I had to. She madeth the sleeping chamber rumble as if cleft in twain.'

'Ah! She snored, you mean?' said Arriman. 'Very distressing that. Nothing worse.'

The knight nodded and plashed a little.

'Then I wedded the Lady Mary. Her I took by the throat and fastened my foul fingers around.'

'Strangulation.' Arriman nodded.

'She hath cheateth me of my victuals,' said the knight.

151

'Fiddled the housekeeping, did she? In that case she deserved everything she got. And the next one?'

'Next I espoused the fair Olivia. Her I walled up in the privy for looking with favour upon the knave who emptied of her slops.'

Arriman shook his head. 'Terrible, terrible. What you've been through!'

Sir Simon went on to tell the magician about the Lady Julia whom he'd stabbed in the buttery because she had a horrid little dog that yapped, and the Lady Letitia whom he'd thrown over a cliff because she guzzled, and he was just about to start on the Lady Henrietta whom he'd knocked off with a poisoned halibut because she drove him nutty walking in her sleep, when there was a knock at the door and the ogre entered.

'The Kraken's in his tureen waiting for you to say goodnight, sir, and I've laid out your pyjamas. Is there anything else you require?'

'No, no, Lester, that's fine. You can go to bed.'

'I've put Sir Simon in the Green Room,' said Lester, winking at Mr Moon, 'on account of it being handy for the bathroom, like.'

'Good, good,' said the magician impatiently. There was still one more wife to go and he wanted to hear about her.

'There was a postcard from the Wizard Watcher by the late post, sir,' the ogre continued. 'It has reached Skegness and hopes to be back the day after tomorrow.'

He had got through to the magician at last. 'Now that is good news! I'm really glad about that. I wouldn't have liked it to miss the wedding.'

But the word 'wedding' had a bad effect on Arriman. His brooding face darkened and he drained his whisky in a single desperate gulp. 'You've no idea what women do, Lester. Sir Simon's been telling me. They snore and have little dogs and walk in their sleep. And those are just *ordinary* women! I mean, this witch . . . she must be really very black to do necromancy. I should think a witch as black as that would have some pretty nasty habits.'

'Not necessarily, sir,' said Lester.

'And if she's blacker than me . . . I mean, I don't want to be *henpecked*. I can't imagine anything sillier than a henpecked wizard.'

'Sir,' said Lester, losing his patience, 'you haven't even *seen* Witch Number Seven. And anyway, what about your duty to wizardry and darkness? What about this blighting black baby you're going to have? What,' said Lester, 'did we have this blinking contest *for*?'

The magician sighed. 'Yes, yes, you're quite right, Lester. I'll go and see her first thing in the morning and fix the date.'

As Lester left the room, Arriman was leaning forward eagerly and saying, 'And the last one? The Lady Beatrice, wasn't it? What did she do?'

'Smelled,' said Sir Simon gloomily. 'Most vilely and horribly hath she smelled.'

And having come to the end of his wives, the knight poured himself another whisky and began again at the beginning.

Arriman kept his word, and the next morning saw him climbing the curved steps to Belladonna's tower.

153

The magician wasn't feeling too good. Sir Simon had told him about his murdered wives not once but three times, and though Arriman understood how much the wife-slayer needed to talk after four hundred years of only plashing, he did feel very tired. Nor were the ogre and the secretary, following close behind him, exactly full of beans. They'd spent the night worrying in case the real Sir Simon burst clanking through the panelling and gave the game away, and they didn't really like the way Monty Moon was settling into his part. That was the trouble with actors. You could get them *on* stage, but getting them off was another matter.

'Leadbetter, you wouldn't lie to me,' said Arriman, turning round. 'Is she covered in warts? I mean, *covered*?'

'No, sir. Not at all.'

'What about her fingers and toes? All there, are they? No . . . stumps, for example? Nothing webbed, or anything? Nothing *clawed*?'

'No, sir.'

The magician climbed a few more steps and turned again.

'And . . . er . . . nothing personal, you understand, because yours is charming. I mean, it's part of you, but it could be awkward in a wife. In short, Leadbetter, has she got . . . a tail? You know, one of those forked jobs, a bit black and bushy?'

'No, sir,' said the secretary. 'Witch Number Seven is tail-less.'

'And her name is Belladonna?'

'That's right.'

'Belladonna Canker. Ah, well.'

154

And reaching the top step, Arriman paused, took a deep breath – and threw open the door.

Belladonna was sitting up in bed. The sun, streaming through the East Window, had turned her hair into a shower of gold; her eyes were bright with happiness and blue as a summer sky and she was singing a sweet and foolish little song: the kind with roses in it and springtime and love. Rather a lot of love.

Arriman stood stock-still in the doorway, unable to move.

'Who . . . is this?' he stammered.

'That is Belladonna, sir. Witch Number Seven. The winner of the contest!'

'You're not pulling my leg?'

'No, sir.'

'She's not . . . er . . . in an enchanted state? I mean, she hasn't taken on another shape just to bamboozle me? She looks like that all the time?'

'All the time, sir.'

Belladonna, meanwhile, was gazing rapturously at Arriman, her heart in her eyes. This was the closest she had ever been to him and she was drinking in the flaring nostrils, the tufty ears, the curve of his noble nose.

'Belladonna!' said the magician, stepping forward. His voice throbbed, his eyes burnt and his chest heaved like a pair of bellows.

'Arry?' murmured Belladonna shyly, from beneath lowered lashes.

'Arry! All my life I've wanted someone to call me Arry.'

Lester and Mr Leadbetter exchanged glances.

155

Things were turning out exactly the way they'd hoped, but they hadn't reckoned on being quite so embarrassed.

'Leadbetter, we must be married at once! Tomorrow at the latest!' said Arriman, who was now sitting on Belladonna's bed and grasping both her hands.

Mr Leadbetter sighed. It was just like Arriman to spend weeks grumbling about having to get married and then fall in love like a ton of bricks and make trouble for everyone.

'I'm afraid that's impossible, sir. There are the wedding invitations to be sent, the food to be ordered, the bride's clothes to be bought. Three weeks is the shortest I can manage it in.'

'Three weeks! I can't wait three weeks! Can you wait three weeks, my pretty?'

'Oh, my Gawd,' murmured Lester. He had forgotten how absolutely ridiculous people sounded when they were in love.

But now at last the really peculiar look of the Tower Room had got through to Arriman, and without letting go of Belladonna's hands, he looked with surprise at the exquisite snow flakes, the strings of gold and silver tinsel, the shimmering moonstones now dripping from the mouth of the wash jug.

Catching every movement of her Beloved's eyes, Belladonna flushed and said, 'I'm sorry about all this. It happened while I was asleep. You see, Arry, I feel I should tell you that I used to be white.'

'No, no, my treasure,' said the magician dotingly. 'That's quite impossible. Your hair is so golden, your cheeks are so pink, your eyes are such a lovely, lovely blue.'

'I don't mean that,' said Belladonna. 'I mean, my *magic* was white. I was a white witch.'

She had got through to Arriman at last. A spasm crossed his face. 'My dearest love, you musn't *say* such things!'

'Oh, it's all right. I'm not white now. I'm very, very black. Well, you saw how black I was. *Rover* made me—' She broke off with a little cry. 'Oh, how dreadful of me! How selfish and cruel! I left Rover in his matchbox all night! Oh, poor, poor Rover; he'll be so dry and sad – Terence will never forgive me.'

She had freed her hands from Arriman's, and jumping out of bed, ran to the chair where her gown was lying.

'Here it comes!' whispered the ogre.

Belladonna had found the matchbox, had opened it, was staring at it while the colour drained from her face.

When she spoke it was in a voice so full of anguish and disbelief that they hardly recognized it. 'Rover's gone,' said Belladonna. 'He's *gone!*'

There was a long and dreadful pause. 'I have to find him, Arry, I have to. He's my familiar, you see. Without him, I'm nothing.'

She began to search desperately, lifting up the Knickerbocker Glories, pushing aside the snow flakes. Arriman had started to help her when he saw the ogre beckoning to him from the other side of the room.

'Sir,' said Lester, when he'd got his master outside the door. 'It's my belief that it ain't no good looking

157

because that worm ain't lost. He's been stolen. I've thought so all along.'

'All along? But Belladonna's only just noticed that he's gone,' said Arriman, looking puzzled.

Lester saw that he'd made a mistake. If he told Arriman that Rover had been gone before the raising of Sir Simon, he'd get suspicious at once. Belladonna had made it clear that her blackness came from Rover, so if there was no Rover there was no blackneses, and that led right back to Sir Simon not being Sir Simon at all but an actor called Monty Moon.

'I can't go into that now, sir,' he said. 'But I can tell you one thing. Rover may be a good performer, but he's not up to shutting a matchbox after he's crawled out of it. No, that worm's been nicked and I'll bet my bottom dollar I know who did it.'

'Who?'

'Witch Number Six. That Madame Olympia. Leadbetter thinks the same.'

'Oh no! Surely not!' Arriman was very shocked. 'The one with the interesting cruel smile and the . . . er . . . rats?'

Lester nodded. 'And if I'm right we ought to be getting down to her caravan quick. The witches are due to go back tomorrow.'

Arriman was frowning. The more he remembered the 'Symphony of Death', the more he thought it would be better not to meet the enchantress head on.

'I think we'd better take her by surprise,' he said. 'And that means disguises. How would you like to be a rabbit, Lester?'

'Not at all, sir.'

'Oh, come on! Be a sport!'

'No, sir. Absolutely and definitely, *no*.'

While Arriman and the ogre were talking, Madame Olympia was packing her things.

Since Belladonna had won the competition, the enchantress had been in such a towering rage that she had made three holes in the floor of the caravan where she had stamped her feet. She had also come out in a rash from sheer temper, and it was this which made her decide to go back to London immediately, to her Beauty Parlour, where she could mix some creams and ointments to get rid of it. Then she planned to come back like the Queen in *Snow White* with a poisoned apple or some poisoned stays which she would sell Belladonna at the door and which would kill her. Except that probably Belladonna did not *wear* stays – people did not seem to nowadays – so she would have to think of something else.

So now she came out of the caravan to do one last job and that was to throw some rubbish she did not want on to the fire. Some nasty, useless, disappointing rubbish that she wanted to get rid of once and for all. And as she did so, a rabbit and a fox ran between her legs and bounded into the caravan.

If she had bothered to look, she might have noticed that the fox was an unusually handsome one with a great bushy autumn-coloured tail, and that the rabbit, which looked cross, had only a single eye. But she only turned round furiously and said, 'Get out at *once*, you dirty animals. Shoo!'

But of course they weren't dirty animals any more.

Sitting round the table were Arriman the Awful and the ogre.

'Good morning,' said Arriman, polite as always.

'How dare you!' screamed the enchantress. 'How *dare* you break in like this?'

Arriman looked at her. An enchantress's power is useless on someone who is truly in love. Arriman could see her now as she really was and he did not like what he saw.

'We believe you may have something which belongs to my fiancée,' said the magician. 'Her familiar, to be exact.'

'Her familiar? What on earth are you talking about? I've a perfectly good familiar of my own, as you can see.' Madame Olympia kicked the cowering aardvark with the heel of her shoe.

Then she shut her eyes and began to gabble something under her breath. But before she could get any further, Lester, following a signal from his master, had taken the full milk jug and upended it over the enchantress's head.

'*Phloo*,' spluttered Madame Olympia. '*Guggle*!'

Milk is a well-known antidote to magic, almost as good as eating roses or holding a rowan twig.

'Quick! Search the caravan!' ordered Arriman, while the enchantress, groping for a towel, used some words that even Lester had not heard before.

So they searched the caravan, turning out the built-in cupboards, opening Madame Olympia's half-packed suitcase, feeling under the bed.

Nothing. Not a sign of Rover.

'You see,' jeered the enchantress. 'Turn the caravan inside out for all I care.'

She flung out of the caravan and, picking up the little bundle of rubbish, walked with a gleeful smile towards the fire.

It was Arriman who caught on first and ran after her, the ogre following.

'Stop! Stop! Let's see what you're burning.'

'Never!' shouted the enchantress, and laughed.

Then she brought her arm over in an arc and threw her bundle on to the flames.

Arriman did not stop for any of the spells that would have made him fireproof, or any magic words that would have doused the flames. Instead, he plunged his hand into the red-hot blaze and drew out the crumpled bundle just as it had begun to catch.

And there – dry and bewildered-looking at the bottom of a cornflake packet – was Rover!

Belladonna, sitting wistfully in a chair in the Tower Room, greeted the earthworm with a shriek of joy. But then she saw the magician's hand.

'Oh, Arry! You're hurt! How dreadful!'

And she took his hand and bent over it and began to croon one of her wholeness songs about the beauty of new skin and the cleverness of having five fingers, and almost at once, the pain disappeared and the blisters also.

'My angel! My little blossom! You've healed me!' cried Arriman, growing more and more besotted.

'Yes, but that was the *old* me,' said Belladonna hastily. 'The new me is quite different, Arry. If you give me Rover, I'll show you.'

The ogre handed her the worm which he'd damped

161

down and fettled up with some moist earth as they came.

'What would you like, Arry?' she said. 'Shall I turn the tinsel into some mouldering thigh bones, perhaps? Sort of in a criss-cross pattern? And what about making the snowflakes into gaping wounds? You do *like* gaping wounds?'

'I adore them, my angel. They're almost my favourite thing.'

So Belladonna closed her eyes while the ogre and Mr Leadbetter and Arriman stood and watched.

The next half hour was one that none of them ever forgot. Belladonna worked and she worked and she worked, not once letting the strain and puzzlement show on her face. But at the end of the time, she put down Rover and threw herself with a wail of anguish on to the bed.

'It's hopeless!' she cried. 'Quite, quite hopeless. You must forget me, Arry. You must wed another. My blackness has absolutely and completely gone!'

The others looked round the room once more. The strings of gold and silver tinsel were still there, but between them there sparkled a chain of most delightful fairy dolls. In the centre of each exquisite, still unmelted snowflake, shone a diadem of flawless pearls. But it was the pots of pink and rather blobby flowers which had sprung up all over the place which made Lester's voice, when he spoke, sound like a voice from the tomb.

'Begonias,' said the ogre, shaking his gigantic head. 'Bloomin' *begonias*.'

*

162

It was in this moment of complete despair that Arriman showed himself a most true and noble lover.

'My angel!' he said, gathering Belladonna into his arms. 'What does it matter? You can fill the whole place with Knickerbocker Glories and those . . . er . . . pink blobby things, and it wouldn't matter to me. All I care about is you!'

But though she let her head rest for a moment on his manly shoulders, Belladonna was firm.

'No, Arry; you have a duty. Remember what the competition was about? "Darkness is All", you said. Suppose we had—' Her voice broke but she pulled herself together. 'Suppose we had a white baby? Or even a grey baby? What could a baby like that do with a devilish maze and a fiendish laboratory and all the other lovely things you've worked so hard to make? How could a white baby keep wizardry and darkness alive in the land? You don't just belong to yourself, Arry. You belong to all the doom and dastardy and devilment in the world and I'd never forgive myself if I let you forget what was right.'

And nothing that the desperate wizard could say would shake her.

'I'll go as soon as I can get my things together,' she said, keeping her voice steady with an effort. 'If I'm so white that I can ruin a powerful familiar like that, the further away I am the better. Only I must say goodbye to Terence and give Rover back to him.' She turned to Mr Leadbetter and the ogre who were standing miserably by the door. 'By the way, where *is* Terence? I haven't seen him for ages.'

The ogre frowned. 'He wasn't at the campsite,' he said.

163

'Are you sure?' said Mr Leadbetter sharply. 'He said he was going down to the campsite to get Bella-donna's things and help the witches clear up. I was sure he'd spent the night down there. You know what boys are with tents.'

And, their great sorrow laid aside for a moment, they all looked at each other with a new anxiety.

Where *was* Terence?

Eighteen

Terence at that moment, was locked in a small dark room with high barred windows in the place he feared and hated more than any other in the world. For the worst thing that could have happened to Terence had happened. Matron had come unrooted; she sent out an alarm; he'd been recaptured as he ran across the road to go to the campsite and now he was back in the Home.

It had happened so suddenly that he'd had no chance to defend himself. A police car had been waiting outside the gates (even policemen didn't dare to go *inside* the gates at Darkington). Two men had stepped out of the car and grabbed him, and before he knew where he was, he was inside the car and driving at seventy miles an hour back to Todcaster.

The policemen had been quite kind, only telling him what a stupid thing it was to run away: children were always caught in the end, they said. Apparently a tradesman who delivered groceries to the Home had seen Terence at the station on the day he went to find Miss Leadbetter and had noticed him buying a ticket back to Darkington.

But if the policemen had been fatherly enough, Matron had received the woebegone little boy with a gloating triumph. She said nothing about the rooting; most probably she had forgotten it (there is often loss of memory after rooting), but she had not forgotten her grudge against Terence. And now, after a night spent on a lumpy mattress with only a bowl of claggy porridge for his breakfast, he was waiting for her to come and punish him.

The door opened and Matron entered. She was yellower and more like a camel than ever and she began at once:

'Now then, what are we going to do with you? Beat you? Send you to Borstal? Keep you locked up for good?

On she went, scolding and threatening, while Terence cowered against the wall and wondered why God hadn't given people earlids as well as eyelids so that they could shut out such dreadful sounds. And all the while, his anxious thoughts raced back to Darkington. Had Belladonna noticed yet that Rover had gone? Had Arriman learnt that Sir Simon was a fake? Would anyone miss him and try to find him or would they think he'd run away because he didn't like it at the Hall? No, they couldn't think that; they *couldn't*.

Matron was still standing over him, shouting and blustering, the steam of ugly words pouring out of her mouth like pitch. She'd have liked to hit Terence, to knock him against the wall, but there were stupid health inspectors who came round these days and made trouble. One had actually had the nerve to tell her that her methods were old-fashioned. Still, there were plenty of things you could do that didn't leave marks. A pinch under the wrist, for example. Matron had a special line in pinches.

'So just you remember, my boy. One squeak out of

you, one more bit of trouble and you'll stay in this room for the rest of your life, do you understand?'

Terence nodded. In the few hours since he'd been back at the Home, all his sparkle and bounce had gone. Terence could stand the blackest magic and enjoy it, but unkindness and spite just finished him.

And so the greyness and misery of the Home closed over Terence once again. By the time he'd eaten his boiled fish and black-eyed potatoes at the scrubbed dining table, had his fingernails inspected, and put on his mackintosh for the boring walk they always took when there was no school – past the formica factory, left at the gas works and back down a long road of seedy terrace houses – he'd almost forgotten that only a few hours ago life had been an exciting and wonderful thing.

But just as the crocodile, led by the Assistant Matron, a watery lady called Miss Kettle, was crossing the road back to the Home, a strange thing happened. Terence heard his name called and looking up he saw Miss Leadbetter carrying a shopping basket and waving her umbrella.

'Wait!' she shouted. 'I want to speak to you!'

She marched up to Terence, ignoring Miss Kettle who was wittering away at the top of the crocodile, and said, 'Just the person I wanted to see. Though what you're doing here, I don't know. I thought you were staying with my brother.'

'I was,' said Terence. 'But they caught me.' He looked up at her eagerly. 'If you could tell Mr Leadbetter I'm here, *please*. I don't want him to think—'

'Come along, Terence Mugg. No loitering,' called Miss Kettle sharply.

167

But Miss Leadbetter, who had once thrown a drunken actor down three flights of stairs, was not at all cowed by Miss Kettle.

'What I was going to say,' she said, bending down and speaking quickly into Terence's ear, 'was that I've just had a message from the hospital. From poor Monty Moon. He's so sorry he's had to let you down. It was the van – the one belonging to the electrician. Monty says the tyres were worn to a shred, but he wouldn't listen. Anyway, they ran into a ditch on the way to Darkington and the whole lot of them were taken to hospital. Just cuts and bruises, but poor Monty didn't really come round till this morning. It was last night, wasn't it, that he was supposed to do the show?'

Terence was looking at her in amazement.

'Yes,' he said. 'It was last night. But he didn't let us down. He did do the show. He was there.'

'No, he wasn't. Not Monty. He's been in hospital since Sunday and the stage manager and electrician with him. He never got to Darkington at all. That's what's worrying him, on account of having taken the five hundred pounds.'

But now Miss Kettle had had enough. She left the front of the crocodile, yanked Terence by the arms, and marched him away.

Terence made no move to resist. He had too much to think about.

If Monty Moon had never got to Darkington, who had appeared from behind the tapestry? Who was the Elizabethan knight they had 'raised'? Could it be . . . didn't it *have* to be . . . Sir Simon Montpelier himself?

So Belladonna had really done it! But Rover hadn't

168

been there, that was certain. The box Terence had handed Belladonna was empty. And without Rover, Belladonna was absolutely white.

Where had all that darkness come from, then? What did it mean?

'Take your coat off, you lazy boy, and don't stand there dreaming,' said Miss Kettle, who took her tone from Matron.

Terence didn't even hear.

The afternoon darkened, the children had beans on toast. Miss Kettle read them a story from *Struwelpeter* about a boy who had his thumbs cut off, and then they all trooped up to bed. Lying in his iron cot, looking at the same crack in the ceiling that he'd looked at for years and years, Terence heard Billy, in the next bed, begin to snuffle and cry.

'What is it, Billy?' asked Terence.

'I'm thirsty; I want a drink.'

'Well, why don't you go and get one?'

'I'm scared,' said Billy. He was partly deaf and wet his bed and was always in trouble too.

'I'll go,' said Terence.

He slipped out of bed and tiptoed out into the corridor towards the bathroom. Matron and Miss Kettle were talking in the hall below – and they were talking about him.

'Of course, he is a troublemaker,' Miss Kettle agreed. 'But I've always felt, Matron, that you dislike him particularly.'

'Dislike him? Of course I dislike him. And I've every reason to. Look!'

She held up her hand, and Miss Kettle peered at it.

'The little finger, do you mean?'

169

'Yes,' shouted Matron. 'The little finger I do mean. The little finger that Terence Mugg bit to the bone and mutilated when he was brought to me, a babe in arms, and I bent over to say "Ickle Bickle Boo" to him as I do to all my babies. Even now I get shooting pains in it when I knit.'

'Goodness,' said Miss Kettle. 'And he was only three weeks old, wasn't he, when they brought him from the kiosk? Most unusual!'

'Everything about that horrible child is unusual. He gives me the creeps. Do you know, whatever you do to him, he never cries? Never. He'll sit there with his eyes like saucers and he'll wince with pain, but he's never shed a tear in all the time he's been here. It's unnatural, that's what it is, and I'll knock it out of him, see if I don't!'

A sharp noise from the top of the stairs made them both turn round. Terence was standing on the landing in his pyjamas. He was standing perfectly still, as though in a state of shock, and the glass of water he'd been fetching for Billy lay in splinters at his feet.

'How *dare* you, Terence Mugg! How *dare* you get out of bed! Just you wait, you've gone too far this time. You've gone too far!'

Terence waited. He felt very queer. There was a sort of roaring in his ears and the landing felt as though it was rocking and swaying beneath his feet.

Matron was on the first step . . . the second . . . Now she was almost up to him, her arms outstretched to get him by the shoulders and shake him.

Terence took a long deep breath. He closed his eyes . . .

170

Nineteen

The Wizard Watcher, returning from a holiday it hadn't enjoyed at all, arrived at Darkington the following morning, and as all three heads agreed, it was like coming back to a blinking funeral.

Arriman and Belladonna sat hopelessly entwined on the big sofa in the Black Drawing Room, gazing into each other's eyes. Belladonna had packed her straw basket and folded her tent and was only waiting for Terence to be found before going away for ever to a life of loneliness, begonias and pain.

Except that it was beginning to look as though Terence never *would* be found. Mr Leadbetter (who'd quite forgotten that the little boy was not really his nephew) had rung every hospital in the district in case there'd been an accident, but no one had news of him and the anxiety was dreadful.

Meanwhile the Kraken wasn't exactly helping by tottering back and forth saying 'Daddy!' to Arriman and 'Mummy!' to Belladonna and making both of them extremely wet. Nor did the wife-slayer take any notice of the fact that everyone was so upset, but plashed up and down droning on about how he'd smothered Lady Beatrice, strangled Lady Mary and knocked off Lady Henrietta with a halibut.

It was to this scene of misery that the Wizard

171

Watcher returned and it made no bones about saying that it wasn't the sort of homecoming it had expected.

Not that Arriman wasn't terribly pleased to see it; he was, and immediately introduced Belladonna whom the monster took to at once.

'Very nice,' said the Middle Head, looking her up and down.

'Better than all those goose-pimpled girls at Brighton,' said the Left-Hand Head who had not felt really happy at the seaside.

'When's the wedding?' asked the Right-Hand Head.

But this, of course, started all the unhappiness off again, and the lovers went back to the business of sighing and looking into each other's eyes, leaving the ogre and Mr Leadbetter to explain the events that had led up to this day.

The Wizard Watcher did what it could to cheer everybody up, but after half an hour during which the Kraken kept trying to climb up its tail, Sir Simon told it in horrid detail what Lady Olivia had said to the lavatory attendant, and Arriman had declared for the hundredth time that he would die without Belladonna, the monster had had enough.

'Proper carry-on in here,' said the Middle Head. 'It's worse than Blackpool.'

'Let's go out and get some fresh air,' said the Right-Hand Head.

'Good idea,' said the Left-Hand Head. 'Get that little perisher off our tail, anyway.'

And twitching the Kraken carefully on to the floor, the monster waddled out into the park.

An hour passed. Mr Leadbetter had made a list of

police stations and was just about to pick up the phone to try again for news of Terence, when they heard the great oak door in the hall burst open with a resounding crash. Next came the sound of footsteps pounding upstairs, then the drawing room door flew open as if pushed by a hurricane and the Wizard Watcher came skidding into the room. Its heads were trembling, its eyes were blazing and they could actually *see* its heart pounding in its chest. Never had anyone known the monster in such a state, and for a moment its excitement was such that it simply could not speak. Then the Middle Head began and the other two joined in.

'The New Wizard Cometh!'

'He *Cometh*!'

'Right *Now*. He Cometh!'

Arriman rose with shaking knees and went to the window, and everybody followed him.

Stumbling with exhaustion, his small face lifted to the windows of the Hall, Terence Mugg was coming up the drive.

Twenty

'Are you suggesting we don't know our job?' said the Middle Head, looking very hurt.

'Yes, are you? I mean, you *made* us, you know,' said the Left-Hand Head.

'No, no, my dear fellow,' said Arriman, who knew how sensitive the monster was. 'It's just . . . well, you see, this is Leadbetter's nephew. We've all been rather anxious about him. Of course you haven't met him, you were away during the contest, but that's who it is. Terence's the name. Terence Mugg.'

Terence was sitting on the sofa next to Belladonna who had rushed up to him, half carrying him into the room, and was now feeding him with cauliflower soup and bananas, pale things she'd been able to magic up quickly till Lester could get to the kitchen and rustle up a steak.

Now he stood up. Already being with the people he loved had made his cheeks glow and chased the weariness from his face.

'Actually, sir,' he began. 'Actually, I think maybe—' But here he broke off because it was so difficult to explain. He didn't really believe it himself yet and had walked all the way from Todcaster rather than try anything that might not work and prove him wrong. So instead he felt in his pocket and took out a piece of string, an apple core, an India rubber – and at last a blue sellotape tin punched with holes.

Terence opened the tin. Inside it was a small spider with hairy legs and a black cross on its back.

'What is it?' asked Arriman as they all craned forward. Terence swallowed.

'It's . . . Matron, sir,' he said.

So then he began to explain, growing more confident as his story unfolded. And as he talked it all became quite clear, and the only surprising thing was that no one had suspected it before.

He began by telling what he'd overheard at the Home and as he spoke they could see the tiny baby carried in and snapping at Matron with his full set of teeth so that she had hated him bitterly from that day. They could see a small boy who never cried because wizards, like witches, cannot shed tears, but a small boy who knew nothing of his powers because unlike Mr and Mrs Canker who had wisely encouraged their little Arriman, Terence had grown up in a place where people were ignorant and blind.

And then, when he'd first met Belladonna, Terence went on, he'd felt – oh, not just that he loved her ('Everyone,' said Terence, 'loves Belladonna,') but a sort of feeling of *belonging* and from the first moment, when she'd tried to root Matron, Terence had said her spells along with her and worked with her and *felt* with her. 'Whatever she did,' he said, 'I had to do it and sometimes I said extra spells of my own. Only I thought it was Rover the blackness came from – we both did. I was *sure* it was Rover. But then I met Miss Leadbetter and she told me that Mr Moon had never come to the Hall at all, he'd had an accident. But Sir

Simon *did* appear and I knew it couldn't be Rover because Rover had already gone. So—'

But this part was news to Lester and Mr Leadbetter, and gobbledegook to Arriman and Belladonna, and Terence had to stop while everybody explained everything to everyone else. Arriman was most displeased to think that his servants had tried to play a trick on him, but when they explained that it was only because they were so sure that Belladonna was the wife for him, he couldn't really make a fuss.

'Anyway,' Terence went on, 'I couldn't understand *what* had happened because I knew Belladonna was quite white without the earthworm. So if it wasn't Rover and it wasn't her, who was it? And then when they said that about me biting so hard when I was a tiny baby, everything sort of clicked into place, and when Matron came charging upstairs at me, I just shut my eyes and – well, there she is.'

And he held out the sellotape tin inside which the spider was scuttling dementedly to and fro.

The rejoicing after Terence had finished his story may be imagined. Belladonna hugged him and kissed him, Lester seized a sabre and gulped it down joyfully in a single swallow, Arriman came and pumped him by the hand.

'My dear, dear boy, what happiness, what joy! What a relief! Don't you see, all our problems are solved. You shall stay here and attend to wizardry and darkness, and Belladonna and I can be married and live happily ever after!'

'Oh, Arry, so we can, so we can!' cried Belladonna, rushing into his arms. 'It doesn't matter what colour

our babies are now, does it, with a mighty wizard like Terence to take charge of things?'

'Am I really going to be a *mighty* wizard?' said Terence, his eyes shining.

Arriman turned to him, his dark face serious for a moment.

'You have a great gift, my boy,' he said. 'A great gift. Necromancy at your age! I couldn't have touched it. Why, if I called the thunder before the lightning I was as pleased as punch. No, it's my belief you're going to extend the frontiers of wizardry and darkness to unheard of depths. Of course, there's a lot of work before you, but you understand that, I'm sure.'

'Oh, yes, sir; I'll work like *anything*.'

In the excitement and happiness which followed, everyone was careful to give the Wizard Watcher his due and the useful monster sat there, contented smiles on its faces, receiving the congratulations it knew it had deserved.

'Yes, it's a relief,' said the Middle Head nodding graciously. 'No use pretending it isn't.'

'Those nine hundred and ninety days just sitting there took it out of us,' said the Left-Hand Head, 'not to mention the chilblains.'

'Still, all's well that ends well,' said the Right-Hand Head.

There was only one slight snag which Mr Leadbetter, drawing aside his employer, pointed out to Arriman.

'If Sir Simon's real, sir, which it seems he is, what's to become of him? Because it's my belief that if anyone else has to hear about Lady Mary or Lady

Julia or Lady Letitia who guzzled, there'll be murder done and it won't be him doing it.'

Arriman nodded. A look of deep wickedness had come into his fiery eyes.

'Actually, Leadbetter, I have just had a very neat idea about Sir Simon. A very neat idea indeed. But first we must have our wedding party. I want you to invite everybody. All the witches that took part in the contest for a start.'

'Even the enchantress, sir?' said Mr Leadbetter frowning.

Arriman smiled.

'*Particularly* the enchantress,' he said.

Twenty-one

The day of the wedding dawned, and from all over the land there came kobbolds and kelpies, goblins and niggets, furies and fiends, to share the magician's happiness and to meet the new wizard whose coming had been foretold by the gypsy Esmeralda and whose power was said to be greater even than Arriman's own.

No handsomer couple than the Bridal Pair could be imagined. Arriman was in antlers and a gold-patterned cloak; Belladonna's ink-black dress was loose and flowing and in her glorious hair she wore only a single, simple bat. It was the little short-eared bat that had invented an Aunt Screwtooth for her at the coven and it had flown up specially to be with her on her great day.

In the centre of the table, on a blue velvet cushion which the ogre had fitted with a special sprinkler, lay Rover, looking rosy and peaceful now that it was understood that he was not a powerful familiar but just an ordinary worm. Opposite him in a high chair sat the Kraken, squeaking with excitement. Belladonna had managed to put him into nappies in spite of his eight legs, and with his underneath wrapped in snow-white muslin, he looked, as Terence said, almost like a bridesmaid or perhaps a page.

None of their friends had failed them. Mr Chatterjee had flown back from Calcutta, the ghoul had left his slaughterhouse. Even Miss Leadbetter, though she didn't hold with magic, was there, bringing news of the Sunnydene Home's new Matron, a fat and friendly lady whom the children loved. (The old Matron had been let loose in the Rose Garden where she was making herself useful eating greenfly and other insect pests, as spiders will.)

And the witches were there. However much they had sneered at Belladonna, now that she was Mrs Canker and Wizardess of the North, they were only too ready to be friendly.

Belladonna, of course, forgave them everything. Not only that, but when the feasting and roistering had died down a little she laid a hand on Arriman's arm and said: ''Arry, shouldn't we grant everyone a wish? Isn't that the thing to do at weddings?'

'Well, my treasure, if that's what you want. Of course, granting wishes isn't exactly *black*. Still, on such a happy day . . . We'll get Terence to do it; it'll be good practise.'

It would take too long to tell what all the brownies and kelpies and niggets wanted, and anyway it was mostly money. Mr Chatterjee didn't need a wish because he'd tracked down the Princess Shari (the one who'd been a penguin) and was engaged to be married. The ghoul and Miss Leadbetter didn't hold with wishes, and Ethel Feedbag had fallen asleep with her head on her plate and couldn't be roused.

But Mother Bloodwart knew exactly what *she* wanted.

'It's that turning-myself-young-again spell,' she said to Terence. 'I can't get it right myself, but you can. About twenty, I'd like to be, or maybe eighteen. Gladys Trotter, the name was, and I'd like to be dressed nice.'

But when the wish had been granted and Mother Bloodwort stood staring into the mirror at the young girl she had been, a very odd look spread across her face.

'I don't like it,' she said at last. 'I'm sorry, but you'll have to turn me back again. All that swollen flesh and those bulgy pink cheeks . . . And what did I want all that hair *for*?'

So Terence turned her back again and the old woman went back contentedly to her shack where she lived for many more years being sometimes a coffee table and sometimes a witch, and not doing any harm to anyone because she had forgotten how.

After that it was Mabel Wrack's turn and what *she* wanted was to have her legs turned back into a mermaid's tail. She said she was sick of them itching and sick of humping Doris about in polythene buckets and she felt bad, she said, about the way she had treated her aunts. 'For when all's said and done, water's thicker than blood and you can't beat a wet family,' said Mabel, 'so if you'll drop me off at that bit of cliff where I did my trick, I'll find them soon enough.'

So the wedding guests, glad of some fresh air after all that eating, trooped off to the Devil's Cauldron and Terence gave Mabel a splendid tail and two gill slits for breathing under water and Belladonna kissed Doris lovingly above her vile red eyes. And sure enough, as Mabel hit the waves, they could all see,

181

distinctly, a set of plump and motherly arms pulling the witch and her octopus down into the foam.

But when Nancy Shouter told the little boy what *she* wanted, Terence turned pale. For what Nancy wanted was no less than the impossible. She wanted Terence to reverse the bottomless hole, to turn it inside out and see if somewhere in its bottomlessness, her sister Nora might be found.

'I don't know if I can do that,' said Terence anxiously.

But with Arriman's hand reassuringly on his shoulder, he walked bravely to the East Lawn and the wedding guests followed.

If anyone had doubted up to then that Terence was a great and mighty wizard, they did not doubt again. For Terence just walked up to the hole with its notices saying *Danger* and *Keep Out* and took them down. Next, with his shoes, he scuffed out the pentacle of protection. And then he stepped forward and spoke to the hole.

No one heard the words he used. What passed between him and it remains secret till the end of time. But the hole obeyed him, it knew its master – and with a frightful scream, a roaring judder and a fearful lurch, it gave up its bottomlessness, turned inside out, and from its new-found bottom, dredged up the crumpled, bewildered body of Nancy Shouter's twin.

'Nora!' cried Nancy, rushing forward and sending her chickens flying.

'Nancy!' cried Nora, rushing into her sister's arms.

Taking no notice of anyone, the two sisters stood there, hugging each other and laughing for joy.

Then, 'You look a proper mess,' said Nancy Shouter. 'You're all crumpled.'

'Of course I'm crumpled, you stupid faggot,' said Nora. 'What do you expect? You shouldn't have pushed me into the hole in the first place.'

'I didn't push you, you fell.'

'I didn't.'

'You did.'

And quarrelling happily, the two sisters picked up their chickens and walked away.

But when Terence, carried shoulder-high by the wedding guests, got back to the Banqueting Hall to grant the enchantress *her* wish, he found her chair empty except for a pair of moth-eaten stays which she had bought in the Portobello Road and poisoned in her Parlour. Madame Olympia, it seemed, had returned to London – and with her had gone no less a person than Sir Simon Montpelier!

'So my plan worked!' said Arriman gleefully, rubbing his hands.

'I'll say it worked,' said the ogre. 'I put the love philtre in each of their drinks like you told me, and you should have seen them! The plasher down on his knees asking her to marry him and measuring her neck for a noose at the same time. And her accepting him and trying to get a squint at his molars to see how they'd look on her necklace. I nearly died!'

'A well-matched pair,' said Arriman. 'I wonder which of them will knock the other off first.' He turned to Belladonna. 'Am I not clever, my little kitten?'

And Belladonna, gazing at him adoringly, said: 'The cleverest person in the world!'

*

But the best part of any party is the bit where the guests have gone and the family is left alone, tired and content.

Terence lay on the hearth rug, chatting to Rover; Lester was sharpening his bedtime sword. Arriman had taken off his antlers, and he and Belladonna were curled up on the sofa making plans. They were going to build a little house on the other side of the park – quite close to the Hall but not too close, so that Terence would learn to manage on his own. Arriman was going to write a book and Mr Leadbetter was already wondering how to stop the magician jumbling up the pages and getting the typewriter ribbon jammed and putting the carbon paper in the wrong way round.

So happy and peaceful did everybody feel that it was quite a while before they noticed that the Wizard Watcher wasn't quite itself. Its round and beautiful eyes were suspiciously moist and it was allowing the Kraken to slide down its tail as though it didn't really care what happened.

'Is anything the matter?' asked Arriman. Now he came to think of it, the Watcher hadn't really been itself at the party. It'd eaten hardly anything and talking had seemed an effort.

The monster shook its head.

'It's nothing,' said the Middle Head in a low voice.

'Not anything, really,' said the Left-Hand Head.

'We're only making a fuss,' the Right-Hand Head agreed.

By this time, of course, everyone was desperate, and Terence, who had loved the monster from the

184

moment he saw it, put down Rover and came over, quite pop-eyed with concern.

'Please!' said Arriman. 'You must tell us! That's what friends are for. To share things with.'

The monster sighed heavily.

'Well,' said the Middle Head. 'It's obvious really, isn't it?'

'I mean, what are Wizard Watchers *for*?' said the Left-Hand Head.

'They're for watching for wizards, aren't they?' put in the Right-Hand Head.

'So when a wizard's been *found*,' said the Middle Head, 'there isn't much use for a Wizard Watcher, is there?'

'Sort of *spare*, a Wizard Watcher is then, isn't he?'

'You could say, useless. Redundant. Finished,' said the Right-Hand Head, dashing away a tear.

There was an absolutely ghastly silence while everyone took in the monster's grief and pain.

Then Belladonna stepped forward, her eyes alight.

'How *could* you be so foolish?' she said to the three heads. 'Surely you know that Wizard Watchers aren't just for watching FOR wizards? They're for watching OVER wizards. I thought everyone knew that!'

The monster lifted its heads.

'Terence may be a mighty and terrible wizard, but he's a very young one,' Belladonna went on, while the little boy nodded eagerly.

'And skinny with it,' said the Middle Head.

'Undernourished, you could say,' said the Right-Hand Head.

'Short of sleep, I shouldn't wonder,' said the Left-Hand Head.

185

'It's my belief a cup of Bovril in the middle of the day wouldn't hurt,' said the Middle Head.

'Nor some hot soup at night. You can't beat hot soup, I always say.'

'And plenty of fresh air . . .'

Everyone sighed with relief. The monster had withdrawn into a corner, busy and interested, and they could hear it working out a routine in which a young wizard could blight and smite and blast and wither, but *sensibly*.

'You'll be all right now,' said Belladonna, drawing the little boy close.

And the wizard who in years to come would be known as Mugg the Magnificent, Flayer of the Foolish and Master of the Shades, looked up at her with shining mud-coloured eyes and said:

'Oh, yes! There'll be no one in the world as all right as me!'

The Secret of Platform 13

For Laurie and for David

One

If you went into a school nowadays and said to the children: 'What is a *gump*?' you would probably get some very silly answers.

'It's a person without a brain, like a chump,' a child might say. Or:

'It's a camel whose hump has got stuck.' Or even:

'It's a kind of chewing gum.'

But once this wasn't so. Once every child in the land could have told you that a gump was a special mound, a grassy bump on the earth, and that in this bump was a hidden door which opened every so often to reveal a tunnel which led to a completely different world.

They would have known that every country has its own gump and that in Great Britain the gump was in a place called the Hill of the Cross of Kings not far from the River Thames. And the wise children, the ones that read the old stories and listened to the old tales, would have known more than that. They would have known that this particular gump opened for exactly nine days every nine years, and not one second longer, and that it was no good changing your mind about coming or going because nothing would open the door once the time was up.

But the children forgot – everyone forgot – and

1

perhaps you can't blame them, yet the gump is still there. It is under platform thirteen of King's Cross railway station, and the secret door is behind the wall of the old Gentlemen's Cloakroom with its flappy posters saying 'Trains Get You There' and its chipped wooden benches and the dirty ashtrays in which the old gentlemen used to stub out their smelly cigarettes.

No one uses the platform now. They have built newer, smarter platforms with rows of shiny luggage trolleys and slot machines that actually work and television screens which show you how late your train is going to be. But platform thirteen is different. The clock has stopped; spiders have spun their webs across the cloakroom door. There's a Left Luggage Office with a notice saying NOT IN USE and inside it is an umbrella covered in mould which a lady left on the 5.25 from Doncaster the year of the Queen's Silver Jubilee. The chocolate machines are rusty and lopsided and if you were foolish enough to put your money in one it would make a noise like 'Harrumph' and swallow it, and you could wait the rest of your life for the chocolate to come out.

Yet when people tried to pull down that part of the station and redevelop it, something always went wrong. An architect who wanted to build shops there suddenly came out in awful boils and went to live in Spain and when they tried to relay the tracks for electricity, the surveyor said the ground wasn't suitable and muttered something about subsidence and cracks. It was as though people knew

2

something about platform thirteen, but they didn't know what.

But in every city there are those who have not forgotten the old days or the old stories. The ghosts, for example ... Ernie Hobbs, the railway porter who'd spent all his life working at King's Cross and still liked to haunt round the trains, he knew – and so did his friend, the ghost of a cleaning lady called Mrs Partridge who used to scrub out the parcels' office on her hands and knees. The people who plodged about in the sewers under the city and came up occasionally through the manholes beside the station, they knew ... and so in their own way did the pigeons.

They knew that the gump was still there and they knew where it led. By a long, misty and mysterious tunnel to a secret cove where a ship waited to take those who wished it to an island so beautiful that it took the breath away.

The people who lived on it just called it the Island, but it has had all sorts of names; Avalon, St Martin's Land, the Place of the Sudden Mists. Years and years ago it was joined to the mainland, but then it broke off and floated away slowly westwards, just as Madagascar floated away from the continent of Africa. Islands do that every few million years; it is nothing to make a fuss about.

With the floating island, of course, came the people who were living on it: sensible people mostly who understood that everyone did not have to have exactly two arms and legs, but might be different in shape and different in the way they thought. So they lived peacefully with ogres who had one eye or dragons (of whom there were a lot about in those days). They didn't leap into the sea every time they saw a mermaid comb her hair on a rock, they simply said, 'Good morning.' They understood that Ellerwomen had hollow backs and hated to be looked at on a Saturday and that if trolls wanted to wear their beards so long that they stepped on them every time they walked, then that was entirely their own affair.

They lived in peace with the animals too. There were a lot of interesting animals on the Island as well as ordinary sheep and cows and goats. Giant birds who had forgotten how to fly and laid eggs the size of kettle drums, and brollachans like blobs of jelly with dark red eyes, and sea horses with manes of silk which galloped and snorted in the waves.

But it was the mistmakers that the people of the Island loved the most. These endearing animals are found nowhere else in the world. They are white and small with soft fur all over their bodies, rather like baby seals, but they don't have flippers, they have short legs and big feet like the feet of puppies. Their black eyes are huge and moist, their noses are whiskery and cool, and they pant a little as they move because they look rather like small pillows and they don't like going very fast.

The mistmakers weren't just *nice*, they were exceedingly important.

Because as the years passed and newspapers were washed up on the shore or refugees came through the gump with stories of the World Above, the Islanders became more and more determined to be left alone. Of course they knew that some modern inventions were good, like electric blankets to keep people's feet warm in bed or fluoride to stop their teeth from rotting, but there were other things they didn't like at all, like nuclear weapons or tower blocks at the tops of which old ladies shivered and shook because the lifts were bust, or battery hens stuffed two in a cage. And they dreaded being discovered by passing ships or aeroplanes flying too low.

Which is where the mistmakers came in. These sensitive creatures, you see, absolutely adore music. When you play music to a mistmaker its eyes grow wide and it lets out its breath and gives a great sigh.

'Aaah,' it will sigh. 'Aaah . . . aaah . . .'

And each time it sighs, mist comes from its mouth: clean, thick white mist which smells of early morning and damp grass. There are hundreds and hundreds of mistmakers lolloping over the turf or along the shore of the Island and that means a lot of mist.

So when a ship was sighted or a speck in the sky which might be an aeroplane, all the children ran out of school with their flutes and their trumpets and their recorders and started to play to the mistmakers . . . And the people who might have landed and poked and pried, saw only clouds of whiteness and went on their way.

Though there were so many unusual creatures on the Island, the royal family was entirely human and always had been. They were royal in the proper sense – not greedy, not covered in jewels, but brave and fair. They saw themselves as servants of the people which is how all good rulers should think of themselves, but often don't.

The King and Queen didn't live in a golden palace full of uncomfortable gilded thrones which stuck into people's behinds when they sat down, nor did they fill the place with servants who fell over footstools from walking backwards from Their Majesties. They lived in a low white house on a curving beach of golden sand studded with cowrie shells – and always, day or night, they could hear the murmur and slap of the waves and the gentle soughing of the wind.

The rooms of the palace were simple and cool; the windows were kept open so that birds could fly in and out. Intelligent dogs lay sleeping by the hearth; bowls of fresh fruit and fragrant flowers stood on the tables – and anyone who had nowhere to go – orphaned little hags or seals with sore flippers or wizards who had become depressed and old – found sanctuary there.

And in the year 1983 – the year the Americans put a woman into space – the Queen, who was young and kind and beautiful – had a baby. Which is where this story really begins.

The baby was a boy and it was everything a baby should be, with bright eyes, a funny tuft of hair, a button nose and interesting ears. Not only that, but the little Prince could whistle before he was a month old – not proper tunes but a nice peeping noise like a young bird.

The Queen was absolutely besotted about her son and the King was so happy that he thought he would burst, and all over the Island the people rejoiced because you can tell very early how a baby is going to turn out and they could see that the Prince was going to be just the kind of ruler that they wanted.

Of course as soon as the child was born there were queues of people round the palace wanting to look after him and be his nurse: Wise Women who wanted to teach him things and sirens who wanted to sing to him and hags who wanted to show him weird tricks. There was even a mermaid who seemed to think she could look after a baby even if it meant she had to be trundled round the palace in a bath on wheels.

But although the Queen thanked everyone most politely, the nurse she chose for her baby was an ordinary human. Or rather it was three ordinary humans: triplets whose names were Violet and Lily and Rose. They had come to the Island as young girls and were proper trained nursery nurses who knew how to change nappies and bring up wind and sieve vegetables, and the fact that they couldn't do any magic was a relief to the Queen who sometimes felt she had enough magic in her life. Having triplets seemed to her a good idea because looking after babies goes on night and day and this way there would always be someone with spiky red hair and a long nose and freckles to soothe the Prince and rock him and sing to him, and he wouldn't be startled by the change because however remarkable the baby was, he wouldn't be able to tell Violet from Lily or Lily from Rose.

So the three nurses came and they did indeed look after the Prince most devotedly and everything went beautifully – for a while. But when the baby was three months old, there came the time of the Opening of the Gump – and after that nothing was ever the same again.

There was always excitement before the Opening. In the harbour, the sailors made the three-masted ship ready to sail to the Secret Cove; those people who wanted to leave the Island started their packing and said their goodbyes, and rest houses were prepared for those who would come the other way.

It was now that homesickness began to attack Lily and Violet and Rose.

Homesickness is a terrible thing. Children at boarding schools sometimes feel as though they're going to die of it. It doesn't matter what your home is like – it's that it's yours that matters. Lily and Violet loved the Island and they adored the Prince, but now they began to remember the life they had led as little girls in the shabby streets of north London.

'Do you remember the Bingo Halls?' asked Lily. 'All the shouting from inside when someone won?'

'And Saturday night at the Odeon with a bag of crisps?' said Violet.

'The clang of the fruit machines in Paddy's Parlour,' said Rose.

They went on like this for days, quite forgetting how unhappy they had been as children: teased at school, never seeing a clean blade of grass and beaten by their father. So unhappy that they'd taken to playing in King's Cross Station and been there when the door opened in the gump, and couldn't go through it fast enough.

'I know we can't go Up There,' said Lily. 'Not with the Prince to look after. But maybe Their Majesties would let us sail with the ship and just look at the dear old country?'

So they asked the Queen if they could take the baby Prince on the ship and wait with him in the Secret Cove – and the Queen said no. The thought of being parted from her baby made her stomach crunch up so badly that she felt quite sick.

It was because she minded so much that she began to change her mind. Was she being one of those awful drooling mothers who smother children instead of letting them grow up free and unafraid? She spoke to the King, hoping he would forbid his son to go, but he said: 'Well, dear, it's true that adventures are good for people even when they are very young. Adventures can get into a person's blood even if he doesn't remember having them. And surely you trust the nurses?'

Well, she did, of course. And she trusted the sailors who manned the ship – and sea air, as everybody knows, is terribly good for the lungs.

So she agreed and had a little weep in her room, and the nurses took the baby aboard in his hand-woven rush basket with its lace-edged hood and settled him down for the voyage.

Just before the ship was due to sail, the Queen rushed out of the palace, her face as white as chalk, and said: 'No, no! Bring him back! I don't want him to go!'

But when she reached the harbour, she was too late. The ship was just a speck in the distance, and only the gulls echoed her tragic voice.

Two

Mrs Trottle was rich. She was so rich that she had eleven winter coats and five diamond necklaces and her bath had golden taps. Mr Trottle, her husband, was a banker and spent his days lending money to people who already had too much of it and refusing to lend it to people who needed it. The house the Trottles lived in was in the best part of London beside a beautiful park and not far from Buckingham Palace. It had an ordinary address but the tradesmen called it Trottle Towers because of the spiky railings that surrounded it and the statues in the garden and the flagpole.

Although Larina Trottle was perfectly strong and well and Landon Trottle kept fit by hiring a man to pummel him in his private gym, the Trottles had no less than five servants to wait on them: a butler, a cook, a chauffeur, a housemaid and a gardener. They had three cars and seven portable telephones which Mr Trottle sat on sometimes by mistake, and a hunting lodge in Scotland where he went to shoot deer, and a beach house in the South of France with a flat roof on which Mrs Trottle lay with nothing on so as to get a sun tan which was *not* a pleasant sight.

But there was one thing they didn't have. They didn't have a baby.

As the years passed and no baby came along, Mrs Trottle got angrier and angrier. She glared at people pushing prams, she snorted when babies appeared on television gurgling and advertising disposable nappies. Even puppies and kittens annoyed her.

Then after nearly ten years of marriage she decided to go and adopt a baby.

First, though, she went to see the woman who had looked after her when she was small. Nanny Brown was getting on in years. She was a tiny, grumpy person who soaked her false teeth in brandy and never got into bed without looking to see if there was a burglar hiding underneath, but she knew everything there was to know about babies.

'You'd better come with me,' Mrs Trottle said. 'And I want that old doll of mine.'

So Nanny Brown went to fetch the doll which was one of the large, old-fashioned ones with eyes that click open and shut, and lace dresses, and cold, china arms and legs.

And on a fine day towards the end of June, the chauffeur drove Mrs Trottle to an orphanage in the north of England and beside her in the Rolls Royce sat Nanny Brown looking like a cross old bird and holding the china doll in her lap.

They reached the orphanage. Mrs Trottle swept in.

'I have come to choose a baby,' she said. 'I'm prepared to take either a boy or a girl but it must be healthy, of course, and not more than three months old and I'd prefer it to have fair hair.'

Matron looked at her. 'I'm afraid we don't have

12

any babies for adoption,' she said. 'There's a waiting list.'

'A *waiting list!*' Mrs Trottle's bosom swelled so much that it looked as if it was going to take off into space. 'My good woman, do you know who I am? I am Larina Trottle! My husband is the head of Trottle and Blatherspoon, the biggest merchant bank in the City and his salary is five hundred thousand pounds a year.'

Matron said she was glad to hear it.

'Anyone lucky enough to become a Trottle would be brought up like a prince,' Mrs Trottle went on. 'And this doll which I have brought for the baby is a real antique. I have been offered a very large sum of money for it. This doll is priceless!'

Matron nodded and said she was sure Mrs Trottle was right, but she had no babies for adoption and that was her last word.

The journey back to London was not a pleasant one. Mrs Trottle ranted and raved; Nanny Brown sat huddled up with the doll in her lap; the chauffeur drove steadily southwards.

Then just as they were coming into London, the engine began to make a nasty clunking noise.

'Oh no, this is too much!' raged Mrs Trottle. 'I will *not* allow you to break down in these disgusting, squalid streets.' They were close to King's Cross Station and it was eleven o'clock at night.

But the clunking noise grew worse.

'I'm afraid I'll have to stop at this garage, Madam,' said the chauffeur.

They drew up by one of the petrol pumps. The chauffeur got out to look for a mechanic.

Mrs Trottle, in the back seat, went on ranting and raving.

Then she grew quiet. On a bench between the garage and a fish and chip shop sat a woman whose frizzy red hair and long nose caught the lamplight. She was wearing the uniform of a nursery nurse and beside her was a baby's basket . . . a basket most finely woven out of rushes whose deep hood sheltered whoever lay within.

The chauffeur returned with a mechanic and began to rev the engine. Exhaust fumes from the huge car drifted towards the bench where the red-haired woman sat holding on to the handle of the basket. Her head nodded, but she jerked herself awake.

The chauffeur revved even harder and another cloud of poisonous gas rolled towards the bench.

The nurse's head nodded once more.

'Give me the doll!' ordered Larina Trottle – and got out of the car.

For eight days the nurses had waited on the ship as it anchored off the Secret Cove. They had sung to the Prince and rocked him and held him up to see the sea birds and the cliffs of their homeland. They had taken him ashore while they paddled and gathered shells and they had welcomed the people who came though the gump, as they arrived in the mouth of the cave.

Travelling through the gump takes only a moment. The suction currents and strange breezes that are stored up there during nine long years have their own laws and can form themselves into wind

14

baskets into which people can step and be swooshed up or down in an instant. It is a delightful way to travel but can be muddling for those not used to it and the nurses made themselves useful helping the newcomers on to the ship.

Then on the ninth day something different came through the tunnel . . . and that something was – a smell.

The nurses were right by the entrance in the cliff when it came to them and as they sniffed it up, their eyes filled with tears.

'Oh Lily!' said poor Violet, and her nose quivered.

'Oh Rose!' said poor Lily and clutched her sister.

It was the smell of their childhood: the smell of fish and chips. Every Saturday night their parents had sent them out for five packets and they'd carried them back, warm as puppies, through the lamplit streets.

'Do you remember the batter, all sizzled and gold?' asked Lily.

'And the soft whiteness when you got through to the fish?' said Violet.

'The way the chips went soggy when you doused them with vinegar?' said Rose.

And as they stood there, they thought they would die if they didn't just once more taste the glory that was fish and chips.

'We can't go,' said Lily, who was the careful one. 'You know we can't.'

'Why can't we?' asked Rose. 'We'd be up there in a minute. It's a good two hours still before the Closing.'

'What about the Prince? There's no way we can leave him,' said Lily.

'No, of course we can't,' said Violet. 'We'll take him. He'll love going in a swoosherette, won't you my poppet?'

And indeed the Prince crowed and smiled and looked as though he would like nothing better.

Well, to cut a long story short, the three sisters made their way to the mouth of the cave, climbed into a wind basket – and in no time at all found themselves in King's Cross Station.

Smells are odd things. They follow you about when you're not thinking about them, but when you put your nose to where they ought to be, they aren't there. The nurses wandered round the shabby streets and to be honest they were wishing they hadn't come. The pavements were dirty, passing cars splattered them with mud and the Odeon Cinema where they'd seen such lovely films had been turned into a bowling alley.

Then suddenly there it was again – the smell – stronger than ever, and now, beside an All Night garage, they saw a shop blazing with light and in the window a sign saying FRYING NOW.

The nurses hurried forward. Then they stopped.

'We can't take the Prince into a common fish and chip shop,' said Lily. 'It wouldn't be proper.'

The others agreed. Some of the people queuing inside looked distinctly rough.

'Look, you wait over there on the bench with the baby,' said Rose. She was half an hour older than the others and often took the lead. 'Violet and I'll go in and get three packets. We're only a couple of streets away from the station – there's plenty of time.'

So Lily went to sit on the bench and Rose and Violet went in to join the queue. Of course when they reached the counter, the cod had run out – something always runs out when it's your turn. But the man went to fetch some more and there was nothing to worry about: they had three quarters of an hour before the Closing of the Gump and they were only ten minutes walk from the station.

Lily, waiting on the bench, saw the big Rolls Royce draw up at the garage . . . saw the chauffeur get out and a woman with wobbly piled-up hair open the window and let out a stream of complaints.

Then the chauffeur came back and started to rev up . . .

Oh dear, I do feel funny, thought Lily and held on tight to the handle of the basket. Her head fell forward and she jerked herself awake. Another cloud of fumes rolled towards her . . . and once more she blacked out.

But only for a moment. Almost at once she came round and all was well. The big car had gone, the basket was beside her, and now her sisters came out with three packets wrapped in newspaper. The smell was marvellous and a greasy ooze had come up on the face of the Prime Minister, just the way she remembered it.

Thoroughly pleased with themselves, the nurses hurried through the dark streets, reached Platform Thirteen and entered the cloakroom.

Only when they were safe in the tunnel did they unpack the steaming fish and chips.

'Let's just give him one chip to suck?' suggested Violet.

But Lily, who was the fussy one, said no, the Prince only had healthy food and never anything salty or fried.

'He's sleeping so sound,' she said fondly.

She bent over the cot, peered under the hood . . . unwound the embroidered blanket, the lacy shawl . . .

Then she began to scream.

Instead of the warm, living, breathing baby – there lay a cold and lifeless doll.

And the wall of the gentlemen's cloakroom was moving . . . moving . . . it was almost back in position.

Weeping, clawing, howling, the nurses tried to hold it back.

Too late. The gump was closed and no power on earth could open it again before the time was up. But in Nanny Brown's little flat, Mrs Trottle stood looking down at the stolen baby with triumph in her eyes.

'Do you know what I'm going to do?' she said.

Nanny Brown shook her head.

'I'm going to go right away from here with the baby. To Switzerland. For a whole year. And when I come back I'm going to pretend that I had him over there. That it's my very own baby – not adopted but *mine*. No one will guess; it's such a little baby. My husband won't guess either if I stay away – he's so busy with the bank he won't notice.'

Nanny Brown looked at her, thunderstruck. 'You'll never get away with it, Miss Larina. Never.'

'Oh yes, I will! I'm going to bring him back as my own little darling babykins, aren't I, my poppet? I'm going to call him Raymond. Raymond Trottle, that sounds good, doesn't it? He's going to grow up like a little prince and no one will be sorry for me or sneer at me because they'll think he's properly mine. I'll sack all the servants and get some new ones so they can't tell tales and when I come back it'll be with my teeny weeny Raymond in my arms.'

'You can't do it,' said Nanny Brown obstinately. 'It's wicked.'

'Oh yes, I can. And you're going to give up your flat and come with me because I'm not going to change his nappies. And if you don't, I'll go to the police and tell them it was you that stole the baby.'

'You wouldn't!' gasped Nanny Brown.

But she knew perfectly well that Mrs Trottle would. When she was a little girl Larina Trottle had tipped five live goldfish on to the carpet and watched them flap themselves to death because her mother had told her to clean out their bowl, and she was capable of anything.

But it wasn't just fear that made Nanny Brown go with Mrs Trottle to Switzerland. It was the baby with his milky breath and the big eyes which he now opened to look about him and the funny little whistling noise he made. She wasn't a particularly nice woman, but she loved babies and she knew that Larina Trottle was as fit to look after a young baby as a baboon. Actually, a lot *less* fit because

19

baboons, as it happens, make excellent mothers. So Mrs Trottle went away to Switzerland – and over the Island a kind of darkness fell. The Queen all but died of grief, the King went about his work like a man twice his age. The people mourned, the mermaids wept on their rocks and the schoolchildren made a gigantic calendar showing the number of days which had to pass before the gump opened once more and the Prince could be brought back.

But of all this the boy called Raymond Huntingdon Trottle knew nothing at all.

Three

Odge Gribble was a hag.

She was a very young one, and a disappointment to her parents. The Gribbles lived in the north of the Island and came from a long line of frightful and monstrous women who flapped and shrieked about, giving nightmares to people who had been wicked or making newts come out of the mouths of anyone who told a lie. Odge's oldest sister had a fingernail so long that you could dig the garden with it, the next girl had black hairs like piano wires coming out of her ears, the third had stripey feet and so on – down to the sixth who had blue teeth and a wart the size of a saucer on her chin.

Then came Odge.

There was great excitement before she was born because Mrs Gribble had herself been a seventh daughter, and now the new baby would be the seventh also, and the seventh daughter of a seventh daughter is supposed to be very special indeed.

But when the baby came, everyone fell silent and a cousin of Mrs Gribble's said: 'Oh dear!'

The baby's fingernails were short; not one whisker grew out of her ears; her feet were absolutely ordinary.

'She looks just like a small pink splodge,' the cousin went on.

21

So Mrs Gribble decided not to call her new daughter Nocticula or Valpurgina and settled for Odge (which rhymed with splodge) and hoped that she would improve as she grew older.

And up to a point, Odge did get a little more hag-like. She had unequal eyes: the left one was green and the right one was brown, and she had one blue tooth – but it was a molar and right at the back; the kind you only see when you're at the dentist. There was also a bump on one of her feet which just could have been the beginning of an extra toe, though not a very big one.

Nothing is worse than knowing you have failed your parents, but Odge did not whinge or whine. She was a strong-willed little girl with a chin like a prize fighter's and long black hair which she drew like a curtain when she didn't want to speak to anyone and she was very independent. What she liked best was to wander along the sea shore making friends with the mistmakers and picking up the treasures that she found there.

It was on one of these lonely walks that she came across the Nurse's Cave.

It was a big, dark cave with water dripping from the walls, and the noise that came from it made Odge's blood run cold. Dreadful moans, frightful wails, shuddering sobs . . . She stopped to listen, and after a while she heard that the wails had words to them, and that there seemed to be not one wailing voice but three.

'Ooh,' she heard. 'Oooh, *ooh* . . . I shall never forgive myself; never!'

'Never, never!' wailed the second voice.

'I deserve to die,' moaned a third.

Odge crossed the sandy bay and entered the cave. Three women were sitting there, dressed in the uniform of nursery nurses. Their hair was plastered with ashes, their faces were smeared with mud – and as they wailed and rocked, they speared pieces of completely burnt toast from a smouldering fire and put them into their mouths.

'What's the matter?' asked Odge.

'What's the *matter*?' said the first woman. Odge could see that she had red hair beneath the ashes and a long, freckled nose.

'What's the *MATTER*?' repeated the second one, who looked so like the first that Odge realized that she had to be her sister.

'How is it that you don't know about our sorrow and our guilt?' said the third – and she too was so alike that Odge knew they must be triplets.

Then Odge remembered who they were. The tragedy had happened before she was born but even now the Island was still in mourning.

'Are you the nurses who took the Prince Up There and allowed him to be stolen?'

'We are,' said one of the women. She turned furiously to her sister. 'The toast is not burnt enough, Lily. Go and burn it some more.'

Then Odge heard how they had lived in the cave ever since that dreadful day so as to punish themselves. How they ate only food that was burnt or mouldy or so stale that it hurt their teeth and never anything they were fond of, like bananas. How they never cleaned their teeth or washed, so that fleas could jump into their clothes and bite them, and

23

always chose the sharpest stones to sleep on so that they woke up sore and bruised.

'What happened to the Prince after he was stolen?' asked Odge. She was much more interested in the stolen baby than in how bruised the nurses were or how disgusting their food was.

'He was snatched by an evil woman named Mrs Trottle and taken to her house.'

'How do you know that,' asked Odge, 'if the door in the gump was closed?' (Hags do not start school till they are eight years old, so she still had a lot to learn.)

'There are those who can pass through the gump even when it is shut and they told us.'

'Ghosts, do you mean?'

Violet nodded. 'My foot feels comfortable,' she grumbled. 'I must go and dip it in the icy water and turn my toes blue.'

'What did she do with him? With the baby?'

'She pretended he was her own son. He lives with her now. She has called him Raymond Trottle.'

'Raymond Trottle,' repeated Odge. It seemed an unlikely name for a prince. 'And he's still living there and going to school and everything? He doesn't know who he is?'

'That's right,' said Rose, poking a stick into her ear so as to try and draw blood. 'But in two years from now the gump will open and the rescuers will go and bring him back and then we will stop wailing and eating burnt toast and our feet will grow warm and the sun will shine on our faces.'

'And the Queen will smile again,' said Lily.

'Yes, that will be best of all, when the Queen smiles properly once more.'

Odge was very thoughtful as she made her way back along the shore, taking care not to step on the toes of the mistmakers who lay basking on the sand. The Prince was only four months older than she was. How did he feel, being Raymond Trottle and living in the middle of London? What would he think when he found out that he wasn't who he thought he was?

And who would be chosen to bring him back? The rescuers would be famous; they would go down in history.

'I wish I could go,' thought Odge, nudging her blue tooth with her tongue. 'I wish *I* could be a rescuer.'

Already she felt that she knew the Prince; that she would like him for a friend.

Suddenly she stopped. She set her jaw. 'I *will* go,' she said aloud. 'I'll make them let me go.'

From that day on, Odge was a girl with a mission. She started school the following year and worked so hard that she was soon top of her class. She jogged, she threw boulders around to strengthen her biceps, she studied maps of London and tried to cough up frogs. And a month before the gump was due to open, she wrote a letter to the palace.

When you have worked and worked for something, it is almost impossible to believe that you can fail. Yet when the names of the rescuers were announced, Odge Gribble's name was not among them.

It was the most bitter disappointment. She would have taken it better if the people who *had* been chosen were mighty and splendid warriors who would ride through the gump on horseback, but they were not. A wheezing old wizard, a slightly batty fey and a one-eyed giant who lived in the mountains moving goats about and making cheese . . .

The head teacher, when she announced who was going in Assembly, had given the reason.

'Cornelius the Wizard has been chosen because he is *wise*. Gurkintrude the fey has been chosen because she is *good*. And the giant Hans has been chosen because he is *strong*.'

Of course, being the head teacher she had then gone on to tell the children that if they wanted to do great deeds when they were older they must themselves remember to be wise and good and strong and they could begin by getting their homework done on time and keeping their classroom tidy.

When you are a hag it is important not to cry, but Odge, as she sat on a rock that evening wrapped in her hair, was deeply and seriously hurt.

'I am wise,' she said to herself. 'I was top again in Algebra. And I'm strong: I threw a boulder right across Anchorage Bay. As for being good, I can't see any point in that – not for a mission which might be dangerous.'

And yet the letter she had written to the King and Queen had been answered by a secretary who said he felt Miss Gribble was too young.

Sitting alone by the edge of the sea, Odge Gribble ground her teeth.

But there was another reason why those three people had been chosen. The King and Queen wanted their son to be brought back quietly. They didn't want to unloose a lot of strange and magical creatures on the city of London – creatures who would do sensational tricks and be noticed. They dreaded television crews getting excited and newspaper men writing articles about a Lost Continent or a Stolen Prince. As far as the Island was a Lost Continent they wanted it to stay that way, and they were determined to protect their son from the kind of fuss that went on Up There when anything unusual was going on.

So they had chosen rescuers who could do magic if it was absolutely necessary but could pass for human beings – well, more or less. Of course, if anything went wrong they had hordes of powerful creatures in reserve: winged harpies with ghastly claws; black dogs which could bay and howl over the roof tops; monsters with pale, flat eyes who could disguise themselves as rocks ... All these could be sent through the tunnel if the Trottles turned nasty, but no one expected this. The Trottles had done a dreadful thing; they would certainly be sorry and give up the child with a good grace.

Yet now, as the rescuers stood in the drawing room of the palace ready to be briefed, the King and Queen did feel a pang. Cornelius was the mightiest wizard on the Island; a man so learned that he could divide twenty-three-thousand-seven-hundred-and-forty-one by six-and-three-quarters in the time it took a cat to sneeze. He could change the weather, and strike fire from a rock, and what was most important he had once been a university professor and lived Up There so that he could be made to look human without any trouble. Well, he *was* human.

But they hadn't realized he was quite so old. Up in his hut in the hills one didn't notice it so much, but in the strong light that came in from the sea, the liver spots on his bald pate did show up rather, and the yellowish streaks in his long white beard. Cor's neck wobbled as if holding up that domed, brain-filled head was too much for it, you could hear his bones creaking like old timbers every time he moved, and he was very deaf.

But when they suggested that he might find the journey too much, he had been deeply offended.

'To bring back the Prince will be the crowning glory of my life,' he'd said.

'And I'll be there to help him,' Gurkintrude had promised, looking at the old man out of her soft blue eyes.

'I know you will, dear,' said the Queen, smiling at her favourite fey. And indeed, Gurkintrude had already brought up a little patch of hair on the wizard's bald head so as to keep him warm for the journey. True it looked more like grass because she was a sort of growth goddess, a kind of agricultural fairy, but the wizard had been very pleased.

If the Queen couldn't go herself to fetch back her son (and the Royal Advisors had forbidden it) there was no one she would rather have sent than this fruitful and loving person. Flowers sprang from the ground for Gurkie, trees put out their leaves – and she never forgot the vegetables either. It was because of what she did for those rich, swollen things like marrows and pumpkins – and in particular for those delicious, tiny cucumbers called gherkins which taste so wonderful when pickled – that her name (which had been Gertrude) had gradually changed the way it had.

And Gurkintrude, too, would be at home in London because her mother had been a gym mistress in a girls' school and run about in grey shorts shouting, 'Well Played!' and 'Spiffing!' before she came to the Island. Gurkie had adored her mother and she sometimes talked to her plants as though they were the girls of St Agnes School, crying, 'Well grown!' to the raspberries or telling a lopsided tree to, 'Pull his Socks Up and Play the Game.'

The third rescuer was lying behind a screen being tested by the doctor. Hans was an ogre – a one-eyed giant – a most simple and kindly person who lived in the mountains putting things right for the goats, collecting feathers for his alpine hat, and yodelling.

As giants go he was not very big, but anyone bigger would not have been able to get through the door of the gentlemen's cloakroom. Even so, at a metre taller than an ordinary person, he would have been noticed, so it had been decided to make him invisible for the journey.

This was no problem. Fernseed, as everyone knows, makes people invisible in a moment, but just a few people can't take it on their skin. They come out in lumps and bumps or develop a rash

29

and it was to test the ogre's skin that the doctor had taken him behind the screen. Now he came out, carrying his black bag and beaming.

'All is well, Your Majesties,' he said. 'There will be no ill effects at all.'

Hans followed shyly. The ogre always wore leather shorts with embroidered braces and they could see on his huge pink thigh a patch of pure, clear nothingness.

But he was looking a little worried.

'My eye?' he said. 'I wish not seed in my eye?' (He spoke in short sentences and with a foreign accent because his people, long ago, had come through a gump in the Austrian Alps.)

Everyone understood this. If you have only one eye it really matters.

'I don't think anyone will notice a single eye floating so high in the air,' said the Chief Advisor. 'And if they do, he could always shut it.'

So this was settled and the Palace Secretary handed Cornelius a map of the London Underground and a briefcase full of money. There was always plenty of that because the people who came through the gump brought it to the treasury, not having any use for it on the Island, and the King now gave his orders.

'You know already that no magic must be used directly on the Prince,' he said – and the rescuers nodded. The King and Queen liked ruling over a place where unusual things happened, but they themselves were completely human and could only manage if they kept magic strictly out of their private lives. 'As for the rest, I think you understand what you have to do. Make your way quietly to the Trottles' house and find the so-called Raymond. If he is ready to come at once, return immediately and make your way down the tunnel, but if he needs time—'

'How could he?' cried the Queen. 'How could he need time?' The thought that her son might not want to come to her at once hurt her so much that she had to catch her breath.

'Nevertheless, my dear, it may be a shock to him and if so,' he turned back to the rescuers, 'you have a day or two to get him used to the idea, but whatever you do, don't delay more than—'

He was interrupted by a knock on the door and a palace servant entered.

'Excuse me, Your Majesties, but there is someone waiting at the gates. She has been here for hours and though I have explained that you are busy, she simply will not go away.'

'Who is it?' asked the Queen.

'A little girl, Your Majesty. She has a suitcase full of sandwiches and a book and says she will wait all night if necessary.'

The King frowned. 'You had better show her in,' he said.

Odge entered and bobbed a curtsey. She looked grim and determined and carried a suitcase with the words ODGE GRIBBLE – HAG painted on the side.

The Queen smiled – almost a proper smile now that she was soon to see her son. 'Aren't you Mrs Gribble's youngest?' she said in her soft voice.

'Yes, I am.'

'And what can we do for you, my dear? Your sisters are well, I trust?'

Odge scowled. Her sisters were very well, showing off, shrieking, flapping, digging the garden with their long fingernails and generally making her feel bad. But this was no time for her own problems.

'I want you to let me go with the rescuers and fetch the Prince,' said Odge. 'I wrote a letter about it.'

The King's secretary now stepped forward and said that Miss Gribble had indeed offered her services but he had felt that her youth made her unsuitable.

The King nodded and the Queen said gently: 'You *are* too young, my dear – you must see that yourself.'

'I'm the same age as the Prince,' said Odge. 'Almost. And I think it would be nice for him to have someone young.'

'The rescuers have already been chosen,' said the King.

'Yes, I know. But I don't take up much room. And I think I know how he might feel. Raymond Trottle, I mean.'

'How?' asked the Queen eagerly.

'Well, a bit muddled. I mean, he thinks he's a Trottle and he thinks Mrs Trottle is his mother and—'

'But she isn't! She isn't! She's a wicked woman and a thief.'

'Yes, that's true,' said Odge. 'But if he's a royal

32

prince it will be difficult for him to hate his mother and—' She broke off, not wanting to say more.

'It could be a dangerous journey,' said the Queen.

Odge drew herself up to her full height which was not very great. Her green eye glinted and her brown eye glared. 'I am a hag,' she said huffily. 'I am Odge-with-the-Tooth.' She stepped forward and opened her mouth very wide, and the Queen could indeed see a glimmer of blue right at the back. 'Darkness and Danger is meat and drink to hags.'

The King and Queen knew this to be true – but it was absurd to send such a little girl. It was out of the question.

'Sometimes I cough frogs,' said Odge – and blushed because it wasn't true. Once she had coughed something that she thought might be a tadpole, but it hadn't been.

'Why do you want to go?' asked the King.

'I just want to,' said Odge. 'I want to so much that I feel it must be *meant*.'

There was a long pause. Then the Queen said: 'Odge, if you were allowed to go, what would you say to the Prince when you first saw him?'

'I wouldn't *say* anything,' said Odge. 'I'd bring him a present.'

'What kind of a present?' asked the King.

Odge told him.

Four

'Well, this is it!' said Ernie Hobbs, floating past the boarded-up Left Luggage Office and coming to rest on an old mailbag. 'This is the day!'

He was a thin ghost with a drooping moustache, still dressed in the railway porter's uniform he'd worn when he worked in the station. Ernie hated the new-fangled luggage trolleys, taking the bread out of the mouths of honest men who used to carry people's suitcases. He also had a sorrow because after he died his wife had married again, and when he went to haunt his old house, Ernie could see a man called Albert Fisher sitting in Ernie's old chair with a napkin tied round his nasty neck, eating the bangers and mash that Ernie's wife had cooked for him.

All the same, Ernie was a hero. It was he who had seen Mrs Trottle snatch the baby Prince outside the fish shop and tried to glide after the Rolls Royce and stop her – and when that hadn't worked he'd bravely floated through the gump (although wind tunnels do awful things to the stuff that ghosts are made of) and brought the dreadful news to the sailors waiting in the Cove.

Since then, for nine long years, Ernie and the other station ghosts had kept watch on the Trottles' house and now they waited to welcome the rescuers and show them the way.

'Are you going to say anything?' asked Mrs Partridge. 'About . . . you know . . . Raymond?'

She was an older ghost than Ernie and remembered the war and how friendly everyone had been, with the soldiers crowding the station and always ready for a chat. Being a spectre suited her: her legs had been dreadful when she was alive – all swollen and sore from scrubbing floors all day and she never got over feeling as free and light as air.

Ernie shook his head. 'Don't think so,' he said. 'No point in upsetting them. They'll find out soon enough.'

Mrs Partridge nodded. She never believed in making trouble – and a very pale, frail ghost called Miriam Hughes-Hughes agreed. She'd been an apologizing lady – one of those people whose voices come over the loudspeaker all day saying 'sorry' to travellers because their trains are late. No one can do that for long and stay healthy and she had died quite young of sadness and pneumonia.

They were a close band, the spectres who haunted platform thirteen. The Ghosts of the Gump, they called themselves, and they didn't have much truck with outsiders. There was the ghost of a train spotter called Brian who'd got between the buffers and the 9.15 from Peterborough, and the ghost of the old woman who'd lost her umbrella and still hovered over the Left Luggage Office keeping an eye on it . . . And there were others haunting shyly in various parts of the station, not wanting to put themselves forward, but ready to lend a hand if they were needed.

The hands of the great clock moved slowly forward. Not the clock on platform thirteen which was covered in cobwebs, but that of the main one. Eleven-thirty . . . eleven forty-five . . . midnight . . .

And then it happened! The wall of the gentlemen's cloakroom moved slowly, slowly to one side. A hole appeared . . . a deep, dark hole . . . and from it came swirls of mist and, very faintly, the smell of the sea . . .

Mrs Partridge clutched Ernie's arm. 'Oooh, I am excited!' she whispered.

And indeed it was exciting; it was awesome. The dark hole, the swirling mist . . . and now in the hole there appeared . . . figures. Three of them . . . and hovering high above them, a clear blue eye.

'Welcome!' said Ernie Hobbs. He bowed, the women curtsied.

And the rescuers stepped forward into the light.

It has to be said that the ghosts were surprised. They knew that the Prince was to be brought back without a fuss, but they had expected . . . well . . . something a bit fiercer.

Of course they could see that the ancient gentleman now tottering towards them was a wizard. His face was very wise and there seemed to be astrological signs on his long, dark cloak though when they looked more carefully they saw they were pieces of very old spaghetti in tomato sauce. The wizard's ear trumpet, which he wore on a string around his neck, had tangled with the cord holding his spectacles so that it looked as if he might choke to death before he ever set out on his mission, and though they could see a place on his shoulder where a mighty eagle must have once perched, it was definitely not there any more. Yet when he came forward to shake hands with them, the ghosts were impressed. How you shake hands with a ghost matters, because of course you feel nothing and someone who isn't a true gentleman can just wave his hands about in mid-air and make a ghost feel really small.

'I am Cornelius the Mighty,' said Cor, 'and I bring thanks from Their Majesties for your Guardianship of the Gump.'

He then introduced Gurkintrude.

The fey was wearing a large hat decorated with flowers, but also with a single beetroot. It was a living beetroot – Gurkie would never have worn anything that was dead – and she carried a straw basket full of important things for gardening: a watering can, some brown paper bags, a roll of twine . . . The ghosts knew all about these healing ladies who go about making things better for everyone, and they had seen fairy godmothers in the pantomime, but Mrs Partridge was a bit worried about the hat. The beetroot suited Gurkie – it went with her kind pink face – but of course vegetables are not worn very much in London.

But it was the third person who puzzled the Ghosts of the Gump particularly. Why had the rulers of the Island sent a little girl?

Odge's thick black hair had been yanked into two pigtails and she wore a pleated gym slip and a blazer with 'Play Up and Play the Game' embroidered on the pocket. The uniform was an exact copy of the one that the girls of St Agnes wore in the photograph that Gurkie's mother had had on her mantelpiece, but the ghosts did not know that – nor did they understand why the suitcase she was clutching, holding it out in front of her like a tea tray, was punched full of holes.

Fortunately the Eye at least belonged to the kind of rescuer they had expected. Because they themselves were often invisible, the ghosts could make out the shape of the ogre even though he was covered in fernseed. They could see his enormous muscles, each the size of a young sheep, and his sledgehammer fists and while the embroidered braces were a pity, they thought that he would do very well as a bodyguard.

Cornelius now explained that they were disguised as an ordinary human family. 'I am a retired university professor, Gurkintrude is my niece who works for the Ministry of Agriculture and Odge is her god-daughter on the way to boarding school.' As for the ogre, he told them, he would stay invisible, closing his eye when necessary but not, it was hoped, bumping into things.

'And the dear boy?' Gurkintrude now asked eagerly. 'Dear little Raymond? He is well?'

There was a pause while Ernie and Mrs Partridge looked at each other and the ghost of the apologizing lady stared at the ground.

'He's very well,' said Ernie.

'In the pink,' put in Mrs Partridge.

'And knows nothing?'

38

'Nothing,' agreed Ernie.

It now struck the rescuers that there was very little bustle round the gentlemen's cloakroom and that this was unusual. Last time the gump had opened there'd been a stream of people going down: tree spirits whose trees had got Dutch Elm Disease, water nymphs whose ponds had dried up, and just ordinary people who were fed up with the pollution and the noise. But when they pointed this out to Ernie, he said: 'Maybe they'll come later. There's nine days to go.'

Actually, he didn't think they'd come later. He didn't think they'd come at all and he knew why.

'Let us plunge into the bowels of the earth,' said Cornelius who wanted to be on his way.

But the Underground had stopped running and so had the buses. 'And I wouldn't advise waking Raymond Trottle in the middle of the night,' said Ernie. 'I wouldn't advise that at all!'

So it was decided they would walk to Trottle Towers and rest in the park till morning. There was a little summer house hidden in the bushes, and close to Raymond's back door where nobody would find them. The only problem was the wizard who was too tottery to go far and the giant solved that by saying: 'I pig him on back.'

This seemed a good idea. Of course they'd have to watch out for people who'd be surprised to see an old gentleman having a piggy back in mid-air, but as the ghosts were coming along to show them the way, that wouldn't be difficult.

Odge had gone back into the cloakroom to do something to her suitcase. They could hear a tap running and her voice talking to someone. Now, as she stomped after the others down the platform, Ernie took a closer look at her. At the unequal eyes, the fierce black eyebrows which met in the middle . . . at a glimmer of blue as she yawned.

Not just a little girl, then. A hag. Well, they could do with one of those with what was coming to them, thought Ernie Hobbs.

'Goodness, isn't it grand!' said Gurkintrude, looking at the house which was as famous on the Island as Buckingham Palace or the castle where King Arthur had lived with his knights.

Gurkie was right. Trottle Towers was *very* grand. It had three storeys and bristled with curly bits of plasterwork and bow windows and turrets in the roof. The front of the house was separated from the street by a stony garden with gravel paths and a high spiked gate. On the railings were notices saying TRADESMEN NOT ADMITTED and IT IS STRICTLY FORBIDDEN TO PARK – and on the brick-work of the house were three burglar alarms like yellow boils.

The back of the house faced the park and it was from here that the rescuers had come. The ghosts had returned to the gump. Dawn was just breaking but inside the house everything was silent and dark.

Then as they stood and looked, a light came on downstairs, deep in the basement. The room had barred windows and almost no furniture so that they could see who was inside as clearly as on a stage.

A boy.

A boy with light hair and a friendly, intelligent face. He was dressed in jeans and a sweater – and he was working. On a low table stood a row of shoes – shoes of all shapes and sizes: boots and ladies' high-heeled sandals and gentlemen's lace-ups – and the boy was cleaning them. Not just rubbing a cloth over them, but working in the polish with a will – and as he worked, he whistled; they could just hear him through the open slit at the top of the window.

And the rescuers turned to each other and smiled, for they could see that the Prince had been taught to work; that he wasn't being brought up spoilt and selfish as they had feared. Something about the way the ghosts had spoken about Raymond Trottle had worried them, but the boy's alert face, the willing way in which he polished other people's shoes, was a sign of the best possible breeding. This was a prince who would know how to serve others, as did his parents.

The boy finished the shoes and carried them out. A second light went on and they saw him enter a scullery, fill a kettle and lay out some cups and saucers on a tray. This job too he did neatly and nimbly, and Odge sighed for it was amazing how right she had been about the Prince; he was just the kind of person she wanted for a friend, and she held on even tighter to the suitcase, glad that she had brought him the best present that any boy could have.

The scullery light went off and a light appeared between the crack in a pair of curtains which the boy now drew back. As he did this, they could see

41

his face turned towards them: the straight, light hair lapping the level brows, the wide-set eyes and the pointed chin. Then he made his way to the bed and set the tray down beside a fierce-looking lady who didn't seem to be thanking him at all, but just grabbed her cup.

'That must be Mrs Trottle,' whispered Gurkintrude. 'She doesn't look very loving.'

The boy's tasks were still not done. Back in the scullery, he took out a mop and a bucket and began to wipe the floor. Was he perhaps working a little *too* hard for a child who had not yet had breakfast? Or was he on a training scheme? Knights often lived like this before a joust or a tournament – and boy scouts too.

But nothing mattered except that the Prince was everything a boy should be and that the day they brought him back to his rightful home would be the most joyful one the Island had ever known.

'Can't we go and tell him we're here?' asked Odge.

There was no need. The boy had come out of the back door carrying a polythene bag full of rubbish which he put in the dustbin. Then he lifted his head and saw them. For a moment he stood perfectly still with a look of wonder on his face and it was almost as though he was listening to some distant, remembered music. Then he ran lightly up the basement steps and threw open the gate.

'Can I help you?' he asked. 'Is there anyone you want to see?'

Cor the Wise stepped forward. He wanted to greet the Prince by his true name, to bow his head before him, but he knew he must not startle him, and trying to speak in an ordinary voice (though he was very much moved) he said: 'Yes, there is someone we want to see. You.'

The boy drew in his breath. He looked at Gurkie's round, kind face, at the grassy patch on the wizard's head, at Odge who had turned shy and was scuffing her shoes. Then he sighed, as though a weight had fallen from him, and said: 'You mean it? It's really me you've come to see?'

'Indeed it is, my dear,' said Gurkintrude and put her arm round him. He was too thin and why hadn't Mrs Trottle cut his hair? It was bothering him, flopping over his eyes.

The boy's next words surprised them. 'I wish I could ask you in, but I'm not allowed to have visitors,' he said – and they could see how much he minded not being able to invite them to his house. 'But there's a bench there under the oak tree where you could rest, and I could get you a drink. No one's up yet, they wouldn't notice.'

'We need nothing,' said Cor. 'But let us be seated. We have much to tell you.'

They made their way back into the park and the boy took out his handkerchief and wiped the wooden slats of the seat clear of leaves. It was as though he was inviting them to his bench even if he couldn't invite them to his house. Nor would he himself sit down, but stood before them and answered their questions in a steady voice.

'You have lived all your life in Trottle Towers?' asked Cor.

'Yes.' A shadow spread for a moment over his

43

face as though he was looking back on a childhood that had been far from happy.

'And you have learnt to work, we can see that. But your schooling?'

'Oh, yes; I go to school. It's across the park in a different part of London.'

Very different, he thought. Swalebottle Junior was in a rowdy, shabby street; the building was full of cracks and the teachers were often tired, but it was a good place to be. It was the holidays he minded, not the term.

The ogre had managed to follow them to the bench with his eye shut, but the Prince's voice pleased him so much that he now opened it. Cor frowned at him, Gurkie shook her head – they had been so careful not to startle the Prince and invisible ogres *are* unusual; there is nothing to be done about that. But the boy didn't seem at all put out by a single blue eye floating halfway up the trunk of the tree.

'Is he . . . or she . . . I don't want to pry, but is he a friend of yours?'

Hans was introduced and the visitors made up their minds. The Prince was entirely untroubled by magic; it was as though the traditions of the Island were in his blood even if he hadn't been there since he was three months old. It was time to reveal themselves and take him back.

'Was that Mrs Trottle to whom you brought a cup of tea?' asked Cor. 'Because we have something to say to her.'

The boy smiled. 'Oh, goodness, no!' he said. 'Mrs Trottle lives upstairs. That was the cook.'

Cor frowned. He was an old-fashioned man and a bit of a snob and he did not think it absolutely right that a prince should have to take morning tea to the cook.

But Odge had had enough of talking.

'I've brought you something,' she said in her abrupt, throaty little voice. 'A present. Something nice.'

She put the suitcase down on the grass. The words ODGE GRIBBLE – HAG had been painted out. Instead she'd written THIS WAY UP. HANDLE WITH CARE.

The boy crouched down beside her. He could hear the present breathing through the holes. Something alive, he thought, his eyes alight.

It was at this moment that, on the first floor of Trottle Towers, someone began to scream.

All of them were used to the sound of screaming. Odge's sisters practically never stopped, banshees wailed through the trees of the Island, harpies yowled and the sound of bull seals calling to their mates sometimes seemed to shake the rafters. But this was not that sort of a scream. It was not the healthy scream of someone going about their business; it was a whining, self-pitying black-mailing sort of scream. Odge re-fastened the catch of her suitcase in a hurry; Gurkintrude put her arm round the Prince, and the Eye soared upwards as Hans got to his feet.

'What is it, dear boy?' asked Gurkie, and put her free hand up to her head as though to protect the beetroot from the dreadful noise.

'Is it someone having an operation?' said Cornelius. 'I thought you had anaesthetics?'

The boy shook his head. 'No,' he said. 'It's nothing like that. It's Raymond.'

A terrible silence fell.

'What do you mean, it's Raymond?' asked Cor when he could speak again. 'Surely you are Raymond Trottle, the supposed son of Mr and Mrs Trottle?'

The boy shook his head once more. 'No. Oh, goodness, no! I'm only the kitchen boy. I'm not anybody. My name is Ben.'

As he spoke, Ben moved away and stood with his back to the visitors. It was over, then. It wasn't him they'd come to see; he'd been an idiot. When he'd seen them standing there he'd had such a feeling of . . . homecoming, as though at last the years of drudgery were over. It was like that dream he had sometimes – the dream with the sea in it, and soft green turf and someone whose face he couldn't see clearly, but who he knew wanted him.

Only dreams were things you woke from and he should have known that it was not him but Raymond the visitors had come to find. Everything had always belonged to Raymond. All his life he'd been used to Raymond living upstairs with everything he wished for and parents to dote on him. Raymond had cupboards full of toys he never even looked at and more clothes than he knew what to do with; he was driven to his posh school in a Rolls Royce and just to tear the wrapping paper from his Christmas presents took Raymond hours.

46

And so far Ben hadn't minded. He was used to living with the servants, used to sleeping in a windowless cupboard and working for his keep. You couldn't envy Raymond who was always whining and saying: 'I'm bored!'

But this was different. That these strange, mysterious, interesting people belonged to Raymond and not to him was almost more than he could bear.

'You're sure he isn't being tortured?' asked Cor as the screams went on.

'Quite sure. He often does it.'

'*Often*?' said the wizard and shook out his ear trumpet in case he had misheard.

Ben nodded. 'Whenever he doesn't want to go to school. Probably he hasn't done his homework. I usually do it for him but I couldn't yesterday because I was visiting my grandmother in hospital.'

'Who is your grandmother?' Odge wanted to know.

'She's called Nanny Brown. She used to be Mrs Trottle's Nanny and she still lives here in the basement. She adopted me when I was a baby because I didn't have any parents.'

'What happened to them?'

Ben shrugged. 'I don't know. They died. Mr Fulton thinks they must have been in prison because Nanny never mentions them.'

Talking about Nanny Brown was difficult because she was very ill. It was she who protected him from the bullying of the servants – even the snooty butler, Mr Fulton, respected her – and if she died . . .

The rescuers were silent, huddled together on the bench. Hans had closed his eye and was covering his face with his invisible hand. He was used to the silence of the mountains and felt a headache coming on. Odge was crouched over the suitcase as though to comfort what was inside.

It was a *child* who was making that noise; the child they had come so far to find. And the boy they liked so much had nothing to do with them at all!

Five

'What is it, my angel, my babykins, my treasure?' said Mrs Trottle, coming into the room.

She had been making up her face when Raymond's screams began. Now her right cheek was covered in purple rouge and her left cheek was still a rather nasty grey colour. Mrs Trottle's hair was in curlers and she gave off a strong smell of Maneater because she always went to bed covered in scent.

Raymond continued to scream.

'Tell Mama; tell your Mummy, my pinkyboo,' begged Mrs Trottle.

'I've got a pain in my tummy,' yelled Raymond. 'I'm ill.'

Mrs Trottle pulled back the covers on Raymond's huge bed with its padded headboard and the built-in switches for his television set, his two computers and his electric trains. She put a finger on Raymond's stomach and the finger vanished because Raymond was extremely fat.

'Where does it hurt, my pettikins? Which bit?'

'Everywhere,' screeched Raymond. 'All over!'

Since Raymond had eaten an entire box of chocolates the night before this was not surprising, but Mrs Trottle looked worried.

'I can't go to school!' yelled Raymond, getting to the point. 'I can't!'

49

Raymond's school was the most expensive in London; the uniform alone cost hundreds of pounds, but he hated it.

'Of course you can't, my lambkin,' said Mrs Trottle, drawing her finger out of Raymond's middle. 'I'll send a message to the headmaster. And then I'll call a doctor.'

'No, no – not the doctor! I don't want the doctor; he makes me worse,' yelled Raymond – and indeed the doctor was not always as kind to darling Raymond as he might have been.

Mr Trottle now came in looking cross because he had sat on his portable telephone again and asked what was the matter.

'Our Little One is ill,' said Mrs Trottle. 'You must tell Willard to drive to the school after he has dropped you at the bank and let them know.'

'He doesn't look ill to me,' said Mr Trottle – but he never argued with his wife and anyway he was in a hurry to go and lend a million pounds to a property developer who wanted to cover a beautiful Scottish island with holiday homes for the rich.

Raymond's screams grew less. They became wails, then snivels . . .

'I feel a bit better now,' he said. 'I might manage some breakfast.' He had heard the car drive away and knew that the danger of school was safely past.

'Perhaps a glass of orange juice?' suggested Mrs Trottle.

'No. Some bacon and some sausages and some fried bread,' said Raymond.

'But, darling—'

Raymond puckered up his face, ready to scream again.

'All right, my little sugar lump. I'll tell Fulton. And then a quiet day in bed.'

'No. I don't want a quiet day. I feel better now. I want to go to lunch at Fortlands. And then shopping. I want a laser gun like Paul has at school, and a knife, and—'

'But, darling, you've already got seven different guns,' said Mrs Trottle, looking at Raymond's room which was completely strewn with toys which he had pushed aside or broken or refused to put away.

'Not like the one Paul's got – not a sonic-trigger activated laser, and I want one. I *want* it.'

'Very well, dear,' said Mrs Trottle. 'We'll go to lunch at Fortlands. You do look a little rosier.'

This was true. Raymond looked very rosy indeed. People usually do when they have yelled for half an hour.

'And shopping?' asked Raymond. 'Not just lunch but shopping afterwards?'

'And shopping,' agreed Mrs Trottle. 'So now give your Mumsy a great big sloppy kiss.'

That was how things always ended on days when Raymond didn't feel well enough to go to school – with Raymond and Mrs Trottle, dressed to kill, going to have lunch in London's grandest department store.

The name of the store was Fortlands and Marlow. It was in Piccadilly and sold everything you could imagine: marble bath tubs and ivory elephants and sofas that you sank into and disappeared. It had a

Food Hall with a fountain where butlers in hard hats bought cheeses which cost a week's wages, and a bridal department where the daughters of duchesses were fitted for their wedding gowns – and none of the dresses had price tickets on them in case people fainted clean away when they saw how much they cost.

And there was a restaurant with pink chairs and pink tablecloths in which Raymond and his mother were having lunch.

'I'll have shrimps in mayonnaise,' said Raymond, 'and then I'll have roast pork with crackling and Yorkshire pudding and—'

'I'm afraid the Yorkshire pudding comes with the roast beef, sir,' said the waitress. 'With the pork you get apple sauce and redcurrant jelly.'

'I don't like apple sauce,' whined Raymond. 'It's all squishy and gooey. I want Yorkshire pudding. I *want* it.'

It was at this moment that the rescuers entered the store. They too were having lunch in the restaurant. When Ben had told them how Raymond was going to spend the day, they decided to follow the Prince and study him from a distance so that they could decide how best to make themselves known to him.

'Only I want Ben to come,' Odge said.

Everyone wanted Ben to come, but he said he couldn't. 'I don't have school today because they need the building for a council election and I promised my grandmother I'd come to the hospital at dinner time.'

But he said he would go with them as far as

Fortlands and point Raymond out because the Trottles had gone off in the Rolls and no one had seen him yet. Hans, though, decided to stay behind. He didn't like crowded places and he lay down under an oak tree and went to sleep which made a great muddle for the dogs who didn't understand why they couldn't walk through a perfectly empty patch of grass.

Gurkie absolutely loved Fortlands. The vegetable display was quite beautiful – the passion fruit and the pineapples and the cauliflowers so artistically arranged – and she had time to say nice things to a tray of broccoli which looked a little lonely. In a different sort of shop, the rescuers might have stood out, but Fortlands was full of old-fashioned people coming up from the country and they fitted in quite well. The only thing people did stare at a bit was the beetroot in Gurkie's hat so she decided to leave it in the fountain to soak quietly while she went up to the restaurant. It was as she was bending over the water to look for a place where the beloved vegetable would not be noticed, that she saw, beneath the water weed, a small, sad face.

Bending down to see more clearly, she found that she had not been mistaken.

'Yes, it's me,' said a slight, silvery voice. 'Melisande. I heard you were coming.' And then: 'I'm not a mermaid, you know, I'm a water nymph. I've got feet.'

'Yes, I know, dear; I can see you've got feet. But you don't look well. What are those marks on your arms?'

'It's the coins. People chuck coins into the

53

fountain all day long, heaven knows why. I'm all over bruises – and the water isn't changed nearly often enough.'

And her lovely, tiny face really did look very melancholy.

'Why don't you come down with us, dear?' whispered Gurkintrude. 'The gump's open. We could take you wrapped in wet towels, it wouldn't be difficult.'

'I was going to,' said the nymph sadly. 'But not now. You've seen him.'

'The Prince, do you mean? We haven't yet.'

'Well, you will in a minute; he's just gone up in the lift. There was a lot of us going, but who wants to be ruled by *that*?'

She then agreed to hide the beetroot under a water lily leaf and Gurkie hurried to catch up with the others. The nymph's words had upset her, but feys always think the best of people and she was determined to look on the bright side. Even if Mrs Trottle had spoilt Raymond a little, there would be time to put that right when he came to the Island. When children behave badly it is nearly always the fault of those who bring them up.

'There he is,' whispered Ben. 'Over there, by the window.'

There was a long pause.

'You're sure?' asked Cor. 'There can be no mistake?'

'I'm sure,' said Ben.

He then slipped away and the rescuers were left to study the boy they had come so far to find.

'He looks . . . healthy,' said Gurkintrude, trying to make the best of things.

'And well-washed,' agreed the wizard. 'I imagine there would be no mould behind his ears?'

Odge didn't say anything. She still carried the suitcase, holding it out flat like a tray, and had been in a very nasty temper since she discovered that Ben was not the Prince.

What surprised them most was how like his supposed mother Raymond Trottle looked. They both had the same fat faces, the same podgy noses, the same round, pale eyes. They knew, of course, that dogs often grew to be like their owners so perhaps it was understandable that Raymond, who had lived with the Trottles since he was three months old, should look like the woman who had stolen him, but it was odd all the same.

The visitors had looked forward very much to having lunch in a posh restaurant, but the hour that followed was one of the saddest of their lives. They found a table behind a potted palm from which they could watch the Trottles without being noticed, and what they saw got worse and worse and worse. Raymond's shrimps had arrived and he was pushing them away with a scowl.

'I don't want them,' said Raymond. 'They're the wrong ones. I want the bigger ones.'

As far as Gurkie was concerned there was no such thing as a wrong shrimp or a right shrimp. All shrimps were her friends and she would have died rather than eat one, but she felt dreadfully sorry for the waitress.

'The bigger ones are prawns, sir; and I'm afraid we don't have any today.'

'Don't have any *prawns*,' said Mrs Trottle in a loud voice. 'Don't have any prawns in the most expensive restaurant in London!'

The waitress had been on her feet all day, her little girl was ill at home, but she kept her temper.

'If you'd just try them, sir,' she begged Raymond.

But he wouldn't. The dish was taken away and Raymond decided to start with soup. 'Only not with any bits in it,' he shouted after the waitress. 'I don't eat bits.'

Poor Gurkie's kind round face was growing paler and paler. The Islanders had ordered salad and nut cutlets, but she was so sensitive that she could hear the lamb chops screaming on the neighbouring tables and the poor stiff legs of dead pheasants sticking up from people's plates made her want to cry.

Raymond's soup came and it did have bits in it – a few leaves of fresh parsley.

'I thought I asked for *clear* soup,' said Mrs Trottle. 'Really, I find it quite extraordinary that you cannot bring us what we want.'

The rescuers had been up all night; they were not only sad, they were tired, and because of this they forgot themselves a little. When their nut cutlets came they were too hard for the wizard's teeth and he should have mashed them up with his fork – of course he should. Instead, he mumbled something and in a second the cutlets had turned to liquid. Fortunately no one saw, and the liquidizing spell is nothing to write home about – it was used by wizards in the olden days to turn their enemies' bones to jelly – but it was embarrassing when they were trying so hard to be ordinary. And then the sweet peas in Gurkintrude's hat started to put out tendrils without even being told so as to shield her from the sight of the Prince fishing with his fingers in the soup.

The Trottles' roast pork came next – and the kind waitress had managed to persuade the chef to put a helping of Yorkshire pudding on Raymond's plate though anyone who knows anything about food knows that Yorkshire pudding belongs to beef and not to pork.

Raymond stared at the plate out of his round pale eyes. 'I don't want roast potatoes,' he said. 'I want chips. Roast potatoes are boring.'

'Now Raymond, dear,' began his mother.

'I want *chips*. This is supposed to be my treat and it isn't a treat if I can't have chips.'

Odge had behaved quite well so far. She had glared, she had ground her teeth, but she had gone on eating her lunch. Now though, she began to have *thoughts* and the thoughts were about her sisters – and in particular about her oldest sister, Fredegonda, who was better than anyone on the Island at ill-wishing pigs.

Ill-wishing things is not all that difficult. Witch doctors do it when they send bad thoughts to people and make them sick; sometimes you can do it when you will someone not to score a goal at football and they don't. Odge had never wanted to ill-wish pigs because she liked animals, but she had sometimes wanted to ill-wish people, and now, more than anything in the world, she wanted to ill-wish Raymond Trottle.

But she didn't. For one thing she wasn't sure if she could and anyway she had promised to behave like the girls of St Agnes whose uniform she wore.

'I want a Knickerbocker Glory next,' said Raymond. 'The kind with pink ice-cream and green ice-cream and jelly and peaches and raspberry juice and nuts.'

The waitress went away and returned with Mrs Trottle's caramel pudding and the Knickerbocker Glory in a tall glass. It was an absolutely marvellous one – just to look at it made Odge's mouth water.

Raymond picked up his spoon – and put it down again.

'It hasn't got an umbrella on top,' he wailed. 'I always have a plastic umbrella on top. I won't eat it unless I have a – Ugh! Eek! Yow! What's happened? I didn't touch it, I didn't, I *didn't*!'

He was telling the truth for once, but nobody believed him. For the Knickerbocker Glory had done a somersault and landed face down on the table, so that the three kinds of ice-cream, the jelly, the tinned peaches and the raspberry juice were running down Raymond's trousers, into his socks, across his flashy shoes . . .

Odge had not ill-wished Raymond Trottle. She had been very good and held herself in, but not completely. She had ill-wished the Knickerbocker Glory.

Six

'I want some brandy for my teeth,' said Nanny Brown.

She lay in the second bed from the end in Ward Three of the West Park Hospital, in a flannel night-dress with a drawstring round the neck because she didn't believe in showing bits of herself to the doctors. She had been old when Mrs Trottle per-suaded her to come to Switzerland with the stolen baby and now she was very old indeed; shrivelled and tired and ready to go because she'd said her prayers every day of her life and if God wasn't waiting to take her up to heaven she'd want to know the reason why. But she was cross about her teeth.

'Now, Mrs Brown,' said the nurse briskly, 'you know we can't let you soak your teeth in that nasty stuff. Just pop them in that nice glass of disin-fectant.'

'It isn't nice, it's smelly,' grumbled Mrs Brown. 'I've always soaked my teeth in brandy and then I drink the brandy. That's how I get my strength.'

And she had needed her strength, living in the Trottles' basement helping to look after Raymond, but keeping an eye on Ben. She didn't hold with the way Larina was bringing up Raymond; she could see how spoilt he was going to be and when

59

he was three she'd handed him over to another nanny, but she wouldn't let Larina turn her out – not with Ben to look after. Mrs Trottle might threaten her with the police if she said anything about the stolen baby, but the threat worked both ways. 'If you turn me out, and the boy, I'll tell them everything and who knows which of us they'll believe,' Nanny Brown had said.

So she'd stayed in Trottle Towers and helped with a bit of sewing and ironing and turned her back on what was going on in the nurseries upstairs. And she'd been able to see that Ben at least was brought up properly. She couldn't stop the servants ordering him about, but she saw to his table manners and that he spoke nicely and got his schooling and he was a credit to her.

That was the only thing that worried her – what would happen to Ben if she died. Mrs Trottle hated Ben; she'd stop at nothing to get him sent away. But I'm going to foil her, thought Nanny Brown. Oh yes, I'm going to stop her tricks.

'There's a burglar under my bed,' she said now. 'I feel it. Have a look.'

'Now, Mrs Brown,' said the nurse, 'we don't want to get silly ideas into our head, do we?'

'It isn't silly,' said Nanny peevishly. 'London's full of burglars, so why not under my bed?'

The nurse wouldn't look though; she was one of the bossy ones. 'What will your grandson say if you carry on like that?' she said, and walked away with her behind swinging.

But when Ben came slowly down the ward, the old woman felt better at once. She'd been strict with him: no rude words, eating up every scrap you were given, yet she didn't mind admitting that if she loved anyone in the world it was this boy. And the other patients smiled too as he passed their beds because he was always so polite and friendly, greeting them and remembering their names.

'Hello, Nanny.'

He always called her Nanny, not Grandma. She'd told him to, it sounded better. Now he laid a small bunch of lilies of the valley down beside her and she shook her head at him. 'I told you not to waste your money.' She'd left him a few pounds out of her pension when she went into hospital and told him it had to last. Waste was wicked, but her gnarled fingers closed round the bunch and she smiled.

'How are you feeling?' Ben asked.

'Oh fine, fine,' lied Nanny Brown. 'And you? What's been going on at home?'

Ben hesitated. He wanted to tell Nanny about his mysterious visitors, about how much he liked them . . . the strange feeling he'd had that they belonged to him. But he'd promised to say nothing and anyway he'd been wrong because they didn't belong to him. So he just said: 'Nothing much. I've got on to the football team and Raymond's had another screaming fit.'

'That's hardly news,' said Nanny Brown grimly. And then: 'No one's been bothering you? That Mr Fulton?'

'No, not really. But . . . do you think you're coming home soon, Nanny? It's better when you're there.'

61

Nanny patted his hand. 'Bless you, of course I am. You just get on with your schooling and remember once you're grown up, no one can tell you what to do.'

'Yes.'

It would be a long time though till he was a man and Nanny looked very ill. Fear was bad; being afraid was about yourself and you had to fight it, but just for a moment he was very much afraid whether it was selfish or not.

It was very quiet in the ward when the visitors had gone. All the other patients lay back drowsily, glad to rest, but Nanny Brown sat up in bed as fierce as a sparrow hawk. There wasn't much time to waste. And she was lucky: it was the nice nurse from the Philippines who came round to take temperatures. Celeste, she was called, and she had a lovely smile and a tiny red rose tucked into her hair behind her ear. You could only see it when she bent down, but it always made you feel better, knowing it was there.

'Listen, dear, there's something I want you to do for me. Will you get me a piece of paper and an envelope? It's really important or I wouldn't ask you.'

Celeste reached for Nanny's wrist and began to take her pulse.

'I'll try, Mrs Brown,' she said. 'But you'll have to wait till I've finished my rounds.'

And she didn't forget. An hour later she came with the paper and a strong white envelope. 'Have you got a pen?'

Nanny Brown nodded. 'Thank you, dear; that's a weight off my mind. You're a good kind girl.'

Celeste smiled. 'That's all right.' She looked closely at the old woman's face. It wouldn't be long now. 'I'll just make sure about the burglars,' she said.

She bent down to look, and as she did so Nanny Brown could see the little red rose tucked in the jet black hair.

'Bless you,' she said – and then, feeling much better, she began to write.

Seven

'Is simple,' said Hans. 'I bop 'im. I sack 'im. We go through gump.'

The others had returned from Fortlands in such a gloomy mood that the poor ogre could hardly bear it. He'd had a good sleep and when he heard what had happened in the restaurant, he decided that he should come forward and put things right.

Cor shook his head. It was tempting to let the giant bop Raymond on the head, tie him up in a sack and carry him back to the Island, but it couldn't be done. He imagined the King and Queen unwrapping their stunned son like a trussed piglet ... realizing that Raymond had had to be carried off by force.

'He must come willingly, Hans,' he said, 'or the Queen will break her heart.'

Ernie Hobbs now glided towards the little summer house where they were sitting. He usually allowed himself a breather in the early evening and had left the other ghosts in charge of the gump.

'Well, how's it going?'

The Islanders told him.

Ernie nodded. 'I'm afraid it's a bad business. We've been keeping an eye on him and he's been going downhill steadily. Mrs Trottle's a fool and Mr Trottle's never there – there's no one to check him.'

64

'I suppose there can be no doubt who Raymond is?' asked Cor.

Ernie shook his head. 'I saw her steal the baby. I saw her come back a year later with the baby in her arms. What's more, he had the same comforter in his mouth. I noticed it particularly with it being on a gold ring. He'll be the Prince all right.'

'And what about Ben?' asked Gurkintrude.

'Ah, he's a different kettle of fish, Ben is. Been here as long as Raymond and you couldn't find a better lad. He can see ghosts too and never a squawk out of him. The servants treat him like dirt – take their tone from Mrs Trottle. It'll be a bad day for the boy when his Grandma dies.'

He then glided off to watch Albert Fisher eat bangers and mash in his old house and make himself miserable, but first he promised the help of all the ghosts in the city if it was needed. 'And not just ghosts – there's all sorts would like to see things come right on the Island,' he said.

He had no sooner gone than Ben came hurrying out of the house towards them, and Odge – who had been exercising her present in the shrubbery – crawled out with her suitcase and said 'hello'.

'How was your grandmother?' Gurkie asked.

A shadow crossed Ben's face. 'She says she's all right but she doesn't look very well to me.' And then: 'How did it go at lunch?'

'Raymond was awful,' said Odge. 'I think he's disgusting. I think we should have a republic on the Island and not bother with a prince once the King and Queen are dead.'

'*Odge*!' said Gurkie in a warning voice.

Odge hung her head. She had not meant to betray the reason for their journey any more than she had meant to ill-wish the Knickerbocker Glory, but she was a girl with strong feelings.

But Cor had come to a decision.

'I think, Ben,' he said, 'that you are a boy who can keep a secret?'

'Yes, sir, I am,' said Ben without hesitation.

'You see, we shall need your help. You know Raymond's movements and where he sleeps and so on. So we had better explain why we are here.'

He then told him about the Island, about the sorrow of the King and Queen, about their quest.

Ben listened in silence and when they had finished his eyes were bright with wonder. 'I always knew there had to be a place like that. I knew it!' But he was amazed that Raymond had been stolen. 'Mrs Trottle's got his birth certificate framed in her room.'

'Well, that just shows she's a cheat, doesn't it?' said Odge. 'Who'd want to frame a crummy birth certificate unless they had something to hide?'

'Now, listen, Ben,' the wizard went on, 'we want you to take us to see Raymond when he's alone. Do you know when that might be?'

'Tonight would be good. The Trottles are going out and Mrs Flint's meant to listen for him – that's the cook – but all she does is switch the telly on full blast and stay in her sitting room.'

'That will do then. And now we must think how to win Raymond's trust and make him come with us. What sort of things does he like?'

This was difficult. Ben could think of a lot of

things Raymond *didn't* like. After a pause he said: 'Presents. He likes getting things.'

'Ah, in that case—'

'*No!*' Odge broke in most rudely. She was clutching the suitcase and her green eye gave off beams of fury. 'I won't give this present to that pig of a boy.'

Cornelius rose. 'How *dare* you speak like that to your superiors?'

But Odge stood her ground. 'This present is special. I brought it up from when it was tiny and it's still a baby and I'm not going to give it to Raymond because he's horrible. I'm going to give it to Ben.'

Gurkintrude now knelt down beside the hag. 'Look, Odge, I know how you feel. But it's our duty to bring back the Prince. The Queen trusted you as much as she trusted us and it was because you thought of such a lovely present for her son that she said you could come. You can't let her down now.'

But it was Ben who changed her mind. 'If you promise to do something, Odge, then you have to do it, you know that. And if giving Raymond ... whatever it is ... will help, then that's part of the deal.'

'Oh, all right,' said Odge sulkily. 'But if he doesn't treat it properly I'll let my sisters loose on him, and that's a promise.'

It was nine o'clock before the servants were settled in front of the telly and Ben could creep upstairs with his new friends.

Raymond was sitting up in bed with his ghetto-blaster going full tilt, wriggling in time to the music.

'What do you want?' he said to Ben. 'I don't need you. I haven't got any homework to do today because tomorrow's Saturday and anyway you're supposed to stay in the kitchen.'

'I've brought some people to see you,' said Ben. 'Visitors.'

The rescuers entered, and Ben introduced them – all except Hans who had to crawl through the door on his hands and knees and settled himself down with his eye shut.

Raymond stared at them. 'They look funny,' he said. 'Are they in fancy dress?'

'No, Your Roy—' began Cor and broke off. He had been about to call Raymond Your Royal Highness but it was too early to reveal the full truth. 'We come from another place.'

'What place?' asked Raymond suspiciously.

'It's called the Island,' said Gurkintrude. Feys are used to kissing children and being godmother to almost everyone, but Raymond, bulging out of his yellow silk pyjamas, looked so uninviting that she had to pretend he was a vegetable marrow before she could settle down beside him on the bed. 'It's a most beautiful place, Raymond. There are green fields with wild flowers growing in the grass and groves of ancient trees and rivers where the water is so clear that you can see all the stones on the bottom as if they were jewels.'

Raymond didn't say anything, but at least he'd switched off his radio.

'And all round the Island are beaches of white

sand and rock pools and cliffs where the sea birds come to nest each spring.'

'And there are seals and buzzards and rabbits and crabs,' said Odge.

'I don't like crabs,' said Raymond. 'They pinch you. Is there a pier with slot machines and an amusement arcade?'

'No. But you don't need an amusement arcade – the dolphins will come and talk to you and the kelpies will take you on their backs and gallop through the waves.'

'I don't believe it,' said Raymond. 'You're telling fibs.'

'No, Raymond, it's all true,' said Gurkie, 'and if you come with us we'll show you.'

Cor opened his briefcase and took out a cardboard folder. 'Perhaps you would like to see a picture of our King and Queen?'

He handed the photograph to Raymond. It wasn't one of the official palace portraits with the royal family in their robes. The Queen was sitting on a rock by the sea with one hand trailing in the water. Her long hair was loose and she was smiling up at the King who looked down at her, his face full of pride. The picture had been taken before the Prince was stolen and what came out of it most was – happiness.

'They look all right,' said Raymond. 'But they don't look royal. They're dressed like ordinary people. If I was royal I'd wear a gold uniform and medals.'

'Then you'd look pretty silly by the sea,' said Odge, 'because the salt spray would make the gold braid go all green and nasty and your medals would clank and frighten away—'

'Now, Odge!' said Gurkie warningly.

'Could I look?' asked Ben – and Cor took the picture from Raymond and handed it to him.

Ben said nothing. He just stood looking at the photograph – looking and looking as if he could make himself part of it . . . as if he could vanish into the picture and stay there.

But now Raymond sat up very straight and pointed to the door. 'Eeek!' he shouted. 'There's a horrible thing there! An eye! It's disgusting; it's creepy. I want my Mummy!'

The others turned their heads in dismay. They knew how sensitive the ogre was and to call such a clean-living person 'creepy' is about as hurtful as it is possible to be. And sure enough, a tear welled up in Hans' clear blue eye, trembled there . . . and fell. Then the eye vanished and from the space where the giant sat, there came a deep, unhappy sigh.

But Odge now came to the rescue. She had promised to behave like the girls of St Agnes who said: 'Play Up and Play the Game' and she said: 'Raymond, I've brought you a present, a really special one. I brought it all the way from the Island. Look!'

The word 'present' cheered Raymond up at once and he watched as she lifted her suitcase on to the bed and opened it.

'What is it?' Raymond asked.

But he didn't shudder this time; he looked quite pleased. And the person who wasn't pleased with

70

what lay inside, cradled in layers of moss, would have been made of stone. A very small animal covered in soft, snow-white fur, with big paws lightly tipped with black. His eyes, as he woke from sleep, were huge and very dark, his blob of a nose was moist and whiskery and cool, and as he looked up at Raymond and yawned you could see his strawberry pink tongue and smell his clean milky breath.

'I've never seen one of them,' said Raymond. 'It's a funny looking thing. What is it?'

Odge told him. 'It's a mistmaker. We have hundreds of them on the Island; they get very tame. I got this one because his mother got muddled and rolled on him. She didn't mean to, she just got mixed up.'

She lifted the little animal out and laid him on the satin quilt. The mistmaker's forehead was wrinkled like a bloodhound's; he had a small, soft moustache and his pink, almost human-looking ears had big lobes like you find on the ears of poets or musicians.

'Why is it called a mistmaker?' asked Raymond.

'I'll show you,' said Odge. 'Can you sing?'

'Of course I can sing,' said Raymond. 'Everyone can sing.'

'Well, then, do it. Sing something to it. Put your head quite close.'

Raymond cleared his throat. 'I can't remember any words,' he said. 'I'll play it something on my radio.' He turned the knob and the room was filled with the sound of cackling studio laughter.

'You try, Ben,' ordered Odge. 'You sing to it.'

71

But Ben didn't sing. He whistled. None of them had heard whistling quite like that; it was like bird-song, but it wasn't just chirruping – it had a proper tune: a soaring tune that made them think of spring and young trees and life beginning everywhere. And as Ben whistled, the little animal drew closer . . . and closer still . . . he pressed his moist nose against Ben's hands; the wrinkles on his worried-looking forehead grew smoother . . .

'Aaah,' sighed the mistmaker. 'Aaah . . .'

Then it began. At first there was only a little mist; he was after all very young . . . and then there came more . . . and more . . . Even from this animal only a few weeks old there came enough cool, swirling mist to wreathe Raymond's bed in whiteness. The room became beautiful and mysterious; the piles of neglected toys disappeared, and the fussy furniture . . . and the Islanders drank in the well-remembered freshness of early morning and of grass still moist with dew.

Raymond's mouth dropped open. 'It's weird. I've never seen that. It isn't natural.'

'Why isn't it natural?' asked Odge crossly. 'Skunks make stinks and slugs make slime and people make sweat so why shouldn't a mistmaker make mist?'

Raymond was still staring at the little creature. No one at school had anything like that. He'd be able to show it off to everyone. Paul had a tree frog and Derek had a grass snake but this would beat them all.

'You'd be able to play with mistmakers all day

72

long if you came to the Island,' said Gurkie. 'You will come, won't you?'

'Nope,' said Raymond. 'I'd miss my telly and my computer games and my Scalextric set. But I'll keep him.'

He made a grab for the mistmaker but the animal had given off so much mist that he was less pillow-shaped now, and nimbler. Jumping off the bed he landed with a thud on his nose and began to explore the room.

They watched him as he ran his whiskery moustache along Raymond's toy boxes, rolled over on the rug, rubbed himself against a chest of drawers. Sometimes he disappeared into patches of mist, then reappeared with one ear turned inside out which is what happens to mistmakers who are busy.

The wizard cleared his throat. Now was the time to come out with the truth. Such a snobby boy would surely come to the Island if he knew he would live there as a prince.

'Perhaps we should tell you, Raymond, that you are really of noble—'

He was interrupted by another and even louder shriek from Raymond.

'Look! It's lifted its leg! It's made a puddle on the carpet. It's dirty!'

Odge looked at him with loathing. 'This mist-maker is *six weeks old*! They can be housetrained perfectly well but not when they are infants. You made enough puddles when you were that age and it's a *clean* puddle. It isn't the puddle of someone who guzzles shrimps and roast pork and greasy potatoes.'

Ben had already been to the bathroom for a cloth and was mopping up. Mopping up after Raymond was something he had been doing ever since he could remember. Then he gathered up the mist-maker who was trembling all over and trying to cover his ears with his paws. You cannot be as musical as these animals are without suffering terribly from the kind of stuck-pig noises that Raymond made.

'You keep him downstairs, Ben,' ordered Raymond. 'You can feed him and see he doesn't mess up my room. But remember, he's *mine*!'

Eight

Odge and Gurkie spent the night curled up on the floor of the little summer house. It was a pretty place with a fretwork verandah and wooden steps but no one used it now. Years ago the roof had begun to leak and instead of mending it, the head keeper had put up a notice saying: PRIVATE. NO ADMITTANCE. Dark privet bushes and clumps of laurel hid it from passers by. Only the animals came to it now: sparrows to preen in the lop-sided bird bath; squirrels to chatter on the roof.

Near by, a patch of snoring grass showed where the ogre rested. Ben had smuggled the mistmaker into his cupboard of a room.

But Cornelius could not sleep. He longed to conjure up a fire to keep his old bones warm, but he thought it might be noticed and after a while he took his stick and wandered off towards the lake. The Serpentine it was called because it was wiggly and shaped like a serpent, and he remembered it from when he had lived Up Here. Londoners were fond of it; people went boating there and caught tiddlers and brave old gentlemen broke the ice with their toes in winter and swam in it, getting goose pimples but being healthy.

But it wasn't just old men with goose pimples or lovers canoodling or children sailing their boats that came here. There were . . . others. There had been mermaids in the lake when Cor was a little boy, each tree had had its spirit, banshees had wailed in the bushes. And on Midsummer's Eve they had gathered together and had a great party.

Midsummer's Eve was in two days' time. Did they still come, the boggarts and the brownies, the nymphs and the nixies, the sproggans and the witches and the trolls? And if so was there an idea there? If Raymond saw real magic – saw the exciting things that happened on the Island, would that persuade him to come?

Cor's ancient forehead wrinkled up in thought. Then he raised his stick in the air and said some poetry – and seconds later Ernie Hobbs, who had been sleeping on a mail bag on platform thirteen of King's Cross Station, woke up and said: 'Ouch!' Looking about him, he saw that Mrs Partridge, who'd been flat out on a luggage trolley, was sitting up and looking puzzled.

'I've got a tingle in my elbow,' she said. 'Real fierce it is.'

At the same time, Miriam Hughes-Hughes, the ghost of the apologizing lady, rolled off the bench outside the Left Luggage Office and lay blinking on the ground.

It was Ernie who realized what had happened.

'We're being summoned! We're being sent for!'

'It'll be the wizard,' said Mrs Partridge excitedly. 'There isn't no one else can do tricks like that!'

Wasting no more time, they glided down the platform and made their way to the park. They found

Cornelius sitting on a tree stump and staring into the water.

'Did you call us, Your Honour?' asked Ernie.

'I did,' said Cor. He then told them what had happened earlier in Raymond's room: 'We went to tell him who he was, but the noise he made was more than anyone could bear. We had to leave.'

The ghosts looked troubled. 'We should have warned you, maybe,' said Ernie, 'but we thought he might be better with you.'

'Well, he wasn't.' Cor rubbed his aching knees. 'Hans wants to bop the Prince on the head and carry him through the gump in a sack, but I think we must have another go at persuading him to come willingly. So I want you to call up all the . . . unusual people who are left Up Here and ask them to put on a special show for Raymond. Wizards, will o' the wisps . . . everyone you can find. Ask them to do the best tricks they can and we'll build a throne for Raymond and hail him as a prince.'

'A sort of Raymond Trottle Magic Show?' said Mrs Partridge eagerly.

Ernie, though, was looking worried. 'There's always a bit of a do on Midsummer's Eve, that's true enough. But . . . well, Your Honour, I don't want to throw a damper but magic isn't what it was up here. It's what you might call the Tinkerbell Factor.'

'I don't follow you,' said the wizard.

'Well, there's this fairy . . . she's in a book called *Peter Pan*. Tinkerbell, she's called. When people say they don't believe in her she goes all woozy and feeble. It's like that up here with the wizards and the witches and all. People haven't believed in them so long they've lost heart a bit.'

'We can only do our best,' said Cornelius. 'Now, tell me, what's the situation about . . . you know . . .' He spoke quietly, not knowing who might be listening in the depths of the lake. '*Him*. The monster? Is he still there?'

'Old Nuckel? They say so,' said Ernie. 'But no one's seen him for donkey's years. Have you thought of calling him up?'

'I was wondering,' said Cor. 'I happen to have my book of spells with me. It would make a splendid ending to the show.'

The ghosts looked respectful. Raising monsters from the deep is very difficult magic indeed.

'Well, if that doesn't fetch the little perisher, nothing will,' said Mrs Partridge – and blushed, because nasty or not, Raymond Trottle was, after all, a prince.

It was incredible how helpful everyone was. Witches who worked in school kitchens trying to make two pounds of mince go round a hundred children said they would come, and so did wizards who taught Chemistry and stayed behind to make interesting explosions after the children had gone home. An animal trainer who trained birds for films and television, and was really an enchanter, promised to bring his flock of white doves so that the evening could begin with a fly-past.

Melisande, the water-nymph-who-was-not-a-mermaid, swam through the outlet pipe at Fortlands and spoke to her uncle who was a merrow and worked the sewers, dredging up stuff which people had flushed down the loo by mistake or lost in the plughole of the bath, and he too said he would come and do a trick for Raymond.

'Really, people are so *kind*,' said Gurkie as she ran about jollying along the tree spirits who had agreed to do a special dance for Raymond on the night.

And she was right. After all, it wasn't as though they didn't know what Raymond was like – that kind of thing gets around – but everyone wanted the King and Queen to be happy. The Island mattered to them; it was their homeland even if they themselves hadn't been there, and there seemed to be no end to the trouble they were prepared to take.

The ghosts, during these two days, were everywhere; helping, persuading, taking messages. Even Miriam Hughes-Hughes stopped apologizing and found a Ladies' Group of Banshees – those pale, ghastly women who wail and screech when something awful is going to happen, and they agreed to come and sing sad songs for the Prince. A troll called Henry Prendergast who lived in the basement of the Bank of England said he thought he could manage some shape-shifting, and Hans tried to forget the hurt that Raymond had done him by calling him creepy, and practised weight-lifting till his muscles threatened to crack. As for Odge Gribble, she went off by herself in the Underground to visit an aunt of her mother's. The aunt was an Old Woman of Gloominess and absolutely marvellous at turning people bald, and she promised to bring some friends along from her sewing circle and amuse Raymond by making donkey's tails come out of people's foreheads and that kind of thing.

But it was Cor who worked himself hardest. Hour after hour, he sat by the lake with his black book practising his monster-raising spell. He didn't eat, he scarcely slept, but he wouldn't stop. There was something special about the Monster of the Serpentine, only, he couldn't remember what it was. There was a lot he couldn't remember these days, but he wasn't going to give up. There was nothing Cor wouldn't have done to bring back the Prince – un-bopped and un-sacked – to the parents who wanted him so much.

The only thing that still worried the rescuers was how to make Raymond Trottle come to the park. Of course it would be easy to call him by magic as Cor had called the ghosts, but they had promised faithfully not to use any magic directly on the Prince.

It was Ben who thought of what to do. 'There's a boy at Raymond's school called Paul who's the son of a duke. Raymond would do anything to keep up with him. If we pretend that Paul's giving a secret party by the lake, I'm sure Raymond will come.' Then his face became troubled. 'Of course, it's cheating, I suppose. It's a lie.'

But Cor was firm about this. 'Bringing Raymond back to the island is like a military campaign. Like a war. In a war, a soldier might have to tell a lie but he'd still be serving his country.'

Ben's plan worked. Melisande knew a siren who worked in Fortlands showing off the dresses, and she 'borrowed' a posh invitation card and Ben pretended that Paul had bribed him to deliver it.

And just before twelve o'clock on Midsummer's Eve, Raymond Trottle, in his jazziest clothes, arrived at the edge of the lake – and found a great throne which the trolls had built for him, and a host of people who raised their arms and hailed him as a prince.

'A prince?' said Raymond. 'Me?'

'Yes, Your Highness,' said the Wizard, and told Raymond the story of his birth.

Raymond listened, and as he did so a smug, self-satisfied smile spread across his face.

'I always knew I was special,' he said. 'I knew it,' – and he climbed on to his throne.

Nine

There had been nothing like it for a hundred years.

The witches had made a circle of protection round the lake which no one could cross; everything inside it was invisible to any stray wanderers. Light came from the flaring torches of the wizards and from the glow-worms which Gurkie had coaxed into the trees – hundreds of them, glimmering and winking like stars. And there were real stars too: the night was clear, the moon shone down calmly on the revels.

'Doesn't it look *beautiful*!' whispered Ben. He hadn't expected to be allowed to watch, but Odge had told him not to be silly.

'Of course you're watching. We'll hide in the shrubbery with the mistmaker; no one will mind you being there.'

And they didn't. It was strange how well Ben fitted in. He spoke to the ghosts as easily as the Islanders and even Odge's aunt, the Old Woman of Gloominess, had patted him on the head without turning him the least bit bald.

The Raymond Trottle Magic Show began with a fly-past of Important Birds.

First a skein of geese flew in perfect formation across the moon, dipping their wings in salute as they passed over the Prince. Next the enchanter who had brought them called up a cloud of coal black ravens who swooped and circled over Raymond's head – and then he stretched out an arm, and from a tree full of nightingales came music so glorious that Ben and Odge vanished for a moment as the mistmaker folded his paws over his chest and sighed.

Last came three dozen snow-white doves which did the most amazing aerial acrobatics and turned to green, to orange, to pink, as the wizards changed the light on their flares. Then one bird left the flock, pulled a sprig of greenery from a laurel bush, flew with it in his beak to Raymond's throne – and laid it in his lap. It was just like this that the dove in the ark had come to Noah and shown him that his troubles were over, and all the watchers were very much moved.

And what did Raymond Trottle say? He said: 'I've seen that on the telly.'

But now the waters of the lake began to shimmer and shine. Then slowly, very slowly – three spouts of water rose from the centre, and on the top of each spout sat a beautiful girl who began to sing and comb her hair.

'Of course, there are far more mermaids than this on the Island, Your Royal Highness,' said Cor who was standing beside the Prince.

Not only more, but of better quality, thought the wizard, who was beginning to realize what Ernie had meant when he said magic wasn't what it was. One of the mermaids came from the Pimlico Swimming Baths and the chlorine in the water hadn't done much for her voice; the second had cut her hair into spikes after a pop group came to give an open air concert by the lake where she lived, so though she could sing, she couldn't really comb. As for the third lady, she was Melisande from the fountain at Fortlands and as she sang and combed, she kept pointing to her feet. No one knew why she minded so much about being taken for a mermaid, but she did.

Everyone clapped when it was over, though Raymond didn't seem very excited, and then Melisande's uncle, whom they called the Plodger, came forward. He was wearing his wellies and the woolly hat he wore to work in the sewers, but he bowed very respectfully to the Prince and said: 'I shall search for the treasure of the lake.'

He then walked to the water's edge . . . plodged into the shallows, kept on till the water came to his waist, his chin, his woolly hat . . . and disappeared!

No one was worried about this because merrows can breathe under water, but they were very interested.

The Plodger was gone a long time and when he came back he was holding a large fish by the tail. The fish was flopping and wriggling and the Plodger, though covered in slime and waterweed, looked pleased.

The wizards and witches whispered among themselves because they knew what was coming, and in the bushes Odge said: 'This is going to be good; he's found a Special Carp!'

The Plodger came right up to Raymond; he still held the fish upside down and the fish went on wriggling and thrashing its tail. Then suddenly it

gave a big hiccup and out of its mouth there came
– a beautiful ring! Swallowing rings is something
certain fish do – one can read about it in the fairy
tales – but finding a fish who has done it when
you're wandering about on the bottom of a grey
and murky lake is really difficult, and from the
watchers there came another burst of clapping.

The Plodger then thanked the fish and threw him
back into the lake and Raymond looked at the ring.

'It isn't gold,' he said. 'It isn't a proper one. You
couldn't get money for it in a shop.'

Cor shook his head and the merrow went off
looking hurt. It was true that the ring had come out
of a Christmas cracker, but what had that to do with
anything? The special fish had trusted him; he had
given up the ring that had been in his stomach for
ten years – the ring that was part of his life as a
fish – and all the Prince wanted to know was if he
could sell it in a shop.

After that came the chorus of banshees. They'd
had a busy week wailing in a football stadium
because they knew that England was going to lose
the European Championship, but they'd taken a
lot of trouble, putting on their white shrouds and
looking properly sinister and sad. And the songs
were sinister and sad too – songs about darkness
and dread and doom and decay.

When the banshees had finished, Raymond
wanted to know if they were going to be sawn in
half.

'There's always people sawn in half when there's
magic on the telly,' he said.

Needless to say, the banshees didn't stay around

after that and Hans came on to do some weight lifting.

The ogre had washed off his fernseed and looked truly splendid in his leather shorts and his embroidered braces and the knee socks with the tassel on the side.

First he picked up a park bench, twirled it over his head, and put it down. Then he plucked out a concrete drinking fountain, balanced it on his nose – and put it back. And then he turned to the statue of Alderman Sir Harold Henfitter which had been put up a month before. The Alderman was cast in bronze and rested on a slab of marble and even Hans had to pull and tug several times before he could free him from the ground.

But he did it. Then he counted to one . . . to two . . . to three . . . and threw the ten ton Alderman into the air!

Everyone waited. They waited and waited but nothing happened. Nothing ever *would* happen – and that was the point, of course. The Alderman had been thrown with such force that he would never come down again. Even now, Sir Harold Henfitter is going round and round somewhere in space and will go on doing so until the end of time.

It is not easy to believe what Raymond did after this amazing trick. He pointed with his fat finger at the giant's midriff. He giggled. And then he said: 'A button's come off his braces!'

No one could believe their ears. Making personal remarks is rude at any time, but at a moment like this! It was true there had been a slight twang as the button went missing – but it was only on one side and the ogre's leather shorts had hardly slipped at all.

Still, the show had to go on. The wizards did some tricks with the weather, making it rain on one side of the lake and snow on the other, and calling up a rumble of thunder with lightning following *afterwards* – and then it was time for refreshments.

Gurkie was in charge of these, and instead of arranging for an ice-cream lady to come with her tray, she had laid on something very special. She ran to the big elm growing by the water and called to the glow-worms to come so that the tree was lit as brightly as on a stage. Then she tapped the bark and spoke softly to the tree – and lo, every one of its branches began to bear fruit. There were peaches like golden moons; apples whose red skins glistened; pears as big as two fists put together.

'We beg Your Highness to refresh himself,' said Gurkie.

Raymond got out of his throne and waddled over to the tree. Then he said: 'I don't like fruit; it's got pips in it. I want a gobstopper.'

Everyone lost heart a little after that. Cor didn't know what a gobstopper was; they hadn't had them when he lived Up Here and even when the troll called Henry Prendergast drew one for him he didn't feel like conjuring one up. There is very little magic done with gobstoppers anywhere in the world – and in the end a kind witch who worked as a school cook got on her bicycle and found an all-night garage which sold sweets and brought one for Raymond who sucked it, moving it from cheek to bulging cheek all through the second part of the show.

This began with Odge's aunt and her sewing circle. There were seven of these Old Women of Gloominess, and though all of them were fierce and hairy, Odge's aunt was definitely the fiercest and the hairiest. The ladies struck each other with baldness, they made newts come out of each other's nostrils; they gave each other chicken pox . . . And in the bushes, Odge sighed.

'Do you think I'll ever be like that?' she asked.

'Of course you will,' said Ben stoutly. 'You've just got to get a little older.'

Gurkie's tree spirits came next. To get a spirit to leave his tree is not easy, but Gurkie had such a way with her that one by one they all stepped out: the old, gnarled spirit of the oak, the tall, grey slightly snooty spirit of the ash; the wavery spirit of the willow . . . The dance they did was as ancient as Stonehenge – only three humans had been allowed to watch it in a thousand years – and Raymond Trottle sat there, moving his gobstopper from side to side – and yawned.

And now came Cor's big moment. He walked to the edge of the lake and the wizards and the witches, the banshees and the trolls all held their breath.

The wizard closed his eyes. He waved his wand and spoke the monster-raising spell . . . and nothing happened. Once more he raised his wand, once more he said the spell . . .

Still nothing . . . Cor's shoulders sagged. He was too old. His power was gone. For the third and last time, the wizard drew on his strength and spoke the magic words. He had turned away, the watchers were shaking their heads – and then there appeared on the waters of the lake a kind of . . . shudder. The shudder was followed by a ripple . . . then a whole ring of ripples, and from the centre of the ring there came . . . slowly, very slowly . . . a head.

It was a large head, and human – but unusual. The head was followed by a neck and the neck was followed by shoulders and a chest, but what came after that was not a man's body, it was the body of a horse.

And everybody remembered what it was that was different about a nuckelavee.

It wasn't that it had a man's head and a horse's body. Animals that are partly people, and people that are partly animals, are two a penny where there is magic. No, what was unusual about the nuckelavee was that he didn't have any skin.

As the monster looked about him, wondering who had called him from the deep, they could see the blood rushing about inside his arteries, and his windpipe taking in air. They could see the curving shape of his stomach as it churned the nuckel's food, even the creature's heart, patiently pumping and pumping, was as clear as if they were seeing it through glass.

No one could take their eyes off him; they were entranced! To be able to see a living body in this way – to be allowed to study the marvellous working of the muscles and nerves and glands – was an honour they could hardly believe, and a young cousin of the troll called Henry Prendergast decided then and there to become a doctor.

Of course, they should have known what was to come. They should have known that Raymond Trottle would spoil this amazing and wonderful moment – a moment so special that none of them forgot it as long as they lived. They should have known that this boy with his bulging cheeks and piggy eyes would hurt and insult this awe-inspiring creature, and he did.

'Eeek!' said Raymond. 'Ugh! It's disgusting; it's creepy. I don't like it!'

Well, that was that, of course. The nuckel sank – and from the onlookers there came a great groan for they knew it would be a hundred years before the monster showed himself again and they could once more study this miracle of nature.

After that there was nothing to do except get to the end. The troll called Henry Prendergast shape-shifted himself into a bank manager and a policeman, and the witches did a few interesting things with toads; and then everybody raised their torches and hailed Raymond as Prince of the Island – and it was done.

'Well, Your Highness,' said Cor, but he spoke without any hope. 'Now do you see what powerful forces you would rule over if you came to the Island? Will you come with us?'

Raymond shrugged. 'Well, I dunno. I don't think I fancy it.' And then. 'You didn't make gold, did you? I thought all wizards could make gold. Can you make it?'

'Certainly we can make it. Your Highness. Any

wizard worth his salt can make gold, but it isn't very interesting to watch.'

'I don't believe you. I don't believe you can do it.'

Cor turned and clapped his hands, and three wizards came to him at once.

'His Highness wishes us to make gold,' he said wearily. 'Find me some base metal – a bit of guttering from a drain pipe . . . an old bicycle wheel . . . anything.'

The wizards vanished and came back with a load of junk metal which they laid on the ground close to Raymond. 'Shall we do it, sir?' they asked because Cor was looking desperately tired. But the old wizard shook his head. 'Just light the fire,' he said.

When it was lit, he bent over it. He didn't even bother to get out his wand or to consult his book of spells. Making gold is something wizards learn to do in the nursery.

Raymond, who had hardly seemed interested when the mermaids sang from a water spout, or the nuckel rose from the deep, couldn't take his eyes from what Cornelius was doing.

The old bicycle wheel, the tin cans glowed . . . flared . . . the flames turned green, turned purple, turned red . . . Cor muttered. Then there was a small thud and the centre of the fire was filled with a mass of molten metal which glinted and glittered in the light of the flares.

'Is that it? Is that really gold?' asked Raymond.

'Yes, Your Highness,' said Cor. He blew on the metal, cooled it and handed it to Raymond.

'And if I come to the Island can you make more of it? As much as I want?'

The wizard nodded. 'Yes, Your Highness.' He could have said that no one used gold on the Island – that they either swopped things or gave them away, but he didn't.

'Then I'll come,' said Raymond Trottle.

Ten

'Hurry up, boy,' said Mr Fulton, giving Ben a push. 'You've got the potatoes to bring in from the cellar still, and there's the brass strip to polish and the milk bottles to swill.'

The butler was a tall, grim man who ruled with a rod of iron and never smiled.

'He's in a dream this morning,' said Mrs Flint. 'I've had to tell him three times to wipe down the stove.' Cooks are often fat and cheerful but she was thin and cross and seemed to hate the food she prepared.

Only the housemaid, Rosita, gave Ben a kind glance. The boy looked thoroughly washed out, as though he hadn't slept.

Rosita was right. Ben had scarcely closed his eyes after he crept in from the park the night before. He was glad, of course, that Raymond had agreed to go with the rescuers; he *had* to be glad. Cor and Gurkie had been so relieved that their job was done, but as he dragged the heavy sack of potatoes up the cellar steps he felt as wretched as he had ever felt in his life.

In half an hour, Raymond would leave the house and never come back. On Monday morning, he went to the house of a Mrs Frankenheimer who gave him exercises to cure his flat feet and knock knees. Mrs Frankenheimer was very easy-going and wouldn't notice if he didn't turn up, and he was going to meet the rescuers at the corner of her street instead of going to school. Just about the time that Ben would be sitting in his classroom and opening his arithmetic book, Raymond would be stepping out on to the sands of the Secret Cove.

As he went to fetch his school bag, Ben's foot bumped against the cat tray under his bed. He had already almost house-trained the mistmaker even in the three days he had hidden him in his room. The animal was incredibly intelligent and the realization that he would never see him again suddenly seemed more than he could bear.

Ben had accepted his life – the early morning chores, the drudgery again when he came home at night, but that was before he had found people who really understood him and were his friends.

And he had quarrelled with Odge.

'You're coming with us, of course,' Odge had said. 'You're coming to the Island.'

And he'd said: 'I can't, Odge.'

The hag had been furious. 'Of course you can. If you're worried about Raymond being such a pain you needn't be because if he isn't any better by the time he's grown up, I'll start a revolution and have his head chopped off; you can rely on that!'

'It isn't Raymond, Odge. I don't care about him. It's my grandmother. She took me in because I had nobody and I can't leave her now she's ill. You must see that.'

But Odge hadn't seen it. She'd stamped her feet and called him names and even when Cor had agreed with Ben and said you had to stand by people who had helped you, she went off in a huff.

Well, it didn't matter now. He'd never see any of them again.

Ben usually liked school but this morning the shabby old building, with the high windows, made him feel as though he was in a trap. And to make things worse, his usual teacher was ill and the student who took over was obviously terrified of kids. It would be uproar all morning, thought Ben – and he was right.

At break he didn't join his friends but went off on his own to a corner of the play-yard. You had to take one day at a time when things were bad, Nanny had said. 'You can always take just one more step, Ben,' she told him, but today it seemed as though the steps would lead down the greyest, dreariest road he could imagine.

There was a grating in the asphalt, covering a drain, and he crouched down beside it, wondering if the Plodger was somewhere near by in his wellies . . . and that made him think of Melisande and the nuckel with his interesting face . . . Well, that was over, and for ever. He'd never see magic again, not an ordinary boy like him.

For a moment, he wondered whether to change his mind. The gump was still open. The rescuers had trusted him; they had told him where it was. They hadn't told Raymond, but they'd told him. He closed his eyes and saw the three-masted sailing ship parting the waves . . . saw the green hump of the Island with its golden sands, and the sun shining on the roofs of the palace . . .

Then the picture vanished and there was another picture in its stead. An old woman lying in a high hospital bed, shrunken, ill, watching for him as he came down the ward.

The teacher blew her whistle. The children began to stream back into the building, but Ben still lingered.

Then he looked up. A small girl was coming across the road towards him. She wore an old-fashioned blazer; her thick black hair was yanked into two pigtails, and she was scowling.

Ben scrambled to his feet. He tried to be sensible – he really tried – but a lump had come into his throat and he stretched his hand through the bars like a prisoner.

'Oh, Odge,' he said. 'I am so *terribly* pleased to see you!'

Raymond had not kept his promise. He had not turned up at the corner of Mrs Frankenheimer's street as he said he would. They had waited and waited, but he had not come.

'We should have known that the pig boy would double cross us,' said Odge. 'The others are in an awful state. Gurkie keeps saying that if she'd been a fuath it wouldn't have happened, which is perfectly ridiculous.'

'What's a fuath?'

'Oh, some really vile swamp fairy with all sorts of nasty habits. And the giant keeps talking about bopping and sacking and how it was all his fault because he didn't – and the wizard looks about two hundred years old. He really loves the King and Queen.'

'But where is Raymond, then?'

'Well, that's it; nobody knows. He's not in the house – the ghosts have haunted all over. Mrs Trottle's gone as well – Ernie thinks that Raymond must have blabbed and she's done a bunk with him. And it's serious, Ben. There are only five more days till the Closing. He's got to be found.'

Ben drew himself up to his full height, and the hag thought how fearless he looked suddenly, how strong. 'Don't worry, Odge. We'll find him; I absolutely know we will.'

Ernie was right. Raymond had blabbed. When his mother came to wake him and told him to hurry or he'd be late for Mrs Frankenheimer, Raymond yawned and said: 'I don't have to go to Mrs Frankenheimer again. Not ever.'

Mrs Trottle sat down on the edge of his bed, sending waves of Maneater over the coverlet, and put her pudgy hand on Raymond's forehead.

'Now, don't be difficult, sweetikins. You know Mrs Frankenheimer is going to make your feet all beautiful – and you really can't miss school again. The headmaster was quite cross last week. Just think if you were expelled and had to go to a common school with ordinary children.'

Raymond stretched his arms behind his head and smirked. 'I don't have to go to school again either. I'm never going to school any more. I'm a prince.'

'Well, of course, you're a prince to your Mummy,

dear,' said Mrs Trottle, giving him a lipsticky kiss. 'But—'

'Not that kind of prince; I'm really one. I'm going to go away and rule over hundreds of people on a secret island.'

'Yes, dear,' said Mrs Trottle. 'That's a very nice dream you've had but now please get dressed.'

'It's not a dream,' said Raymond crossly. 'They told me. The old man in the park. And the lady with the beetroot in her hat. I'm going to be a famous ruler and I don't have to do anything I don't want to ever again.'

Mrs Trottle went on tutting and taking no notice. Then as she picked up Raymond's jacket, which he had thrown on the floor, she noticed grass stains on it, and in his buttonhole, a spray of ivy. Her eyes narrowed.

'Raymond! What is the meaning of this? You've been out after I put you to bed!'

Raymond shrugged. 'You can't tell me what to do now,' he said. 'And Dad can't either because I'm a prince and they're coming to show me the secret way back this morning.'

Mrs Trottle now became very alarmed. She hurried into Mr Trottle's dressing room and said: 'Landon, I think Raymond's in danger. People have been giving him drugs – dreadful drugs – to make him believe all sorts of things. It's a plot to kidnap him and hold us up to ransom, I'm sure of it.'

'Nonsense,' said Mr Trottle, stepping into his trousers. 'Who would want to kidnap Raymond?'

This was not a fatherly thing to say, but Mr Trottle's mind was on the bank.

'Anyone who knows we're rich. I'm serious. They've persuaded him that he's a prince so as to lure him away.'

'Well, he isn't, is he?' said Mr Trottle.

'Landon, will you please listen to me. I'm very worried.'

'Then why don't you contact the police?'

'Certainly not!' There were all sorts of reasons why Mrs Trottle didn't want the police snooping around in Trottle Towers. Then suddenly: 'I'm going to take Raymond away. I'm going into hiding. Now. This instant. You can stay here and change the locks and look out for anything sinister.'

She wouldn't wait a minute longer. Mrs Trottle was a stupid woman but when it came to protecting her son, she could move like greased lightning. Taking no notice as Raymond snivelled and whined and said he was a prince, he really was, she packed a suitcase. Half an hour later, she and Raymond drove away in a taxi, and no one who worked in Trottle Towers knew where they had gone.

The search for Raymond went on all that day and well into the next.

Everyone helped. The Ghosts of the Gump got in touch with the ghosts in all the other railway stations and soon there wasn't a train which drew out of London without a spectre gliding down the carriages looking for a fat boy with a wobble in his walk and his even wobblier mother.

The mermaids and the water nymphs checked out the river boats in case the Trottles meant to escape by sea. The enchanter's special pigeons flew the length and breadth of the land delivering notes to road workers and garage men who might have seen the Trottles' car – and the train spotter called Brian (the one who got between the buffers and the 9.15 from Peterborough) sat all day by the computer at Heathrow, checking the passenger lists, though electricity is about the worst thing that can happen to a spectre's ectoplasm.

Ben had not returned to school after Odge came for him. He'd asked the headmaster for the afternoon off and because he'd looked so peaky when he first came, the head had agreed.

'Don't come back till you're properly well,' he had said – and that was something he didn't say to a lot of children.

But though Ben searched Trottle Towers for clues and tried to get what he could out of the servants, he too drew a blank. Mr Trottle had returned at lunchtime with a locksmith and told everyone that his wife and son would be away for a long time. And that was all that anybody could discover.

Ben's first thought was that Mrs Trottle had taken Raymond to her home in Scotland, but one of the banshees, who came from Glasgow, telephoned the station master at Achnasheen and he swore there was no sign of the Trottles.

'You'd notice them soon enough,' he'd said, 'with their posh kilts they've got no right to wear, and their bossy ways.'

The rescuers had returned to the summer house which now became the headquarters of the search. They had bought some blankets, and a primus and kettle, and some folding chairs – and Hans had painted up the notice saying PRIVATE: NO ADMITTANCE which blocked the path. Fortunately the Head Keeper was on holiday so nobody disturbed them, but just to make sure Gurkie had spoken to the bushes who grew so thick and tangled that anybody passing by could see nothing. She had planted out the beetroot from her hat because people did seem to stare rather, and to stop it being lonely she had made a vegetable patch from which huge leeks and lettuces erupted. And a pink begonia on the other side of the lake had made such a fuss because it wanted to be near her that she'd moved it so as to grow beside the wooden steps.

But even though she could feed everyone and make them comfortable, Gurkie still worried dreadfully and thought she should have been a fuath.

'No, you shouldn't, Gurkie,' said Ben firmly. 'You being a fuath, whatever that is, is a perfectly horrible idea and it wouldn't have helped at all.'

Nor would he let the giant moan on because he hadn't bopped and sacked the Prince.

'Raymond'll be found, I'm absolutely sure of it,' said Ben.

Ben was changing, thought Odge; he was becoming someone to rely on. She watched as he put down a bowl of milk for the mistmaker. The animal had taken to lurching after Ben wherever he went and making offended noises when he wasn't immediately scratched on the stomach or picked up and spoken to. There was going to be a fuss from the mistmaker when they had to go back and part from Ben, thought Odge, and she wondered whether she should kill Ben's grandmother. Killing people was the sort of thing hags were meant to do but it had not been allowed on the Island and without any practice it was probably a bad idea.

But what mattered now was finding Raymond. All that afternoon, all the evening and well into the night, they searched and searched – the wizards and the witches, the ghosts and the banshees and the trolls ... and as soon as day broke they began again – but it was beginning to look as though Raymond and his mother had vanished from the face of the earth.

Eleven

The Queen leant out of her bedroom window. She leant out so far that she would have fallen but for a dwarf whom the King had put in charge of holding her feet. He had been holding her feet for days now because she did nothing except look out to sea and watch for the three-masted ship.

'Oh, where is it?' she said for the hundredth time. 'Why doesn't it come?'

There were men all over the Island peering through telescopes, the dolphins searched the seas, and the talking birds – the minahs and the parrots – were never out of the air. The instant the ship was sighted, rockets would flare up, but the Queen went on watching, her long hair streaming over the sill, as though by doing so she could will her son to come to her.

But the dwarf now sighed – he was growing tired – and the Queen dragged herself away and went into the next room which she had prepared for the Prince. His old, white-curtained cradle still stood in the corner, but the palace carpenters had made him a beautiful bed of cedar wood and a carved desk and a bookcase because she knew without being told that the Prince would love to read. She hadn't made the room fussy, but the carpet, with its pattern of mythical beasts and flowers, had taken seven years to make – and there was a wide window seat so that he could sit and look out over the waters of the bay.

But would he ever sit there? Would she ever come in and see his bright head turn towards her?

The King, coming into the room, found her in tears again.

'Come, my dear,' he said, putting his arms round her, 'there are five days still for the rescuers to bring him back.'

But the Queen wouldn't be comforted. 'Let me go to the Secret Cove, at least,' she begged. 'Let me wait there for him.'

The King shook his head. 'What can you do there, my love? You would only fret and worry and your people need you.'

'I would be closer to him. I would be near.'

The King said nothing. He was afraid of letting his wife go near the mouth of the gump. If she lost her head and went through it, he could lose her as he had lost his son.

'Try to have patience,' he begged her. 'Try to be brave.'

The King and Queen were not the only people on the Island to worry and grow afraid. The school-children had been given a holiday during the nine days of the opening, but they had decorated the school with flowers and hung up banners saying WELCOME TO THE PRINCE. Now the flowers were wilting, the banners hung limp after a shower of rain. The bakers who had baked huge, three-tiered cakes for the welcoming banquet began to prod them with skewers, wondering if they were going stale and they should start again. The housewives who had ironed their best dresses, shook them out and ironed them all over again because they'd grown crumpled.

As for the nurses in the cave, they had ordered a crate of green bananas before the Opening so that the second the ship was sighted they could rip it open and help themselves to the firm, just ripened fruit – but when no news came they nailed it up again and now they were back to wailing and eating burnt toast.

Then that night the square began to fill up with some very strange people.

There had been rumours, quite early on, of discontent in the north of the island. Not just the kind of grumbling you always get from people who have not been chosen for a job they are sure they could do. Not just Odge's sisters complaining because their baby sister had been chosen and not them. Not just grumpy giants saying, what do you expect, sending a milksop who yodels to bring back the Prince? No . . . this was more serious discontent, and from creatures that were to be reckoned with.

And that evening, the evening of the fourth day of the Opening, they came, these discontented people of the north. They came in droves, filling the grassy square in front of the palace, and turned their faces up to the windows, and waited . . .

Strange faces they were too: the blue-black faces of the neckies with their lop-sided feet . . . the slavering-tongued sky yelpers, those air-borne hell hounds with their saucer eyes and fiery tongues, and the squint-eyed faces of the harridans.

There were hags in the square who made Odge's sisters look like tinsel fairies; there was a bagworm as long as a railway carriage; there was even a brollachan – one of those shapeless blobs who crawl over the ground like cold jellies and can envelop anyone who gets in the way.

And there were the harpies! They had elbowed their way to the front, these monstrous women with the wings and claws of birds – and even the fiercest creatures who waited with them, gave them a wide berth.

'Tell them to choose a spokesperson and we will hear what they have to say,' said the King.

But he knew why they had come and what they had to say, for these creatures of the North were as much his subjects as any ordinary school child or tender-hearted fey. Not only that, they were useful. They were the police people. There was no prison on the Island – there was no need for one. No burglar would burgle twice if it meant a hell hound flying in through his window and taking pieces out of his behind. Any drunken youth going on the rampage soon sobered up after a squint-eyed har-ridan landed on his chest and squeezed his stomach so as to give him awful dreams – and you only had to say the word 'harpy' to the most evil-minded crook and he went straight then and there.

And it was a harpy – the chief harpy – who pushed the others aside and came in to stand before the King.

She called herself Mrs Smith, but she wasn't married and it would have been hard to think of anyone who would have wanted to sit up in bed beside her drinking tea. The harpy's face was that of a bossy lady politician, the kind that comes on the telly to tell you not to eat the things you like and do something different with your money. Her brassy permed hair was strained back from her forehead and combed into tight curls, her beady eyes were set on either side of a nose you could have cut cheese with and her mouth was puckered like a badly sewn button hole. A string of pearls was wound round her neck; a handbag dangled from her arm and she wore a crimplene stretch top tucked into dark green bloomers with a frill round the bottom.

But from under the bloomers there came the long, scaly legs and frightful talons of a bird of prey, and growing out of her back, piercing the crimplene, was a pair of black wings which gave out a strange, rank smell.

'I have come about the Prince,' said Mrs Smith in a high, piercing voice. 'I am disgusted by the way this rescue has been handled. Appalled. Shocked. All of us are.'

Harpies have been around for hundreds of years. In the old days they were called the Snatchers because they snatched people's food away so that they starved to death, or fouled it to make it uneatable. And it wasn't just food they snatched in their dreadful claws; harpies were used as punishers, carrying people away to dreadful tortures in the underworld.

Mrs Smith patted her hair and opened her handbag.

'No!' said the King and put up his hand. The

handbags of harpies are too horrible to describe. Inside is their make-up – face powder, lipstick, scent ... But what make-up! Their powder smells of the insides of slaughtered animals, and one drop of their perfume can send a whole army reeling backwards. 'Not in the palace,' he went on sternly.

Even Mrs Smith obeyed the King. She shut her bag, but once again began to complain.

'Obviously that feeble fey and wonky wizard have failed; one could hardly expect anything else. And frankly my patience is exhausted. Everyone's patience is exhausted. I insist that I am sent with my helpers to bring back the Prince.'

'What makes you so sure that you can find him?' asked the King.

The harpy twiddled her pearls. 'I have my methods,' she said. 'And I promise he won't escape us.' She lifted one leg, opened her talons, covered in their sick-making black nail varnish, and closed them again – and the Queen buried her face in her hands. 'As you see, my assistants are ready and waiting.' She waved her arm in the direction of the window and sure enough there were four more loathsome harpies, like vultures with handbags, standing in the light of the lamp. 'I'll take a few of the dogs as well and you'll see, the boy will be back in no time.'

By 'dogs' she meant the dreaded sky yelpers with their fiery breath and slavering jaws.

The Queen had turned white and fallen back in her chair. She thought of Gurkie with her gentle, loving ways ... of Odge showing them the baby mistmaker she meant to give to the Prince . . . And old Cor, so proud to do this last service for the court. Why had they failed her? And how could she bear it if her son was snatched by bossy and evil-smelling women?

Yet how long could they still delay?

The King now spoke.

'We will wait for one more day,' he said. 'If the Prince has not been returned by midnight to-morrow, I will send for you all and choose new rescuers to find him. Till then everyone must return to their homes so that the Queen can sleep.'

But when the Northerners had flown and slith-ered and hopped away, the King and Queen did anything but sleep. All night long, they stared at the darkness and thought with grief and longing and despair of their lost son.

Twelve

Mrs Trottle was in the bath. It was an enormous bath shaped like a sea shell. All round the edge of the tub were little cut-glass dishes to hold different kinds of soap and a gold-plated rack stretched across the water so that she could rest her box of chocolates on it, and her body lotions, and the sloppy love story she was reading. On the shelf above her head was a jar of pink bath crystals which smelled of roses, and a jar of green crystals which smelled of fern, and a jar of yellow crystals which smelled of lemon verbena, but the crystals she had put into the water were purple and smelled of violets. Mrs Trottle's face was covered in a gunge of squashed strawberries which was supposed to make her look young again; three heated bath towels waited on the rail.

'Ta-ra-ra *Boom*-de-ray!' sang Mrs Trottle, lathering her round, pink stomach.

She felt very pleased with herself for she had foiled the kidnappers who were after her darling Raymond. She had outwitted the gang; they would never find her babykins now. They would expect her to go to Scotland or to France, but she had been too clever for them. The hiding place she had found was as safe as houses – and so comfortable!

Mrs Trottle chose another chocolate and added

more hot water with her magenta-painted toe. Next door she could hear the rattle of dice as Raymond played ludo with one of his bodyguards. She'd told Bruce that he had to let Raymond win and he seemed to be doing what he was told. The poor little fellow always cried when he lost at ludo and she was paying the guards enough.

Reaching for the long-handled brush, she began to scrub her back. Landon was staying at home to find out what he could about the kidnappers. They would probably go on watching the house and once she knew who they were she could hire some thugs to get rid of them. That was the nice thing about being rich; there was nothing you couldn't do.

And that reminded her of Ben. She'd rung the hospital and though they never told you what you wanted to know, it didn't look as though Nanny Brown was ever coming out again. The second the old woman was out of the way, she'd move against Ben. Thinking of Ramsden Hall up in the Midlands, made her smile. They took only difficult children; children that needed breaking in. There'd be no nonsense there about Ben going on too long with his schooling. The second he was old enough he'd be sent to work in a factory or a mine.

How she hated the boy! Why could he read years before Raymond? Why was he good at sport when her babykin found it so hard? And the way Ben had looked at her, when he was little, out of those big eyes. Well, she'd found a place where they'd put a stop to all that!

As for Raymond, she'd frightened him so thoroughly that there was no question of him wandering off again. He knew now that all the things he thought he'd seen in the park, and earlier in his bedroom, were due to the drugs he had been given.

'There's nothing people like that won't do to you if they get you in their clutches,' she'd said to him. 'Cut off your ear ... chain you to the floor ...'

She'd hated alarming her pussykin, but Raymond would obey her now.

What a splendid place this was, thought Mrs Trottle, dribbling soapy water over her thighs. Everything was provided. And yet ... perhaps the violet bath crystals weren't quite strong enough? Perhaps she should add something of her own; something she had brought from home? Sitting up, she reached for the bottle of Maneater on the bathroom stool. The man who mixed it for her had promised no one else had a scent like that.

'You're the only lady in the world, dear Mrs Trottle, who smells like this,' he'd said to her.

Upending the bottle, she poured the perfume generously into the water. Yes, that was it! Now she felt like her true and proper self.

She leant back and reached for her book. The hero was just raining kisses on the heroine's crimson lips. Mr Trottle never rained kisses on her lips, he never rained anything.

For another quarter of an hour, Mrs Trottle lay happily soaking and reading.

Then she pulled out the plug.

The Plodger liked his job. He didn't mind the smell of the sewage; it was a natural smell, nothing fancy

112

about it, but it belonged. He liked the long dark tunnels, and the quiet, and the clever way the water-courses joined each other and branched out. He could tell exactly where he was – under which street or square or park – just from the way the pipes ran. It was a good feeling knowing he could walk along twenty feet under Piccadilly Circus and not be bothered by the traffic and the hooting and the silly people trying to cross the road.

It wasn't a bad living either. It was amazing what people lost down the loo or the plughole of a bath, especially on a Saturday night. Not alligators – the stories about alligators in the sewers were mostly rubbish – but earrings or cigarette lighters or spectacles. His father had been in the same line of business, and his grandfather before him: flushers they were called, the people who made a living from the drains. Of course, having some fish blood helped – that's what merrows were, people who'd married things that lived in water. Not that there had been any tails in the family; merrows and mermen are *not* the same. Melisande was quite right to be proud of her feet; tails were a darned nuisance. No one could work the sewers with a tail.

Thinking about Melisande brought a frown to the Plodger's whiskery face. Melisande was all churned up. She'd got very fond of the fey – of all the rescuers – and now she worried because they couldn't find that dratted boy. All yesterday they'd searched and they were at it again today, scuttling about up there, but there wasn't any news.

Over his woolly hat the Plodger wore a helmet with a little light in it and now, bending down, he saw a pink necklace bobbing in the muck. Not real – he could see that at once; plastic, but a pretty thing. It would fetch a few pence when it was cleaned up and that was good enough for him; he wasn't greedy. Scooping it up in his long-handled net, he tramped on along the ledge beside the stream of sludge. He was near the Thames now, but he wouldn't go under it, not today. There were good pickings sometimes from the busy street that ran beside the river.

He turned right, plodded through a storm relief chamber, and made his way along one of the oldest tunnels close to Waterloo Bridge. You could tell how old it was with the brickwork being so neat and careful. No one made bricks like that nowadays.

Then suddenly he stopped, and sniffed. His snout-like nose was wrinkled, his mouth was pursed up in disgust. Something different had just come down. Something horrid and yucky and *wrong*. Something that didn't belong among the natural, wholesome smell of the drains.

'Ugh!' said the Plodger, and shook his head as though he could escape the sickly odour. A rat scuttled past him and he fancied that it was running away from the gooey smell just as he wanted to do himself. Rats were sensible. You could trust them.

It wasn't just nasty – it was familiar. He'd smelled it before, that sweet, overpowering, clinging smell.

But where? He thought for a moment, standing on the ledge beside the slowly moving sludge. Yes, he remembered now. Not here – in quite a different part of the town.

He was excited now. Moving forward he exam-

114

ined the inlet a few paces ahead. Yes; that was where it was coming from, running down in a slurp of bath water. He tilted his head so as to shine the torch down the pipe, making sure he knew exactly where he was.

Then he turned back and hurried away, turning left, right . . . left again. A lipstick case bobbed up quite near him – brand new it looked too – but he wouldn't stop.

Half an hour later, he was lifting the manhole cover on the path between the Serpentine and the summer house inside the park.

No one, at first, could believe the wonderful news. They stood round the Plodger and stared at him with shining eyes.

'You really mean it? You've found the Prince?' asked Gurkie, holding a leek which had sprung out of the ground before she could stop it.

The Plodger nodded. 'Leastways, I've found his mother.'

'But how?' Cornelius was completely bewildered. Surely the Trottles weren't hiding in the sewer?

The Plodger answered with a single word.

'Maneater,' he said.

'Maneater?' The wizard shook out his ear trumpet, sure he had misheard.

'That rubbishy scent Mrs Trottle uses. It's got a kick like a mule. I used to smell it when I worked the drains under Trottle Towers. And just now I smelled it again.'

The ring of faces stared at him, breathless with suspense.

115

'Where – oh, please tell us? Where?' begged Gurkie.

'I can tell you for certain,' said the Plodger with quiet pride, 'because I followed the outlet right back. It came from the Astor. That's where Mrs Trottle's taken Raymond. She's holed up here in London, and in as clever a place as you can find. Getting the perisher out of there'll be like getting him out of Fort Knox.'

The Astor was a hotel, but it was not an ordinary one. It was a super, luxury, five star, incredibly grand hotel. The front of the hotel faced a wide street with elegant shops and night clubs, and the back of the hotel looked out over the river Thames with its bridges and passing boats. Gentlemen were only allowed to have tea in the Astor lounge if they were wearing a tie, and the women who danced in the ballroom wore dresses which cost as much as a bus driver earned in a year. The Astor had its own swimming pool and gym and in the entrance hall were show cases with one crocodile-skin shoe in them, or a diamond bracelet, and there was a flower shop and a hairdresser and a beauty salon so that you never had to go outside at all.

Best of all was the famous Astor cake. This was not a real cake; not the kind you eat. It was a huge cake made out of plywood, painted pink and decorated with curly bits that looked like icing – and every night while the guests were at dinner, it was wheeled into the restaurant and a beautiful girl jumped out of it and danced!

Needless to say, ordinary people didn't stay in a

116

hotel like that. It was pop stars and business tycoons and politicians and oil sheiks who came to the Astor, and people of that kind are usually afraid. Pop stars are afraid of fans who will rush up to them and tear their clothes, and politicians are afraid of being shot at by people they have bullied, and oil sheiks and business tycoons like to do their work in secret.

So the Astor had the best security service in the world. Guards with arm bands and walkie talkies patrolled the corridors, there were burglar alarms everywhere and bomb-proof safes in the basement where the visitors could keep their jewels. Best of all there was a special penthouse on the roof built of reinforced concrete and the rooms in it had extra thick walls and secret numbers and lifts which came up inside them so that they weren't used by the other guests at all. What's more, the penthouse was built round a helicopter pad so that these incredibly important people could fly in and out of the hotel without being seen by anyone down in the street.

And it was one of these secret rooms – Number 202 – which Mrs Trottle had rented for herself and Raymond. Actually, it wasn't one room: it was a whole apartment with a luxurious sitting room and a bedroom with twin beds so that Mrs Trottle could watch over her babykin even when he slept. Even so, she had checked into the hotel under a different name. She'd called herself Lavinia Tarbuck and Raymond was Roland Tarbuck and both of them wore dark glasses so that they stumbled a lot, but felt important.

Although the Astor bristled with security men,

Mrs Trottle had hired two bodyguards specially for Raymond. Bruce Trout was a fat man with a pony tail, but the fatness wasn't wobbly like Raymond's; it was solid like lard. His teeth had rotted years ago because he never cleaned them and his false ones didn't fit, so they weren't often in his mouth. They were usually behind the teapot or under the sofa. Not that it mattered. If there was trouble, Bruce could kill someone even without his teeth and had done so many times.

But it was the other bodyguard that was the most feared and famous one in London. Doreen Trout was Bruce's sister, but she couldn't have been more different. She was small and mousy with a bun of grey hair and weak blue eyes behind round spectacles. Doreen wore lumpy tweed skirts and thick stockings – and more than anything, she loved to knit. She knitted all day long: purple cardigans and pink bootees and heather mixture ankle socks . . . Clackety-click, clickety-clack, went Doreen's needles from morning to night – and they were sharp, those needles. Incredibly sharp.

There are certain places in the human body which are not covered by bones and someone who knows exactly where these soft places are does not need to bother with a gun. A really sharp needle is much less messy and scarcely leaves a mark.

Bruce was costing Mrs Trottle a hundred pounds a day, but for Soft Parts Doreen, as they called her, she had to pay double that.

Mrs Trottle had made a good job of scaring Raymond. He believed her when she said that everything he'd seen in the park and in his bedroom had been due to dangerous drugs that the kidnappers had put into his food, and when she told him not to move a step without his bodyguards, he did what he was told.

Life in the Astor suited Raymond. He liked the silver trolley that came in with his breakfast, and the waiters calling him 'sir', and he liked not having his father there. Mr Trottle sometimes seemed to think that Raymond wasn't absolutely perfect and this hurt his son. Best of all, Raymond Trottle liked not having to go to school.

Because the bodyguards were so careful, Mrs Trottle soon allowed her son to leave his room. So he sat and giggled in the jacuzzi beside the swimming pool and went to the massage parlour with his mother and bought endless boxes of chocolate from the shop in the entrance hall. In the afternoon, the Trottles ate cream cakes in the Palm Court Lounge which had palm trees in tubs, and a fountain, and at night (still followed by the bodyguards) they went to the restaurant for dinner and watched the girl come out of the Astor cake.

She was a truly beautiful girl and the dance she did was called the Dance of the Seven Veils. When she first jumped out she was completely covered in shimmering gold, but as she danced she dropped off her first veil . . . and then the next . . . and the next one and the next. When she was down to the last layer of cloth, all the lights went out – and when they came on again both the girl and the cake had gone.

Raymond couldn't take his eyes off her. He thought he would marry a girl like that when he grew up but when he said so to his mother, she told him not to be silly.

'Girls who come out of cakes are common,' said Mrs Trottle.

What she liked was the man who played the double bass. He had a soaring moustache and black soulful eyes and he called himself Roderigo de Roque, but his real name was Neville Potts. Mr Potts had a wife and five children whom he loved very much, but the hotel manager had told him that he must smile at the ladies sitting close by so as to make them feel good, and so he did.

Mrs Trottle liked him so much that on the second night she decided to go downstairs again after Raymond was in bed and listen to him play.

First though, she put a call through to her husband.

'Have you done what I told you? About Ben?'

'Yes.' Mr Trottle sounded tired. 'Are you sure . . .?'

'Yes, I'm perfectly sure,' snapped Mrs Trottle. 'Tell the servants he may leave very suddenly and I don't want any talk about it.' She paused for a moment, tapping her fingers on the table. It was important that there weren't any bumps or bruises on the boy when he was taken away. 'You can tell them to let him off his work till then – and remember, Ben is to be told *nothing*. What about the kidnappers – any sign of them?'

'No.'

'Well, go on watching,' said Mrs Trottle. Then she sprayed herself with Maneater and went downstairs to make eyes at Mr Potts as he sawed away on his double bass and wished it was time to go home.

Thirteen

Absolutely everyone wanted to help in rescuing Raymond from the Astor. The ghosts wanted to, and so did the banshees and the troll called Henry Prendergast – and Melisande sent a message to say that she was moving into the fountain in the Astor so as to keep an eye on things.

But before they could make a plan to snatch the Prince, there was something they felt had to be done straightaway, and that was to send a message to the Island.

'They'll be getting so worried, the poor King and Queen,' said Gurkie. 'And even if everything goes smoothly it could take another two days to get Raymond out. If they thought he was lost or hurt it would break their hearts.'

But how to do this? Ernie offered to go through the gump again and speak to the sailors in the Secret Cove, but Cor shook his head.

'Your poor ectoplasm has suffered enough,' he said.

This was true. There is nothing worse for ecto-plasm than travelling in a wind basket and using ghosts as messengers is simply cruel.

Luck, however, was on their side. The nice witch who worked as a school cook and had fetched Ray-mond's gobstopper during the Magic Show, had decided to go through the gump immediately and make her home on the Island. She'd gone to work on Monday morning and been told she was being made redundant because the school had to save money and she didn't think there was any point in hanging about Up Here without any work.

'I don't say as I like Raymond because I don't, but I dare say by the time he's on the throne I'll be under the sod,' she said, coming to say goodbye.

Needless to say she was very happy to take a message to the sailors in the Secret Cove, so that problem was solved.

'Tell them there is nothing to worry about. The Prince is found and we hope to bring him very soon,' said Cor, who actually thought there was quite a lot to worry about, such as how to get into the Astor, how to bop and sack the detestable boy, how to carry the wriggling creature to the gump. But he was determined not to upset the King and Queen.

So the witch, whose name was Mrs Frampton, said she would certainly tell them that, and made her way to King's Cross Station, and in no time at all she was stepping out on to the sands of the Secret Cove.

No one can be a school cook and work with children and be gloomy, and Mrs Frampton was perhaps more cheerful than she needed to be. At all events, the message that a sailor (travelling like the wind in a pinnace) carried back to the Island was so encouraging, that the Queen started to laugh once more and the school children put fresh flowers in the classroom and everyone rejoiced. Any day now, any hour, the Prince would come! The nurses opened the crate of bananas again – and most importantly, the harpies and the sky yelpers and all the other dark people of the North were told that they would not be needed; that the Prince was found, and coming, and all was wonderfully well!

By the second day of watching Raymond, Bruce was thoroughly fed up. When you are a thug and used to being with gangsters, you aren't choosy, but he'd never met a boy who opened a whole box of chocolates and guzzled it in front of someone else without offering a single one. Bruce didn't like the way Raymond whined when he looked like being beaten at ludo and he thought a boy sending up for someone to give him a massage when he hadn't taken any exercise was thoroughly weird.

All the same, Bruce did his job. He never let Raymond out of his sight, he kept his gun in its holster, he tasted the food that was sent up in case it was poisoned – and each morning he went into the bathroom as soon as Raymond woke so as to make sure there were no crazed drug fiends lurking behind the tub or in the toilet.

Now, though, he came out looking rather pale.

'There's something funny in there. It felt sort of cold, and the curtain moved, I'm sure of it.'

Doreen Trout went on knitting. She knitted as soon as she woke. This morning it was a pair of baby's bootees – very pretty, they were, in pink moss stitch, and the steel of the needles glinted in the sun.

'Rubbish,' she said. 'You're imagining things.'

She got up and went into the bathroom. Her empty needle flashed. She waited. No screams followed, no blood oozed from behind the pierced curtains.

'You see,' she said. 'There's nobody there.'

But she was wrong. Mrs Partridge was there, and a nasty time she was having of it. She was a shy ghost and hated nakedness, but she had set herself to haunt the Trottles' sleeping quarters and get the lay-out, and though the sight of Mrs Trottle in her underwear spraying Maneater into her armpits had made her feel really sick, she was determined to stick to her job.

Mrs Partridge was not the only person watching the Trottles. Cor had decided that a day spent studying their movements was necessary before a proper plan to rescue Raymond could be made. So Ernie was floating through the kitchen quarters looking for the exits, peering at the switch boards which controlled the lights . . . The troll called Henry Prendergast, disguised as a waiter, loaded Raymond's breakfast trolley . . .

And there were others. Down in the laundry room, an immensely sad lady had got herself taken on as a temporary laundry maid and wept a little as she counted the sheets and studied the chute which sent the dirty washing down into the basement. She didn't cry because she was particularly troubled, but because she was a banshee, and weeping is what banshees do.

By ten-thirty, Raymond said he was bored.

'I want to go and buy something,' he said.

So the Trottles went down in the lift with their

124

bodyguards and Raymond went into the gift shop in the hotel and grumbled.

'They haven't got the comic I want. And the toys are rubbish.'

Mrs Trottle went shopping too. She decided to buy a beautiful red rose to tuck into her bosom at dinner so that the double bass player would notice it and smile at her.

The flower shop though looked different today, and the lady who served in it seemed to be puzzled.

'Everything's taken off,' she said. 'Look at that rubber plant – I'll swear it's grown a foot in the night. And that wreath . . . it's twice the size it was.'

The wreath was made of greenery and lilies. The hotel always kept wreaths because a lot of the people who stayed at the Astor were old and had friends who died.

Mrs Trottle bent her head to smell a lily, wondering if the double bass player would prefer her with one of those – and jerked her head back. If it wasn't impossible, she'd have said that someone had pinched her nose.

Someone had. Flower fairies look much like they do in the pictures: very, very small with gauzy wings – but they are incredibly bad tempered because of people sticking their faces into the places where they live and *sniffing*. Seeing the hairy insides of someone's nostrils is not amusing, and though this particular fairy had offered to go to the Astor and help Gurkie, she certainly wasn't going to be *smelled*.

By lunch time, the secret watchers were feeling thoroughly gloomy. It wasn't just that the body-

125

guards never let Raymond out of their sight, it was that Raymond himself was such a horrible boy. But it was Melisande who found out just what they were up against in rescuing him.

She had got her uncle to move her into the fountain in the Palm Court and she was not having a nice time. This was because of the goldfish. In the Fortlands fountain she had been alone. Here she had to share with a dozen, droopy, goggle-eyed fantailed goldfish who flapped their tails in her face and dirtied the water with their droppings and their food.

But Melisande was a trooper. She peeped out from under the leaves, she watched Raymond and Mrs Trottle guzzle a slab of fudge cake not an hour after they had finished breakfast; she watched the daft way Mrs Trottle leered at the double bass player when the orchestra played for the guests at tea.

And she watched as Doreen Trout came over to the fountain, sat down on the rim and – with her eyes still fixed on Raymond – took out her knitting bag.

'Knit two, slip one,' murmured Doreen.

Then she turned slightly – so slightly that Melisande hardly noticed it – and one of her needles plunged down into the water.

It was all over in a second and then she got up and went back to stand beside Raymond – but the fan-tailed goldfish she had speared lay floating, belly up, between the leaves while his life's blood, draining away, came down on Melisande's shocked and bewildered head.

There was only one thing that cheered up the hidden watchers – and that was the cake!

The cake was beautiful! The way it came in, all pink and glowing, from a door beside the orchestra, the balloons and streamers that came down on top of it . . . and the lovely girl who burst out of it and danced, tossing away her golden veils, while the band played music so dreamy and romantic that it made you weep.

And it was the cake which gave Cor his idea.

All day the watchers had reported to him where he sat in the summer house with his briefcase beside him, taking notes, making maps of the hotel and the street outside – and thinking. Now he was ready to speak.

It was close on midnight and everyone had come to listen. The Plodger had brought Melisande, carrying her wrapped in a wet towel, and now she sat in the bird bath looking worried because she felt no one knew quite how dreadful Doreen Trout could be. The ghosts hovered on the steps, the troll called Henry Prendergast lay back in a deck chair eating a leek which Gurkie had put into his hand. He did not care for leeks but he cared for Gurkie and was doing his best with it. Ben had crept out of Trottle Towers, and he and Odge were crouched on the wooden floor watching the mistmaker. Among the banshees and the flower fairies were Odge's great aunt and a couple of ducks.

Cor's plan, like all good plans, was simple. They would use the moment when the girl in the cake finished her dance and the lights went out to capture the Prince.

'Hans will bop him – very, very carefully, of course, using only his little finger – and drop him into the cake as it is wheeled away. No one will think of looking for him there.'

'But won't the girl in the cake get a shock when the Prince is thrown in on top of her? Won't she squeak?' asked Gurkie.

Cor shook his head. 'No,' he said. 'Because the girl in the cake won't be there. The girl in the cake will be somebody else.' He looked at Gurkie from under his bushy brows. 'The girl in the cake,' said the wizard in a weighty voice, 'will be – you!'

'Me!' Gurkie blushed a deep and rosy pink. She had always longed to come out of a cake – always – but when her mother was alive it was no good even thinking about it. Gym mistresses who run about blowing whistles and shouting 'Play Up and Play the Game' are not likely to let their daughters within miles of a cake. 'You mean I'm to do that dance? The one with the Seven Veils? Oh, but suppose I was left standing in only my—' She didn't say the word knickers – she never *had* said it. Saying knickers was another thing her mother had not allowed.

'You won't be,' said Cor. 'The lights will go off before that, when you still have one veil on.'

'You'll do it beautifully, Gurkie,' said Ben. 'They'll go mad for you.' And everyone agreed.

'But after that?' said the troll. 'How will you get the Prince out of the cake and away? Hans may be invisible, but Raymond won't be, if we're not

128

allowed to use magic on him, and the cake only gets wheeled as far as the artists' dressing room.'

Cor nodded. 'But there are other things in the dressing room. Such as the instruments that the players in the orchestra use. Among them a large double bass case.'

He paused, and everyone looked at him expectantly, beginning to get the drift.

'As soon as the cake arrives in there, Hans will transfer the Prince into the case – and the double bass player will carry him out of the hotel by the service stairs where a van will be waiting.'

'But surely he'll notice,' said Ernie. 'Raymond must weigh about five times as much as a double bass.'

'Yes. But you see it won't be the real double bass player. It'll be Mr Prendergast.' He turned to the troll. 'You shape-shifted yourself into a bank manager and a policeman. Surely you can manage a double bass player with a black moustache and a cow's lick in the middle of his forehead?'

The troll nodded. 'No problem,' he said. 'I got a good look at him tonight.'

The other details were quickly settled. Since they still had over a thousand pounds in banknotes, they were sure they could pay the real girl in the cake to let Gurkie take her place. 'And I shall call Mrs Trottle away with a phone message just before the cake comes in,' said Cor. 'Odge will pretend to be the double bass player's little daughter and tell the doorman that her father has to come home early. As for you, Ben, you must wait on the fire escape and signal to the van driver as soon as Raymond is packed and ready, so that he can back up against the entrance. And then off we go, all of us, through the gump with a whole day to spare!'

Ben, when the jobs were given out, sighed with relief. He'd been afraid that they wouldn't let him help and he wanted more than anything to be part of the team.

But he felt guilty too because he knew that Odge thought he was going with them to the island.

'This time you're coming!' said Odge. 'You *have* to!'

And Ben had said nothing. It was no good arguing, but you had to do what was right, and leaving Nanny Brown alone, ill as she was, couldn't ever be right. Only he wouldn't let himself think what it would be like after the rescuers had gone. He wouldn't let himself think of anything except how to get Raymond Trottle out of the Astor and bring the King and Queen their long-lost son.

Fourteen

Nanny Brown moved her head restlessly on the pillow. She was worried stiff. Why had Larina Trottle phoned to ask how she was? Larina didn't care tuppence how she was, Nanny knew that. Surely she couldn't be planning to send Ben away already? In which case Ben ought to have the letter now ... But what if the police came to the hospital to ask questions? Perhaps they'd pull her out of bed and take her to prison? Ben wouldn't like that; he felt things far too much.

And here he was now! As he sat down beside her and took her hand, she thought what a handsome boy he was turning out to be.

'You've had your hair cut.'

Ben nodded. Gurkie had pruned his hair with her pruning shears. She'd offered to curl it too, like she curled the petals of a rose, but Ben didn't think Nanny would like him with curly hair. Thinking of the rescuers made him smile – they were all so excited about tonight and getting Raymond out. Then he looked more closely at Nanny and his heart gave a lurch. She was nothing but skin and bone.

'Does it hurt you, Nanny? Are you in pain?'

'No, of course not,' she lied. They'd offered her some stuff to take away the pain but she'd never let them dope her when Ben came. 'What about Mrs Trottle? How's she been?'

'She's still away – and Raymond too.'

Nanny nodded. That was all right then. If Larina was away she couldn't harm Ben, so the letter could wait. The nurses had promised faithfully to give it to Ben when the time came.

'And the servants?'

'They've been all right. They seem to let me do what I like, almost.' But he was puzzled. The servants were almost *too* nice, and Mr Fulton gave him an odd look now and again, as though he knew something. It made Ben uncomfortable, but he wasn't going to worry Nanny Brown.

And Nanny wasn't going to worry Ben about the nonsense the young doctor had come up with that morning. She knew her time was up and she certainly didn't mean to go up to heaven stuck full of tubes.

But as Ben left the ward, he found the nice nurse Celeste, waiting for him.

'Sister'd like a word with you, Ben,' she said. 'Would you come along to her room?'

The Sister had dark hair and kind eyes. 'Ben, you're very young but you're a sensible boy and there's doesn't seem to be anyone else.'

Ben waited.

'You're the next of kin, dear, aren't you? I mean, you're the only relation Mrs Brown has?'

'Yes. I'm her grandson.'

The nurse sighed and stabbed her pencil on to a note pad.

'You see, Ben, the doctors are thinking of opera-

132

ting on your grandmother. It would be a shock to her system and cause her some pain, but it might give her a bit longer.'

Ben bit his lip. 'When would that be?'

'The day after tomorrow. We thought you should know.'

The day after tomorrow. The last day of the Opening. It would be all over then and the rescuers gone. Well, if he'd had any doubts, that settled it. To let her go through an operation by herself was not to be thought of.

'I'd like to be there when she comes round,' he said. 'I'd like to be with her.'

'I'll ask the doctor,' said the Sister – and smiled at him.

Fifteen

Mrs Trottle had got the table she wanted – on the left of the band which was where the cake came in, and really close to the double bass player. She was sure he fancied her; every so often when he wasn't sawing away with his bow, his eyes seemed to meet hers. What a lovely player he was, and what a lovely man!

Raymond was sitting opposite, dressed to kill in a new silk shirt and spotty bow tie and, as she leant forward to wipe the dribble of cream from his chin, Mrs Trottle thought there wasn't a better looking boy in the world. Her husband said she spoiled him, but Mr Trottle didn't understand Raymond. The boy was sensitive. He *felt* things.

Bruce was standing by the far wall, his eye on Raymond. He was hungry, but no one thought of sending anything over for him to eat. His sister Doreen sat on a chair by the big double doors. Ordinary guests would have been surprised to see a woman knitting all through dinner, but there were enough people there who had used bodyguards in their time and it gave them a good feeling to know that Soft Parts Doreen was in the room. No terrorists or assassins would get far with her around!

In the phone box across the street from the hotel, Cor was reading the instructions. Or trying to, but his spectacles kept falling off the end of his nose, and he didn't like the look of all those buttons.

'Insert money,' mumbled the wizard. 'Dial number . . .' But when he dialled it, something gloomy flashed on to the little grey screen and everything went dead. He tried again and the same thing happened. Then suddenly he lost patience. They weren't supposed to use magic on the Prince, but a telephone was different. He spoke the number of the Astor; he turned to the East, he uttered the Calling Spell – and on the reception desk of the hotel, the phone began to ring.

'Oh no! I can't come now.' Mrs Trottle glared at the page who had come to say that she was wanted on the telephone. The double bass player was playing something so dreamy that he must surely be playing it for her alone and she almost decided to pluck the rose from her chest and throw it at him.

'The gentleman said it was very urgent, Madam,' said the page – and Mrs Trottle got up sulkily and followed him, while Bruce moved closer to Raymond and Doreen shifted slightly in her chair.

Hans now entered the room. He had been incredibly brave and offered to have fernseed even in his eye so that he could be completely invisible and still see where he was going. His little finger was stretched out ready to bop Raymond, and it trembled because the ogre was very much afraid. Suppose he bopped too hard and brought the Prince to the Island with a broken skull? On the other hand, suppose he didn't hit him hard enough so that he squealed when he was thrown into the cake?

135

If Hans was nervous, poor Gurkie was terrified.

'Oh Mother, forgive me,' she muttered. She had been to Fortlands and bought some of the stuff they used for black out curtains to make the last veil – the one she wore over her underclothes – and the underwear itself was bottle green chilprufe because her mother had always told her that it was what you wore next to the skin that mattered, so even if the lights didn't go out at exactly the right time she would still be decent. All the same, as she stepped into the cake, Gurkie's teeth were chattering. At least the girl who usually did the Dance of the Seven Veils was happy! She'd grabbed the money Cor had given her and even now was going up in a Jumbo on the way to sunny Spain.

'Ready?' asked the porter, coming to wheel her in.

'Ready!' squeaked Gurkie, from inside the layers of tissue.

The orchestra burst into a fanfare; balloons and streamers came down from the ceiling – and Gurkie burst out of the cake and began to dance.

Raymond didn't recognize her because even her face was veiled, and the light was rosy and dim, but everyone felt that something beautiful was going to happen, and they were right. Feys have always loved dancing – they dance round the meadows in the early morning, they twirl and whirl on the edge of the sea, and of all the twirlers and whirlers on the Island, Gurkie was the best. She forgot that her mother would have turned in her grave to see her in the dining room of the Astor Hotel like any chorus girl, she forgot that any minute Raymond Trottle would land with a thump on top of her. And as she danced, the orchestra followed the way she moved . . . got slower when she went slowly and quicker when she went fast and there wasn't a single person in the dining room who could bear to take his eyes off her.

Gurkie dropped the first of her seven veils on the floor. She was thinking of all the lovely things that grew on the Island and of her cucumbers and how she would soon be home, but the people watching her did not know that. They thought she was thinking of them.

And Hans had reached Raymond's table. He was standing in the space left by Mrs Trottle. He was ready.

The sixth veil dropped. The music got even soupier. Now as she danced, Gurkie was strewing herbs into the room, the sweet-smelling herbs she had brought in her basket to make people sleepy, to make them forget their troubles.

By the back entrance, Odge Gribble was explaining to the porter that her father had to leave early.

'My Mummy isn't well,' she said with a lisp – and he nodded and pinched her cheek.

In the lavatory which led out of the dressing room, the troll waited. He looked so like the double bass player that his own mother wouldn't have known him. Ben, crouching on the top of the fire escape, kept his eyes on the waiting van.

Back in the dining room Gurkie dropped her fifth veil . . . her fourth . . . She still spun and whirled, but more slowly now – and the lights were turning mauve . . . then blue.

'Coo!' said Raymond Trottle as she danced past his table.

The third veil now . . . the second. And now Gurkie did begin to worry. What if the lights didn't go out? Was her last veil *really* thick enough?

But it was all right. Hans' little finger was stretched out over Raymond's head.

The orchestra went into its special swirly bit. The lights went out.

And at that moment, Hans bopped!

The getaway van was parked in the narrow road which ran between the back of the Astor and the river. It had been dark for some time; the passing boats had lit their lamps and light streamed from the windows of the hotel.

The inside of the van was piled with blankets so that the Prince could be made comfortable on the way to the gump. All the rescuers' belongings were there because they were driving straight to the station.

And Odge's suitcase was there, carefully laid flat. The door of the van was open and plenty of fresh air reached the mistmaker through the holes that Odge had drilled in it, so he should have been content, but he was not. He was too old for suitcases; he was a free spirit; he was used now to being part of things!

Rustling about in the hay, complaining in little whimpers, he put his sharp front teeth against the fibre of the case and found a weak place where

138

the rim round one of the holes had frayed. Getting interested, beginning to see hope, he began to gnaw.

The driver noticed nothing. He had his eyes fixed on the boy who crouched on top of the fire escape. As soon as Ben signalled with his torch he'd back up against the entrance.

In the dining room of the Astor, the guests waited for the cake; the orchestra played a tango.

'It's awfully hot in here,' complained a girl at one of the tables, and called a waiter.

The mistmaker went on gnawing. He was pleased. Something was happening. The hole was getting bigger ... and bigger ... and bigger still. His whiskers were already through, and his nose ...

Then quite suddenly he was free!

Trembling with excitement, he sat up on his haunches and looked about him. And at that moment, one of the waiters opened a window in the dining room, sending the sound of the orchestra out into the night.

Music! And what music! The mistmaker had never heard a full orchestra in his life. His eyes grew huge, his moustache quivered. Then with a bound he leapt out of the van and set off.

The driver's eyes were still on Ben.

Lolloping along like a lovesick pillow, the mistmaker crossed the road, leapt on to the bottom rung of the fire escape, missed ... tried again. Now he was on and climbing steadily.

'Oom-pa-pa, oom-pa-pa,' went the band. The violins soared, the saxophones throbbed ...

Ben peered down the iron stairs, wondering if he

had seen something white crossing the road. No, he must have been mistaken . . .

The Astor was beside the river and the river bank was full of rats. Large, intelligent rats who had dug paths for themselves into the hotel. Panting up the first rung of the fire escape, the mistmaker found a hole in the brick and plunged into it. It came out near the kitchens, behind a store cupboard, and from there another rat-run led into the pantry where the waiters set out the trays to carry into the dining room. He only had to cross a passage, run through an open door . . .

And now he was where he wanted to be – where he absolutely had to be, facing that wonderful sound! He had arrived just as the cake was wheeled away and the room was in darkness, but that didn't matter because the band was still playing and it was a Viennese waltz!

The mistmaker made his way into the middle of the room and sat down. Never, never had he heard anything so beautiful! The fur on the back of his neck lifted; he shivered with happiness; his ear lobes throbbed.

'Aaah!' sighed the mistmaker. 'Aaah . . . aaah!'

The waves of mist were slight to begin with; he was puffed from the climb and he was over-whelmed. But as the beauty of the music sank deeper and deeper into his soul, so did the clouds of whiteness that came from him.

At one of the tables, an old gentleman began to cough. An angry lady leant across her husband and told the man at the next table to stop smoking.

'I'm not smoking,' the man said crossly.

But as the lights came on again, the guests could see that something odd was happening. The room was covered in a thick white mist – so thick that the Trottles' table could hardly be seen.

'It's smoke! The room's full of smoke,' shouted a girl in a glittery dress.

'No, it isn't. It's tear gas!' yelled a bald man and put his napkin to his face.

'It's a terrorist bomb!' cried a fat lady.

Bruce was blundering round Raymond's chair, feeling for the boy. Perhaps he was hiding under the table, trying to get away from the creeping gas? Clutching his gun, he dived under the cloth.

The mistmaker was upset by the ugly shrieking. He moved closer to the band which was still playing. A good orchestra will play through thick and thin.

Once more he gave himself up to the beauty of the music; once more he sighed. But he was getting thinner now; he was no longer pillow shaped. The whiteness that came from him was not so thick, and in a break in the mist, a woman in a trouser suit stood up and pointed: 'Look! It's coming from that horrible thing!' she screeched.

'It's a poisonous rat! It's a rodent from Outer Space!'

'It's got the plague! They do that, they give off fumes and then they go mad and bite you!'

The cries came from all over the room. A waiter rushed in with a fire extinguisher and squirted foam all over a group of Arabs in their splendid robes. One of the Astor's own guards had seized a walking stick and was banging it on the floor.

141

And now something happened which put the mistmaker's life in mortal danger. The band gave up. The music stopped . . . and with it, the supply of mist which had helped to hide and shelter him. Suddenly cut off from the glorious sound, the little animal blinked and tried to come back to the real world. Then he began to run hither and thither, looking for the way back.

And Doreen Trout reached for her knitting bag.

In the artists' dressing room, Gurkie had climbed out of the cake. She had a bruise on her shoulder where Raymond's chin had hit her, but she was being brave. The Prince looked crumpled, but his breathing was steady. Only a few minutes now and he'd be stretched out in the van where she could make him comfortable.

'I bopped well?' asked Hans who had followed her into the dressing room.

'You bopped beautifully,' said Gurkie.

The troll came out of the toilet and opened the double bass case.

'I'll take the feet,' he said, and Hans nodded and went to Raymond's shoulders.

Everything was going according to plan.

It was at that moment that the door to the fire escape burst open and Ben, ashen-faced and frantic, rushed into the room.

'The mistmaker's escaped,' he said. 'He's in the dining room. And they're going mad in there. They'll kill him.'

'No!' Hans let go of Raymond, who fell back into

the cake. 'Our duty is to the Prince. You must not go!'

Ben did not even hear him. Before the ogre could move to stop him, he had reached the other door and was gone.

In the dining room everyone was shrieking and joining in the hunt for the dangerous rodent from Outer Space. The Arabs whose robes had been squirted with foam were yelling at the waiter; a lady had fainted and fallen into her apple pie.

'There he is!' screamed a woman. 'Behind the trolley!' And Bruce aimed, fired – and hit a bottle of champagne which exploded into smithereens.

The mistmaker was terrified now. The shrieks and thumps beat on his ears like hammer blows; his head was spinning, and he ran in circles, trying to find the way out.

'He's got rabies!' yelled a fat woman. 'That's how you tell, when they go round and round like that.'

'If he bites you, you're finished,' shouted a red-faced man. 'Get on a table; he'll go for your ankles.'

The fat lady did just that and the table broke, sending her crashing to the ground. 'Don't let him get me!' she screamed. 'Squash him! Finish him!'

Bruce had seized a chair and was holding it above his head as he stalked the desperate little beast. Now he brought it down with a thump and one leg came off and rolled away.

'He's missed,' moaned the woman on the floor.

Once again Bruce raised the chair, once again he brought it down, and once again he missed.

Doreen Trout had not screamed. She had not

thumped. She had not picked up heavy chairs or reached for her gun. All she had done was take out her favourite knitting needle. It was a sock needle of the finest steel and sharper than any rapier. She had judged its length and it would skewer the animal neatly without any waste.

'Get out of the way, oaf,' she hissed at her brother. 'I'm dealing with this. Just corner him.'

This was easier said than done. The mistmaker, caught in the nightmare, scuttled between the tables, vanished into patches of whiteness, skittered on the foam. But his enemies were gathering. The saxophone player had jumped down from the bandstand and shooed him against the wall; a waiter with a broom handle blocked him as he tried to dive behind the curtains.

And now he was cornered. His eyes huge with fear, he sat trembling and waited for what was to come.

'Stand back!' said Doreen to the crowd – and began to move slowly towards the terrified animal. 'Come on, my pretty,' she cooed. 'Come to your Mummy. Come and see what I've got for you.'

The room fell silent. Everyone was watching Doreen Trout, holding her needle as she moved closer, and all the time talking in a coaxing, wheedling voice.

The mistmaker's whiskers twitched. He blinked; the delicate ears became flushed. Here was a low voice; a kind voice. He turned his head this way and that, listening.

'I've got lovely things for you in my bag. Carrots . . . lettuce . . .'

More than anything, the desperate creature wanted kindness. Should he risk it? He took a few steps towards her . . . paused . . . sat up on his haunches. Then suddenly he made up his mind, and in a movement of trust he turned over on his back with his paws in the air as he had done so often when he was playing with Ben and Odge. He knew what came next – that moment when they scratched him so soothingly and deliciously all down his front.

Soft Parts Doreen looked down at the rounded, unprotected stomach of the little beast; at the pink skin still showing where his grown-up fur had not yet come.

Then she smiled and raised her arm. The next second she lay sprawled on the floor. A boy had come from nowhere and leapt at her, fastening his arms round her throat.

'You murderess! I'll kill you; I'll kill you if you harm him!' shouted Ben.

The attack was so sudden that Doreen dropped her needle which quivered, point down, in the carpet. Scratching and spitting, she tried to shake Ben off while her free hand crawled like a spider towards the embedded needle.

'Get the boy, idiot!' she spluttered at Bruce.

But that was easier said than done.

Every time it looked as though he could get a shot at Ben, some bit of Doreen got in the way. Anyway his sister was sure to win – the boy fought like a maniac, but he was half her size and her hand was almost on the needle. Now she was clawing at his face and as he pushed her away and tried to free himself his arm was clear of Doreen's body. Blowing a hole in the boy's arm was better than nothing and carefully, Bruce lifted his gun and aimed.

The next second he staggered back, reeling, while pieces of splintered wood rained down on his shoulders. The double bass player had gone mad and hit him on the head with his instrument.

Except that the real double bass player was up on the bandstand with his hand to his mouth staring down at the man who seemed to be him.

But Doreen's crawling fingers had reached the needle, pulled it out. Holding the glittering steel, above Ben's throat, she brought it down in a single, violent thrust – just as Ben, with a superhuman effort, rolled out of her grasp.

'Ow! Help! Gawd!'

Bruce clutched his foot, hopped, tried to pull the needle out of his shoe. Maddened by pain, half stunned by the blow the troll had given him, he seized a brass table lamp.

Ben had turned, trying to catch the mistmaker. He had no time to dodge, no time to save himself. The base of the heavy lamp came down on his skull in a single crushing blow – and as the blood gushed from the wound, he fell unconscious to the ground.

'He's dead!' screamed a woman.

'I hope so,' said Doreen softly. 'But if not . . .'

She pulled the needle out of her brother's shoe and knelt down beside Ben, searching for the soft hollow beneath his ear.

But then something terrifying happened. As she bent over the boy, she was suddenly pushed back

146

as if by an invisible hand – pushed back so hard that she fell against the plate-glass window which broke with a crash.

It was incredible but they could all see it – slowly, gently, the wounded boy rose into the air . . . Higher he rose, and higher . . . Blood still trickled from his scalp, he lay with one arm dangling and his head thrown back . . . lay *in the air*, unsupported and clearly visible above the mist.

'He's going to heaven!' cried someone.

'He's been called up to Paradise!'

And that was how it looked to everyone there. They had seen pictures of saints and martyrs who could do that . . . levitate or lift themselves up and lie there in the clouds.

But that wasn't the end of it. Now the boy who *had* to be dead – began to float slowly, gently, away, high over everyone's head . . . until he vanished through the door.

Sixteen

On the morning of the eighth day of the Opening, the Royal Yacht set off from the Island, bound for the Secret Cove.

Not only was the Queen aboard, but the King and several of his courtiers, for he understood now that the Queen had to get as close as she could to the place where the Prince would appear – if he appeared at all. Two days had passed since the cheerful message from the witch and still there was no sign of their son. All along the King had tried to comfort his wife, but now even he was finding it hard to be brave.

Down below, a special cabin had been prepared for the Wailing Nurses. They had begged to be allowed to come along, but since they hadn't washed for nine years they had to be kept well away from the other passengers. With them had come a new crate of bananas because the first batch had become overripe, and the Queen had managed a smile as she saw it carried aboard because it meant the triplets, at least, still hoped.

As the Royal Yacht drew out of the harbour, a second and much larger boat pulled up its anchors, ready to follow. This was a ship chartered by people on the Island who could not fit on to the King's yacht but who also wanted to be there for the last day of the Opening. Most of these were people who cared very much about the little Prince and longed and longed for him to be brought back safely, even now at the eleventh hour. But some – just a few – were peevish grumblers: people who wanted to gloat over the old wizard and the loopy fey and the conceited little hag when they came back in disgrace. And there were some – there are always such people even in the most beautiful and best-ruled places – who just wanted an outing and a chance to gawp at whatever was going to happen, whether it was good or bad.

The Royal Yacht skimmed over the waves. The charter boat followed more slowly. In their cabin the nurses wailed and tried to think of ways of punishing themselves, but not for long because they became sea-sick and no one can think of a worse punishment than that.

The Queen would not go below. She stood leaning over the rails, her long hair whipped by the wind, and over and over again she said: 'Dear God, please let him come. Please let him come. I will never do anything bad again if only you let him come.'

Poor Queen. She never *had* done anything bad; she was not that sort of person.

They had been at sea for only a short time when something happened. The sky darkened; a black thunder cloud moved in from the west, and a few drops of rain fell on the deck.

Or was it rain?

The sailors who had been below hurried up the ladders, preparing for a storm. The gulls flew off with cries of alarm; the dolphins dived.

149

It was not a storm, though, and the swirling blackness was not a cloud. The sky yelpers came first: a pack of baying, saucer-eyed dogs racing overhead, dropping their spittle on the deck where it hissed and sizzled and broke into little tongues of flame which the sailors stamped out.

But it was the harpies which made the Queen sway and the King run to her side.

They flew in formation like geese, with Mrs Smith at their head and the others in a V shape behind her: Miss Green, Miss Brown, Miss Jones and Miss Witherspoon. Their handbags dangled from their arms; their varnished talons hung down from their crimplene bloomers . . . and their unspeakable stench beat against the clean, salty air of the sea.

From the charter ship, a cheer went up. These were the real rescuers, the proper ones. And about time too! The King and Queen had waited till the last possible moment before sending in these frightful women, and there were those who thought they had delayed too long.

The harpies flew on, the dogs racing before them. In an hour they would be through the gump. The Queen's knuckles whitened on the rail, but she would not faint; she would bear it.

'There was nothing else to do, my dear; you know that,' said the King.

The Queen nodded. She did know it. There were twenty-four hours left; only one day. These ghastly creatures were her only hope.

Seventeen

Ben lay on the floor of the summer house, his head pillowed on the wizard's rolled up cloak. His eyes were closed; his face, in the light of the candles, was deathly pale. Since Hans had carried him out of the Astor he had not stirred.

Gurkie sat beside him, holding his hand. She had rubbed healing ointment into his scalp; the bleeding had stopped, the wound was closing – but the deeper hurt, the damage to his brain, was beyond her power to heal. And if he never came round again ... if he lived for ever in a coma ... or if he died ...

But no one could bear to think of that. Cor sat still as stone in the folding chair. He was shivering but they hadn't been able to stop him giving his cloak to Ben.

'I am too old,' he thought. 'I have failed in my mission and brought harm to as brave a child as I shall ever see.'

Hans was crouched on the steps. His fernseed had gone blotchy and every so often a moan escaped him. 'Oi,' murmured the giant. 'Oi.' If he had followed Ben at once into the dining room instead of waiting by the Prince he could have prevented this dreadful accident, and he knew that he would never forgive himself.

The manhole cover on the path now lifted slowly and the Plodger climbed out, still in his working clothes.

'Any news?' he asked. 'Has he come round?'

The wizard shook his head and the Plodger sighed and made his way back into the sewer. Melisande was going to be dreadfully upset.

It was well past midnight. In Trottle Towers the servants slept, believing that Ben had already been taken to his new 'home'. The ghosts had come to stand round Ben as he lay unstirring, and then gone back to the guarding of the gump.

It was amazing how many people had come to ask after Ben, people who should scarcely have known the boy. Wizards and witches, the banshee who had worked in the laundry room of the Astor . . . the flower fairy who had pinched Mrs Trottle on the nose. It was extraordinary how many people cared.

It was the last day of the Opening. They had expected to be back on the Island by now, but no one even thought of leaving. Ben had helped them from the first moment they had seen him cleaning shoes in the basement of Trottle Towers; he had seemed at once to belong to them. Not one of the rescuers dreamt of abandoning him.

Odge was not with the others as they clustered round Ben. She had gone off by herself and was sitting by the edge of the lake, wrapped in her long black hair.

Ben was going to die; Odge was sure of it.

'And it's my fault,' she said aloud. 'I brought the

mistmaker and it was because he went to save him that Ben was hurt.'

The mistmaker lay beside Ben now; Odge had been able to snatch him up when the ogre brought Ben out of the dining room. If Ben woke he would see the little animal at once and know that he was all right, but he wouldn't wake. No one could lie there so white and still and not be at death's door.

And if Ben died, nothing would go right ever again. She could grow an extra toe – she could grow a whole *crop* of extra toes – she could learn to cough frogs, and none of it would be any use. Only yesterday her great aunt had taught her the Striking People with Baldness Spell, but what did that matter now? Hags don't cry – Odge knew that – but nothing now could stop her tears.

Then suddenly she lifted her head. Something had happened – something horrible! An evil stench spread slowly over the grass, and crept through the branches of the trees . . . The roosting birds flew upwards with cries of alarm. A cloud passed over the moon. Running back to warn the others, she saw that they had risen to their feet and were staring at the sky.

The smell grew worse. A mouse in the bushes squealed in terror; a needle of ice pierced the warmth of the summer night.

And then she came! Her rancid wings fluttered once . . . twice . . . and were folded as she came in to land. Her handbag dangled from her arm; the frill round the bottom of her bloomers, hugging her scaly legs, was like the ruff on a poisonous lizard.

'Well, well,' sneered Mrs Smith. 'Quite a cosy

little family party, I see.' She opened her handbag to take out her powder puff – and the rescuers fell back. The smell of a harpy's face powder is one of the most dreaded smells in the world. 'One might think that people who have fallen down on their job so completely would at least show some signs of being sorry.'

No one spoke. The nail polish on the harpy's ghastly talons, the loathsome hairspray on her permed hair, were making them feel dizzy and sick.

'Candles! Flowers! Giants in embroidered braces! Pshaw!' said Mrs Smith. She put her claws on Gurkie's begonia and tore it out of the ground. 'Well, you know why I'm here. To tell you you're finished. Demoted. *Kaput*. Off the job. I don't know if the King and Queen will forgive you, but if they've got any sense they won't. You're failures. You're feeble. Pathetic. A disaster. Rescuing a kitchen boy and leaving the Prince!'

Still the rescuers said nothing. They were guilty of everything the harpy accused them of. For they *had* put Ben before the Prince. Hans had struggled with himself for a few minutes but in the end he and the troll had run back to help Ben and left the true Prince of the Island in a squelchy heap inside the cake. They had forgotten him, it was as simple as that. And Raymond had come to himself and climbed out and even now was probably guzzling Knickerbocker Glories in his room in the hotel. What's more, they hadn't even thought of going back and having another go at getting him out; all they'd thought of was carrying Ben away to safety. They weren't fit to be rescuers; the harpy was right.

'The ghosts told me what happened,' said Mrs Smith. 'And if I was the King and Queen I'd know what to do with you. All that fuss about a common servant boy!'

'He's not a common servant boy, he's *Ben*,' raged Odge – and took a step backward as the harpy lifted her dreadful claw and sharpened it once, twice, three times against the step.

'Well, the most useful thing you can do now is keep out of our way,' Mrs Smith went on. 'Get yourself through the gump and let us finish the job.'

Gurkie put her hand to her heart. She didn't care for Raymond but the idea of him being carried away in the talons of Mrs Smith was too horrible to bear.

'How will you operate?' asked the wizard.

'That's none of your business. But some of my girls are sussing out the Astor now. There seems to be a helicopter pad.'

She said no more, but in the distance they could hear the baying of a hell hound and a high, screeching voice ordering him to: '*Sit!*'

The harpy flew off then, but the evil she had left in the air still lingered. Then from behind them came a strong young voice.

'Goodness!' said Ben, sitting up and rubbing his head. 'What an absolutely *horrible* smell!'

Eighteen

'And, please, let us get this clear,' said Mrs Smith. 'It is I who will actually snatch the boy. You will help me, of course, you will take care of his mother and the guards, but the Prince is *mine!*'

'Yes, Mrs Smith,' said the other harpies gloomily. 'We understand.'

They sat in a circle round their chief in a disused underpass not far from the Astor. No one went there after dark; it was the sort of place which muggers loved and ordinary people avoided. All of them would have liked to be the one to snatch the Prince but they hadn't really expected to be chosen – their leader always kept the best jobs for herself.

Miss Brown, Miss Green, Miss Jones and Miss Witherspoon were a little smaller than Mrs Smith, but they had the same rank black wings, the same evil talons, the same stretch tops and bloomers ending in the same frills. They too had handbags full of make-up but Miss Witherspoon kept a whistle and some dog biscuits in hers. She was the sporting one; the one who trained the dogs.

'You have the sack, Lydia?' asked Mrs Smith – and Miss Brown nodded.

'And you have the string, Beryl?' she went on – and Miss Green held up the ball of twine.

'Good. We'll parcel him up in the cloakroom – I

156

don't fancy any wriggling as we go through the tunnel.' She turned to Miss Witherspoon: 'As for the dogs, they'd best stay on the lead till the last moment. I'll give the signal when you should let them go.'

One of the black yelpers stirred and got to his feet.

'Sit!' screeched Miss Witherspoon – and the dog sat.

'Now *grovel*!' she yelled – and the great saucer-eyed beast flopped on to his stomach and crawled towards her like a worm.

'Well, that settles everything, I think,' said Mrs Smith. 'Just time for a little sleep.' She opened her handbag and took out a packet of curlers which she wound into her brassy hair. Then she tucked her head into her wings, as birds do, and in a moment the others heard her snores.

There were only a few more hours before the closing of the gump for nine long years, but it was clear that Mrs Smith didn't even think of failure. Much as they had wanted to snatch the Prince themselves, the other harpies had to admit that she was the best person for the job.

On the roof of the Astor, Mrs Trottle waited with her husband and her son. Her suitcase, ready packed, was beside her, and a travelling rug. In ten minutes the helicopter would be there to take them to safety. Mr Trottle's uncle, Sir Ian Trottle, who lived in a big house on the Scottish border, had offered to shelter them from the madmen who were chasing Raymond.

Her darling babykin hadn't realized that the gang of dope fiends were after him again. When he came round inside the cake he couldn't remember anything and she hadn't told him what had happened. And actually she herself wasn't too clear about what had gone on in the Astor dining room. Bruce had told her that he'd thrown the boy for safety into the cake to save him from the clutches of the kidnappers and she'd rewarded him, but he wasn't much good any more, limping about and with a bruise on his head the size of a house. And Doreen, who'd been thrown through a window, had cut her wrist so badly that it would be a long time before she could knit. She'd sent them both home and it was two of the Astor's own guards who were protecting them until the helicopter came.

As for the rest of the babble – something about some boy being lifted up and taken to heaven – Mrs Trottle put that down to the effect of the poisonous gas that had been let off in the room. By the time she'd got back after some idiot kept her talking on the phone, the dining room was in a shambles and what everyone said was double-dutch.

'I'm hungry!' said Raymond.

'We'll have some sandwiches in the helicopter, dear,' said Mrs Trottle.

'I don't want them in the helicopter, I want them *now*,' whined Raymond. He began to grope in Mrs Trottle's hold-all, found a bar of toffee, and put it in his mouth.

Mrs Trottle looked up, but there was no sign yet of the helicopter. It was a beautiful clear night.

They'd have an easy flight. And as soon as Raymond was safe at Dunloon, she was going to call the police. Once Ben was out of her way and there was no snooping to be done, she'd get proper protection for her Little One. And Ben *would* be out of the way – she'd left clear instructions at the hospital. Even now he might be on the way to Ramsden Hall. She'd had a scare with Ramsden – some meddling do-gooders had tried to get the place shut down, but the man who ran it had been too clever for them. Whatever it was called, Ramsden was a good old-fashioned reform school. They didn't actually send children up chimneys because most people now had central heating, but they saw to it that the boys knew their place and that was what Ben needed. And oh, the relief she'd feel at having him out of the house!

'Here it comes!' said Mr Trottle, and the guards moved aside the cones and turned up the landing lights, ready for the helicopter to land.

The pilot who'd been sent to fetch the Trottles was one of the best. He had flown in the Gulf War; he was steady and experienced and of course he would never have taken even the smallest sip of drink before a flight.

And yet now he was seeing things. He was seeing dogs. Which meant that he was going mad because you did not see dogs in the sky; you didn't see stars blotted out by threshing tails; you didn't see grinning jowls and fangs staring in at the cockpit.

The pilot shook his head. He closed his eyes for an instant, but it didn't help. Another slobbering face with bared teeth and saucer eyes had appeared beside him. There were more of them now ... three ... four ... five.

There couldn't be five dogs racing through the sky. But there were – and they were coming closer. He dipped suddenly, expecting them to be sliced by his propellers, but they weren't. Of course they weren't because they didn't exist.

High above him, Miss Witherspoon, her handbag dangling, encouraged the pack.

'Go on! See him off!' she shouted. 'Faster! Faster!'

Excited by the chase, the dogs moved in. Sparks came from their eyes, spittle dropped from their jaws. The pack leader threw himself at the cockpit window.

The pilot could see the roofs of the Astor below, but every time he tried to lose height the phantom dogs chivvied him harder – and what if those sparks were real? What if they burnt the plane?

'Tally ho!' cried Miss Witherspoon, high in the sky. She blew her whistle and the dogs went mad.

The pilot made one more attempt to land. Then suddenly he'd had enough. The Astor could wait, and so could the people who had hired him. The Trottles, staring at the helicopter's light as it came down, saw it rise again and vanish over the rooftops.

'Now what?' said Mrs Trottle, peevishly.

She was soon to find out.

The people of London had forgotten the old ways. They had heard the baying of the phantom yelpers in the sky, and now they could smell the evil stench

160

that came in with the night air, but they spoke of drains, of blocked pipes, and shut their windows.

And the harpies flew on.

'Yuk!' said Raymond, chewing his toffee bar. 'It stinks. I feel sick!'

'Well, my little noodle-pie, I did tell you not to eat sweets before—'

Then she broke off, and all the Trottles stared upwards.

'My God!' Mr Trottle staggered backwards. 'What are they? Ostriches . . . vultures?'

The gigantic birds were losing height. They could see the talons of the biggest one now, caught in the landing lights.

And they could see other things.

'B . . . Bloomers,' babbled Mrs Trottle. 'F . . . frills.'

'Shoot, can't you!' yelled Mr Trottle at the guard. 'What are we paying you for?'

The guard lifted his gun. There was a loud report, and Mrs Smith shook out her feathers and smiled. The wings of harpies have been arrow proof and bullet proof since the beginning of time.

'Ready, girls!' she called.

The second guard lifted his gun . . . then dropped it and ran screaming, back into the building. He had seen a handbag and could take no more.

And the harpies descended.

Each of them knew what to do. Miss Brown landed on Mrs Trottle who had fainted clean away, and sat on her chest. Miss Green picked up the remaining guard and threw him on to the fire escape. Miss Jones pinned the gibbering Mr Trottle against a wall.

Only Raymond still stood there, his jaws clamped so hard on his treacle toffee that he couldn't even scream.

And then he stood there no longer.

Nineteen

By the evening of the ninth day, the rescuers could put off their return no longer, but as they made their way to King's Cross Station they felt sadder than they had ever felt in their lives. To come back in disgrace like this . . . to know that they had failed!

Odge, trudging along with the mistmaker's suitcase, was silent and pale and this worried the others. They had expected her to rant and rave and stamp her feet when Ben once more refused to come with them, but she had behaved well and that wasn't like her. If Odge was sickening for something that would really be the end.

They had waited till the last minute to make sure Ben had completely recovered from the blow to his head. He'd kept telling them he was fine; he'd helped them to clear up the summer house, sweeping and tidying with a will, and that had made the parting worse because they'd remembered the moment when they first saw him in the basement of Trottle Towers. How happy they'd been when they thought he was the Prince! How certain that they could bring him back!

But there'd been no changing Ben's mind; he wouldn't leave his grandmother. 'She's having an operation,' he'd said. 'I can't leave her to face that alone. Maybe I can come down next time, when the gump opens again.'

He'd turned away then, and they knew how much he minded – but Odge hadn't lost her temper the way she'd done before; she'd just shrugged and said nothing at all.

The ghosts were waiting on platform thirteen. They looked thoroughly shaken though it was hours since the harpies had come through on their way to rescuing Raymond.

'I tell you, it was like the armies of the dead,' said Ernie. 'I wouldn't be Raymond Trottle for all the rice in China. They've had engineers here all afternoon looking for blocked drains.'

And indeed the harpies' vile stench still lingered. Even the spiders on the stopped clock looked stunned.

Now it was time to say goodbye and that was hard. The ghosts and the rescuers had become very fond of each other in the nine days they had worked together, but when Cor asked them if they wouldn't come through the gump, they shook their heads.

'Ghosts is ghosts and Islanders is Islanders,' said Ernie. 'And what would happen to the gump if we weren't here to guard it?'

But the ogre was looking anxiously at the station roof.

'I think we go now?' he said. 'I wish not to be under the smelling ladies when they return.'

No one wanted that. No one, for that matter, wanted to see the Prince brought back in the harpies' claws like a dead mouse.

They went through into the cloakroom and shook

164

hands. Even the ghost of the train spotter was upset to see them go.

'Please could you take the mistmaker's suitcase for me,' said Odge suddenly. 'My arm's getting tired.'

Gurkie nodded and Odge went forward to the Opening. 'I'll go ahead,' she said. 'I'm missing my sisters and I want to get there quickly.'

It says a lot about how weary and sad the rescuers were that they believed her.

When he came into the ward, Ben saw that the curtains were drawn round Nanny's bed.

'Has she had the operation?' he asked the nurse. It was Celeste, the one with the red rose in her hair whom everyone loved.

'No, dear. She's not going to have the operation. She's – very ill, Ben. You can sit with her quietly – she'd like to have you there but she may not say much.'

Ben drew aside the curtain. He could see at once that something had happened to Nanny. Her face was tiny; she looked as though she didn't really belong here any more. But when he pulled a chair up beside the bed and reached for her hand, the skinny, brown-flecked fingers closed tightly round his own.

'Foiled 'em!' said Nanny in a surprisingly clear voice.

'About the operation, do you mean?'

'That's right. Going up there full of tubes! Told them my time was up!'

Her eyes shut . . . then fluttered open once again.

'The letter . . . take it . . .' she whispered. 'Go on. Now.'

Ben turned his head and saw a white envelope with his name on it lying on her locker.

'All right, Nanny.' She watched him, never taking her eyes away, as he took it and put it carefully in his pocket. And now she could let go.

'You're a good boy . . . We shouldn't have . . .'

Her voice drifted away; her breathing became shallow and uneven; only her hand still held tightly on to Ben's.

'Just sleep, Nanny,' he said. 'I'll stay.'

And he did, as the clock ticked away the hours. That was what he had to do now, sit beside her not thinking of anything else. Not letting his mind follow Odge and the others as they made their way home . . . Not feeling sorry for himself because the people he loved so much had gone away. Just being there while Nanny needed him, that was his job.

The night nurse, coming in twice, found him still as stone beside the bed. The third time she came in, he had fallen asleep in his chair – but he still held his grandmother's cold hand inside his own.

Gently, she uncurled his fingers and told him what had happened.

It was hard to understand that he was now absolutely alone. People dying, however much you expect it, is not like you think it will be.

The Sister had taken him to the rest room; she'd given him tea and biscuits. Now, to his surprise, she said: 'I've been in touch with the people who are going to fetch you and they're on their way. Soon you'll be in your new home.'

Ben lifted his head. 'What?' he said stupidly.

'Mrs Trottle has made the arrangements for you, Ben. She's found a really nice place for you, she says. A school where you'll learn all sorts of things. She didn't think you'd want to go on living with the other servants now your grandmother is dead.'

Ben was incredibly tired; it was difficult to take anything in. 'I don't know anything about this,' he said.

The Sister patted his shoulder. Mrs Trottle had sounded so kind and concerned on the telephone that it never occurred to her to be suspicious.

'Ah, here they are now,' she said.

Two men came into the room. They wore natty suits – one pin-striped, one pale grey – and kipper ties. One of them had long dark hair parted in the middle and trained over his ears; the other was fair, with thick curls. Both of them smelled strongly of after shave, but their fingernails were dirty.

Ben disliked them at once. They looked oily and untrustworthy and he took a step backwards.

'I don't want to go with you,' he said. 'I want to find out what all this is about.'

'Now come on, we don't want a fuss,' said the dark-haired man. 'My name's Stanford by the way, and this here is Ralph – and we've got a long drive ahead of us so let's be off sharpish.'

'Where to? Where are we going?'

'The name wouldn't mean anything to you,' said Ralph, putting a comb through his curls. 'But you'll

167

be all right there, you'll see. Now say goodbye to the Sister and we'll be on our way.'

The Sister looked troubled. The men were not what she had expected, but her orders were clear. Ben must not leave the hospital alone and in a state of shock.

'I'm sure everything will be all right, dear,' she said. 'And of course you'll come back for your Granny's funeral.'

The men caught each other's eye and Ralph gave a snigger. One thing the children at Ramsden Hall did *not* get, was time off to go to funerals!

Ben was so tired now that nothing seemed real to him. If the Sister thought it was all right, then perhaps it was. And after all, what was there for him now in Trottle Towers?

He picked up his jacket. The letter was still in his pocket, but he didn't want to read it in front of these unpleasant men.

'All right,' he said wearily. 'I'm ready.'

And then, sandwiched between the two thugs Mrs Trottle had hired to deliver him to as horrible a place as could be found in England, he walked down the long hospital corridor towards the entrance hall.

It was very late. As she trudged through the streets, Odge was dazzled by the headlights of cars and the silly advertisements flashing on and off. Advertisements for stomach pills, for hairspray, for every sort of rubbish. For a moment she wondered if she was going to be able to stand it. On the Island now it would be cool and quiet; the mistmakers would be

168

lying close together on the beaches and the stars would be bright and clear. It wasn't a very nice thought that she would never see the Island under the stars again. Well, not for nine years. But in nine years she might be as silly as her sisters, talking about men and marriage and all that stuff.

She stopped for a moment under a lamp to look at the map. First right, first left, over a main road and she'd be there.

London wasn't very beautiful, but there were good things here, and good people. The Plodger was kind, and Henry Prendergast, and even quite ordinary people: shop assistants and park keepers. It wouldn't be too bad living here. And she wouldn't miss her bossy sisters – well, perhaps Fredegonda a little. Fredegonda could be quite funny when she was practising squeezing people's stomachs to give them nightmares.

The mistmaker she'd miss horribly, that was true, but she couldn't have kept him. The way those idiots had carried on in the Astor had shown her that, and he was old enough now to fend for himself. When the others realized that she hadn't gone ahead – that she'd doubled back and hidden in the cloakroom – they'd see to him, and explain to her parents. And even if she wanted to change her mind, it was too late. In an hour from now, the gump would be closed.

'I am a hag,' she reminded herself, because rather a bad attack of homesickness was coming on. 'I am Odge with the Tooth.'

She turned left . . . crossed the road. She could see the hospital now, towering over the other buildings.

169

Ben would be in there still and when she imagined him watching by the old woman's bed, Odge knew she'd done the right thing. Ben was clever, but he was much too trusting; he needed someone who saw things as they really were. No one was going to get the better of Ben while she was around and if it meant living in dirty London instead of the Island, well that was part of the job.

Up the steps of the hospital now. Even so late at night there were lights burning in the big entrance hall. Hospitals never slept.

'I am Miss Gribble,' she said, and the reception clerk looked down in surprise at the small figure, dressed in an old-fashioned blazer, which had come in out of the dark. 'And I have to see—'

She broke off because someone had called her name – and spinning round, she saw Ben coming towards her, hemmed in by two men. His face was white, he looked completely exhausted, and the men seemed to be helping him.

'Odge!' he called again. 'What are you doing here? Why aren't you—'

The man on Ben's right jerked his arm. 'Now then – we've no time to chat.'

He began to pull Ben towards the door, but Ben twisted round, trying to free himself.

'She's dead, Odge!' he cried. 'My grandmother. She's dead!' His voice broke, it was the first time he'd said that word.

Odge drew in her breath. Then she looked at the big clock on the wall. A quarter past eleven. They could do it if they hurried. Just.

'Then you can come with me!' she said joyfully. 'You can come back to the Island.'

Ben blinked, shook himself properly awake. He had lost all sense of time, sitting by his grandmother's bed; he'd thought it was long past midnight and the gump was closed. Hope sprang into his eyes.

'Let me *go*!' he said, and with sudden strength he pulled away from his guard. 'I'm going with her!'

'Oh no, you aren't!' Stanford grabbed his shoulders; Ralph bent Ben's arm behind his back and held it there. 'You're coming with us and pronto. Now walk.'

Ben fought as hard as he knew how, but the men were strong and there were two of them. And the receptionist had gone into her office. There was no one to see what was happening and help. They were close to the door now, and the waiting car.

But Odge had dodged round in front of them.

'No, Ben, no! You mustn't hurt the poor men,' she said. 'Can't you see how ill they are?'

'Get out of the way, you ugly little brat or we'll take you too,' said Stanford, and kicked out at her.

But Odge still stood there, looking very upset.

'Oh, how dreadful! Your poor hair! I'm so *sorry* for you!'

Without thinking, Stanford put his hand to his head. Then he gave a shriek. A lump of black hair the size of a fist had come out of his scalp.

'That's how it starts,' said Odge. 'With sudden baldness. The frothing and the fits come later.'

'My God!' Stanford grabbed at his temples and

171

another long, greasy wodge of hair fell on to the lapel of his suit.

'And your friend – he's even worse,' said Odge. 'All those lovely curls!'

It was true. Ralph's curls were dropping on to the tiled floor like hunks of knitting wool while round patches of pink skin appeared on his scalp.

'Usually there's no cure,' Odge went on, 'but maybe they could give you an injection in here. Some hospitals do have a vaccine – it gets injected into your behind with a big needle – but you'd have to hurry!'

The thugs waited no longer. Holding on to their heads, trying uselessly to keep in the rest of their hair, they ran down the corridor shrieking for help.

'Oh, Odge!' said Ben. '*You* did it! You struck them with baldness!'

'Don't waste time,' said the hag.

She put her hand into Ben's and together they bounded down the steps and out into the night.

Twenty

The three-masted schooner was at anchor off the Secret Cove. Beside it lay the Royal Yacht with its flying standard, and the charter boat. A number of smaller craft – dinghies and rowing boats – were drawn up on the beach. The tide was out; the clean firm sand curved and rippled round the bay. In the light of the setting sun, the sea was calm and quiet.

But the King and Queen stood with their backs to the sea, and facing the round dark hole at the bottom of the cliff. The cave which led to the gump was surrounded by thorn bushes and overhung by a ledge of rock. It was from there that the Prince would come.

If he came at all . . .

Flanking the King and Queen were the courtiers and the important people on the Island. The head teacher of the school had come on the charter boat and the Prime Minister and a little girl who had been top in Latin and won the trip as a prize.

And standing behind the King and Queen, but a little way off because they still hadn't allowed themselves to wash, were Lily and Violet and Rose. Each of them held a firm, unopened banana in their hand, and their eyes too were fixed on the cave.

There were just two hours still to go before the Closing.

'Your Majesty should rest,' said the royal doctor, coming forward with a folding stool. 'At least sit down, you're using up all your strength.'

But the Queen couldn't sit, she couldn't eat or drink, she could only stare at the dark hole in the cliff as if to take her eyes from it would be to abandon the last shred of hope.

At ten-thirty the flares were lit. Flares round the opening, flares along the curving bay now crowded with people ... A ring of flares where the King and Queen waited. It was beautiful, the flickering firelight, but frightening too for it marked the ending of the last day.

But not surely the end of hope?

Five minutes passed ... ten ... Then from the crowd lining the shore there came a rustle of excitement ... a murmuring – and from the Queen a sudden cry.

A lone figure had appeared in the opening. The King and Queen had already moved towards it, when they checked. It was not their son who stood in the mouth of the cave – it was not anyone they knew. It was in fact a very tired witch called Mrs Harbottle, holding a carrier bag and looking bewildered. She'd heard about the gump from a sorcerer who worked in the Job Centre and decided she fancied it.

The disappointment was bitter. The Queen did not weep, but those who stood close to her could see, suddenly, how she would look when she was old.

Another silence – more ticking away of the minutes. A cold breeze blew in from the sea. Rose and Lily and Violet still held their closed bananas, but Lily had begun to snivel.

Then once more the mouth of the cave filled with figures. Well known ones this time – and once more hope leapt up, only to die again. There was no need to ask if the rescuers had, after all, brought back the Prince. Cor was bent and huddled into his cloak; Gurkie carried her straw basket as if the weight was too much to bear – and where the fernseed had worn off, they could see the ogre's red, unhappy face.

From just a few people on the shore there came hisses and boos, but the others quickly shushed them. They knew how terrible the rescuers must feel, coming back empty handed, and that failure was punishment enough.

Cor was too ashamed to go and greet the King and Queen. He moved out of the light of the flares and sat down wearily on a rock. Gurkie was looking for Odge in the crowd gathered on the beach. She could make out two of Odge's sisters but there was no sign of the little hag – and trying not to think what a homecoming this might have been, she went to join Cor and the ogre in the shadows.

'We must go and speak to them,' said the King. 'They will have done their best.'

'Yes.' But before the Queen could gather up her strength, the child who had won the Latin prize put up her hand.

'Listen!' she said.

Then the others heard it too. Baying. Barking Howling. The sky yelpers were back!

They burst out of the opening – the whole pack – tumbling over each other, slobbering, slavering, their saucer eyes glinting. Freed suddenly from the tunnel they hurled themselves about, sending up sprays of loose sand.

But not for long! The smell came first – and then Miss Witherspoon, holding her whistle.

'Sit!' screamed the harpy – and the dogs sat.

'Grovel!' she screeched, and the dogs flopped on to their stomachs, slobbering with humbleness.

'Stay!' she yelled – and they stayed.

Then she stepped aside. The smell grew worse, and out of the tunnel, feet first, came Miss Green, Miss Brown and Miss Jones. The monstrous bird-women's wings were furled and one look at their smug faces showed the watchers what they wanted to know.

Turning, the harpies took their place on either side of the tunnel and stretched out their arms with their dangling handbags. 'Lo!' they seemed to be saying as they pointed to the opening. 'Behold! The Great One comes!'

A cheer went up then and to the sound of hurrahs and the sight of waving hands, Mrs Smith appeared in the mouth of the cave.

And in her arms – a sack! A large sack, tied at the top but heaving and bulging so that they knew what was inside it was very much alive.

The Prince! The Prince had come!

All eyes went to the King and Queen. The Queen stood with her hand to her heart. He had come in a sack, as a prisoner – but he had come! Nothing mattered except that.

176

But before she could move forward, the chief harpy put up her arm. She had decided to drop Raymond at the feet of the King and Queen – to sail through the air with him, like the giant birds in the stories. Now she picked up the sack in her talons; unfurled her wings – and circling the heads of the crowd, holding the squirming bundle in her iron claws, she came down and with perfect timing, dropped it on a hummock of sand.

'I bring you His Royal Highness, the Prince of the Island,' said Mrs Smith – and patted her perm.

The cheering had stopped. No one stirred now, no one spoke. This was the moment they had waited for for nine long years.

The harpy bent down to the sack – and the King banished her with a frown. Later she would be rewarded, but no stranger was going to unwrap this precious burden.

'Your scissors,' he said to the doctor.

The doctor opened his black bag and handed them over. The Queen was deathly pale, her breath came in gasps as she stood beside her husband.

With a single snip, the King cut the string, unwound it, loosened the top of the sack. The Queen helped him ease it over the boy's shoulders. Then with a sudden slurp like a grub coming out of an egg, the wriggling figure of Raymond Trottle fell out on the sand.

He wasn't just wriggling; he was yelling, he was howling, he was kicking. Snot ran from his nose as he tried to fight off the Queen's gentle hands.

'I want my Mummy! I want my Mummy! I want to go home!' sobbed Raymond Trottle.

The nurses stepped forward, their unzipped bananas in their hands – and stepped back, zipping them up again. And a great worry fell over the watchers on the shore because even from a distance they could see the Prince kicking out at his parents and hear his screams, and now as the King set him firmly on his feet, they saw his piggy, swollen face and the hiccuping sobs that came from him. Would the Queen not be terribly hurt at the way her son was carrying on?

They needn't have worried. The Queen had straightened herself; and as she lifted her face, they saw that she was looking most wonderfully and radiantly happy. The years fell away from her and she might have been a girl of seventeen. Then the King followed her gaze and the watching crowd saw this brave man become transfigured too and change into the carefree ruler they had known.

On the ground, the boy the harpies had brought continued to kick and scream and the Queen very politely moved her skirt away from him, but she did not run. She moved the way people do in dreams, half gliding, half dancing, as though there was all the time and happiness in the wide world – and the King moved with her, his hand under her arm.

Only then did the onlookers turn their heads to the mouth of the cave and see two figures standing there. One was the little hag, Odge Gribble. The other was a boy.

A boy who for an instant stood quite still with a

look of wonder on his face. Then he let go of Odge's hand and he *did* run. He ran like the wind, scarcely touching the ground – nor did he stop when he reached the King and Queen, but threw himself into their arms as though all his life had led to this moment.

And now the three figures became one, and as the King and Queen held him and encircled him, the watchers heard the same words repeated again and again.

'My son! My son! My *son*!'

Twenty-One

Odge Gribble had moved into the nurses' cave. A week had passed since Ben had gone to the palace to live and she hadn't heard a single word from him. Now she was going to retire from the world and become a hermit. She had left a note for her mother and her sisters and she was settling in.

The nurses had eaten burnt toast and slept on stones and poked sticks into their ears, but the things Odge was going to do were much more interesting than that. She was going to sleep on rusty spikes and eat slime and raw jellyfish. She wasn't going to talk to a living soul ever again and every day and in every way she was going to get more awful and fearful and hag-like. By the time she was grown up, she would be known as Odge of the Cave, or Odge of the Ocean, or just Odge the Unutterable. The cave would be full of frogs she had coughed; *all* her teeth would be blue, and the bump on her left foot would have turned not into one extra toe, but into seven of them at least.

Now she unpacked her suitcase. It was the one the mistmaker had travelled in, but of course Ben had taken the mistmaker with him to the palace. It was her pet really, but Ben hadn't cared; he'd just gone off with his parents to be a prince and never given her another thought. They said that when people became grand and famous they forgot their friends and Ben certainly proved it.

She found a flat boulder which would do as a table and decided to have mouldy bladderwrack for lunch. She wouldn't eat with a knife and fork either; she'd eat with her fingers so as to become disgusting as quickly as possible. Now that the nurses did nothing but guzzle beautiful bananas and parade around in frilled dresses which they washed three times a day, it was time someone remembered sorrow and awfulness.

She found the bladderwrack all right; it even had some little worms crawling on it, but she decided to have lunch a bit later. Not that she was going to be beaten; she'd eat it in the end, all of it. She wasn't going to be beaten by *anything*. No one was going to hurt her again and she wasn't going back to school either. She had enjoyed school, but she wasn't going to enjoy anything any more *ever* and that would show them!

But as she sat with her toes in an icy pool, waiting for them to turn blue and perhaps even drop off with frost-bite, she couldn't help thinking how cruel and unfair life was. For it was she who had brought Ben through the gump and if she hadn't made him open his grandmother's letter as the taxi took them to King's Cross, he might still have argued about coming and perhaps not being welcome on the Island.

Odge could remember every word that Nanny Brown had written.

'Dear Ben,' the letter began. 'I have to tell you that something very bad was done to you when you were little. You see, you were kidnapped by Mrs Trottle. She snatched you from your basket near King's Cross Station and carried you off to Switzerland, meaning to pass you off as her own child. But when she got there she found she was expecting a baby of her own and after Raymond was born to her, she turned against you and would have sent you away, only I wouldn't let her. No one knows who your real parents are, but they must have loved you very much because you were wearing the most beautiful clothes and the comforter in your mouth was on a golden ring.

So you must go to the police at *once*, Ben, and tell them the truth and ask them to help you find your family – and please forgive me for the lies I told you all those years.'

The whole thing had made sense to Odge at once. Ben must have been so much nicer to look at than Raymond, and cleverer, and better able to do things. No wonder Mrs Trottle had got annoyed and tried to send him away.

And Ben *was* nice – he was as nice as Raymond was nasty – so that it hurt all the more that he had forgotten her. True, the King and Queen had hugged her and the other rescuers and said how grateful they were – and it was true too that the short time between Ben coming through and the Closing had been incredibly busy. Raymond had had to be packed up and thrown into one of the last of the wind baskets that went up to King's Cross, and what the ghosts of the gump thought when they saw him was anybody's guess. And just as Raymond went up, there was a great surge of last-minute people coming down: the Plodger with a bundle of wet cloths which turned out to be his niece Melisande, and the troll called Henry Prendergast, and two of the banshees who'd got wind of the fact that Raymond wasn't the Prince and decided to come to the Island after all.

Even so, Odge had at first not believed that she was forgotten. Every day she had waited at least to be asked to tea at the palace, or thought Ben might ride by her home and ask how she was. Everyone told stories about him – about his white pony, his intelligence, the great wolf hound his father had given him, and the happiness of the Queen who looked so beautiful that the King had had to post a special guard at the palace gates to take in the bunches of flowers which besotted young men left for her.

Well, that's nothing to do with me, thought Odge. I shall stay here in the darkness and the cold and get shrivelled and old and one day they'll find a heap of bones in the corner – and then they'll be sorry.

She was sitting in the mouth of the cave, her hands round her knees, and coughing, when she saw a boy picking his way between the mistmakers on the sands. As he came closer she saw who it was, but she didn't take any notice, she just went on coughing.

'Hello!' said Ben. He looked incredibly well and incredibly happy. She'd have liked to see him wearing silly clothes to show he was royal but he wasn't – he wore a blue shirt and cotton trousers, and he'd come alone.

'What are you doing?' asked Ben, surprised.

'I'm trying to cough frogs, if you really want to know,' said Odge. 'Not that it's any business of yours.'

Ben looked round to see if there were any frogs there, but there weren't.

'Odge, I don't know why you're so keen on coughing them. What would you do with them if you did cough them? Ten to one, they'd start thinking they were enchanted princes and wanting you to kiss them and what then?'

Odge sniffed. 'I haven't the slightest idea why you've come,' she said. 'As you see, I've moved in here and I'm going to live here for the rest of my life.'

'Why?' asked Ben, sitting down beside her.

Odge drew her hair round her face and disappeared. 'Because I want to be alone. I don't want to live in the world which is full of ingratitude and pain. And I can't help wondering what you're doing sitting on the ground? Why didn't you bring your throne, an important prince like you?'

Ben looked at her amazed. 'What on earth's got into you?' he asked.

'Nothing. I told you, I'm going to live here for the rest of my life.'

But Ben had seen, in a chink between her hair, the glint of tears. 'I see. Well that's rather a waste because we've spent a whole week decorating your room and furnishing it so as to be a surprise. I suppose I shall just have to tell my parents that you don't want to come, but they'll be terribly disappointed.'

184

'What room?' asked Odge faintly.

'Your room; I've told you. The next one to mine in the palace. It was painted pink and we didn't think that was right for a hag so my mother chose a midnight blue wallpaper with a frieze of bats, and she put a cat door in for the mistmaker and you've got a huge bed stuffed with raven's feathers – the ravens *gave* their feathers because you're a heroine. It's pretty nice. And my mother drove over to your mother this morning to ask if you could come and live and your mother said it was all right as long as you visit once a week. So it's kind of a pity about the cave.'

He waited. Odge turned her head. Her green eye appeared; then her brown one as she shook back her hair.

'Really? You want me to live with you?'

'Of course. We decided it on the first day, my parents and I,' said Ben, and when he said 'my parents' his whole face seemed to light up. 'Perhaps we should have told you, only I love surprises and I thought maybe you do too.'

'Well, yes, I do actually.' She scuffed her shoes on the sand. 'Only . . . what if I don't turn out to be . . . you know . . . mighty and fearful? Would they want to have a hag that's just . . . ordinary . . . living in a palace? I mean, I may *never* get an extra toe?'

Ben got to his feet. 'Don't be silly, Odge,' he said. You're *you* and it's you we want.'

Odge blew her nose and put her pyjamas back in the suitcase. Then she gave Ben her hand, and together they walked along the shore towards the welcoming roofs of the palace.